To (

enjoy!

Jane Bennett
Munro

MURDER UNDER THE MICROSCOPE

MURDER UNDER THE MICROSCOPE

Jane Bennett Munro

iUniverse, Inc.
Bloomington

Murder Under the Microscope

This is a work of fiction. All of the characters, names, incidents, organizations, and dialogue in this novel are either the products of the author's imagination or are used fictitiously.

iUniverse books may be ordered through booksellers or by contacting:

iUniverse
1663 Liberty Drive
Bloomington, IN 47403
www.iuniverse.com
1-800-Authors (1-800-288-4677)

ISBN: 978-1-4502-9862-9 (sc)
ISBN: 978-1-4502-9861-2 (ebook)

Printed in the United States of America

iUniverse rev. date: 6/21/2011

For Semih

Introduction

The inspiration for this novel comes from thirty-plus years as a pathologist in a small rural town. Twin Falls, Idaho, is a real city, but Perrine Memorial Hospital, Southern Idaho Community College, and the Intermountain Cancer Center are completely fictitious, as are all the characters, and there is no Montana Street.

My heartfelt thanks to my best friend, Rhonda Wong, for her patience, support, and constructive criticism; to all the people I met at Murder in the Grove, particularly Janet Reid of FinePrint Literary Management, whose advice has been invaluable; to Dennis Chambers, formerly of the Twin Falls Police, currently county coroner, for information on police procedure; to Marilyn Paul, Twin Falls county public defender, for information on courtroom procedure; and finally, to all the people at iUniverse, without whom this book would not exist.

Any anachronisms, medical misstatements, or other errors are entirely mine.

Chapter 1

By the pricking of my thumbs,
Something wicked this way comes.
—Shakespeare, *Macbeth*

There was a dead body in my office.

It wasn't mine, and I didn't put it there.

I found it when I got called in for a frozen section at the ungodly hour of five o'clock in the morning.

Hurrying into my office, I tripped and damn near brained myself on the corner of my desk. The desk lamp fell over on me. That, plus my hangover, nearly did me in.

I picked up the lamp and switched it on.

On the floor lay the body of a woman in tight white pants and a red tank top. Long, black hair fell over her face, obscuring it, but there was no doubt in my mind who it was. My first instinct was to run right back home and crawl under the covers.

"Oh, shit," I said, bending down and sweeping the hair away from her face.

She felt cold and stiff, and her puffy contorted face had taken on a blue-gray tint.

It was bad enough finding a dead body in the first

1

place, but why did it have to be this one? And what the hell was she doing in my office?

I picked up the phone and called the police.

My name is Antoinette Day Shapiro, but everyone calls me Toni. Ten years ago, when Perrine Memorial Hospital in Twin Falls, Idaho, recruited me as their hospital pathologist, I jumped at the chance to create and run my own pathology department. My husband, Hal, jumped at the chance to get out of Southern California. Now I have a successful career in a peaceful rural setting, without the ghost from my past that had stalked me in Long Beach. Most of the time I can handle anything that comes up, and I go home to my husband each night feeling like I've done a good day's work, no longer afraid.

But I'd just had the worst month of my life, work-wise, and it was all because of the person lying on the floor of my office. So was the hangover I was currently nursing.

Sally Maria Shore, MD, had come here to Perrine Memorial to fill in for Joe Fortner, whose sudden heart attack had left us short one surgeon. Her job required her to see his patients, do his surgeries, and take his turns covering the emergency room. When Joe recovered from his quadruple bypass, she would leave, and everything would get back to normal.

That's not what happened.

So it was with mixed feelings that I awaited the arrival of the police. On the one hand, I wouldn't have to deal with her any more, but on the other hand, I had a feeling that she would cause me even more trouble dead than she had alive.

Chapter 2

O, how full of briers is this working-day world!
—Shakespeare, *As You Like It*

When our administrator, Bruce Montgomery, brought Dr. Sally Shore to my office last month, I had no idea what was in store for me.

My job at that point was to give a brief tour of the lab and answer any questions she might have about it. Our lab was embarrassingly small, consisting of two rooms with alcoves for blood bank and microbiology, every square inch crammed with cabinets, instruments, and technologists, in what seemed to be a constant state of chaos, phones ringing, and people yelling back and forth, pushing past one another with papers and specimens in their hands. The lab "office" was actually a desk out in the hall, and the patient waiting area consisted of chairs lining the hall on both sides. One of our sales reps had recently quipped that he was forced to grease his body in order to walk through our lab. Usually, when I gave my little tours, I could just stand in one place and point.

Sally Shore stood close to six feet tall, which pissed me off right away because I'm short, and it was giving me a crick in my neck to keep looking up at her. Her shapely legs went all the way up to *here*, and so did the skirt of her little black suit, which fit her like a second skin. Her full lips matched her red spike heels. With luxurious black hair that hung nearly to her waist, she could have been Cher's twin sister. She looked about twenty-five, but the tiny lines around her eyes and mouth put her closer to my own age, forty-one. Monty, a Mormon bishop and usually proper to the point of stuffiness, couldn't seem to take his eyes off her.

She took an inordinate amount of time looking around my office, but there wasn't much to see. My office was smaller than the crate our chemistry analyzer came in. Along with Monty and myself, we were putting quite a strain on it.

After introductions, I led her out of my office and into the lab, expecting this to be the usual quickie.

Boy, was I ever wrong. Once she opened her mouth, it was nearly impossible to get her to shut it. In the next ten minutes I learned more about Dr. Sally Shore than I cared to, and so did my techs: about her divorce, her daughter's impending marriage, her problems with the prestigious neurosurgery group with whom she had been affiliated in Boston, her unhappy love affair with one of her colleagues there, and her fear of malpractice suits, which bordered on paranoia. Apparently several of her former colleagues had already been sued, and she had left because she feared she would be next. We even heard about the allergy shots she'd been taking, for God's sake.

Chatty Cathy really wasn't interested in the lab; I realized this after trying to introduce her to the techs and to point out the various departments and the instruments in them—all to no avail. She didn't ask a single question about me or my qualifications, or about how long it took to get a blood gas done. She expressed no interest in the usual topics that interested other physicians. Conversation was not an option; she seemed to be interested only in herself. I don't much care for giving these tours at the best of times, but this one was a real pain in the ass.

Finally she and Monty left. My techs clustered around me, wanting to know what was going on.

I couldn't help them. I didn't know any more than they did at that point.

Dr. Shore's problems with the lab and the lab's problems with her started the first day she was on duty. One of my techs complained that Dr. Shore would not allow her to draw the patient's blood in the usual manner, with a syringe and needle, but instead insisted on starting an IV and letting the blood drip into the tubes from the IV line. Of course, all the tubes were clotted, and blood for some of the tests would have to be redrawn. A minor problem, to be sure—except to the patient.

"I tried to explain that to her," the tech told me, "but she screamed at me, 'Who's the doctor here, you or me?' I couldn't get a word in edgewise!"

A couple of days later, another tech showed me a culture plate that was absolutely plastered with white colonies of various sizes. "This is one of her GC cultures," she ranted. "She squashes the head of the penis into the plate like this, and just look at it! How the hell are we supposed to isolate anything out of all those skin contaminants?"

"Didn't you explain that to her?" I asked in my innocence.

"I tried," she told me, "but she yelled at me. 'When you've been to medical school,' she says, 'you can tell me how to do this, and not before!' I couldn't get a word in edgewise!"

Apparently Dr. Sally "Can't-Get-A-Word-In-Edgewise" Shore had a real problem with non-physician personnel trying to tell her things. Maybe she was just uncomfortable doing ER call. Maybe once she started getting surgical cases, things would smooth out.

They didn't.

Maybe she'd respond to a little chat from the pathologist; after all, we were both doctors.

I found her at the hospital nurses' station, writing a note on a chart.

She looked like something out of Frederick's of Hollywood—tight white pants, low-cut red tank top, and the same red stiletto heels she'd had on the day I first met her. Two male physicians leaned on the counter on either side of her, eyeing her appreciatively. Gosh, I hated to interrupt such an idyllic scene, but somebody had to.

"Excuse me, Dr. Shore, I need to talk to you when you're done here," I said from behind her.

She whirled around, and when she saw me, she smiled widely. I noted with some satisfaction that there was lipstick on her teeth.

"Oh, hi!" she squealed. "I need to talk to you too. Can you boys excuse us for just a minute?" She rolled her eyes at her male companions, and I swear to God, she *batted her eyelashes* at them. It was so cute I wanted to just vomit all over their shoes, but I restrained myself.

"It's so nice of you to come all the way up here to talk to me," she went on in the same sugary tone she had used on the "boys," and the smile remained unchanged. "So, can you tell me something I've always wanted to know?"

I shoved both hands into my lab coat pockets, unconsciously searching for the insulin I was going to need to keep me out of diabetic ketoacidosis. "What's that?"

"Why you pathologists can't give me a straight answer." Her voice had suddenly gone steely, and she shoved the chart at me. "This patient's pleural fluid, for example. Your cytology report says 'Atypical cells present, cannot rule out malignancy.' What does that mean? Does this man have cancer or doesn't he? I'm trying to provide quality medical care here, and you're not helping."

"I do the best I can with what you send me," I explained. "If I don't see unequivocally malignant cells, I can't say I do, now, can I?"

"I must say I don't appreciate your attitude," she stated, slapping the chart back on the counter and folding her arms. "If you're this way with the other physicians, I'm surprised they keep you here."

A frisson of fear and sensation of dread came over me. The threat was unmistakable, and yet that creepy smile was undiminished. How did she *do* that, I wondered.

I also wondered why I should be fearful of a locum tenens, for God's sake. A temp doctor had no power to fire me, or so I thought at the time.

I folded my arms in turn and refused to back down. "Okay, my turn. Here's the thing. My techs have tried to tell you the proper way to collect specimens, and you have refused to listen to them and have spoken to them in an abusive manner. No, I'm not finished," I added, as she tried to interrupt me. "I listened to you; now you listen to me. My techs know what kinds of specimens are needed for every test we do. It's their job to know that. My advice to you is to listen to them, because if you don't, you will compromise specimen integrity, and that's not fair to the patients; they shouldn't have to be restuck or have to collect another urine or stool sample because you didn't listen to my techs. Our lab results are only as good as the specimen we get. Do you understand?"

"I understand all too well," she said. "You had better slap your people into line or I will. Who do they think they are, telling physicians what to do with no more education than they've had? I've never had to take that in any of the other hospitals I've worked at, and I'm not about to take it now. Do *you* understand?"

Well, that went well.

Her manner toward me had gone from effusive to hostile in a matter of nanoseconds. I knew that further retaliation on my part would no doubt degenerate into a totally unprofessional, hair-pulling cat-fight, for which I would probably get blamed, since Hard-Hearted Hannah seemed to have all that testosterone on her side.

I beat a strategic retreat.

I managed to stay out of her way and out of trouble for exactly one day. Then I got called in at night on an appendectomy in which the surgeon had found something unexpected; and wanted me to find out what it was.

Whereupon, I walked into World War III.

As I unlocked the door to my office, I heard loud voices in the lab and went to investigate. I found one of my techs in a screaming match with one of the doctors. They were practically nose to nose.

"She's lying," insisted Lucille Harper, in a voice made husky from years of smoking.

"How dare you accuse a physician of lying?" demanded an outraged Tyler Cabot. "Just who do you think you are?"

"Hey!" I interrupted. "What's this all about?"

They both started talking at once.

"One at a time!" I attempted to separate the combatants, now both in *my* face. "Lucille, you first."

Lucille's beehive hairdo fairly quivered with indignation. "Dr. Cabot just fired me for refusing to come in and set up a throat culture for Dr. Shore—but I didn't."

"Not only did she refuse, but she used obscenities," interjected Dr. Cabot. "That is not acceptable behavior."

"It certainly isn't," I agreed.

"But Dr. Day—" began Lucille.

I held up a hand. "But Lucille says she didn't do it, Tyler. What about that?"

"Of course she says she didn't do it. What did you expect?" he snorted.

This was a potential disaster.

Our lab is so small that we don't have a night shift. The techs take night call. If this tech was fired, someone would have to come in and finish her shift, and the lab would be shorthanded until she could be replaced.

Furthermore, there is a protocol for firing an employee, and having a physician do it on the spot in the middle of the night isn't it.

I opened my mouth to explain all this to the physician when a surgical tech in scrubs arrived, bearing a stainless steel basin covered by a towel.

"Okay," I said. "This conversation is over. Lucille, you're not fired. You finish your night on call. Tyler, I'll talk to you later."

"But—"

"Later," I repeated firmly. "We'll talk later. I have to deal with this specimen now. We can talk about this tomorrow."

I turned and left to go across the hall to Histology, and Tyler followed me, still talking.

"We'll settle this right now," he insisted, and I stopped and turned to face him.

"No, we won't. You're not going to harass me while I do this. It's not fair to the patient."

Even Tyler Cabot could see the logic in that, so he backed down. "Okay, Toni, you win this round, but we are *not* done discussing this!"

I hadn't asked Tyler why Dr. Sally Shore couldn't do her own firing.

I didn't need to.

She was the surgeon who'd called me in.

The basin contained a rather nasty-looking segment of bowel covered with pus. Further examination showed a diverticular abscess in the cecum that had created a huge mass and then ruptured, causing peritonitis. The symptoms were identical to those of acute appendicitis, but the appendix looked normal. I did a frozen section to rule out colon cancer, which can sometimes do the same thing.

I ruled it out, but Dr. Shore refused to talk to me. She insisted that I give the diagnosis to the nurse, which is something I really don't like to do. I had never forgotten the time I'd told a surgical nurse that a specimen wasn't cancer, and she told the surgeon it *was* cancer, and the patient ended up having a radical procedure she didn't need to have.

I told the nurse it wasn't cancer and hoped for the best.

Now I had two things to talk to Sally Shore about, and I dreaded both of them.

Once I called Surgery with my report and put the specimen into a bucket of formalin, I could have gone home. But I knew I wouldn't sleep until I had at least tried to resolve the problem.

Lucille hadn't left yet, having received a set of blood gases from ICU, so I went back over to the lab to hear her side of the story.

Lucille, a large bleached blonde with a voice like a foghorn and a vocabulary that would make a sailor blush, did double duty in the lab. In the morning she prepared the slides that I looked at and made diagnoses on every day. In the afternoon she worked in the lab, and at night she took call. She frequently got into trouble because of her mouth, and periodically some physician would threaten to fire her, but it never happened. For one thing, she's the only one who seems to be able to fix lab instruments.

She had just hung up the phone, having given the blood gas report to someone in ICU. Not for the first time I wished I had my sunglasses with me; Lucille looked like an explosion at the Crayola factory—purple stirrup pants, red high-top Reeboks, and a yellow Betty Boop sweatshirt under her unbuttoned lab coat.

"So what happened here?" I asked her.

"Well, first, the ward clerk called me at eight, because Dr. Shore wanted me to set up a throat culture, and I said, okay, fine. I figured I'd do it when I came in to do the cardiac enzymes at nine o'clock."

"Did you tell the ward clerk that?"

"No, why would I do that?"

Maybe if she had, I thought, the ward clerk could have passed that information to Dr. Shore, and avoided this whole situation; but on the other hand, Dr. Shore could have turned that against Lucille, too.

"No reason. Go on."

"So I came in at nine, and while I was there, Dr. Cabot admitted a new patient and ordered a CBC, BUN, creatinine, lytes, and a four-unit crossmatch. So I got that done. About nine-thirty Dr. Shore came in and asked if I'd set up the throat culture yet, and I told her I had, and then she said she wanted the results by eight in the morning, and I said okay, fine."

"You did? You know that's impossible; unless she ordered a Rapid Strep."

"She didn't, but that's okay," Lucille explained, "she never checks anything. I figured that out after the first week. I don't argue with her, I just agree with everything she says."

"You do?" That surprised me. Lucille may not have as much education as the other techs, but she was clearly not stupid.

"Sure. We've been gettin' along real good lately. Oh, I told her once when she first came here that we didn't make a special trip to set up Rapid Streps or throat cultures on call—but not since then. It ain't worth the hassle to tell her anything, so I just quit trying."

"So then what?"

"Well, then, around ten, Dr. Cabot came in and told me I was fired and said, 'I want you out of here. Now.'"

He can't do that, damn it. I pulled up a lab stool and sat down. "Then what?"

"Well, then, I asked him why, and he told me what Dr. Shore said, and I got mad and said I never did any such thing, and he said I was lying, and then you came in."

Lucille's round face looked as red as her Reeboks. I wondered about her blood pressure, and then decided I really didn't want to know. One crisis at a time is my motto.

"Lucille, I wouldn't blame you, no matter what you said. I know how unreasonable she is. Did anybody else hear this conversation?"

"You can ask the ward clerk if you don't believe me." Lucille was obviously upset at my lack of trust.

It hadn't been my intention to piss her off. I hastened to smooth things over. "Come on, Lucille, give me a break. If I'm going to straighten this out, I have to be one hundred percent sure you're telling the truth. I can't just accept it at face value without checking, you know."

"I guess so." Lucille didn't sound convinced.

I heaved my reluctant butt off the lab stool and walked out of the lab, wishing I could just go home to bed and forget about this mess. The last thing I wanted to do was talk to either Tyler Cabot or Sally Shore; but this problem would not be resolved unless I talked to both of them.

I decided to start with Tyler.

Chapter 3

He comes of the Brahmin caste of New England.
This is the harmless, inoffensive, untitled aristocracy.
—Oliver Wendell Holmes

*I*n any situation, there is always that one person without whom life would be so much easier. In my case, Tyler Cabot, MD, filled that role.

Tyler Cabot was an internist, a tall and incredibly handsome man with a cap of silver curls and intensely blue eyes that matched his Porsche. In the summertime, he wore pastel shirts and matching sneakers, which set off his golf-course tan. His wife, the former Desiree Baumgartner of Ketchum, was nearly as gorgeous as he was. Her grandfather was one of the first ski instructors at Sun Valley and went on to found a multimillion-dollar business, Baumgartner Boots & Bindings, of which Desiree was the sole heiress. To Tyler's credit, however, he was an excellent physician, and his patients loved him.

However, his relentless criticism of the lab did not endear him to me or my techs. Not a day went by that I didn't get a phone call from him.

"Toni, I don't have Mary Smith's CBC yet. What

are they doing down there, exchanging recipes instead of doing their jobs? If I have to admit her for a transfusion, I'd like to know sometime in this century ..."

"Toni, I know you did a basic metabolic profile on John Doe because I have it in my office, but it's not on his hospital chart. Are your techs too busy knitting baby booties to deliver hospital reports, or what?"

"Toni, I've got a problem with the lab. Last week, Betty Jones had a CK of 300, and two days later it was 762. I thought CK was supposed to go *down* after a heart attack, not *up*. Can you explain that to me?"

"Why didn't you say something at the time?" I would say. "We could have investigated it then, but we can't do anything now."

He would sigh. "I figured it was useless to complain, because nothing ever changes."

Arrgh!

I would walk into staff meetings to hear him waxing eloquent on the failure of those goof-offs in the lab to get his lab reports to his office while the patient was still there, sarcasm dripping from his delicately sculptured lips. It was almost a pleasure to listen to him, so finely honed was his rapier wit, if one could forget about whom he was talking. To make it worse, Tyler was also one of those dinosaurs who absolutely refused to use his computer to check lab reports.

"The hard copies are in the box on your door," I would inform him. "I put them there myself two hours ago."

"So you have to do their jobs for them because they can't handle it themselves? Too busy reading movie magazines, no doubt. So what about the electrolytes yesterday? All the potassiums were too high."

Crap. "I'll check into it, Tyler, but you should have told me yesterday."

Then I would go into the hospital information system to review somebody's chart, and see a progress note from Tyler that said the patient's lab report was "strangely not on the chart, again." In my opinion, it was unprofessional to put complaints about the lab right in the electronic medical record like that; what if we got sued? How would it look in court? Once I complained to Monty about it, but nothing changed.

However, I did find out that the lab wasn't alone. Tyler was that way with all the departments, and there was nothing personal about it. Even so, I could always count on him to cut me down to size whenever I got to feeling too cocky.

If Dr. Shore really had a vendetta against the lab, she couldn't have chosen a better ally.

I found him in the doctors' dictation room upstairs in the hospital, dictating the history and physical on his newly admitted patient in ICU. I leaned on the counter and waited patiently until he had finished. Then I attacked.

"What makes you think you can just walk into the lab and fire one of my employees without so much as talking to me?"

He looked down his nose at me, quite a feat since I was standing and he was sitting. "As a member of the medical staff, I can fire any hospital employee, no matter where she works," he said.

"Oh, really? Then how would you like it if I fired your office nurse? Huh? How about that? Without saying anything to you about it. I can do that; I'm a member of the medical staff too, you know!"

He opened his mouth to respond, but I didn't give him a chance to say anything.

"You've clearly never heard of professional courtesy!"

"Well, really, Toni, she had it coming. She's been shooting off her mouth for years around here; how much of that are we supposed to put up with? I realize she's going to be hard to replace, but after all, her conduct and attitude are just not acceptable. Her behavior is most unprofessional. We just don't need that."

"She's been here twenty years," I said. "How is this incident worse than all the others that she didn't get fired for? Is there some kind of quota system now? Or is it just because it happened to Dr. Shore?"

To my surprise, Tyler blushed.

Aha! I thought. *There's more here than meets the eye.*

"Well, she's had a tough time. And you people aren't giving her much cooperation. Why doesn't she get the same courtesy the rest of us get?"

Obviously the two of them had discussed this in some detail. How else would he know that, and why would he care? His reasons had to go beyond professional concerns, considering the pheromones that practically dripped from the ceiling wherever Dr. Shore went.

"She does," I said. "We don't make a special trip to set up throat cultures or Rapid Streps at night for anybody. You didn't know that? The swabs are stable for twenty-four hours. We're supposed to be cutting back on overtime; and there's absolutely no reason why a tech can't wait to set it up the next time she gets called in."

"I didn't think of that," Tyler said, "but it doesn't

excuse Lucille's language. She actually told Dr. Shore to go fuck herself and then hung up on her. We can't have that. Doctors shouldn't have to take abuse like that."

I narrowed my eyes at him. "You're right. They shouldn't. Nobody should, including my techs. What about that, Tyler?"

Tyler seemed temporarily at a loss for words.

"Also, Lucille says she didn't say that."

Tyler miraculously regained his vocabulary. "Naturally she denied it. She's trying to cover her ass."

Infuriated, I put my hands on the arms of Tyler's chair and pushed it all the way back against the wall. Had I been taller, I might have hauled him up out of it by his throat; but this seemed to be working well, judging by the astonishment on his face.

"Did you actually hear this conversation, Tyler?"

Tyler suddenly seemed to have difficulty looking me in the eye. "No," he admitted. "I tell you what," he went on, still not looking at me. "Why don't you explain to Sally about the overtime? If you can get her to change her mind, I'll go along."

Did I just hear what I thought I heard?

I straightened up and stared at him in disbelief. "That doesn't make any sense! You and I are on the staff. She's a locum tenens. What gives her so much authority?"

Tyler's discomfort was now almost palpable. His smooth tanned forehead was beaded with sweat.

"I'm sorry, Toni, but that's the way it has to be," he said. "We need her here while Joe's recovering. She insisted that Lucille be fired or she would leave. If you want Lucille to stay, you'll have to talk to Sally."

We seemed to have reached an impasse.

Unbelievable. Replacing Joe was one thing, but come on. Why should that make Tyler blush and break out in a sweat, for God's sake? Was he hiding something?

Could Dr. Shore have something on him?

Chapter 4

*She was a woman of mean understanding,
little information, and uncertain temper.*
                                           —Jane Austen

The ward clerk had gone off duty, so I would have to wait till tomorrow or the next time she worked, whichever came first, to talk to her.

So I went to Surgery to talk to Dr. Shore.

I found her, still in her scrubs, dictating her operative note in the little dictating room next to the dressing rooms. I waited, leaning on the doorjamb, until she had finished. She looked up at me and smiled brilliantly. She had lipstick on her teeth again.

She greeted me in her usual, overly effusive manner. It didn't fool me.

"I need to talk to you," I said.

Her smile shrank a bit. "Of course. What about?"

"Why did you send Tyler Cabot down to the lab to fire my tech on call?" I asked.

"I'd be happy to tell you," she replied, still smiling. "I had a five-year-old girl with fever and vomiting. Her mother was frantic. When the ward clerk told me the tech on call refused to set up a throat culture, the mother heard every word. I wouldn't be surprised if she sued. I had the ward clerk call the tech back, and I got on the phone myself and talked to her. She had the gall to tell me that the lab doesn't set up throat cultures at night. I told her I wanted results by eight in the morning, and she said it wouldn't grow that fast. Who does she think she is? Where did she get her medical degree? I'm not accustomed to arguing with *lab people*," she added, with a contemptuous eye roll.

My blood ran cold.

"She's right," I said. "I would have told you the same thing."

"She had no right to talk to me like that, with the mother standing right there, hearing every word; and I simply cannot even repeat what else she said."

"Lucille says she didn't talk to you like that. She says she came in at nine and set it up."

Dr. Shore shook her head impatiently. "Of course she denied it. Those people always lie."

I felt a wave of fury and struggled to maintain my composure.

"*Those people*? What do you mean, *those people*?"

She waved a hand negligently. "Oh, you know. All the inferior life forms that work in hospitals, including in the lab."

"Really." I gritted my teeth. "You do realize that I also work in the lab."

Dr. Shore just shrugged. "Present company excluded, of course," she said, but she didn't sound like she meant it. "As I was saying, I was trying to deal with a desperately ill child. I had a frantic mother hanging over my shoulder. I was trying to provide quality medical care. That's what I would have wanted if that had been my child. The other doctors are all so good. How can they manage with the type of service your lab provides? I'm not sure I want to be on the staff here if I can't get better lab support than I'm getting from your lab."

That was too much. I lost my temper. "Then don't stay here. Nobody's forcing you. Just go away and leave me and my techs alone."

"How dare you talk to me like that?"

"Were you actually waiting for morning to treat that patient?"

"Don't be silly. It's just their whole attitude. They don't seem to care about the patient at all."

What a crock. My techs grew up with these families.

"Their personal lives take precedence," Dr. Shore continued. "Do you know that one of them couldn't come in last Saturday because she was grocery shopping?"

"They have to do it sometime," I said. "They have families to feed, whether they're on call or not."

She scratched at a large red welt on her upper arm. "Well, they can do it some other time. Since when is shopping more important than a patient?"

I felt as if I was beating my head against a stone wall. No, that's not right. I felt like the stone wall was actively attacking me.

I decided to cut to the chase and not bother with the overtime issue. "Okay, here's the thing. You cannot fire my employees. Is that clear? You don't just walk into my lab and tell my tech on call that she's fired."

She drew back her head like a cobra about to strike, but before she could say anything, I struck first. "And you don't send Tyler to do your dirty work for you, either. If you want someone fired, you go to administration and make a complaint, and there's a whole process to go through. If we don't follow it, we could get in trouble with the labor laws in this state. Lucille is *not* fired, got it?"

She rolled her eyes again. "At the other hospitals I have worked at, the techs are respectful and do anything that's asked of them without questioning it. Now the X-ray techs here are wonderful. I've had no trouble at all with radiology. Their chief tech is just outstanding. You have your work cut out for you with those people of yours. Small wonder, when you're so preoccupied with money that you've lost sight of the patient. This has to change. If I were you, I'd fire them all and start over."

That did it. She'd finally rendered me speechless. I realized there would be no reasoning with her. Behind that terrible smile, her attitude was cast in cement. She had an agenda, and nothing I could say to her would make the slightest difference. Screw it. I'd had enough of this conversation.

"Stay out of my lab," I told her, "or this hospital won't be big enough for both of us."

Chapter 5

*I do not want people to be very agreeable, as it
saves me the trouble of liking them a great deal.*
—Jane Austen

I got home shortly after one o'clock in the morning. Killer and Geraldine met me at the door with soft whines and wagging tails. I knelt and hugged and petted them both, told them what good doggies they were, gave them Milk-Bones and let them out, hoping Hal would not wake up. Our cat, Spook, was undoubtedly hiding somewhere, waiting to leap out at me when I least expected it, thereby living up to his name.

Hal, bless him, only woke up enough to roll over and throw an arm around me when I slid into bed. As he pulled me into the warm curve of his body, I wished I could tell him all about what had happened tonight and have him comfort me, but I was not about to wake him up for that. He'd be a lot more sympathetic after a good night's sleep.

And maybe, after a good night's sleep, I would be able to see tonight's events in a whole new light. In any case, Lucille had not been fired. I didn't need to worry about that, or so I thought, and it wasn't long before I was asleep too.

I awoke to hear the wind howling around the corner of the house and driving snow against the windows. Hal snored peacefully, and I snuggled up against him, and dropped off again, only to find myself in the embalming room of a large and shadowy mortuary. The naked body of a woman lay on the embalming table with her arms crossed over her bosom. Bloodshot eyes stared sightlessly from a swollen purplish face.

I turned to the mortician, who had not spoken a word. "Blood alcohol? Is that all you want me to do?"

He nodded.

I took a 20 cc syringe and a cardiac needle and drew blood from the heart. It wasn't easy. Her ham-like arms were in the way, and the degree of rigor mortis was extraordinary. I literally had to drape her right arm over my shoulders, and it felt as if she were trying to crush me. I handed the syringe to the mortician, and in the process I chanced to look directly into her eyes. They were fixed on mine. Frozen, I stared back.

"Hey," I whispered to the mortician. "Are you sure she's dead?"

He said nothing but gave me an eye roll.

"Look, you, I've seen plenty of dead bodies, and they don't bother me. So don't roll your eyes at me! *Look* at her!"

The woman smiled and stretched her arms over her head, lacing her fingers behind it. There was lipstick on her teeth. Her pits needed shaving.

It was Dr. Shore.

I screamed and woke up. Hal leaned over me.

"Toni, for God's sake!"

My bedside clock said 4:45 a.m.

I lay awake clinging to Hal until the alarm went off.

I had a tough time shaking off that nightmare. Every time I closed my eyes, I saw that awful face.

When the alarm went off, I got up and went to my aerobics class. As long as I was doing something, I didn't feel too bad.

Histology was still dark when I got to work, which was unusual. I walked into the lab and found my chief tech, Margo, on the phone. "Morning," I said.

She slammed down the phone, a very uncharacteristic gesture for her, and snarled, "What's good about it?"

"What's got into *you*?" I asked.

"I'm sorry, Doctor, but wait till you hear," she said. "Lucille got herself fired last night. Since I got here at five, they've taken two patients to surgery, admitted a GI bleeder who's gone through twelve units of blood already and a patient in respiratory failure, and I've been doing blood gases every half hour since. We're still doing them. And that was Mary Kay on the phone, calling in sick *again*. So we're two people short, and we're swamped already, and the day hasn't even started yet."

I was still derailed back at the second sentence. "What do you mean, Lucille got fired? I thought I made it clear to both of them that they couldn't—"

"Both of who?" she demanded. "You knew about this already?"

"Who else? Drs. Cabot and Shore, Incorporated," I said and told her the whole story.

She gasped. "Surely Lucille didn't actually say *that*!"

"She says not," I said. "Dr. Shore says she did. So now I have to talk to the ward clerk who was on duty last night and supposedly heard the whole conversation."

But of course the ward clerk was not on duty again until three in the afternoon. So I decided to talk to Monty.

"I'm not surprised," Monty said. "She's been asking for it for twenty years. What can I do? Dr. Cabot can fire anybody he wants to. The only way to reverse that would be if you could show that he didn't have sufficient cause."

"His *cause*," I replied, "is that Dr. Shore wanted her fired. Then he said that if I could convince Dr. Shore to let her have her job back, it was okay with him. Does that make sense to you? Since when does a locum tenens get to fire people around here?"

"She's not going to be a locum tenens much longer. The Board votes today whether or not to recommend her for appointment to the medical staff."

My breakfast turned to lead in my stomach. "Are you kidding?"

Monty sighed. "No. Dr. Cabot wants her, and he's on the Board, and he's pretty influential, you know."

"But then the entire staff has to vote, don't they?"

"Yes. It takes a two-thirds majority vote."

Well, thank God for that.

I embedded, cut, and stained my own surgicals. This was Lucille's job, which she was no longer here to do, and I wasn't particularly enjoying it. As a former medical technologist, I had been trained in histology, but it had been a long time ago, and the task was a slow process.

I suppose I should have been feeling smug, since most pathologists would have been totally helpless in my situation, but instead I felt abused. So I'm afraid I was a little less than sympathetic when Tyler stopped by and wanted to know if there was going to be a pathology report today on the patient Sally Shore had operated on last night.

"You fired my histotech," I snapped. "I wouldn't count on it if I were you."

He looked down his nose at me. "There's no need to be rude, Toni."

I shot out of my chair and confronted him face to face. "Rude? No need to be *rude*?" I mimicked. "Let's try *homicidal*. Did you or Dr. Shore give any thought to how I'm supposed to function without a histotech? Do you have any idea how long it's going to take to get another one? Do you realize that we're going to have to send all our tissue cassettes out to another lab somewhere to be embedded, cut, and stained and that the turnaround time is going to be about a week instead of twenty-four hours? You did that, Tyler, and I hope you're satisfied. You're going to be the one who explains it to the surgeons, because every time they ask, I'm going to refer them right to you."

By the time I had finished my tirade, I had backed Tyler toward the door and right out into the hall, where he turned and walked very fast back to his own office without another word.

Not for the first time, I wondered why Tyler was talking to me on Dr. Shore's behalf. Maybe she was at home sleeping after her long night in surgery.

As I read my slides and dictated the reports, constant phone calls interrupted me. It took me two hours to read out ten cases.

Things were no better in the lab. Work was still backed up, and tempers were frazzled. An irate internist called at five, wanting to know what the hell the lab was doing with all his blood counts, and if my techs didn't get their asses in gear he was going to fire them all.

Why this obsession with firing my techs? Why did everyone seem to think that would speed things up in the lab? I wondered if things would have been better if I'd stayed in Southern California.

Then I remembered what I had left behind in Long Beach and decided perhaps not.

It was quarter past seven by the time I finished grossing. The lab was dark, and most of the doctors had gone home as well. I could go home too, if I wanted to, but Hal had told me he'd be working late, and I wanted to talk to the ward clerk. She confirmed Lucille's story.

The charge nurse embellished it. "I don't know what kind of a doctor she is, and that's a fact. I've never seen anything like it. That little girl was not just febrile and vomiting, but she also had a headache and stiff neck. Now that says meningitis to me, but Dr. Shore just did a throat culture, gave her some Tylenol elixir, and sent her home. She'll be back, you mark my words!"

On my way out, I noticed lights still on in Administration, and I took a detour, hoping Monty was still there and that I could settle this once and for all. Monty wasn't there, but Charlie Nelson, the assistant administrator was, and nobody was with him, and he wasn't on the phone. I walked right in and sank into a chair with a huge sigh.

Charlie was short and portly and favored three-piece suits with a watch on a chain, like Grandpa Day. Maybe that was why I felt so comfortable with him. He was one of those people who never seemed to get upset at anything, and he was never too busy to talk. In fact, talking was what Charlie did best.

"What can I do for you, Doc?"

"I suppose you know that Dr. Shore had Dr. Cabot fire Lucille last night."

"I heard something of the sort, yes," he said, leaning forward with his elbows on his desk.

"I thought there was a procedure for firing employees here. It's in the employee handbook. I told her that. But I came to work today, and guess what? No Lucille. How can they do that?"

Charlie cracked his knuckles. "I guess that when a doctor wants somebody fired, they're fired; unless someone comes up with a good reason why not."

I told him about my conversation with the ward clerk and the charge nurse.

Charlie leaned back in his chair. "That sounds like a good reason why not to me. But you'll have to talk to Monty in the morning."

I wasn't through. "What's her problem, Charlie? Why does she have such a vendetta against the lab? Do you know she suggested firing all the techs and starting over?"

"Jesus Christ!"

"On the other hand, she thinks radiology is wonderful."

Charlie chuckled. "Radiology doesn't think *she's* wonderful. She waits until the last minute to order X-rays, and they end up having to call in the tech on call because the regular shift is over before they can finish the procedure."

"She also said she might not stay here because she can't get good lab support. Is she really supposed to be joining the staff?"

"She's been asked to stay on permanently," Charlie informed me. "They were supposed to vote on it at the Board meeting today, but I wasn't there, and I don't know what happened."

"What about Joe? Isn't he coming back?" *Christ on a crutch*, I thought. What would I do if *that* happened? Spend the rest of my working life fighting with Dr. Jekyll and Mrs. Hyde? She would either drive me away or insane, whichever came first, and it would be a short trip.

"Apparently, Dr. Cabot thinks there's enough surgery to go around."

"Well, Tyler said if I could get her to change her mind about Lucille, he'd consider reinstating her. But she took everything I said and turned it against me. She was just impossible, Charlie! Totally unreasonable!" I jumped to my feet, gesticulating. "If I ever have to talk to her again, I swear to God, I just might have to kill her!"

"Now, now, take it easy, Toni," Charlie reassured me. "If she has any more problems, you just tell her to talk to Monty or me, okay?"

I remained unappeased, pacing back and forth in front of Charlie's desk. "Fine, but how long is that going to work? She's already gotten my histotech fired. Is she going to work her way through the lab firing all my techs one by one?" I stopped and leaned on Charlie's desk with both hands. "Is she trying to destroy the lab? What's her problem, Charlie? Why am I the only one having trouble with her?"

Charlie sat back in his chair and turned his palms up. "I don't know, Toni. I haven't got the faintest idea what her agenda is."

Well, that was helpful.

Chapter 6

Those serpents! There's no pleasing them!
—Lewis Carroll

D r. Shore wasn't through with me.
When I got to work the next morning, there was a letter on my desk. Typed, single spaced.

Dear Mr. Montgomery,

I think you should be aware of what is going on in your lab. For your information, the technicians have been rude, and obstructive, and are seriously jeopardizing my attempts to provide quality medical care. They are constantly questioning my orders. When they have been to medical school they can question my orders. In the meantime, I am not obligated to justify anything to them.

She went on with a litany of complaints, including slow turnaround times for tests sent to reference labs, the inability to get certain tests done at night, and the cavalier attitude of the laboratory staff in general, which of course was my fault.

Then she started in on me personally.

And speaking of your pathologist, I find that she is unable to give me the slightest support when I need a diagnosis. At other hospitals, the pathologists have bent over backward to give me diagnoses when I need them, but Dr. Day has been extremely uncooperative in that regard. I can't help but think that her attitude is covering up a disturbing degree of incompetence.

In the future, if I do not get better laboratory support, I shall be forced to reconsider my decision to stay on here.

Very truly yours,
Sally M. Shore, MD

Furious, I crumpled the letter and threw it in the wastebasket. Incompetence, my ass! The other doctors had no problem with my expertise, and there was no way she could have gotten anything back from a reference lab any faster in any of the places she used to work than she could get it here. And why was she complaining about any of these things when none of the other doctors ever had in the past ten years?

I doubted very much that the lab was really doing anything to interfere with her ability to provide "quality medical care," as she called it, so this was an obvious attempt to get me in trouble. Why? What was her problem?

My first instinct was to run out of my office, find Sally Shore, and beat the crap out of her, which used to work just fine when I was a kid; but instead, striving to maintain a professional attitude, I consulted Margo, who knew about these complaints and was able to bring me up to speed on each one of them. Most of our send-outs went to the reference lab at the University of Utah, and results were usually available within two days. Results from that lab were interfaced with our laboratory information system, so we didn't have to depend on the mail. The fungus culture Dr. Shore complained about took ten days because nothing grew, and that's how long we held them before reporting out a negative.

Personally, I thought she was just trying to show off; she had told both Margo and me at different times that she had a number of articles on various subjects in her car that she would be happy to share. One day as I walked to work, she drove past me in a white Cadillac convertible. I caught up with her in the parking lot as she got out of her car and asked her about the articles. She favored me with a brilliant smile as she told me that since no one had asked about them, she had left them home. *Right.*

The thyroid screen at midnight was troublesome; the medical staff had approved a policy that the lab didn't do certain tests on call unless the pathologist gave permission, and thyroid screens were on that list. If she had called me and explained the patient's situation, I could have told the tech to go ahead and do the test; but she didn't call. Dale Scott, the tech on call the night before, had drawn the patient at midnight and run the test this morning; it had been normal.

As far as I could see, we were doing nothing wrong. But apparently Dr. Shore could not live with lab policies that had been in place for years. There are bound to be misunderstandings when a new physician comes into a hospital and doesn't know what the policies are, but this was ridiculous. She'd yell at my techs, and my techs would complain to me; then she'd complain to Tyler, and Tyler would complain to me. When I'd try to talk to her, she'd ignore my explanation and start talking about something else that was wrong with the lab.

Was Tyler giving her lessons, or what?

I went back to my office with the intention of retaliating. I couldn't let Sally Shore say these things to the other doctors; it threatened my job and those of my techs. I was going to have to defend myself. I retrieved the crumpled up letter from the trash, fired up the computer, and started to write a blistering reply. It was difficult. She had attacked me on so many fronts, I didn't know where to start.

Then I noticed something I hadn't seen before. At the bottom of the letter, it said:

cc: Antoinette Day, MD
Tyler Cabot, MD

At this, my heart sank right to the soles of my feet. *No point in writing letters back,* I thought. This was not just between her and me.

I deleted my unfinished letter. Then I went to see Monty.

Monty's office was much larger and more luxurious than mine. It contained four chairs and a love seat, tastefully upholstered in dark green tweed, and a massive and ornately carved antique desk, which undoubtedly had come all the way from Missouri with the Mormon migration. Framed pictures of his wife and their eight (or was it nine?) children sat on one corner, while Monty sat behind his desk talking to Charlie. Jack Allen, MD, the chief of staff, sat on the love seat drumming his fingers impatiently on his knee. Tyler leaned negligently against the wall, looking like an ad from *Gentleman's Quarterly*.

When I stuck my head inside the door, Tyler greeted me with, "Toni, you're just the person we wanted to see."

I brandished the letter. "I suppose you've all seen this?"

They nodded.

"Just exactly what the hell am I supposed to do with this masterpiece of bullshit?" I demanded.

"Nothing," said Jack.

I stared at him in disbelief. "*Nothing?*" I echoed. "She can slander the lab and my techs and me and send copies to the entire medical staff, and I'm supposed to do *nothing*? She shouldn't be allowed to get away with this. The lab has done nothing wrong, and you know it."

"Just leave it, Toni, okay?" Jack said. "Don't antagonize her. She's a wonderful physician, and she's saving our butts by filling in while Joe's gone. If she were to leave, we'd be in a world of hurt. We know the lab's okay. Just forget it."

"Just forget it? Don't antagonize her? That's easy for you to say. You don't have to deal with all the complaints from my techs. She's *abusive*, Jack. She can't seem to comprehend that there are some things we simply cannot do, and she's making call a nightmare for them."

"Well, they're not perfect either," Tyler put in. "They've been surly and uncooperative to her. She's doing us a great favor, filling in for Joe, and also taking some of our night call upstairs in the hospital. We'd hate to lose her, but we might if she doesn't get better lab support."

"She'll get better cooperation if she quits treating them like dirt," I said, struggling to keep my temper. "For God's sake, Tyler, she treats *me* like dirt, and I'm a doctor!"

Tyler shrugged elegantly. "Well, now that you mention it, Toni, she's complained about you too. She thinks you don't know what you're doing. The business about the pleural fluid, for example."

I lost the struggle. "Damn it, Tyler, you know as well as I do that cytology's not an exact science. You've never complained about that before, and neither has anybody else."

"All right then, what about Emma Grainger?"

God, give me strength. "Who the hell is Emma Grainger?"

"She was supposed to have a bone marrow. You sent her home without doing it and didn't have the decency to tell Dr. Shore about it. She didn't find out about it until the patient came in for her follow-up appointment."

Just shoot me now. "For your information, Dr. Shore didn't have the decency to tell *me* about it. The patient just showed up. No clinical history, the patient couldn't tell me anything, Dr. Shore wasn't here to tell me anything, and there was nothing useful in the electronic medical record. We had no record of any lab work on her. What would *you* have done? Would you just do it without any clinical indication? Well, I wouldn't. For all I know, she didn't even *need* a bone marrow." As I spoke, I advanced on Tyler, and he stepped back until his back was to the wall. I was now practically nose to nose with him.

"Toni, take it easy!" exclaimed Jack.

Tyler sidestepped me. "Calm down, Toni. There's no need to get physical."

I ignored him. I was on a roll. "And my techs have been as cooperative as they can, considering that she keeps insisting they do things that we simply cannot do here. My lab policies have been in place for years, none of you have had any problems with them, but she won't listen when they try to explain that to her, and I can't help them because she won't listen to me either." I folded my arms across my chest and glared at him.

Tyler looked down his nose at me and sighed. "Well, I can't understand that, Toni, because the rest of us have had no problems like that. She's an excellent clinician and will be a real addition to our staff. She's very well-trained, you know."

"What do you mean, an addition to our staff? I thought she was a locum tenens. I thought she was only going to be here until Joe comes back."

"I plan to recommend to the Board that she be appointed to the medical staff."

"You can't be serious!"

"He's serious, all right," put in Jack.

"What about Joe? Isn't he coming back?"

"In a couple of weeks, last I heard," said Charlie.

"So you're really going to have to think about why you're having problems with Dr. Shore, Toni," advised Tyler. "Because you're the only one who is."

"You think about this," I retorted. "Which do you need more, an extra surgeon or a pathologist?"

"Oh, now wait, Doctor," objected Monty, "I don't think you need to go that far."

I had gone too far to back down now. "You choose, gentlemen," I replied calmly as I opened the door to leave. "It's either her or me."

Chapter 7

I would 'twere bedtime, Hal, and all well.
—Shakespeare, Henry IV

While it was nice to know the chief of staff wasn't concerned about the lab, it was not too encouraging to know the Sweetheart of Sigma Chi was going to be allowed to continue her abusive behavior with impunity, and moreover, might be on our medical staff permanently.

What was I going to tell my techs? I'd always been honest with them up till now. If I told them the truth, they might start leaving.

I was in an untenable position. My techs and I were being singled out for abuse and disrespect, and I was unable to do anything about it, getting absolutely no support from the medical staff or administration.

If worse came to worst and Dr. Shore was in fact appointed to the medical staff, I would have to resign.

I had dug myself a hole too deep to get out of.

What on earth was Hal going to say?

This was one of those times that I wished that I'd married a physician instead of becoming one; then I wouldn't have to work. I knew that some of the other physicians' wives worked before they married. I think George Marshall's wife, Teresa, had been a med tech, and Jack Allen's wife, Rita, an X-ray tech, but most of them had been nurses— even Tyler's wife, Desiree, but that was before she became CEO of Baumgartner Boots & Bindings.

Right now would be a wonderful time to not have to work; but that wasn't practical in my situation. Living on Hal's salary as a college professor wouldn't be impossible, but would require a major lifestyle change.

Or we could move somewhere else; but I hoped it wouldn't come to that.

When Hal asked me about my day, I fished the letter out of my purse and handed it to him. "It started with this."

He read it all the way through, and laid it down. "Well, this is a crock of shit if I ever saw one."

I poured two glasses of wine, and gave him one. "I know. I tried to write a rebuttal, but there's so much stuff in there that I didn't know where to start."

"So what did you do?"

I sat down on the edge of the couch. "I went to talk to Monty about it, and when I got there, Tyler and Jack and Charlie were already there. They all had copies. It was almost as if they were expecting me."

"So what did they say?"

"They told me not to worry about it. They said the lab's okay."

Hal cranked up the footrest on his recliner and settled back. "Good. Then there's no problem."

"Oh yes, there is too a problem." I couldn't sit still. I got up and started pacing. "Jack told me not to *antagonize* her. They need her. So my techs and I are supposed to keep quiet and take any shit she dishes out. My techs won't have any recourse. They're already angry about the way she treats them. They're going to start leaving, Hal. And once they start leaving, the others will be under even more pressure, and then more will leave, and the rest of the medical staff will figure they can just replace them. But the replacements won't stay long, and it'll become a vicious circle, replacing a tech every month or so, and nobody staying long enough to get familiar with the routine, and it's just going to be chaos."

"Toni, you can't let that happen."

"Oh, I know that, but wait, there's more. Did you notice the bit about how she might not want to stay on here if she doesn't get better lab support?"

Hal looked at the letter again. "Does that mean what I think it means?"

"Tyler said he was going to recommend to the Board that she be appointed to the medical staff."

"Oh no," said Hal.

"Oh yes. So I asked them to think about what they need more, another surgeon or a pathologist."

"You didn't!"

"I did. I said it was either her or me."

There! It was out.

Hal put his head in his hands. "*Oy vey.*"

I sat down and put my wineglass on the coffee table.

"Damn it, Hal, I refuse to work with her on a permanent basis, just being a good little pathologist, sitting back and letting my techs take all her shit and not being able to do anything about it because I'm not supposed to *antagonize* her, for God's sake!"

Hal looked up. He was smiling. No, by God, he was chuckling.

"Toni, I'm proud of you. Not everybody would have the courage to challenge those assholes."

"You're not mad?"

"No, honey, of course I'm not mad. Besides, it's not going to happen. She's probably made the same impression on the other docs as she has on you. You haven't talked to anybody but Tyler. You can't tell me that twenty-five intelligent physicians are going to put up with her bullshit permanently. Doesn't the entire medical staff have to vote on it?"

I wasn't sure how intelligent those other twenty-three sex-mad physicians would be, since they would be voting with their dicks. "Yes," I said. "It has to be a two-thirds majority of the medical staff."

Hal snorted. "No way that's going to happen."

"Either way, I've got nothing to lose now."

"What are you going to do?"

I picked up my wineglass and curled my legs up under me. "What do you think I'm going to do? I'm gonna *antagonize* her ass. I'm gonna antagonize the pure livin' *bejesus* out of her."

Hal threw me a kiss. "That's my girl."

Chapter 8

The smallest worm will turn, being trodden on.
              —Shakespeare, *Henry VI*

I should have known what kind of day it was going to be when the alarm failed to go off.

When the phone rang, Hal, who hates being awakened suddenly, cursed and answered it.

The frozen section case originally scheduled for ten o'clock had already started, and I was needed posthaste by none other than my biggest fan, Dr. Sally Shore. I decided to skip the shower. Quickly, I threw on pants and turtleneck sweater, and stuffed my feet into boots. I ran a brush through my curly black hair—which was rapidly becoming streaked with white, due, no doubt, to all these unscheduled frozen sections—applied minimal makeup, and was out the door in ten minutes.

Outside, it was still dark. I picked my way carefully across Montana Street, where the snow had turned to deep slush. I sincerely hoped nobody would drive by and soak me before I made it to the relative safety of the hospital parking lot.

It was 7:15 when I got to my office. The specimen,

a breast biopsy, waited on the desk in the lab. I did the frozen section and diagnosed cancer. Dr. Shore decided to proceed with the mastectomy, as the patient had requested, and I went back to the lab to check and see if a type and screen had been done on the patient. By that time, everybody was there.

Dr. Shore had actually ordered a crossmatch rather than a type and screen, which most surgeons no longer do since nowadays the idea is to avoid transfusion if at all possible; but it wasn't done yet, naturally, because the surgery was scheduled for ten. So I gave the blood bank tech a heads-up.

A type and screen consists of determining the patient's blood type, and performing an antibody screen. Then if the patient has no antibodies and has not been pregnant or received a transfusion in the last three months, type-specific blood can be given as needed without a crossmatch, thereby saving time and money.

But the patient had an antibody. When Surgery called for the first unit, the blood bank tech was still struggling. She had tried crossmatching every unit of O positive we had. They were all incompatible, and the young tech, just out of training, was practically in tears.

We had no record of the patient having received blood here, but that didn't mean she hadn't received it somewhere else. Obviously we weren't going to be able to solve the problem in time to do her any good.

The phone rang again. I picked it up. It was the Surgery supervisor, Roger Elquist, a fat, overbearing tyrant who ruled Surgery by intimidation and was not overly cooperative with the lab or anybody else. Usually I tried to stay on his good side, but not today.

"What the hell's going on down there? Dr. Shore's having a shit-fit about that blood. You better get your ass up here with it right now!"

His voice sounded raspy, and I guessed he'd been getting the rough side of Sally Shore's tongue. But that was no excuse.

"This is Dr. Day. Tell Dr. Shore there's a problem with the blood and that I'm coming up there to tell her all about it. And might I suggest that you also watch your mouth?"

I hung up before he could reply.

Roger was nowhere in sight when I got to surgery. Clothed in cover gown, mask, cap, and shoe covers, I entered the operating room, tucking my ungloved hands into my sleeves so as not to contaminate anything. Dr. Shore and several unidentifiable, green-shrouded persons were grouped around the patient, also shrouded in green. Dr. Shore's assistant, Dave Martin, MD, was the first to notice I was there.

"Oh, hi, Toni," he said.

Dr. Shore turned her head and saw me.

"Why can't I get blood for this patient? What's wrong with you people in the lab?"

Now I've got you, you bitch. "Your patient was scheduled for ten, Dr. Shore," I told her calmly. "Nobody, including me, was told that it was going to be at seven!"

"Well, if you'd done all this last night, none of this would have happened!"

"She's incompatible with every unit we have. We'll have to get the antibody identification done in Boise and get specially typed blood from Boise. We couldn't have done that last night."

"If I'd known about this last night, I could have cancelled the surgery," she protested. "I'm trying to provide quality medical care here. How can I do that when I get no support from the lab?"

If I heard the words "quality medical care" one more time, I thought, I would just puke right up.

"If we'd known she was going to surgery at seven, you would have known last night. We aren't mind readers, Dr. Shore. I refuse to accept the blame for this. Communication goes both ways, you know."

"Okay, suppose you tell me what I'm supposed to do with this patient who needs blood now."

I shook my head. "I'm sorry. Unless you want to give her incompatible blood, there's nothing I can do."

"And I'd have to sign my life away, I suppose."

"Naturally."

"I'll do without," she snarled.

"Wise choice," I muttered as I left the room.

Roger waited for me outside the room, red-faced. "Dr. Day, I apologize. I didn't know it was you on the phone."

"I know," I replied tartly. "You thought it was only a tech. Well, my techs deserve as much respect as I do. Kindly see that they receive it in the future."

He opened his mouth and shut it again without saying anything.

Ass-kicking rocks!

I left. I hummed as I ran down the stairs to the first floor. I was feeling pretty good. The world looked like a better place.

At least for a while.

Arms folded, I stood in front of Monty's ornate desk while he shuffled papers and paid no attention to me. "Well, Monty?"

He looked up, startled. "Well what, Doctor?"

"What was the Board's decision?"

"Oh." Monty shuffled papers some more. He seemed to be looking for something and not finding it. "They voted to recommend Dr. Shore for appointment to the medical staff. Three to two. There was quite a bit of discussion."

"Well, there's going to be quite a bit more."

"Oh? How's that?"

"Lucille categorically denied everything Dr. Shore and Dr. Cabot said."

"Naturally."

"Naturally nothing. The ward clerk backed her up. And so did the charge nurse. I think you ought to interview them both." I gave him their names. "From what the charge nurse said, we may very well have a malpractice suit on our hands. And that's not just sour grapes on my part."

Finally, I had his attention. "Okay. You'd better tell me about it."

I told him.

Monty put his head in his hands for a moment and then looked up. "Doctor, this is not the first time I've heard this type of thing about Dr. Shore. The nursing supervisor has given me an earful too. But what can I do? The physicians want her to stay, and they sign my paycheck."

"You said the only way Lucille could have her job back was if I could show that Dr. Cabot had insufficient cause to fire her. Well, I think I have shown that. There is absolutely no reason why Lucille should not have her job back."

"Except her mouth."

"Her mouth is not the issue here. The story Dr. Shore told is a pack of lies. Lucille did not argue with Dr. Shore, and she did not refuse to come in and set up the throat culture. She has witnesses who will back her up. If she doesn't get her job back, I think she has a legitimate grievance, and I will see to it that she knows that, if she doesn't already. Of course, if you *want* to be involved in a labor dispute …"

Monty shuddered. "All right, all right. I'll talk to the chief of staff."

Lucille was back at work the next day, the chunk-chunk-chunk of the microtome music to my ears. But my joy was short-lived.

Monday when I came to work, I found out that Lucille had been the victim of a hit-and-run Friday night, and in the hospital parking lot of all places. She'd been on call and was on her way out. She had multiple fractures and a ruptured spleen. They took her to surgery that night and removed the spleen and pinned some of the fractures. The next morning, when she kept drifting in and out of consciousness, they did a CT scan and found a subdural hematoma, whereupon she was life-flighted to Boise where there was a neurosurgeon.

The subdural hematoma was evacuated, but Lucille still had not regained consciousness.

Now what was I supposed to do?

Chapter 9

I am in blood
Stepp'd in so far that, should I wade no more,
Returning were as tedious as go o'er.
—Shakespeare, *Macbeth*

As I embedded, cut, and stained my own surgicals again, I tried not to feel put-upon.

After all, this was more than just an inconvenience. Lucille's life was at stake here, not just my lack of a histotech. On the other hand, without a histotech, I would have to work fourteen-hour days just to keep up. Even if Lucille pulled through, it would probably be months before she was able to come back to work.

If I was ever going to see my husband again, I would have to start sending the tissue cassettes out to another lab as I had threatened Tyler. And speaking of which …

The phone rang. Tyler was calling to request a bone marrow on Emma Grainger, the elderly lady Dr. Shore had scheduled for me that I had refused to do.

I did the bone marrow. I had to pull Brenda out of an already overworked lab to assist me. The patient was morbidly obese and wheelchair-bound. Brenda and I had to horse her up onto the table and put her into position; she didn't help at all. The procedure took twice as long as it should have, and afterward she complained of chest pain and shortness of breath, so I had to call Tyler and try to stabilize the patient until he got there.

I noted with relief that, despite her symptoms, Emma Grainger's plump face remained rosy-cheeked, and she wasn't sweating. I suspected that she was simply hyperventilating and had her breathe into a bag, whereupon her symptoms improved. When Tyler arrived ten minutes later, he grumpily confirmed my suspicion.

Then we had to get her back into her wheelchair.

Back in my office, I sank exhausted into my chair and put my head down on my desk. *This can't go on*, I thought to myself. I would have to hire a histotech. There was no alternative.

As if he'd read my mind at that moment, Monty came smiling into my office accompanied by a tall, statuesque, young girl with long, black hair, intense blue eyes, and a peaches-and-cream complexion that fairly glowed. He introduced her as Natalie Fisher and handed me her application and resume.

Natalie was twenty-two years old, unmarried, trained at Massachusetts General, ASCP registered, and had some training in histotechnology as well.

I handed the paperwork back to him. "Monty," I said, "this is a bloody miracle."

He grinned. "I thought you'd be impressed."

I stuck out my hand. "Welcome to Twin Falls," I said. "Can you start now?"

She giggled. Her teeth were very white.

"I'm serious," I said. "Well, okay, I guess you can start tomorrow. Let's go meet everybody, shall we?"

It was a pleasure to come to work the next morning at five o'clock, show my new histotech what her duties would be and where everything was, and watch while she efficiently set up the embedding center, the water bath, and the slide dryer around the microtome, and began embedding. After about ten minutes, it was obvious that I didn't need to stay there and watch any more.

"I'm right across the hall if you have any questions," I told her and went back to my office.

Natalie had all the slides, including the special stains, done and on my desk by nine. By ten, she had everything cleaned up and put away. The blocks were filed. The special stain jars no longer sat on my cutting board. By eleven, the Paps were also stained and on my desk. By noon, she had logged in all the surgical specimens and labeled cassettes for me. Then she went to lunch, and I sat there just smiling right out loud.

In the afternoon, Margo started her off in Hematology. Natalie already knew how to operate *and* troubleshoot the Coulter counter, and after about ten minutes, Margo left her on her own.

At three, she went back to Histology and logged in the rest of the surgicals for me before she went home.

As I grossed them in, I thought I'd died and gone to heaven.

From what Margo told me over the next few days, she thought so too.

The word got around. Doctors began coming into the lab to check on their own lab reports, instead of calling or sending their nurses. I couldn't help but notice that

Tyler didn't snarl at her the way he did the other techs. Male employees from other departments began coming into the lab to socialize more than ever before, even when we didn't have food. Our own male tech, Dale, couldn't keep his eyes off her.

It was a wonder Natalie could keep her mind on her work with all the attention she was getting, but she did, and her work was excellent. Not only that, she kept Histology spotless. I hated to say so under the circumstances, but Lucille was somewhat of a slob.

Meanwhile, Lucille continued to hang on and remained unconscious.

Sometimes I wondered what would happen if she came back and found she had been replaced. Not that I was complaining, but somewhere in the back of my mind was the nagging thought that this was just too awfully damn convenient.

When something seems too good to be true, they say, it usually is.

The police came to see me Tuesday afternoon. Detective Sergeant Pete Vincent was once one of Hal's students at Southern Idaho Community College. Pete was a home-grown product and had played football at Twin Falls High School. With his ruddy freckled face and shock of sandy hair, Pete still looked like a college kid. His companion was a compact, dark-haired individual with opaque black eyes, who Pete introduced as Detective Lieutenant Bernard Kincaid.

Naturally I was working on a particularly ugly and malodorous specimen at the time. Kincaid looked as if he wished he hadn't come. I was a little worried about him.

His jaw was clenched and he looked slightly green. Sweat beaded his upper lip.

I knew I didn't have to worry about Pete, who'd watched me do a couple of autopsies when he was in college; he'd put on gloves and gotten his hands right in there with mine.

"What *is* that, Toni?" Pete asked me.

"It's a gangrenous bowel," I explained, holding it up out of the sink so Pete could see it better. It was about five feet long, purplish-black, covered with patches of yellow exudate, and dripping blood.

"Isn't that an awful lot?"

"Not really. The small bowel is about twenty-two feet long, and a person can live without an awful lot more than this."

As I spoke, the specimen slipped out of my hands and landed in the sink with a juicy *plop*. "Woops," I said.

Kincaid abruptly left the room.

Pete casually parked one cheek on the counter behind me, and swung his leg gently. "Uh-oh," he said.

I started hosing down the tile backsplash on the wall behind the sink where blood had splattered. "Does he get sick?"

"Not usually. But you've got to admit, *that's* pretty bad."

"What does he do when you get a body that's been in the river for a month?"

"I don't know. We haven't had one since he joined the force. He's from California."

"What's he doing up here?"

"I don't know. He doesn't talk about it. Okay if we

wait in your office until you're done with that thing? No offense, but it really stinks."

When I finished and went back to my office, both Pete and Kincaid were there. Kincaid looked pale and sweaty.

I tried to be sympathetic. "Are you all right, Lieutenant?" I asked. "Here, why don't you take my chair, and I can sit on the desk."

I felt bad enough about making him sick, but apparently this only made things worse. The look he gave me could have frozen molten lava.

"Thank you, Doctor, but that won't be necessary. I'm quite all right."

Actually he looked as if a good sneeze would blow him over, but I shrugged and said, "Okay. What can I do for you two?"

"We're investigating the hit-and-run that took place here Friday night," began Kincaid. "We've already talked to your administrator and he told us the victim was one of your employees."

"That's true. She was my histotech."

"And just what is a histotech?"

Briefly I explained what Lucille did.

"How well do you know Mrs. Harper?"

"As well as you'd know anyone who worked for you for ten years."

"Did she ever talk about anyone who might be trying to harm her?"

"Not to my knowledge."

"Do you know of anyone who would want to get her out of the way for any reason?"

"Only Dr. Cabot. He keeps trying to get her fired; but I can't believe he'd do anything like this."

Kincaid stood up. "Doctor, may we question the lab employees?"

"Sure. Start with my chief tech. She knows Lucille better than anyone else here."

I took them into the lab and let them get on with it.

I was already beginning to regret telling them about Dr. Cabot. No doubt they would mention my name when they questioned him. Just one more thing for him to hold against me.

"So what?" said Hal, when I voiced my fears to him over dinner. "You've already figured out the worst that can happen, haven't you?"

"Well, yeah, but I really don't want to get fired. It wouldn't look good if I ever want to work again."

"You don't need to worry unless the entire medical staff goes along with the Board and votes her onto the staff," Hal continued.

"Maybe I'd better vote for her too."

"Wait a minute. You lost me."

"If she joins the staff, I resign. If she doesn't, I don't. She'll be gone, but Tyler won't, and he'll make my life hell."

"What can he do that he hasn't already done?"

"Fear not, o ye of little faith. He'll think of something."

Chapter 10

*Reputation, reputation, reputation! Oh, I have
lost my reputation! I have lost the immortal
part of myself, and what remains is bestial.*
　　　　　　　　　　　　—Shakespeare, *Othello*

The staff meeting was cancelled.

With all four surgeons tied up in surgery, I was tied up doing frozen sections. An emergency admission claimed the physician on call. We had one physician on vacation, one at a seminar somewhere, and another out sick with the flu, and of course Joe wasn't back yet. The others worked their butts off trying to take care of all the patients. We had a hospital census over 100 percent—with beds in the halls—thanks to the flu, which had reached epidemic proportions. Consequently, we had no quorum.

So, I didn't have to resign yet. I had a reprieve for another week at least.

Maybe Dr. Shore would be too busy to harass my techs. Or maybe she'd get the flu and die.

Shame on you, Toni, I admonished myself.

Emma Grainger had iron deficiency anemia. Of

course, she also had chronic lymphocytic leukemia, but that had nothing to do with the anemia. The cause of her anemia was chronic blood loss, which in a seventy-five-year-old lady was most likely due to bleeding from the GI tract.

Tyler stopped by my office to tell me he was sorry about what had happened to Lucille. I was touched by this unusual display of sympathy, but not for long.

"The police came to talk to me this morning," he said. "They said you practically accused me of being responsible for Lucille's accident. I don't appreciate that, Toni."

I felt my face get hot and was thankful that I had that sort of thick skin that never shows a blush. I forced myself to look him right in the eye. "They were mistaken," I said as coolly as I could manage.

"Then where did they get that idea?" he demanded. "You must have said something. You'd better be careful what you say, Toni, if you don't want the same thing to happen to you someday."

"Is that a threat?" I asked. "Are you threatening me, Tyler? Are you going to run over Dr. Shore in the parking lot and accuse me of doing it?"

Silence. Tyler was speechless. I wished I had a video camera and could record this, because I had never seen Tyler speechless in all the ten years that I had known him. Now what? Should I wait for him to recover or not? Not, I decided and changed the subject. "Emma Grainger has iron-deficiency anemia," I said.

Tyler was definitely disoriented. "Huh? Who?"

"Your bone marrow patient?"

"Oh, her. What about her leukemia?"

"Oh, she has leukemia, all right, but she also has

plenty of functioning marrow that should be providing everything she needs, except that she's probably bleeding from somewhere. Has she been scoped lately? Maybe she has a colon cancer or something."

Tyler's temper flared. "First you accuse me of attempted murder, and then you try to tell me how to practice medicine. Who the hell do you think you are?"

I shrugged and turned my palms up, trying to appear unruffled. "A pathologist. I'm doing my job."

Tyler turned and left without another word.

Ordinarily, Tyler would have accepted my assessment without question and referred his patient for endoscopy, but now I didn't know. I'd never seen Tyler this rattled before. So I sent a copy of the bone marrow report to the gastroenterologist, George Marshall, just to make sure Emma Grainger didn't fall through the cracks.

It wasn't ten minutes before he called me.

"What the hell, Toni," he growled. "This isn't my patient."

"She should be. I think she might have a colon cancer."

"Could be," he conceded. "But it isn't your place to refer patients to me like this, Toni. Tyler should be talking to me."

"I know that, and ordinarily I wouldn't do this. But Tyler isn't quite himself today; I don't know what's going on, but something is, and I told him what I thought, and he chewed me out for telling him how to practice medicine. So I just decided to play it safe."

"Okay, Toni, I'll talk to him. But it's not gonna make him any happier with you, you realize."

Well, I knew that. Tyler had never been happy with me. Why start now?

"Just pretend it's a lab error," I advised him. "He won't have any trouble believing *that*."

I put a slide under my microscope, took one look, and broke out in a cold sweat.

Yesterday, I had confidently diagnosed the frozen section as unequivocally malignant.

This permanent slide showed sclerosing adenosis, a benign lesion.

This patient had had her mastectomy yesterday.

I supposed I had been lucky not to have this happen before; every pathologist's nightmare come true, a certain malpractice suit, one that I had no chance whatever of winning. My heart beat with slow, sickening thuds. I felt nauseated. My hands grew numb. I thought I might faint.

Automatically, I went on to the next slide in the case. Then the next. And the next. Then I saw it.

A focus of metastatic tumor in a lymph node.

What the hell was going on here?

If this patient didn't have cancer, why did she have a metastasis in one of her axillary nodes?

Obviously, I realized with a sigh of relief, the cases had been switched. Natalie must have mislabeled the cassettes.

But we didn't have any other breast cases yesterday. So where did this slide come from?

I keep frozen section slides in a folder on top of my file cabinet. When I get the permanent slides, I put the accession number of the case on the frozen section slide and file it with the permanent slides. That way, if there's a discrepancy between the frozen section and the permanent section, I have the original slide to back me up.

The slide was gone.

This made absolutely no sense.

I went back to the first slide. Natalie hadn't done as good a job of cutting it as she had the others, and the staining was more uneven. The quality of Natalie's work was noticeably better than Lucille's, much as I hated to admit it, and this slide was not up to par for Natalie.

It was almost as if Lucille had cut it.

Perhaps she had. There was a definite air of familiarity about this slide, as if I'd seen it before, and recently too.

I stared at the label. It was a new label, like the others, not yellowed with age, but there was a definite, yellowish tinge to the mounting medium caked along the edges of the coverslip. Natalie did not allow mounting medium to collect at the edges of the coverslip in the first place, but with Lucille's slides, the mounting medium had a tendency to leak and run under the slides as they lay in the slide tray. When they dried, they would stick to the tray and have little bits of cardboard sticking to them when I ripped them out of the tray to read them. She didn't drain them long enough, even though I'd mentioned it to her time and time again.

I turned the slide over. Sure enough, there was a little fragment of cardboard sticking to it along one edge.

I tore the label off. Underneath it, on the frosted end of the slide, was a penciled number, 1148-04.

The number of this case was 421-05, not 1148-04. Lucille *had* cut this section—last year sometime.

I went into the lab and looked up S-1148-04. The

patient's name was Darlene Simmons, the specimen was a breast biopsy, and the diagnosis was sclerosing adenosis.

Bingo.

Natalie had switched cases on me, all right. But *why*?

Only one way to find out.

I found Natalie in Chemistry. "Natalie," I began. "Do you know that you switched cases on me today?"

"I did what?"

I showed her the slide. "You gave me this slide on S-1148-04 instead of the one on S-421-05."

Her hand flew to her mouth, and she stared at me wide-eyed.

"Natalie, where's the slide on S-421?"

"I ... I don't know."

Either the girl was a consummate actress or she really didn't know. Her cheeks flamed and her blue eyes were filled with bewilderment. Then suddenly her face cleared.

"Oh, I know now. I must have sent it to Boise by mistake."

"To Boise?" Now it was my turn to be bewildered.

"Yeah. Now where did I put that?" She rummaged in the pocket of her lab coat and came up with a crumpled slip of paper. She handed it to me.

It bore the patient's name, the accession number S-1148-04, and the name of the oncologist that had requested them at Intermountain Cancer Center in Boise.

The mystery was explained.

Or was it?

Wait a minute, I thought. Why did Natalie have to put a label on that slide? It should have had one already.

"It didn't, though. It must have fallen off or something. So I just made a new one," Natalie explained.

"So then you must have put the S-1148-04 label on the slide you sent to Boise?"

"I guess I must have."

"Well, I need that slide to sign the case out with, so could you cut me a new one?"

"Well … I can't. I sent the block to Boise too."

Crap. Apparently Natalie hadn't gotten around to reading the policy on send-outs, which was that slides and blocks were never sent out together until the blocks were recut so that we had something in our file at all times. I mean, what if the package got lost in the mail?

I handed it back to her. "So where are those slides now?"

"In the mail. Want me to go see if I can get them back?"

"Please."

Natalie sprinted out the door. If I was lucky, she'd be able to intercept the mail before it went out; but it was nearly three o'clock now.

I was not lucky.

Natalie returned, breathless. "They just picked it up not five minutes ago," she said, handing me a letter. "But the lady in the mailroom said to give you this. Do you want me to call Boise? To tell them they've got the wrong case?"

"No, I'll do it. And, Natalie, you'd better be more careful in the future. Do you have any idea what I've been through this afternoon?"

She shook her head slowly.

"I thought I'd misread a frozen section and caused a patient to have a breast removed unnecessarily. Do you know what that would do to my career? It would be the end of the line. I must've aged ten years today."

"So ... how did you figure out you hadn't done that?"

"I found metastatic tumor in a lymph node. Thank God you didn't send the whole case to Boise." I laughed shakily.

"Yeah. I'm sorry, Dr. Day."

"Okay. Just don't let it happen again." I patted her shoulder and went back to my office. I tossed the letter into the pile of mail from this morning that I still hadn't had time to go through. I could deal with it later. There were still several more cases to sign out, and it was getting pretty late. But my mind was going round and round in circles.

Why did IMCC want to see a case of sclerosing adenosis anyway? Did someone think I had misdiagnosed that case?

I called Medical Records and asked for her chart.

When I saw it, I realized why the case had seemed familiar.

The patient had returned six months after her breast biopsy with an enlarged axillary node on the same side as the biopsied breast. It was removed and showed metastatic tumor. It was an undifferentiated tumor that could have come from anywhere. There were no clues to its origin. I had sent the case to Boise for immunostains, since our volume was too small to make them cost-effective, but in this case they were no help.

The most likely source for metastatic tumor in axillary nodes is the breast. The patient's mammogram had shown a very suspicious lesion with microcalcifications, but there had been no question in my mind at the time that her breast biopsy was benign. However, when I saw the lymph node, I went back and reviewed the breast biopsy just to relieve my mind, and I said so in my report.

I also noted she was Tyler Cabot's patient.

Natalie's explanation was plausible enough, but it still bothered me, somehow. I couldn't put my finger on it. As I signed out the rest of my surgicals, my mind continued to wrestle with it.

Hal and I had been invited to dinner by our next-door neighbors and best friends, Elliott and Jodi Maynard. Elliott was a lawyer. Jodi owned and operated a spa called First Resort, patronized by those who could afford facials, massage, manicures, pedicures, and acupuncture on a regular basis along with their hair care. I got my hair cut there. So did Desiree Baumgartner Cabot.

Once the Maynards' five children had finished their dinners and dispersed to their various activities, Hal and I brought them up-to-date on my situation at work.

We had discussed Dr. Shore with them before, and they knew about Lucille because it had been in the *Clarion*, but they didn't know about Natalie. So I told them.

"Why didn't you fire her freakin' ass?" asked Elliott, refilling his wineglass.

The same thing had occurred to me, but the thought of losing my histotech right after I got her made me feel faint.

"If I wasn't such a softie, I probably would have," I said.

"Maybe it was just an honest mistake," said Jodi. "I'm sure she'll be more careful next time."

"I hope so, but I can't be sure."

"Why not?"

"Do you realize what would have happened if I hadn't seen tumor in that lymph node?" I shuddered. "I'd be worried sick."

"It's one of the things you do best," Hal put in.

I turned on him. "And with good reason, don't you think? Of course, there's still tumor tissue left in the container, and I could have put in another section, but I wouldn't have been able to sleep until I saw the slide tomorrow, and she could have sabotaged that too."

"Okay, suppose you're right," said Elliott. "What would have happened?"

I took a sip of wine. "Well, I suppose I would have gotten some clue when I got the report back from Boise on the other case, and ... oh, my God ..." I clapped my hands to my mouth.

"What?" asked Jodi.

I felt myself breaking out in a sweat all over again.

"The slides she sent to Boise were from the cancer case. And the slides she was supposed to send were benign. If I hadn't called and told them to send the slides back, they would have sent a report to the surgeon that it was cancer, and the surgeon would have told the patient that she'd had cancer all along but that the pathologist had missed it, and if they had known then, she might have been cured, but now she has a lymph node metastasis, and will not only lose her breast but have to have chemotherapy as well."

"Jesus freakin' Christ," said Elliott.

I mopped my forehead with my napkin. "So not only would we have a patient who has cancer but thinks she doesn't and lost her breast unnecessarily because the pathologist screwed up, but we also would have one who doesn't have cancer but thinks she does and loses a breast and gets chemo unnecessarily because the pathologist screwed up. What a mess," I moaned. "I wasn't even thinking about the *other* patient. One was bad enough, but two... oh, it doesn't bear thinking about. I just can't believe Natalie would do a thing like this on purpose. She doesn't seem like the vindictive type, but then I don't really know her, do I?"

I couldn't sit still any more. So I got up and started stacking plates to take them to the kitchen.

"You don't have to do that, Toni," Jodi said. "I'll get them."

Hal shook his head. "She hasn't been there long enough to know the routines that well. She wouldn't be able to think up a plot like this, would she? Would she have the knowledge? And even if she did, why would she?"

Suddenly, the light dawned. It was all so clear. And so unbelievable.

"I'll bet it wasn't her idea," I said darkly.

Hal took off his glasses and polished them with his napkin. "You think somebody put her up to it? Who'd do a thing like that?"

I sat down, put my arms on the table and leaned forward. "How about Drs. Cabot and Shore, Incorporated?"

Hal turned his palms up. "But why? And why now? Tyler's had ten years to get you if he wanted to."

"But Dr. Shore hasn't."

Hal put his arms on the table and leaned toward me. "She's had three weeks."

"But Natalie's been here less than a week."

"Why did she have to wait for Natalie? Why couldn't she have used Lucille?"

"You don't give Lucille much credit, Hal. She's pretty loyal. She'd never agree to such a thing, and Dr. Shore knows it."

"I see. She had to wait until you got a new tech that wouldn't be loyal. She didn't have to wait long, did she?"

"No. She certainly didn't. Lucille's accident fit right into her plans, didn't it?"

"But you could have waited *months* for another tech. That's what usually happens."

"But not this time. Natalie showed up almost on cue."

By now we were practically nose to nose, and Jodi and Elliott were following this conversation as if it were a tennis match. "Toni," said Hal, "what are you saying?" He sat back and took another swig of his wine. Elliott poured him some more.

I got up and started pacing. "Hal, the whole thing stinks to high heaven. Dr. Shore arrives, immediately forms an alliance with the *only doctor* on the staff who doesn't like me, and proceeds to make life hell for me and my techs. She gets him to fire Lucille. I get Lucille back. Lucille gets hit by a car and ends up in the hospital. Natalie shows up the *next day*. Next thing I know, she makes an 'honest mistake' that would have left my reputation in tatters and gotten me sued for everything we have and ever will have—if it hadn't been for a fluke of luck. Now, maybe I have a suspicious mind, but I think these things are more than just a coincidence. I think I have a Trojan horse in my lab, and I think Dr. Shore put her there."

"Paranoia is alive and well in the Shapiro household," commented Hal dryly.

I shook my head stubbornly. "I don't think so. She's got an agenda, and it involves getting rid of me, for some unknown reason."

"You don't know?" Jodi asked.

"Well, she doesn't exactly confide in me."

"Maybe she's afraid of you," Hal suggested.

I stared at him in disbelief. "That doesn't make any sense. She started in on me right from the beginning. Did she already know I was someone to be afraid of when she came here? How would she know that?"

Hal stared back. "Maybe somebody told her."

"Like Tyler."

"Now you're catching on."

I clutched my head with both hands. "Are we both being paranoid? Hal, this is unbelievable. And there isn't a particle of proof for any of it. But proof or not, my reputation was very nearly damaged beyond repair today, and I intend to make sure it never happens again."

"So now what?" asked Elliott. "Want to sue her for defamation of character?"

Now, there was an idea. But without proof, I guessed I was just going to have to kill her.

Or get someone else to do it.

Chapter 11

Have you not heard it said full oft,
A woman's nay doth stand for naught?
     —Shakespeare, *The Passionate Pilgrim*

With the morning had come reality and common sense. The scenario Hal and I had evolved the night before seemed more fantastic than ever, once I got to my office. But it left me with a very uncomfortable feeling.

So I decided to go through my mail.

The letter I had tossed into the pile sat right there on top, rather like a snake coiled up and ready to strike.

The return address was that of a law firm: Walker, Atkinson, Simpson, and Price—of Long Beach, California.

Oh my God, I'm being sued. It was an automatic response to mail from law firms.

Or maybe …

Oh, no. Not Robbie. Not after all this time. Surely he'd gotten over me and married someone else by now.

Oh, for God's sake, open it and get it over with! I could

hear Hal saying it as clearly as if he were standing right next to me.

With teeth gritted, I slit the envelope open and removed its contents.

I wasn't being sued.

I was being stalked.

Again.

I have no idea how I got through the rest of the day. I'd thought that chapter of my life was permanently closed. Now, it was as if twenty years had vanished without a trace.

Robbie Simpson always could write the most incredibly sexy letters. He could also be incredibly abusive. Which would this be?

I got up and closed my door. I was embarrassed to even be reading this by myself, let alone having somebody walk in on me and see it. I might just as well run out and buy a copy of *Hustler* and be done with it.

Dearest Toni,

I hardly know how to begin now that so much time has gone by since we saw each other last. So much has happened, and yet it seems like just yesterday.

I never wanted us to break up like we did. I tried and tried to get in touch with you, but you never returned my calls, and your mother wouldn't tell me where you were. I suspect she never liked me anyway. Maybe she didn't tell you how often I called. Dare I hope?

I've been married and divorced twice since

we parted. No children. As you can probably tell from the letterhead, I did go on to law school as planned, passed the California bar (on the first try, hurray) and have been with this firm ever since. My life is complete. Except for one thing.

I've never stopped loving you.

Oh, God. How in the hell did he find me?

Even after all these years, I can still close my eyes and see your beautiful face, taste your delicious kisses, feel your naked body pressed to mine, your legs wrapped around me, the warm wetness of your...

Christ, this is embarrassing. Even worse, I wasn't sure if I was revolted or slightly titillated and ashamed to admit it. Either way, it wasn't good.

And it got worse.

Do you know that the only way I could make love to either of my wives was to make believe that I was making love to you? Then I'd open my eyes and it wasn't you, and I couldn't hide my disappointment. That's probably why I'm divorced now. I couldn't stop wanting you.

I despaired of ever seeing you again, my lost love, let alone holding you in this lifetime, except for a stroke of luck.

The lawyer who handled my last divorce, Stan Snow, left our firm to join another firm up there in Idaho. When I told him about you, he told me that he had actually met you. I couldn't believe my good fortune.

Stanley, you're a dead man. Whatever happened to privileged information?

So, my darling Toni, I'm planning a trip up your way, ostensibly to visit my pal Stan.

This time I won't give up so easily.

Your everlastingly devoted
Robbie

Hal knew about Robbie, of course. I had told him about my old boyfriend who wouldn't take no for an answer, but it wasn't until we were seriously considering marriage that I told him the whole story. For the first few years of our marriage while we were still in Long Beach, we were never quite free of the fear that Robbie, if he was in the area, would resume his activities; but once we moved to Idaho, Robbie just sort of faded into the misty past, and we actually forgot about him.

Until the letter arrived. Then it all came roaring back.

That fateful night back in 1981, my junior year in high school, I had gone to a party at somebody's house, I forget whose, where I distinguished myself by being the only one who knew all the words to "Bad Bad Leroy Brown," which I sang with considerable verve and panache, while casting sidelong glances at the serious-looking, bespectacled young man with a crew cut who gazed admiringly at me as I sang. I knew Robbie Simpson by reputation, of course; he was a senior and one of the smartest students in his class. We started dating and were inseparable for the rest of that year.

"Don't get too attached to him, kitten," Mum warned me. "You need to keep your mind on your grades, not your social life." My mother never stopped reminding me that I needed to keep my grades up and get scholarships, because she couldn't afford to pay for college on a secretary's salary.

But I was only sixteen, and college seemed light-years away. When Robbie graduated and went away to Harvard, I was devastated. My senior year was a desert until Christmas vacation when Robbie came home. We spent every possible moment together, kissing and fondling. He told me that he loved me and wanted to marry me. I was in heaven. Then he went away again.

Summer came, and Robbie came home—with a ring. I wore it proudly for about two hours; then I showed it to my mother. Far from sharing my happiness, she was livid.

"Have you heard *nothing* I've been telling you, Antoinette?" she demanded, hands on hips, impaling me with her glittering, green glare. "I've been working my tail off to give you a better life than I've had, and this is how you show your gratitude? Getting engaged in high school? Getting married right after graduation, getting some *dreary* little job to help put that boy through school while your own brain *shrivels* from years of disuse?"

"No, Mum," I protested, "Robbie's going to be a lawyer, and then he can put me through school."

Mum was unimpressed. "Sure he can, dear. By the time he's a lawyer, you'll have had two or three children, and he'll dump you for some sweet young thing who *doesn't* have stretch marks and varicose veins. Then what?"

"You got married at seventeen," I accused. "And you got pregnant too."

"Let me tell you something, Antoinette. Just because I got married at seventeen is no reason for you to do the same. Oh yes, I was deliriously happy. Right up until your father was killed. Have you any idea how alone I was? I was pregnant. My parents kicked me out of the house. I don't know what I would have done if it hadn't been for Jack's parents. They insisted that I bring you to this country and live with them. They paid our passage. Thanks to them, we live in this nice house, in this nice neighborhood. Without them, we'd be in some *grotty* little flat in some London backstreet, wearing secondhand clothing from Oxfam."

I opened my mouth to argue with her, but my mother was on a roll.

"Now, you listen to me, young lady, and no backchat. I moved in with my in-laws with my two-year-old child. I got a dreary little job so that I could contribute my share. I've been a secretary since you were two, because I didn't know anything else, and I've *hated* every minute of it. I will be *damned* if I let you throw your life away because of some *pimply*-faced boy who just wants to get into your *knickers*."

"Robbie doesn't just want to get into my knickers," I sobbed. "He wants to marry me! He loves me! And he doesn't have pimples, either," I added inconsequentially.

My mother straightened up and folded her arms across her chest. Her curly red hair literally quivered with outrage. "Antoinette. Believe me when I say that I mean every word of what I am about to say. You are my child, my blood, I love you with all my heart, and I would give my life for you if I had to. But you marry that boy, and you can forget about ever coming home again. You will be dead to me."

Well. That got my attention. Mum's words struck fear into my heart, and there was nothing I could say. The choice was clear.

I gave the ring back, and I cried for days. Robbie and I continued to see each other when my mother was at work, and one day she came home unexpectedly to find us on the couch in a state of partial undress. She slapped my face and called me a slut.

That summer was a nightmare. It was almost a relief when Robbie went back to Harvard and I started college at Long Beach State. I dated other boys; a lot of other boys. At one point I had a major crush on one of my professors, who was very married and totally impervious to my feminine wiles. I made a fool of myself for about a month. It failed to cure me of Robbie.

Then I met Hal.

Of course, it was just another crush on a professor, but I was two years older and determined to worship this one from afar and not make a complete idiot of myself.

This resolve lasted approximately two weeks. It seemed that my crush on Dr. Shapiro was mutual. Of course, he was married too, but it didn't seem to matter. My junior year whizzed by. Robbie graduated from Harvard with honors and was accepted at Harvard Law School.

When he came home, I tried to be glad to see him. An affair with a married professor was destined to go nowhere and could only hurt me; but Robbie had been a huge part of my life for four years, and he still wanted to marry me.

He picked me up at the college. As I got into his car and saw the dorky crew cut, the thick glasses, the buck teeth, and the nerd pack, I felt faintly repelled. I wondered what I had ever seen in him.

As he took me in his arms, I stiffened involuntarily. He took me by the shoulders and held me away from him while he scrutinized my face.

"Toni? Darling? What's the matter?"

I assured him that nothing was wrong, and we went to his house. His parents were out, so we had the house to ourselves. We went into his bedroom and sat on his bed. He kissed me deeply and slipped his hands under my clothes, unhooking my bra and fondling my breasts. When he slid his hands under my waistband, I tried to stop him, but he was stronger than I was. "Oh, Toni, my darling," he groaned. "I've wanted this so much, oh please, my love, don't deny me, please love me, love me now," and he started to pull my panties off. He pushed me down on the bed and began to suck on my nipples. Hard. It hurt. I struggled out from under him and stood up, pulling my panties up and trying to rehook my bra. He sat up, staring at me incredulously.

"What's the matter with you?" he asked. "I thought you wanted this just as much as I did."

"I'm sorry, Robbie. I guess I'm just not in the mood."

"Oh, you're not in the mood, huh?" He reached for me and pulled me back down on the bed. "You're not in the *mood*? Well, isn't that just too bad." He no longer sounded loving. In fact, he sounded royally pissed. He grabbed me by my hair with both hands and held my head down on the pillow while he ground his lips onto mine and probed my mouth deeply with his tongue while I tried not to gag. "I've waited four years for this," he informed me. "So you're gonna get in the mood, or else."

Then he raped me.

He hit me. He knocked me onto the floor. He shoved my bra and my shirt up, and bit my breasts. He ripped my underpants off. I struggled. It was no use. He gripped my neck with both hands, and had his way with me, while I struggled to keep breathing and not throw up.

Filthy, bloody, bruised, and shamed, I took a cab home. It was still early, and my mother was still up. I tried to slip past her unnoticed, but not much slips by Mum.

"Antoinette? Come here, please."

Reluctantly, I complied.

"Kitten, what on *earth* happened to you? Where have you been?"

I took a deep breath. Painfully. I wasn't sure I hadn't broken a rib. "At Robbie's house."

"*Robbie* did this to you?"

She insisted on calling the police. I tried to talk her out of it, but nothing doing. Maybe it was just as well. What Robbie had done to me was nothing compared to what she would have done to him given the opportunity.

I ended up in the emergency room, still in my bloody, torn clothes, where my broken nose was set, my lacerated lip was stitched, and rape kit samples were taken. I got a tetanus shot. I hadn't broken a rib, but some cartilage was torn, which was equally painful. The female cop who took the rape kit samples was very disappointed that I refused to press charges. Mum told her that she would be glad to press anything that needed pressing to make sure that bloody sod got what was coming to him, but since she wasn't the one who'd been raped, she couldn't.

Deep down, I wasn't too sure that it hadn't been partly my fault. Of course, that's what women are supposed to think, isn't it? That's why so many rapes go unreported.

In any case, I was finally and completely cured of Robbie.

I refused to take his calls. Night after night, I would hear Mum answer the phone and say in her most upper-crust English accent, "No, Robbie, love, she's not here. *Quite* the social butterfly is our Toni, don't you know," followed by a tinkling laugh. Quite the actress was my Mum, who would have cheerfully killed Robbie if she could have done it legally.

Night after night, after I had gone to bed, Robbie would creep into our backyard and throw pebbles at my window. "Come out," he would plead. "Please, Toni, I have to talk to you." When I ignored him, he would simply raise his voice until either Mum or I told him to shut up or we'd call the police. Once the neighbors did call the police, but Robbie was gone by the time they got there.

Night after night, I prayed that Robbie hadn't managed to get me pregnant.

He hadn't. Summer ended. Robbie went back to Harvard Law School. But he didn't stop calling.

My senior year passed. I graduated and started my medical technology internship at the VA hospital, which was right next door to the college campus. Hal gave most of the chemistry lectures to the med-tech students, so we still got to see each other, but not nearly as much as before. I tried to compensate by dating two of the techs, an intern, and a pathology resident.

At the end of the year, I graduated, got my California license, and went off to medical school. I shared an apartment with a second-year student. I made sure the phone was in her name.

Robbie continued to call my mother. She continued to not tell him where I was. But someone did.

I nearly fainted when I answered the phone and heard his voice. I told him I was seeing someone else. He began asking questions. What did this guy do for a living? What did we do on our dates? Where did we go? And what about the physical relationship? Was it as good as ours had been?

Nauseated, I slammed down the phone. As soon as I could, I moved to an apartment of my own with an unlisted number—but not before he showed up on my doorstep and informed me that he was never going to give up, that if he couldn't have me, nobody else could either.

I slammed the door in his face. He sat in his car at the curb and wouldn't leave until I called the police.

Robbie went back to calling my mother. He called about once a month, until the day Mum told him I was married. That was the last I'd heard from or about Robbie.

Until now.

Chapter 12

Like a dog in the manger, he doth only keep it because it shall do nobody else good, hurting himself and others.
—Robert Burton

"**I** don't know what to tell you, kitten," my mother had said on the phone. "You can't keep running from it, now, can you? You have a life there—a job, responsibilities, don't you know. You're going to have to deal with it on your own, now; I can't help you any more."

Hal, on the other hand, was only too eager to help me deal with it. He was ready to get a gun and go out and hunt Robbie down like a criminal.

I talked him out of it. After all, if Hal got caught and sent to prison, where would that leave me?

So he called Elliott, who came right over.

"Let me see that letter," he said.

"And hello to you, too," I replied, as I fished it out of my purse and handed it to him.

His eyes widened as he read it. "Wow. Hot stuff. Did you read this, Shapiro?"

Hal shook his head, and Elliott handed it to him.

"Oh jeez," I muttered, and put my face in my hands.

"It's okay, honey," he reassured me, but as he read the letter, his face got red, and his lips compressed. He handed it back to Elliott without a word and went straight to the liquor cabinet.

"I've got to wash the taste of that out of my mouth," he remarked with a grimace. "Anybody want anything?"

We both accepted with alacrity.

"Now," Elliott said. "I need to know everything you know about this guy."

Hal and I looked at each other. "Everything?"

"Everything."

"It's really ugly," I said.

"All the more reason why I need to hear it."

So we told him the whole story, about the rape and everything that followed. By the time we finished, Elliott had refilled his Scotch and finished most of it.

He tossed it off and wiped his mouth. "This guy," he said, "is freakin' evil. Toni, I'm sorry. Nobody should have to go through what you did. Unfortunately, we can't do anything to him now except keep him away from you. So, here's the plan. Tomorrow I'll talk to Stan. If he's friends with this creep, maybe he could just make a friendly phone call and convince this guy to leave you alone. But if that doesn't do it, then we'll just go from there."

He took the letter with him when he left. Just having it out of the house made me feel better.

Until the phone rang.

"Sorry to bother you at home, Toni, but this situation has gone on long enough."

"What situation is that, Tyler? Because there are so *many* of them, don't you know?"

"Don't get cute with me, Toni. You know very well what situation. I'm up here in ICU and my patient's chem profile isn't on his chart. I know you did one, because I got my office copy today. In fact, I just went down and got it and put it on the chart myself."

"That was very thoughtful of you, Tyler."

"Dammit, Toni, that's not the point! Your techs are going to have to start doing their jobs or …"

"That isn't their job. The nurses do the charting in ICU."

"Whatever. I'm just not going to put up with it any more. It happens all the time, and there's no excuse for it. I can't think of anything else to do except call you every time it happens from now on. No matter what time it is. Maybe if you get awakened in the middle of the night a few times, you'll start doing your job!"

"Oh, so now it's my job. Make up your mind, Tyler."

"I mean it, Toni. No matter what time it is." He hung up on me.

This was getting to be a habit, all this slamming down of phones.

After a few minutes, during which I could think of absolutely nothing I could have done or said differently, I decided to go back over to the hospital and see if I could find that report. One thing I couldn't do was just sit here all night and stew about it.

I told Hal I was going to run over to the hospital for a minute, and did so. It was an easy matter to check. Outpatients always had an extra copy of their lab work, because there were three copies and only two were needed. Hospital patients used all three of their copies, because one had to go on the hospital chart. So, if there was a copy of Tyler's patient's chem profile in the pile of extra copies, it would mean that we had not taken it upstairs for the nurses to chart.

It wasn't there.

Just to be sure, I went up to ICU and looked at the patient's chart myself. Sure enough, Tyler's copy was there. I could tell it was Tyler's copy because he had written on it in red ink: MY OFFICE COPY, WHICH I PUT ON THE CHART MYSELF! But it was the only copy on the chart. Why in hell, I wondered, not for the first time, couldn't he use the fucking computer like everybody else?

"I don't know where it could be," I told the charge nurse. "It's not in the lab."

She shrugged. "He'll get over it. He always does. You know, he yells at us all the time too."

"I know. But this is the first time he's called me at home about it."

"He's been really tense lately. We've all noticed it. We've been wondering if he's having problems at home. That's what it usually is."

"I wouldn't know. He doesn't confide in me. But I do know that if I don't get out of here, *I'll* be the one with a problem at home!"

She chuckled, and I left, intending to go straight home. The lab was dark when I went by, but I saw a light under the closed door to my office. I could have sworn I'd turned off the lights when I left earlier, but I supposed I could have forgotten. It wouldn't be unheard of.

My door was unlocked too. I could have sworn I'd

locked it when I left. When I opened it, my heart jumped into my throat.

Sally Shore was sitting in my chair, at my desk.

Knowing how she usually reacted to me, I immediately went on the offensive. "What the hell are you doing in my office?" I demanded.

She responded in kind. "What the hell are you doing, going around accusing me of malpractice?"

"What?"

"You heard me."

"Yes, I did. But I don't know what you're talking about."

"You and Bob were talking about that little girl with meningitis today." Meaning Bob Anderson, one of the pediatricians.

"Yes, but I don't recall anyone mentioning malpractice."

She took a sip of her coffee. I hadn't noticed that she had a cup of coffee before, but then I'd been just a bit preoccupied with her accusation.

"Do you deny it?"

I was, by now, just about up to here with this conversation. If she was trying to pick a fight with me, by God, I'd give her one.

"No, I don't deny it. I think your treatment of that child *was* malpractice, from what Bob told me."

"You had better be careful, Doctor, that you haven't committed malpractice yourself before you go around accusing anyone else."

"Is that a threat?"

"When I'm on the staff here, you are going to have to make significant changes, or I will make them for you.

Starting with the lab. And if you think your colleagues are going to help you, think again."

I'd had enough. "Get your ass out of my office before I ..."

She stood up. "Before you what? Are you threatening *me*?"

I swung the door wide open and stood aside. "I told you to stay out of my lab. That includes my office."

She picked up her coffee cup and sauntered slowly through the doorway. She stopped in the hallway and turned back to face me. "Remember what I said."

Hmph. As if there were a chance in hell that I'd forget.

What an idiot! I screamed silently to myself. *How could you be so dumb?* Sally Shore was absolutely right when she said I'd better be careful before accusing others of malpractice. After all, hadn't I been put into a practically indefensible position just yesterday? If I hadn't seen tumor in that lymph node, two patients would have had ample reason to sue me for malpractice. But she didn't know that.

Or did she?

In any case, the battle lines were drawn now. She would be ruthless in her campaign to get rid of me, and I would have to be just as ruthless in my campaign to get rid of her, and each of us knew what the other was trying to do.

"That's actually a good thing," Hal said, as he plied me with Scotch. "Forewarned is forearmed. And another thing. I'll answer the phone at night from now on. If that asshole Tyler Cabot thinks he's going to harass you by calling in the middle of the night, he's got another think coming." Then he chuckled. "One thing about all this—I bet it took your mind off Robbie for a while."

Shit, I thought, he *would* have to mention that. But on the other hand, which was worse, thinking about Robbie or thinking about Sally Shore?

Damned if I knew.

Chapter 13

And so from hour to hour we ripe and ripe,
And then from hour to hour we rot and rot;
And thereby hangs a tale.
  —Shakespeare, *As You Like It*

I'd had less than an hour's sleep when I got called in for that frozen section and tripped over Sally Shore's body. It was only after calling the police that I queasily remembered why I was there in the first place.

Had I really drunk that much Scotch? Yikes.

I had always considered myself pretty tough, but I quailed at the thought of sitting in my office with Sally Shore lying dead on the floor. Even being in there long enough to read the frozen section on my microscope was difficult. Besides, there was the matter of evidence. If there was any, my presence might mess it up.

So I decided to camp out in the lab until the police arrived and got the body out of my office. I just hoped they'd get what they needed quickly so I could get back to work. My initial shock at finding Sally Shore dead was slowly being replaced by indignation. *What business does she have dying in my office? Doesn't she have a perfectly good office of her own to die in? The nerve of some people!*

My office was now roped off by police tape, and a gurney stood in the hallway with an all-too-familiar, shrouded bundle on it—the late Sally Shore, in a body bag. Three men stood next to the gurney, two of them in uniform—Pete and Kincaid. The other was Roland Perkins, county coroner and owner of Parkside Funeral Chapel across the city park from the hospital.

"Here's Dr. Day," announced Charlie.

"Hi, Doc," said Rollie.

"Hi, Toni," Pete said.

Kincaid merely nodded.

Rollie took me aside and spoke in a sepulchral voice. "I'm afraid we're going to need a post on this one," he began.

Kincaid intervened.

"Just a minute. We'll get the autopsy done in Boise by the forensic experts. There might be some delay, depending on what they find, so you'll have to take that into account when making funeral arrangements."

"Why do you need to send her to Boise?" Charlie asked. "We've got a perfectly good pathologist right here."

Kincaid looked at me expressionlessly. "Are you experienced in death investigation techniques? Have you ever been involved in a murder investigation?"

He sounded like Dr. Shore.

"Well, no, but … you mean you think she was murdered?"

"We're not at a point in this investigation where we can say whether she was or not. We certainly can't rule it out at this point. The autopsy will have a bearing on that, so I'd prefer to have it done by someone with experience. The pathologists in Boise have always done our cases."

I shrugged. "Suit yourself. If you don't need me any more, can I get to work?"

"I'm sorry, Doctor, but your office is a crime scene. We can't let you use it for a while."

"Well, then, where am I supposed to work?" I asked. "I can't just close Pathology down and go home! The other doctors are still going to need frozen sections and path reports, you know?"

"Don't worry, Doctor. We'll find a place for you to work," Charlie said.

"Well, then, I'm going to need my microscope, and my Dictaphone, and I'm going to need access to my books, and …"

In the end, they set me up in Dave Martin's office. He was on vacation. Once my microscope and Dictaphone were set up, and I had a pile of my most frequently used reference books on the floor next to me, I got myself a cup of coffee and settled in to wait for my slides and to reflect.

It was just as well, I told myself, that I wasn't doing this autopsy. If it turned out to be murder, I wouldn't be the one who had to testify in court and have my report (and my reputation) ripped to shreds by opposing counsel.

I sensed a definite easing of tension and took a moment to bask in this unaccustomed atmosphere of peace and goodwill—until Lt. Kincaid returned to the scene of the crime (sort of) to interrogate me. He pulled his chair up to the desk and took out a notepad. I tensed.

"I've been informed that you were here talking to the

deceased last night," he began. "Could you tell me what time that was?"

"Not really. I do know it was a quarter to eight when I got home."

"How long did it take you to get home?"

"Oh, about five minutes, I should think."

"Is there anyone who could substantiate that, Doctor?"

I smiled. "Other than Killer and Geraldine, no."

Kincaid looked up. His eyes met mine for the first time, and a chill went through me. "And just who are Killer and Geraldine?"

Damn. I guessed that Kincaid wasn't in the mood for humor. "Our dogs. My husband wasn't home."

"When did your husband come home, Doctor?"

What was this preoccupation with what time Hal and I got home? What did that have to do with … oh, no. Was I a suspect? Perhaps it was time to get serious now.

"He left me a note saying he was next door. So I went over there, and then we came home together at about ten."

"So, between eight and ten, your neighbors can substantiate your whereabouts, and after that, your husband. Anyone else?"

Other than the dogs, no. I shook my head.

"Could you tell me, please, Doctor, what was the subject of your conversation with the deceased?"

"She accused me of going around accusing her of malpractice."

"And did you?"

"Not until she accused me."

"Why?"

"Why what?"

We were certainly not making it easier for each other.

"Why would you accuse her of malpractice?"

I shifted uncomfortably in my chair. How much could I tell Kincaid without further implicating myself?

Implicating myself? In what? I didn't kill her. How could I implicate myself in something I didn't even do?

Kincaid waited patiently, his black eyes locked on mine. I decided to just tell the truth and be damned.

"One of the pediatricians told me about a case that he felt she had mismanaged."

"Did you in fact accuse her of malpractice when you talked to him?"

"No. Neither of us mentioned it."

"Then where did she get the idea that you did?"

I shook my head. "I have no idea, unless he talked to her after I did."

"I gather that your relationship with the deceased was somewhat less than friendly," Kincaid said.

No shit, Sherlock.

"I didn't like her," I said. "She was abusive to my techs and antagonistic to me, and she got one of my techs fired. She complains about the lack of 'lab support' that she gets and seems to think that firing all my techs and hiring new ones would solve the problem. Last night she threatened that she was going to make 'significant changes'"—I made air quotes with my fingers—"starting with the lab when she got on the medical staff."

"What was your response to that?"

"I kicked her out of my office and told her to stay out of my lab."

Kincaid put his notebook down and sat up straight. "You kicked her out of your office? She was in your office?"

I felt myself getting angry all over again as I responded to his question. I got up and began to pace, no small feat in Dave's tiny office. "She was sitting right there in *my* chair, at *my* desk, with a cup of *coffee,* for chrissake, acting like she owned the damn place."

"What were you doing here that late?"

"Dr. Cabot called me at home to complain that a lab report wasn't on his patient's chart, and I came in to check on it. When I left I noticed a light on in my office, and I figured I had forgotten to turn it off. So I opened the door, and there she was."

"Your office wasn't locked?"

"And that's another thing. I was sure I had turned off the light *and* locked my door when I left earlier."

"So, if your door was locked, how did she get in?"

I shook my head again. "I have no idea. Nobody has a key to my office except me and the security guard."

Kincaid had his head down, writing busily in his notebook. "What would you have done if Dr. Shore had gotten onto the medical staff?"

I stopped pacing. Kincaid looked up. His dark eyes bored into mine. "Well, Doctor?"

If I answered that question truthfully, I'd be handing Kincaid a motive on a silver platter. I could lie and say I didn't know, but if Kincaid interviewed the administrators, Tyler, or the chief of staff, he would find out that I'd threatened to resign, and then I'd look even *more* suspicious.

"I was planning to resign."

"And now?"

I sighed and dropped into my chair.

"Well, now I don't have to, do I?"

The next day, the police tape was gone, so I moved back into my office. No sooner had I settled in than Margo appeared in my doorway, a large bouquet of yellow roses in her hands.

"These were just delivered. Where do you want them?"

I stood up and took them from her. "I'll take care of it. Thanks."

Margo left, and Monty replaced her in the doorway, standing there with some papers in his hands. "Nice flowers," he said. "What's the occasion?"

I put the flowers on a bookcase. "I have no idea. What can I do for you?"

"I just need a signature, Doctor. We're making some changes in our malpractice insurance."

I scrawled my signature in the space indicated. "Does this have anything to do with Dr. Shore?"

"Yes, why?"

I sat back in my chair and looked up at Monty, who towered over me, ramrod straight. I wished he'd just relax. "Just something one of the doctors said. You know, for the first couple of weeks I thought everybody but me thought she was wonderful, and then I started hearing complaints; but now that she's dead, they're coming out of the woodwork."

Monty snorted. "You should have been sitting in my office for the last couple of weeks and heard all the complaints that I heard. The only reason we didn't get rid of her sooner is that nobody wanted to go back to doing surgery at night and covering the emergency room."

After Monty left, I looked at the card on the bouquet of roses. It bore the message "Just because I love you" and was unsigned; but that didn't bother me. They were from Hal, of course. He knew yellow roses were my favorite, and anyway, who else would send me flowers?

I called him at the college and found him between classes.

"Thanks for the flowers, sweetie. What's the occasion?"

Hal sounded perplexed. "What flowers?"

"What do you mean, what flowers? You sent me a dozen yellow roses."

"No, hon, they aren't from me. Not that you don't deserve them, but I didn't send them. Wasn't there a card?"

"Yes, but it isn't signed." I read him the message. "I just assumed they were from you. Who else would send me flowers ... oh, no."

"What's the matter?"

"You know who else used to send me yellow roses?"

"No, who?"

I shuddered. "Robbie."

"Oh, no."

"Those roses are going in the trash the minute I get off the phone," I vowed.

"Anything else going on?"

I told him about my interview with Lt. Kincaid. When I came to the part about not having to resign, he said, "Toni, for God's sake, that makes you look like you had a motive!"

"I know that, but what was I supposed to tell him? If I lied, he'd find out, and then I'd look even more like a suspect."

Hal was silent long enough for me to begin wondering if we still had a connection. "Hal? Are you still there?"

"I'm still here. I was just thinking."

"And?"

"What I'm thinking is, you'd better hope for one of two things."

You mean there's something to hope for? Other than somebody else confessing to the crime? "What's that?"

"That somebody saw her alive after you did, or that the autopsy doesn't show anything."

Chapter 14

Steep'd amid honey'd morphine, my windpipe
Throttled in fakes of death.
—Walt Whitman

*P*ete Vincent called while Hal and I were eating dinner, wanting to go over the autopsy report on Dr. Shore.

He showed up, red-faced from the wind, rubbing his hands together and blowing on them, just as I was loading the last of the supper dishes into the dishwasher. "Breezy out there," he said. "Damn near blew the car off the road."

Hal had made a pot of coffee, and we sat around the dining room table. I had replaced the red candles in the menorah with blue ones to go with the décor, using it as a centerpiece, another bone of contention with my mother-in-law. *Oy gevalt*, what next? When I finally finished reading the report and put it down, two pairs of eyes watched me expectantly.

The cause of death was given as "probable cardiac arrhythmia." In addition, there was mild congestion of the lungs, liver, and spleen, which was probably terminal. She had gallstones, mild gastritis, diverticuli in the sigmoid colon, an ovarian cyst, uterine fibroids and endometrial polyps, a hemangioma on the surface of the liver, and an accessory spleen. She'd had an appendectomy and a tubal ligation. No evidence was found of a pulmonary embolus, acute myocardial infarction, congestive heart failure, ruptured aneurysm, cerebrovascular accident, cancer, or anything else that could cause sudden death in an outwardly healthy person. No marks were found on the body with the exception of a puncture mark on the left upper arm, accompanied by a drop of blood and some bruising.

I flashed back to the memory of the body in my office. I remembered seeing a mark on her arm as I bent over it, and that brought back another memory, one of Sally Shore scratching her arm as we talked in Surgery the night Lucille got fired. She'd had a big red welt then, but the autopsy report didn't mention a welt, and I didn't remember seeing one either when I'd found her.

"Well?"

"This seems pretty straightforward," I said. "Exactly what's the problem?"

"What's a cardiac arrhythmia?"

"That means the heart starts beating in an irregular rhythm that doesn't allow it to pump blood efficiently and sometimes causes it to stop altogether. But that's something that can't be proved or disproved by an autopsy, and pathologists just throw it in as a possible cause of death when they can't find anything else. I've done it myself. But it doesn't make sense in this case."

"Why not?"

"Because when I found her, she was cyanotic, and there's nothing to explain that."

"Cyanotic?" Pete asked. "You mean she was blue? Not enough oxygen, right?"

"Exactly, but I can't see why she would be. She didn't have pneumonia, she didn't have a pulmonary embolus, she didn't have any airway obstruction, and she didn't have any marks on her neck to indicate strangling. Her hyoid bone was not broken, her larynx was not fractured, and her lungs were normal, according to this report."

"Well, don't people get cyanotic when they have a cardiac arrest?" asked Hal.

"No, they get cyanotic when they have a *respiratory* arrest."

"So what's the difference?" asked Pete.

"The difference is that if you stop breathing before your heart stops, your heart continues to pump deoxygenated blood around through your body, and you become cyanotic because deoxygenated blood is very dark colored. If your heart stops first, the blood doesn't go anywhere. So you don't get cyanotic. See?"

"But doesn't your heart stop if you stop breathing?"

"Sure, but not right away. It keeps going long enough to circulate deoxygenated blood around the body at least once."

"So, if she did die of a cardiac arrhythmia, she shouldn't have been cyanotic?" asked Pete.

"Not unless someone did CPR on her."

"What are you getting at, Toni?"

"I don't think anybody did CPR on her. What I'm getting at is that something made a perfectly healthy forty-one-year-old woman stop breathing, and we need to know what. There certainly isn't anything in this report that tells us that."

"Perfectly healthy?" Pete was skeptical. "With all that other stuff?"

"All that other stuff is very common and couldn't possibly make anybody stop breathing," I assured him.

"Jesus." Pete sat with his head in his hands. "How am I going to explain this to Bernie?"

"How about the needle mark on the left upper arm? Did you notice it?"

Pete nodded. "Rollie saw it too. We were both wondering about it."

"Well, I can tell you there was no mark on her arm when I saw her that night."

"Do you have any idea what it might have been?" Pete asked me.

"I know she took allergy shots," I said. "Other than that, your guess is as good as mine."

"Who else knew she took allergy shots?"

"Why, practically everybody, I should think. She talked about her allergies to anyone who'd listen. Why?"

"Bernie and I talked to everybody who was on duty that night. Nobody mentioned giving her a shot. 'Course we didn't ask about that specifically. Maybe we better. I don't suppose she could have given it to herself?"

I maneuvered my right hand into position to inject myself in the left upper arm with an imaginary syringe, and shook my head. "Possible," I observed. "But clumsy."

"You didn't give it to her, did you?"

"Hell, no. Why on earth would you ask that?"

"Because she died in your office."

I shook my head. "She didn't die in my office."

"How do you figure that?" Pete asked, perplexed.

"The postmortem lividity," I said. "You know the discoloration of the skin when the blood settles after death? The report describes it as being all in her buttocks, backs of her thighs, and lower legs and feet."

"Which means…?"

"She died sitting up."

"Yeah," Hal chimed in. "If she died lying down, it would have been in her back. She was moved after she died."

Pete cleared his throat. "Couldn't she have died sitting up in your office and then fallen out of your chair onto the floor?"

"Why are you so all-fired anxious to pin it on me?" I demanded in mock anger.

Pete was suddenly grave.

"I'm not, Toni, believe me; but we haven't found anybody who saw her alive after you did."

After Pete left, Hal and I went to bed. But I didn't sleep. There were too many thoughts in my head.

Dr. Shore had to have received that shot after I talked to her, because I didn't give it to her. But nobody admitted to having seen her after I did.

Normally, records were kept of each shot and any reaction to it. I knew that because both Hal and I had taken allergy shots in the past. Southern Idaho is a great place for allergies—dry, dusty, windy, agricultural. Lots of people take allergy shots. Most of my techs had taken them too, at one time or another.

If someone legitimate, like a nurse, had given her an

allergy shot, that person should have entered it on the record sheet at the time it was given.

I needed to get a look at that sheet. Maybe her nurse Marilyn would be able to shed some light on the problem.

I wasn't able to talk to Marilyn until after the Credentials Committee meeting on Monday. Someone with a warped sense of humor had not only put me on the committee but had also designated me chairman. Luckily, Credentials Committee doesn't meet very often.

Marilyn was at the nurses' station when I went into the emergency room and, miraculously, was not busy. Once I explained why I needed to know, she was happy to talk about it. "I always keep the allergy stuff in this little refrigerator here," she told me, indicating a small refrigerator under the counter of the nursing station. "In fact, it should still be here," she went on, opening the door. She took out a handful of envelopes and sorted through them. "Hmm, that's funny."

"What is?"

"Well, it *was* right here. There was an envelope like this with her name on it, and the bottle and the record sheet that go with it were kept in it. But the envelope's gone. If that isn't the darndest thing."

I peered over her shoulder, trying to make out the names on the other envelopes, but she gathered them all together and put them back in the refrigerator.

I leaned on the counter. "Were you the only one who gave shots to Dr. Shore?"

Marilyn shut the refrigerator door. "Usually.

Sometimes Stacey or Katie did, but I gave the last one, so I would have put the bottle back."

"Could you have put it somewhere else?"

She shook her head. "I don't think so, but let me just check a few other places."

I followed her around as she looked in other refrigerators and in the exam rooms. No joy.

"You couldn't have thrown it away by any chance?" I suggested.

"Well, no. It was practically a new bottle. She'd only had three shots out of it."

Finally, we gave up. The bottle was nowhere to be found. The other nurses, when questioned, had no idea either.

"Could someone else have given her a shot after you did?" I asked.

Marilyn gave me a quizzical look. "I don't know why anyone would do that," she answered. "She wasn't due for another one for three days. She only gets shots twice a week."

"Could she have given herself that shot?" I asked finally.

"Her? Don't make me laugh," retorted Marilyn scornfully. "She was the biggest wuss in the state. You should have seen the way she'd carry on just getting these shots. There's no way."

I remembered the itchy red welt that I'd seen. "She got reactions sometimes, didn't she?"

"She *always* had reactions. She'd get this big welt and itch all over and have to take Benadryl. Every time."

Always? Every time? "So then the welt would go away?"

Marilyn laughed. "Eventually, after a couple of days. Just in time for her next shot."

That means she had a welt on her arm and itched all over pretty much all the time. No wonder she was bitchy. She was *itchy*.

"Well, if you get any ideas about what could have happened to that bottle, let me know, will you?"

"Okay. It's bound to turn up somewhere."

"Are you sure you're not making a big deal out of nothing?" asked Hal, as he squeezed a packet of mayonnaise onto his sandwich. He had no noon class today, so he'd come to have lunch with me in the hospital cafeteria.

I arranged the tomato slice and the lettuce leaf precisely atop my cheeseburger. "I'm not making a big deal. I just can't make these things fit. Somebody gave her a shot, but who? And she always had a reaction to her shot, but this time she didn't. Why? And where's that bottle now?" I took a huge bite.

"Well, to take the first question first, the police haven't talked to everybody in the place, just those who were on duty that night."

I chewed thoughtfully and swallowed. Perfect. "Why would someone who was not on duty come back just to give an allergy shot? Besides, her nurse said there were only the three of them who gave those shots."

"Well then, the other possibility is that it was someone who *was* on duty and lied."

I gestured with a dill pickle spear. "Why would anybody lie about giving a routine allergy shot?"

"Because she died, of course."

"Oh. Yeah."

Chapter 15

The pellet with the poison's in the flagon with the dragon,
The vessel with the pestle has the brew that is true.
                    —Norman Panama and Melvin Frank

*P*ete called while I was doing a frozen section, wanting me to come to the station, which I couldn't do because I was doing a frozen section.

Pete didn't mind, but apparently Lt. Kincaid did, because the phone rang again not five minutes later.

"Doctor, perhaps you didn't understand. When a police officer requests your presence, that means *now*. Nothing takes precedence over that, is that clear?"

"Lieutenant, *you* don't understand. I'm doing frozen sections. I'm going to *be* doing frozen sections for at least the next hour—on a patient who is *in* surgery, *under* anesthesia, *right now*. If you think police business takes precedence over that, you can come right over here and explain it to the surgeon."

Then I hung up. *What a jerk.*

When I finally did go to the police station late in the afternoon, Pete intercepted me just inside the door.

"You're in trouble," he warned me. "Kincaid's ready to throw the book at you."

I wiped my brow. I'd walked six blocks to the police station downtown, and despite the wind I'd worked up a sweat.

Luckily, Kincaid was occupied elsewhere at that particular moment; but Commander Ray Harris was available and greeted me with a smile, removing the toothpick from the corner of his mouth with one hand while shaking my hand with the other. Then he put the toothpick back and invited me to sit.

"I'm delighted to meet you, young lady," he told me. "And you're even prettier than they said you were. I hope those two clowns haven't been giving you a hard time. Hey! Get your butts in here!" He made a gesture with his arm, and Pete and Kincaid came in and sat down. Unlike me, the Commander had enough chairs in his office. This meeting would have been impossible in mine.

The Commander said, "Now, as I understand it, we're trying to clear up some misunderstanding about the autopsy report on this Dr. Shore who died at the hospital the other night. I asked you to come here so we could all hear it together at the same time. Now, what was the problem?"

I explained again about the absence of cyanosis in cardiac arrest and its presence in respiratory arrest.

"Well, now, that seems like a pretty big mistake for a forensic expert to make. Here, let me see that report. Who the hell is Nicholas P. Schroeder, MD? I never heard of him. He's not one of the regulars, is he? Maybe we should be asking *him* these questions."

"We tried," said Pete. "Apparently he was just filling

in for Dr. Robertson while he had his coronary bypass, and now Dr. Robertson is back, and this Dr. Schroeder is gone, and nobody knows where to reach him. He's one of those loco … tenum …"

"Locum tenens," I supplied.

"That's it. He's a sub, and Dr. Robertson can't help us, because he wasn't there at the time."

"And maybe Dr. Nicholas P. Schroeder isn't a forensic expert, either," I said.

"We should have had you do the autopsy, Toni," said Pete. "It would have been a lot less hassle."

"Vincent, she's a suspect," Kincaid snapped. "How would it look if we let her do the autopsy? She could say anything, and we wouldn't know the difference. Talk about hassle!"

I felt as if I'd been kicked in the chest and had the wind knocked out of me. I knew I was a suspect, but the way Kincaid said it really slammed me.

The Commander ignored him. "So what do you think, Doctor? What killed her? Any ideas?"

"There was an injection site on the back of her arm," I said. "I know that she took allergy shots, and maybe that's what it is, but there was no mark on her arm when I was there the night before."

"Are you sure?"

"Yes. She always wore sleeveless tops. She was wearing one that night. She had no marks on either arm."

"Obviously, someone gave her the injection after you left," said Kincaid.

"We couldn't find anybody who did," Pete reminded him. "We couldn't find anybody who even saw her after that."

"Maybe she gave it to herself."

"Her nurse says not," I said. "Apparently she was squeamish about needles."

"I fail to see where this is getting us," Kincaid said. "The cause of death is cardiac arrest, or if we are to believe Dr. Day, respiratory arrest. Why quibble over a shot?"

I opened my mouth to tell them why, and then shut it again.

You had better hope for two things, Hal had said. *That someone saw her alive after you did, or that the autopsy doesn't show anything.*

As far as I knew, I was still the last to see her alive. And as far as they knew, the autopsy didn't show anything.

Why couldn't I just leave it like that?

If I told them everything, there'd be no doubt that Sally Shore was murdered, and I was a suspect. I could go to prison. But if I didn't, I'd be withholding evidence in a murder investigation, and I'd go to prison for sure.

Well, that was a no-brainer. I decided to come right to the point.

"Because she always had a reaction to her allergy shots, a big welt. I didn't see a welt on either arm, and the autopsy didn't mention one, either. The other thing is …"

"Hey! Slow down there, girl. Let me get this straight. You say she always had a reaction. How do you know that?"

I don't want to slow down, damn it. I want to get out of here while I still can.

"Because Marilyn, the nurse who usually gave Dr. Shore her shots, said so."

"Okay, so if she always had a reaction to her allergy

shots, and she didn't have a reaction to the shot she got on the night she died, then it couldn't have been her allergy shot, but something else. Is that what you're getting at?"

"Yes."

"So what was it? Any ideas?"

"Well, it occurred to me that it may have been something like a tetanus shot or a flu shot, so I looked in her chart to see if there was any record of it. I also looked her up on the computer."

"And?"

"There wasn't."

"So, whoever gave her the shot forgot to write it down, obviously," said Pete.

If so, that would be a simple explanation. Except that nurses always write things down. It's the way they're trained.

"Also, the bottle that her shots came out of is missing. Three nurses and I looked all over the place and couldn't find it."

"All over the entire hospital?" Pete looked skeptical.

"No, just the emergency room. Marilyn said it was always kept in the little refrigerator under the desk at the nurses' station, but it wasn't there."

"Maybe somebody threw it away."

"Not likely. Marilyn said it was a practically new bottle."

"It's got to be somewhere," Pete said. "Why would anybody throw away a bottle that was practically full?"

The Commander shifted the toothpick from one side of his mouth to the other and slid forward in his chair. "I think the doc, here, has some ideas on that subject. Out with it, girl!"

"Because there was something in it that wasn't supposed to be there."

"Like what?"

"Like poison."

The Commander took off his steel-rimmed spectacles and rubbed his eyes. "I knew I shoulda stayed in bed this morning," he sighed. "Doctor, have you got any ideas on what kind of poison it could have been?"

"I thought that was why you sent the body to Boise for the autopsy. So the *experts* could do it," I couldn't resist adding.

The Commander groaned. "Don't remind me," he said, and shifted the toothpick back to the other side of his mouth.

"Wait a minute, Toni," Pete interrupted. "Dr. Shore can't have been poisoned. The drug screen was negative."

"What drugs did they screen for?"

The Commander picked a folder out of the pile on his desk and handed it to me. "Here," he said. "This'll probably make more sense to you than it does to me."

They had done a screen for drugs of abuse, the same one we used for our patients. It had been sent to the reference lab in Salt Lake City, the same one we sent our drug screens to.

"This only rules out a few drugs," I said, handing the folder back. "There are lots of other things it could have been."

"Like what?" Kincaid asked.

How the hell do I know? I didn't do it, damn it!

But Pete didn't give me a chance to answer, which was good because I had no idea what to say. "How could she have been given poison?" he objected. "She would have put up some kind of a fight. And there was no sign of that. She didn't even knock over her coffee."

Coffee? What coffee? She'd had a cup of coffee the previous night, but I was pretty sure she'd taken that with her when I kicked her out of my office. I didn't remember seeing a coffee cup on my desk the next morning, but then I'd been too busy taking a dive over the body to notice.

"Was there anything in her coffee?" I asked.

"We're having it analyzed," Pete said.

"And besides," I said, "if she thought she was just getting an allergy shot, why would she put up a fight?"

"Wait a minute," Pete said. "Are you suggesting that someone put poison into her allergy shot stuff and then waited for a nurse to give it to her when it was time?"

I shrugged. "Maybe. Why else would the bottle be missing?"

"Jesus Christ," Pete muttered. "I'd sure hate to be that nurse. How would you feel?"

The Commander cleared his throat. "Well, young lady, this certainly rules out death by natural causes. Now, Pete, you and Bernie have your work cut out for you. You're gonna have to go back and interview all those people again that were on duty that night. You know what to ask."

Pete groaned.

The Commander stood up and shook my hand again. "Thank you very much, Doctor, and we'd appreciate it if you'd let us know as soon as possible if you come up with anything else."

"You mean I can go? You're not going to arrest me?"

The Commander chuckled. "Not yet. Just one thing, though."

"What's that?"

"Don't leave town."

I laughed. "You're kidding, right?"

Kincaid didn't share my amusement. As I started to leave, he blocked my way, standing so close that I felt his breath on my face. "Maybe you think this is funny, Doctor, but you're the only viable suspect so far. This isn't the movies or a TV show, and I'm here to tell you that if you even *think* about leaving town, I'll throw you in the slammer so fast you won't know what hit you. Do I make myself clear?"

His black eyes were like lasers, burning their way into mine. He held my gaze for a long moment, then stepped aside and let me pass. Outside, tears pricked my eyes. I felt like a scolded child, and I didn't like that one bit.

But I had absolutely no doubt that Lieutenant Bernard Kincaid meant every word he said.

Chapter 16

Where sits our sulky, sullen dame,
Gathering her brows like a gathering storm.
Nursing her wrath to keep it warm.
—Robert Burns

"Dr. Day?"

Dale Scott poked his head tentatively around my door.

I looked up from my Pap smears and stretched. It was time for a break anyway. "Come in, Dale. What is it?"

He threw his six-foot frame into a chair and ran his fingers through his curly red hair, resulting in that punk look. "Dr. Day, this isn't exactly lab business, so maybe I shouldn't … I mean … Dr. Day, do you know what's eating Natalie? She won't talk to me. She won't talk to anybody."

I hadn't noticed. Obviously, I had not been paying attention. "Really?"

"Well, she's always been kind of quiet, but I didn't really notice anything until after Dr. Shore died, and we were all so glad … I mean …"

I couldn't fault him on that. Nobody was gladder than I was to be rid of Sally Shore.

"Yes, Dale. I know what you mean. So?"

"So we were all sort of celebrating, you know, and Natalie wasn't. It was real obvious. In fact, I think she's been crying a lot. But when I ask her what's the matter, she says it's nothing. So I just wondered if you knew …" He turned his palms up.

Guiltily, I realized that I hadn't noticed anything different about Natalie, even though I spent several hours a day working in the same room with her.

"I don't know, Dale. We don't really talk about anything but work. I'm sorry."

At that point, Margo came in and Dale left.

"Excuse me, Doctor, but I thought you'd like to know. Lucille gets to come home Saturday."

"Oh, good. And also … oh, shit."

"Yes, I know. But we don't have to worry about that just yet. She's not going to be able to work for several more weeks. Kenny says she's supposed to stay in bed for two more weeks, and then she's going to be on crutches for a while, and then she's going to have to have more surgery—to take pins out and stuff—so it could be six months before she can come back to work."

At this point, George Marshall came in and Margo left.

"What is this, Grand Central Pathologist?" I demanded.

He wanted to look at a liver biopsy that he had done the day before yesterday, so I moved my Pap smears out of the way and let him sit at my microscope.

"Toni," he said as he adjusted my eyepieces to suit his eyes, "did you do a post on Dr. Shore?"

"No. The police wanted the forensic experts in Boise to do it."

"Why? Did they think she was murdered or something?"

I didn't feel like discussing the case with George or anybody else right then. Kincaid's rebuke still stung. "I don't know."

He put the slide back in the tray. "Did you do a trichrome stain?" he inquired, peering nearsightedly at the other slides. "Oh, yes, here it is. You know, if she was still here, she wouldn't be here, if you get my drift."

"Really?"

"I don't think there's anybody on the staff who hasn't had her screw up on a patient. If all those people sue us, we'll have to close the hospital."

"Oh, dear," I said.

"If she *was* murdered, somebody did all of us a great big favor." He put the trichrome back in the tray, pushed the chair back, and stood up. "I know this is the new millennium and all, but there are a lot of chauvinists on this medical staff, and I'll tell you something, Toni." He shook a long bony finger in my face. "If you and Mitzi hadn't gotten here first, you wouldn't be here now. It's going to be a cold day in hell before another woman gets on this medical staff."

Then he stomped out the door before I had a chance to say anything.

Well, that was interesting, I thought. It conceivably widened the field of possible suspects to the entire medical staff—and possibly Monty as well.

Except that I was still the only one who had threatened to resign because of her.

Bugger, as my mother would have said.

I went back into the lab and took Margo aside. "Do you know what's bothering Natalie?" I demanded.

"So you've noticed it too?"

"Actually, I didn't, until Dale pointed it out to me."

"You know, don't you, that Dale has been taking her out?"

"No, I didn't, but I'm not surprised."

"I don't know what her problem is," she said with exasperation. "We've all tried to talk to her, but she just goes around looking like she just lost her best friend and says she's just fine."

Obviously, Margo didn't know any more than Dale did; but she knew a whole lot more than I did. I had been treating Natalie the same as Lucille, not taking into account that I'd known Lucille for ten years. I'd only known Natalie a couple of weeks and had no idea what made her tick. Other than the fact that she did her job well, I knew nothing about her.

Maybe it was time I did something about that.

I took the liver slides back across the hall to Histology where Natalie sat cutting the surgicals. I stood there and looked at her, not saying anything, and eventually she looked up.

"Did you want something, Dr. Day?"

Her eyes did look a little red, and her voice was soft and husky.

"Natalie, is something bothering you?"

"No, why?"

"Dale seems to think something is."

A startled expression crossed Natalie's face. "Dale talked to you? About me?"

"He seems to think that Dr. Shore's death has something to do with it."

Natalie turned away from me, and her black hair obscured her face. "He had no right to do that. Talk to you, I mean. He should mind his own business."

"Margo says the two of you are dating."

Natalie faced me, her red-rimmed eyes ablaze. "So is everybody in the lab talking about me behind my back? Don't they have anything else to do?"

I leaned on the counter next to her. "I think that everybody in the lab likes you very much and wants to help."

"Well, they can't." Her full lips compressed stubbornly into a straight line.

"And I suppose that includes me? And Dale?"

She nodded, lips still pressed together.

I moved away from the counter. "Okay. It's okay if you don't want to talk to me. But if you and Dale are in a relationship, you need to be honest with him about it. Don't you think you owe him an explanation? At least so he doesn't think *he's* the problem?"

A smile struggled to appear on Natalie's mouth. "Maybe you're right."

"Good. I'll just go mind my own business now."

Maybe it was wishful thinking on my part, but I thought I heard a giggle as I crossed the hall.

Chapter 17

No, no, go not to Lethe, neither twist
Wolf's bane, tight-rooted, for its poisonous wine.
—John Keats

I went home with the intention of doing some serious research on poisons.

After dinner, I retired to the den upstairs, which was originally intended to be a bedroom. Hal and I had turned it into a shared office. It had two desks and was lined with bookcases, all of which were overflowing with books. The carpet on the floor was dark red, as were the draperies, and there were mirrored tiles on the ceiling. What the previous owner had used the room for was anybody's guess. It was very cozy up there with the wind howling outside the windows.

It was Hal's turn to do the dishes, and he joined me after a while with two cups of coffee. Then he settled down at the other desk to grade exams.

I had fired up my computer, logged onto the Internet, and systematically gone through the *Physician's Desk Reference* online, listing all the respiratory depressants I could find. Then I Googled all the drugs I had listed and found links that led me to other poisonous substances.

The phone rang in the hall. I started to get up to go answer it, but Hal stopped me. "I'll get it. I hope it's that asshole Tyler. I'll give him a piece of my mind."

But whoever it was had apparently hung up. Hal snarled and slammed the receiver down. Grading exams always makes him testy. So do people who hang up when he answers the phone.

Me too, especially because I can usually manage to forget about Robbie until the phone rings. Then I get scared all over again.

Because the drug screen had been negative, I knew I could eliminate marijuana, phencyclidine, propoxyphene, methadone, methaqualone, cocaine and anything else classified as an opiate, amphetamine, benzodiazepine, or barbiturate, which were on the drug screen the police had ordered. That left such things as fentanyl, ketamine, and the neuromuscular blocking agents used in anesthesia; plant poisons such as hyoscine, aconitine, taxine, coniine, ricin, nicotine, and cyanide; and the sympathomimetics and parasympathomimetics.

At that point, Killer, who'd apparently been drinking out of the toilet, came up to me and planted his dripping muzzle on my shoulder, soaking me to the skin. *Yuck.*

I told him to go drip on his brother, the cat, and went to the bedroom to change into my sweats. As I came back past the phone stand in the hall, the phone rang again. I picked it up.

A familiar voice said, "Toni? Darling? Is that you?"

Oh, no. I broke out in a cold sweat. My knees felt as if they were going to buckle under me.

"Robbie," I said, trying to sound nonchalant. "How did you get this number?"

Hal came into the hall. He gestured at the phone. "Give it to me," he mouthed. I covered the mouthpiece and shook my head. "It isn't Tyler," I hissed.

Robbie snickered. "My buddy Stan gave it to me."

"*Stan* gave it to you? He had no right to do that!"

"Oh, it wasn't his fault. I got it off the Rolodex in his office. He doesn't know anything about it."

"Where *are* you?"

"Here. At Stan's house."

I felt as if all the oxygen had suddenly been taken out of the air. I began to hyperventilate.

"Says here," Robbie continued, "your married name is Shapiro. You married a *Jew*?" The contempt in his voice was almost palpable. I felt my face grow hot.

"Yes. I married a Jew," I said, my voice rising. "What's wrong with that? And what business is that of yours?"

He snickered again. "Quite a comedown, don't you think?"

I opened my mouth to answer, but before I got a word out, Hal took the phone away from me and hung up. I was so angry I was shaking. Hal put his arms around me and held me without saying a word. I buried my face in his shirt front. We stood there like that for a long time. Then he spoke.

"Looks like we've got two reasons for me to answer the phone at night from now on."

Back at my desk, I sat staring at my list, struggling to get back into my previous state of mind. Suddenly I realized that I needed to take volumes into consideration. After all, the shot had to *look* like an allergy shot, which are given in tuberculin syringes, with a volume of between 0.05 and 0.5 cc. Anything bigger would arouse suspicion.

So, after a while I came up with a list of drugs that cause rapid death in fairly small quantities, along with some interesting information.

Nicotine: a fatal dose is 40 mg, the amount contained in one drop (0.05 cc) of pure nicotine or two cigarettes. It paralyzes all skeletal muscle, including the diaphragm. Death occurs in five minutes to four hours.

Cyanide: the lethal dose of hydrocyanic acid is 0.5 mg/kg, or 35 mg for a 150-pound human. The lethal dose of potassium cyanide is 2 mg/kg, or 140 mg. Death occurs in one to fifteen minutes, after causing immediate unconsciousness and convulsions.

It occurred to me that cyanide smells like bitter almonds, which most everybody knows. I hadn't noticed a bitter almond smell in my office, but then not everybody can smell it. However, I'd have thought that between Rollie Perkins, Lt. Kincaid, and Pete, one of them would've been able to smell bitter almonds, wouldn't they? But nobody had mentioned it. On the other hand, nobody had asked them, either.

I made a note to ask them.

Neuromuscular blocking agents: These are drugs used in anesthesia to paralyze skeletal muscles so that the patient doesn't move around during surgery. They block the junction between nerve ends and muscles so that the impulse still travels down the nerve, but never reaches the muscle. Two of the most commonly used are pancuronium and succinylcholine. The effect of pancuronium lasts two hours, and succinylcholine, thirty minutes, plenty long enough to suffocate someone not on a ventilator.

I hit "print" and stretched. Hal looked up from his papers. I handed him the list. He looked at it and then at me with a devilish gleam in his eyes. "Wouldn't it be a bummer if you did all this work and then it turns out she was shot with a poison dart or something?"

"Come on, Hal. Where is anybody going to find a poison dart in Twin Falls, Idaho?"

"Well, it was just a thought. Which one do you like?"

"Personally, if I was going to kill someone, I would use a neuromuscular blocking agent. No muss, no fuss—you just stop breathing and that's it. It would be an awful way to die, though. You remain conscious right up till the end, but you can't move, and you can't call for help, and eventually you can't breathe, but you don't lose consciousness until the brain gets hypoxic enough. Why," I warmed to my subject, rubbing my hands together fiendishly, "you'd have time to tell your victim exactly why you had killed him, and he'd have time to think about it before he died!"

Hal shivered. "Toni, you scare me sometimes. Remind me not to get you mad at me. Come on, let's go to bed."

Chapter 18

Things are seldom what they seem;
Skim milk masquerades as cream.
　　　　　　　　　—Sir William Gilbert

Hal and I were both too keyed up to sleep, so we watched the *Late Show* in bed. Unfortunately, the movie was *Arsenic and Old Lace*, and while it was all very amusing, it was hardly the sort of thing to take my mind off poisonings.

I dozed off before it was over, with the light still on, but I slept fitfully. Every time I went back to sleep, I had disquieting dreams and woke up again. The only unbroken sleep I had was between four and seven in the morning.

It was not a good day to be rousted out of bed after three hours' sleep to do frozen sections on a gastrectomy for possible gastric cancer. I'd been unable to make a definitive diagnosis on the endoscopic biopsies taken several days earlier and had sent the slides to Boise. In the meantime, the patient had developed a gastric outlet obstruction and required emergency surgery—and yet another unscheduled frozen section.

You might know that I wouldn't be able to make a definitive diagnosis on the surgical specimens either. The surgeon was not pleased when I had to give him a deferred diagnosis. "You're not helping, Toni," he said testily when I went up to Surgery to give him the news in person. I dislike giving complicated explanations to nurses on the phone, and I like the intercom still less. The surgeon always sounds like he's standing in the bottom of a barrel with a tin can over his head, and I'm sure I sound the same to him. Why on earth we can't get a decent one, I can't imagine. Intercom, I mean, not surgeon.

However, I had no trouble hearing the altercation that was going on in Roger Elquist's office as I was leaving.

"What the hell is going on here?" he rasped. "You came up short last week too. What are you doing, drinking the stuff?"

I could not make out the hapless nurse's reply, but she sounded near tears.

"Well, this better not happen again, or you'll be back out on the floor passing bedpans!"

The Surgery doors swung shut behind me, and I heard no more.

I stood in the hall, undecided. Should I go back into Surgery, find Roger, and ask him what they came up short of—or just go away and mind my own business?

On the other hand, if they'd come up short of a neuromuscular blocking agent that was used to murder Sally Shore, it *would* be my business.

That did it. I went back into Surgery and into Roger's office, but nobody was there.

I went back out and stuck my head into the scrub room. A circulating nurse had just come out of a room with a specimen and was about to put it on a cart when I spoke. "I can take that down for you," I offered. "Do you know where Roger went?"

She jerked a thumb at the door she had just come out of. "He's in there."

Hmmm, I thought, hesitating. *Maybe I'd better come back later.*

The Commander came out of his office to greet me. "Never felt worse or had less," he answered my routine inquiry, smiling. "So what have you got?" he inquired, settling himself behind his desk. He fished a toothpick out of his shirt pocket and stuck it in his mouth. Pete came in after me and sat in one of the chairs.

I handed him my list. "I can narrow it down for you if you can tell me if anybody smelled bitter almonds."

"No … at least I don't think so," said Pete. "Of course, she still had her clothes on, and we sent the body to Boise just as we found it to preserve evidence; but I didn't smell anything. I don't know about Bernie. He isn't here, so I can't ask him."

Thank heavens for that. I would willingly accept not knowing if he'd smelled bitter almonds in exchange for not having him here to threaten and intimidate me. *What's his problem, anyway,* I wondered. The Commander wasn't like that. Maybe he used Kincaid as his junkyard dog, saving him the trouble of being obnoxious, ignorant, and ugly— to use one of the Commander's favorite expressions.

The Commander was already on the phone. "Let's see if Rollie did. Hey, you old bastard!"

Roland Perkins's reply was inaudible.

"Hey, on the Dr. Shore case, did you smell bitter

almonds? No? Well, Dr. Day is here, and she wanted to know. Something about poisons. No, that's all I wanted. Hey, you watch that, boy. Okay, I will. Sure. Give my love to Wilma. Right. So long." He hung up the phone and turned to me. "Rollie sends his love, and no, he didn't smell any bitter almonds."

Okay, so it probably wasn't cyanide. "Was there any evidence that she'd had convulsions?" I asked.

"I wouldn't say so," said Pete. "Like I said the other day, she didn't even knock her coffee over."

That would make atropine and the parasympathomimetics less likely. *Unless someone planted the coffee on my desk after having dumped her body in my office*, I told myself. If she'd been killed in her own office, the killer surely would have cleaned up any incriminating evidence like spilled coffee.

"There was nothing in the coffee, by the way," put in the Commander. "We had that analyzed too. Does that answer all your questions, young lady?"

"More or less," I replied. "And it narrows the possible drugs down to two or three: nicotine and the neuromuscular blockers, succinylcholine, and pancuronium."

"Neuro-what?"

"Drugs given in surgery to keep people from moving around under anesthesia. They paralyze all the muscles, including the diaphragm."

Pete and the Commander looked at each other quizzically and back at me. "So they can't breathe either, right?" Pete asked.

"No, but in surgery they have them on a respirator, so that's okay."

"I see," said the Commander. "Do you mind telling me how you came up with this?"

"I figured it had to be a drug that causes respiratory arrest and is fatal in a dose small enough to fit into the same size syringe used for allergy shots."

Pete whistled.

"Very neat, Doctor. Only one problem," said the Commander. "Can we prove it? Unless we can find poison in her body, there is no proof that a crime was committed."

Excuse me? "The bottle is missing," I reminded him.

"There could be all kinds of reasons for that."

"Like what?"

Pete saved the Commander from having to answer that. "Can they test for those drugs?" he asked me.

"They can test for nicotine and cyanide. I don't know about the others," I said.

"Why don't you check on that, Pete," suggested the Commander. "But I have to tell you, Doctor, that if the tests come up negative, we'll have to close the file on this case. I just want you to realize that. We have other cases to work on, and we can't waste time and manpower when there is no proof that a crime was committed."

To my surprise, I felt a sharp stab of disappointment when I should have been overjoyed. *That's one in the eye for Kincaid*, I thought viciously; but it didn't make me feel nearly as good as it should have.

If the tests came up negative, there would be nothing more I could do.

I rose from my chair and turned to leave, when something occurred to me. I turned back.

"If it's not murder, why was the body moved?" I asked.

The Commander stared at me. "What are you talking about, Doctor?"

"In the autopsy report, the postmortem lividity was in the buttocks and backs of her thighs as if she'd died sitting up, not lying on the floor. Why would anyone move the body if they hadn't murdered her?"

"That's a damn fine question, young lady," the Commander said.

"Couldn't she have died sitting in your chair and then fallen out of it?" asked Pete. "She had a cup of coffee, don't forget."

"That doesn't mean anything," the Commander said. "That could have been planted to make it look like she died there."

Attaboy, I thought.

"Her fingerprints were all over Toni's desk," Pete pointed out.

"I'm sure they were. She was sitting there the night before. Whose prints were on the coffee cup?" I asked.

Pete reached for a folder on the Commander's desk and leafed through it. "Hang on a minute; let me check … holy shit. There weren't any. It was wiped clean."

The Commander took off his glasses and wiped them with his handkerchief. "All righty then. Looks like we're not gonna be closing this case anytime soon."

Chapter 19

Though this be madness, yet there is method in't.
—Shakespeare, Hamlet

Thursday morning I came to work to find a pile of manila folders on my desk.

Oh yeah, I thought. *We talked about this in the meeting. It's that time again.*

According to our bylaws, all members of the medical staff had to apply for renewal of their privileges every two years. They were required to provide copies of their current state licenses, DEA (Drug Enforcement Administration) and Idaho Board of Pharmacy certificates, an updated curriculum vitae, documentation of malpractice insurance, and a completed form that asked questions about medical conditions, problems related to drug and alcohol use, disciplinary actions, and malpractice suits. There was also a form to be completed by a peer, someone who worked with the applicant on a regular basis and was in a position to assess competency. Then the chairman of the Credentials Committee would review all that and recommend for or against renewal, and the Board would act on the chairman's recommendation.

Usually, this was a slam dunk. Unless something very out-of-the-ordinary had occurred, there was no reason not to approve renewal for the majority of the physicians. Any irregularities were discussed by the committee, and none had been addressed in the last meeting. As chairman, all I had to do was sign them.

To my surprise, I found Dr. Shore's folder in the pile. Obviously, this stuff had been sitting on the secretary's desk for quite a while, and she had forgotten to take Dr. Shore's folder out.

I'd say that reviewing the credentials of a dead physician qualifies as out-of-the-ordinary, although my peers on the Credentials Committee would all agree that it qualified for the circular file. I pulled it out and opened it. It contained all the required documentation, including Dr. Shore's curriculum vitae as well as letters to be sent to her medical school, the hospitals at which she had done her internship and residency, the AMA, and the four references she had given. The copies were stapled to the front of the folder, and the originals were paper-clipped to their envelopes, awaiting my signature.

I threw them in the wastebasket. No point in sending them out now.

Or was there?

I retrieved them and sat holding them in my hand, looking at them.

At this point, Surgery called and asked me to come up and look at something, which I did, putting on the required gown, mask, and shoe covers to go into the operating room. Afterward, I stripped off my sterile gear and handed it to the former supervisor, Dixie Duncan. She had been there as long as Margo and had voluntarily stepped down from her previous position. She looked tired, and I told her so.

She threw my gown into a hamper and my cap and shoe covers into a wastebasket, then leaned wearily against a gurney and sighed.

"I'm acting supervisor this week. Roger's on vacation. I had forgotten what a bitch this job could be."

"I was wondering why it was so quiet up here today."

"Ain't it the truth? I guess he really needed the rest. He was really awful last week. The new gal threatened to quit, and I'm still not sure she won't."

"Is she the one he was bawling out one day last week? About coming up short on something? What was that all about, anyway?"

"He's had her doing the inventory, and she came up short by one ampule of succinylcholine two weeks in a row."

"Succinylcholine?"

"Yeah, isn't that crazy? We never did get it straightened out. Maybe our last shipment had a couple of short boxes or something. I can't imagine that anybody would take it, can you? Who'd want succinylcholine outside of Surgery?"

I called Pete and told him what I had just heard. After I hung up, I sat lost in thought. I remembered what Hal had said: *Wouldn't it be a bummer if you did all this work, and then it turns out she was shot with a poison dart or something?*

To which I had replied, sneering, *Come on, Hal. Where is anybody going to find poison darts in Twin Falls, Idaho?*

In Surgery, that's where.

For I had suddenly remembered what was on those poison darts.

It was curare, which does exactly the same thing as those neuromuscular blockers.

Chapter 20

*"There's no use trying," said Alice: "one
can't believe impossible things."
"I daresay you haven't had much practice," said the
Queen. "When I was your age, I always did it for
half-an-hour each day. Why, sometimes I've believed
as many as six impossible things before breakfast."*
—Lewis Carroll

Our state inspection was coming up in a week, and I noticed that Natalie's ASCP certificate wasn't posted in the lab, so I asked her about it.

ASCP, the American Society of Clinical Pathologists, was the organization that examined and registered medical technologists and histotechs. Most hospitals would not hire techs that were not ASCP-registered or eligible.

"I can't find it, Dr. Day. I've looked all over. It must have been lost when I moved, or maybe it's still at the other hospital. Maybe I forgot to take it with me when I left."

"Well, then, I'd better call them and have them mail it here."

Natalie gasped involuntarily. Startled, I looked at her.

She stared back, eyes wide. I was shocked to see that there were deep shadows around them. Her face looked haggard and strained.

"What's the matter?"

"Oh," she said in a small voice, "I ... I ... oh, nothing, I guess."

"Natalie, something is wrong. Now, what is it?"

"Well, I just wish you wouldn't do that."

"Why?"

"Because I don't want anybody back there to know where I am."

"Why not?"

"You'll think this is stupid."

"Try me," I suggested.

"Well, it's my ex-boyfriend. He threatened to kill me if I don't marry him. I don't want anybody back there to tell him where I am."

Her eyes no longer met mine. Okay, I thought, she's making the whole thing up. She's invented an abusive boyfriend to prevent us from checking up on her past. One can hide a shitload of secrets behind the threat of an abusive boyfriend. Well, she's not going to get away with it.

Then I remembered that I had been in a similar situation myself, twenty years ago. Not to mention right now. Maybe I should cut the poor girl some slack.

"Okay. Relax. I won't call them. I can get a copy from ASCP instead."

To my horror, Natalie put her head in her hands and burst into tears.

I went over and closed the door. Then I sat on the counter next to her. "Natalie, for God's sake," I said. "You can't keep on like this. Something is obviously terribly wrong. You've got to tell somebody. You'll make yourself sick if you don't. Come on, what is it?"

She shook her head obstinately. "I can't."

"If you change your mind," I said gently, "you know where to find me."

Again she shook her head. Defeated, I left. Back in my office, I put in a call to ASCP.

They had no record of a Natalie Fisher.

Stricken, I hung up. *Now what?*

Well, now I would have to confront Natalie, that's what. No wonder the poor girl had been so upset.

Worst of all, I would have to fire her. She had lied on her application. Given false credentials.

As if things weren't bad enough, I'd be back to either fourteen-hour workdays or a one-week turnaround time for surgicals.

Damn!

I didn't have the heart to confront Natalie. I needed her too much. Maybe I could put it off for a while. I could tell the inspectors Natalie had lost her certificate, and that the new one hadn't arrived from ASCP yet. That would get us off the hook for a year, anyway. Anything could happen in a year. After all, nobody but me and ASCP knew I had called them and found out Natalie was a fraud.

But what kind of fraud prepared slides as well as or better than most of the registered histotechs that I had known? I knew from what the other techs said that Natalie's work in the lab was exemplary too. Clearly, she had been well trained somewhere. There could be any number of reasons why she wouldn't be registered.

Like what? I tried to name one good reason.

Maybe she trained in a medical technology school that wasn't ASCP approved.

No, that wasn't it. She had trained at Mass General. Surely Mass General was ASCP approved.

Or had she? Maybe she'd lied about that too.

Or maybe she hadn't taken the ASCP examination.

But she had. She'd given a certificate number on her application.

Of course, maybe she just made one up. If she lied about her training, she could lie about her registration too.

Oh, for heaven's sake, all this arguing with myself was ridiculous. Why didn't I just look at her personnel file and find out? I called Monty's secretary and asked her to bring Natalie's personnel file to me. When she brought it to me, I called ASCP back.

The number Natalie had given was registered to a Natalie Maria Cabot.

It didn't necessarily mean she was related to Tyler. It had to be a coincidence.

But it was a hell of a coincidence. And if it was a coincidence, why wasn't she using her real name?

She said she didn't want anybody to know where she was because her ex-boyfriend had threatened to kill her. Should I believe her? Was I overly sympathetic because of what happened to me with Robbie?

And what if it was true? If I called Mass General and asked for her certificate, and then she was raped and murdered in the parking lot, how would I feel?

I went back across the hall into Histology and closed

the door. Natalie looked up, startled. I leaned on the counter, folded my arms, and told her we had to talk. She stopped cutting.

"Am I fired?" she asked in a tremulous voice.

"That depends. How truthful are you prepared to be?"

"Truthful about what?"

I picked up a paraffin block and idly began scraping excess paraffin off the side of the cassette with my thumbnail. "I just talked to ASCP. Know what I found out?"

She didn't answer. She continued to look up at me with that deer-in-the-headlights expression.

"I found out that your name is really Cabot."

"Oh."

"Are you related to Dr. Cabot?"

She looked down at her knees and began picking at a thread on her lab coat. "I don't think so."

"Then why aren't you using your real name?"

She sighed. "I told you. I don't want my ex-boyfriend to find me."

"How likely do you think it is that he'll find you if you use your real name?"

She turned her palms up. "I don't know."

I got off the counter and began to pace, despite the fact that I could take no more than three or four steps in any direction.

I didn't know either. Would I be endangering her life if I insisted that she use her real name? If I insisted that she call ASCP, which is in Chicago, and request a copy of her certificate, would her ex-boyfriend in Boston find out? If he called ASCP, would they tell him where she was? Would he be likely to call ASCP or even know what it was? Was I playing God here?

I stopped pacing. "Natalie, I want you to call ASCP and request a copy of your certificate. When you get it, I want you to let Margo post it in the lab with everybody else's."

"But then I'll have to explain why I was using a different name!"

"True." I nodded. "You can tell them the same thing you told me; about your ex-boyfriend. I know you won't be the only one who's had to deal with *that* problem. You may even get some good advice. But the best part is, you won't get fired."

"You mean you'd fire me if I don't do that?"

I upturned a palm. "I'd have to. If you can't document that you're qualified for this job, then you're not qualified. You gave false information on your application. That alone might be grounds for dismissal; but in your case I think an exception could be made if you do what I ask. Get a copy of your certificate, tell Margo what you've told me, and take a copy of your certificate to administration and tell them the truth too. Tell them to call me if they have questions. I don't want to lose you. Histotechs aren't that easy to find. Do we have a deal?"

Slowly, she nodded. "I guess I can do that."

"I guess you'd better, if you want to keep this job." With that, I left her and went back to my office.

Chapter 21

O villain, villain, smiling, damned villain!
My tables; meet it is I set it down,
That one may smile, and smile, and be a villain.
                                    —Shakespeare, *Hamlet*

The weird stuff didn't end there.

In my mail were letters from two of the four references that Dr. Shore had given. Both referred to her as "outstanding." I filed them in her folder. There was also a computer printout from the AMA. It confirmed that Sally Maria Shore had attended Loyola-Stritch School of Medicine from 1986 to 1990, served her internship at Cook County from 1990 to 1991, did her residency in general surgery from 1991 to 1994, also at Cook County, and a fellowship in neurosurgery at Massachusetts General in Boston from 1994 to 1997.

And there her associations ended—nearly ten years in the past.

How odd.

Perhaps she hadn't paid her dues after finishing her residency. Or would that matter? I didn't know.

Again, I wondered what a neurosurgeon was doing

traveling around doing locum tenens work as a general surgeon and taking call in emergency rooms. Something awful must have happened to make her give up such a lucrative practice.

Then I remembered that she had mentioned multiple partners getting sued.

So why couldn't she just relocate and go into practice in neurosurgery somewhere else? Why do locum tenens work for a relative pittance?

Maybe she was just burned out and taking a rest from neurosurgery. Sure, that could be it. I had heard of other doctors doing the same thing just to refresh themselves and get a new perspective on things.

But she'd been about to become a full member of our medical staff as a general surgeon. That didn't sound like taking a rest to me. It sounded more like dropping out of neurosurgery completely—but why?

I pulled the letters of recommendation out of her folder and looked at them again. They were both from Mass General. I looked at her curriculum vitae. The other two references were both from Mass General too. There were none from Loyola or Cook County.

How odd ... again. Still ...

Hey, I don't need this, I thought. I had work to do. I didn't need to deal with emotionally exhausted techs who lied on their applications or doctors with weird credentials files—especially when the person in question was dead, for God's sake. I could just mark it "Deceased" and get rid of it.

But then I would never know.

What if all these irregularities had something to do with the murder, and I just threw the file in the trash?

Talk about suppressing evidence! Of course, if I just threw it away, nobody would ever know it was evidence.

Except me.

Wondering if I had a death wish or something, I made a series of phone calls. Eventually I reached the secretary of the chief of neurosurgery at Massachusetts General, who told me he was out to lunch. She took the message and promised to have him call me back.

Well, that was that. I didn't see what else I could do at this point.

Chapter 22

What are these
So wither'd and so wild in their attire,
That look not like the inhabitants o' the earth,
And yet are on't?

—Shakespeare, Macbeth

On Saturday, I decided to take all that frozen hamburger left over from the side of beef we'd bought at the county fair back in September down to the Episcopal church for their Neighbors-in-Need program. Obviously, we were never going to use it up, and it seemed a shame to waste it.

On the way back, I took Maple Street in order to avoid the traffic on Blue Lakes Boulevard and happened to see Lucille's son Lonnie out shoveling the walk in front of the house. Impulsively, I pulled over and rolled the window down.

"Is your mom home?" I called out.

"Hi, Dr. Day," he replied, leaning on his shovel. "Go on in. She's in the bedroom."

Kenny came to the door when I knocked. His dirty chinos had a rip in the knee, his potbelly strained at the buttons of his threadbare flannel shirt, and there was a streak of grease across his forehead. He had a wrench in his hand.

"Hi, Doc," he greeted me. "You'll hafta excuse the way I look. I'm tryin' to rig some o' them monkey bars for Lucille so's she can pull herself up in bed."

The open sofa bed, with rumpled sheets and pillows on it, took up most of Lucille's microscopic living room. Partially emptied glasses and beer bottles and overflowing ashtrays nearly hid the end tables. The house reeked of stale cigarette smoke. A paint-stained dropcloth, covered by a welter of stainless steel bars and various hand tools, hid what was left of the floor. Kenny followed me, apologizing.

"I ain't had time to do nothin' about the house, and them kids ain't no help. Lu, honey," he went on, opening the bedroom door, "Doc Day's here to see you."

"Oh, God, wait'll I get my hair on," came Lucille's voice, giggling. "Okay now."

The double bed almost filled the room. Lucille lay in the middle of it, pillows piled behind her. A commode was shoved into the corner.

I tried to picture Kenny and Lucille sleeping in that double bed, and failed. Hal and I had slept in a double bed for the first four years of our marriage, and it had been a bit too cozy for comfort; but Kenny and Lucille could have made two of Hal and me.

Lucille was quite a sight. One massive leg was encased in plaster to the hip; hot pink with black stripes, going around her leg, like a barber pole. It matched the pink sweatpants she wore, with one leg cut off to accommodate the cast. Both clashed dramatically with the bright yellow, fuzzy mules on her feet. An asymmetric bulge under her just-as-yellow Snoopy sweatshirt told me that she had an arm in a cast too. Both her eyes were ringed with dark purple, like a raccoon. Her chin and ears had a greenish-yellow tinge where the hemorrhage had drained. All this was topped by a platinum-blonde, punk wig with hot pink and chartreuse streaks.

I couldn't help it. I stared.

Kenny started to laugh. So did Lucille. Soon the three of us were howling with laughter, tears rolling down our cheeks. Lonnie came in to see what was going on.

"I'm sorry," I gasped, wiping my eyes. "It's not funny. But those colors! What ever happened to white?"

"Where have you been, Doc?" said Lonnie. "White's out. They got designer casts now. Show her your arm, Ma."

Lucille hauled up her sweatshirt with her free hand. The cast on her other arm was chartreuse with black polka dots.

"Holy shit," I said reverently.

"I figured I might as well be color-coordinated," said Lucille, clutching her stomach. "Oh, God. It only hurts when I laugh. Don't feel bad, Doctor. Everybody reacts like that. If I have to be laid up like this, I may as well have fun doing it, right? Traci got me the wig and sprayed it to match my casts."

"I don't know why the hell they had to shave her whole head," Kenny grumbled. "She's only got this little bitty incision about yay long right here," he went on, indicating the spot on his own head. "How come they do that, Doc?"

I shrugged. "I don't know. I'm not a neurosurgeon.

And speaking of that, had you heard that Dr. Shore is dead?"

"I heard about that," Kenny told her, "but I forgot to tell you."

Lucille glared at him. "How the hell could you forget a thing like that!"

"Gimme a break, willya? You were still unconscious. In case you don't know it, I was worried sick about you. We were all afraid you wouldn't wake up. Dr. Shore doesn't mean shit to me. I forgot, okay? You wanna make somethin' out of it?"

Lucille reached for his hand. "I'm sorry, honey." Then she turned to me. "How did she die?"

I didn't think Lucille needed to know all the details of the investigation. "Just dropped dead, I guess."

"Funniest damn thing," Lucille went on. "You know, I still can't remember anything after I left the hospital that night, but I keep having this dream—about a white Cadillac convertible driving away from me."

Sally Shore's white Cadillac convertible? There aren't too many convertibles of any flavor around here, let alone Cadillacs; they're highly impractical for this climate, and too expensive for most locals.

"Driving *away* from you?"

"Yeah. Isn't that the damnedest thing?"

It certainly is. But then it's a dream. Maybe the top was down too.

"Can you see who's driving?"

"No, because I'm layin' on the ground."

"Laying on the ground!"

"Yeah. I musta slipped on the ice or something."

So much for having the top down.

"Did it have Idaho plates?"

Sally Shore's car had Massachusetts plates. I remembered that because I'd wondered whether she'd driven here all the way from Boston or from a previous assignment in a closer location.

"Idaho plates? I don't know." Lucille closed her eyes and screwed up her face in an effort to recall her dream but gave up after a few seconds. "No. I can't remember. Why?"

"Next time you have this dream, try and look at the plates, okay?"

"Sure, but why?"

"Just for the heck of it."

Lucille reached behind her with her good arm and tried to pull her pillow up. She wasn't having much luck. Kenny helped her adjust it.

"Okay, just for that I'll prob'ly never have the damn dream again. Honey, I'm thirsty. Bring me a beer, willya?"

"Okay. Want a beer, Doc?"

"Oh, no thanks. I've got to go."

As I picked my way back to my car, I wondered just how much Lucille's dream had to do with what had actually happened to her.

Chapter 23

Yon Cassius hath a lean and hungry look;
He thinks too much: such men are dangerous.
                    —Shakespeare, *Julius Caesar*

D r. Shore's car wasn't in the parking lot. I walked up and down all the aisles and didn't find it. What I did find was Robbie.

His black Mercedes was parked in the physicians' parking lot. I noticed the California plates and stopped, wondering who was here from California that would park in doctors' parking, when he opened the door and stepped out, smiling.

"Toni," he greeted me. "I would have known you anywhere. You haven't changed a bit. Just as cute and sexy as ever."

He hadn't changed much either. He was still trim and was dressed in a well-cut, lawyerly gray suit with a blue shirt and yellow tie. The thick glasses were gone—contact lenses?—but nothing else had changed.

"Robbie," I said. "What are you doing here?"

"You could at least act glad to see me." He sounded hurt.

I sighed. "I'm not glad to see you. I don't want to see you. I wish you would just go away and leave me alone."

"How can I get you back if I leave you alone?"

"Get me back? Are you nuts? I'm married. I love my husband. You *can't* get me back. If that's what you're here for, you may as well just turn right around and go back to Long Beach."

"Oh, no. No way. You're mine, Toni, and I *will* get you back. Count on it."

There was a smugness in his manner that I had never noticed before. It made my blood run cold. What the hell did he think he was going to do?

I wasn't sure I wanted to know.

"Get away from me, Robbie. Stay away from me. Do you understand?"

"Oh, I understand, all right. You have no idea how well I understand." He just stood there, smiling with those buck teeth.

I turned away and began to walk back toward the entrance. He fell in step with me. I stopped. "You can't come in with me."

"Oh, yes I can. It's a hospital. It's a public facility. You can't keep me out."

I turned to face him. "Oh, yes. You're a lawyer. You know your rights. But I'm working, and if you interfere with me while I'm working, I have grounds to have you arrested."

He laughed. "You wouldn't dare."

"Don't make me call Security, Robbie."

"Call Security all you want, Toni. It won't help you once you leave the hospital grounds."

"Are you threatening me, Robbie?"

"You might tell that kike husband of yours to stay away from windows if he knows what's good for him."

"You stay away from my house, Robbie, if you know what's good for *you*. I'll call the police if you don't," I retorted with an assurance I did not feel.

Robbie seemed to know it, damn him. "That won't do you any good. They're chronically short-handed. They wouldn't come unless you or your Jew boy husband got your brains blown out by a high-powered rifle through one of those picture windows at your house."

Horrified, I stood there speechless. But Robbie wasn't through. He rubbed his hands together and a dreamy expression came over his face. "Wow, if I had one of those babies, I could do it from here," he mused. "Or down the street. By the time the police got there, I'd be long gone, and the rifle would be in the river."

I struggled to keep my voice from trembling. "Get away from here, Robbie. Go back to Long Beach before you do something you'll regret."

"Oh, no," he said, the sunlight glinting off his protruding teeth. "I've already done all the regretting I'm going to do." He turned and walked back to his car. As he opened the door, he turned back to me and delivered his parting words.

"You haven't seen the last of me, Toni. Not by a long shot."

I'd tried to put up a brave front, but my legs trembled so violently that I have no idea how I managed to walk from the parking lot to my office without crumpling to the ground somewhere along the way. My heart was in my throat and beating so hard that I was sure it was visible.

Cold, rancid sweat soaked me from the skin out. I felt nauseated. But nobody I met in the halls seemed to notice anything amiss.

Standing in the center of my desk was a bud vase containing a single yellow rose.

No card.

Well, that just blew my big brave front right out the window. My bowels turned to water. I turned and ran for the bathroom, feeling as if I might faint or throw up.

Robbie had already been here, in my office.

With trepidation, I inquired of everyone in the lab whether they had let anyone into my office, or had seen anyone go into my office, or had accepted the rose from anyone and put it in my office. The response was a uniform and definite negative, accompanied by lively speculation about who my secret admirer might be. Dr. Cabot maybe? I feigned ignorance. My heart failed me at the thought of telling them about Robbie; that was way too private and personal right now, although it might be good for a few laughs in about twenty more years, assuming I survived that long.

Apparently my office was not the safe haven I thought it was. I had told Robbie he couldn't come in here with me and that I would call Security if he tried; but he'd already been in here and nobody had even noticed. He must be laughing himself sick right about now.

He'd laugh even harder if he knew what we called Security around here. In the big cities, hospitals had security cameras, but not us. Oh no, this is God's country, and nothing bad happens here. During the day, Security consisted of Bruce, Howie, Richard, or Earl—slow-moving and corpulent, all on the frangible side of sixty—who wore their dark-gray uniforms with wrinkled light-gray shirts that strained over their ample bellies and were frequently missing buttons. At night we had Walter and Ralph, who were even slower, fatter, and more decrepit than their daytime counterparts. Hell, I wasn't even sure they carried guns. If they did, they probably kept them hidden under all those rolls of fat. How could any of those guys be any match for Robbie—who apparently could melt through walls without anyone seeing or hearing him—even if he *wasn't* armed with a high-powered rifle that could shoot Hal or me through windows from over five hundred yards away? Not only that, the Old Fat Brigade could offer me no protection between the parking lot and 205 Montana Street. However, it did occur to me that one of them could have let Robbie into my office.

I felt like crying, but instead I called the college and asked for Dr. Shapiro. A disembodied secretarial voice said that Dr. Shapiro was in class and would I like to leave a message?

I wondered what that smug-sounding female would tell Hal if I told her what I was calling about, but I decided not to. I just asked her to tell him to call me back ASAP; I didn't add anything about staying away from windows.

Then I tracked down Earl and Howie, who were on duty today, but neither had seen Robbie or let anyone into my office.

Back in my office, I called the police station and asked to talk to Pete, who was apparently unavailable, because the next voice I heard was Kincaid's.

"What can I do for you, Doctor?"

I told him that I was being stalked by an ex-boyfriend who had just intercepted me in the hospital parking lot, threatened to shoot Hal and me through the window with a high-powered rifle, and left flowers on my desk. As I talked, I could feel waves of skepticism coming through the phone even before Kincaid spoke.

His response wasn't good. Robbie was right.

"What do you expect us to do, Doctor? We don't have the manpower to keep your house under surveillance or provide bodyguards. He could shoot you through your office window too, you know, or on the street when you're walking home in the dark. He can also shoot your husband at the college. Or he could use a knife instead of a gun, or some other deadly weapon. Just because he mentioned a gun doesn't necessarily mean that's what he's going to use. There's no way we can cover all those scenarios."

I found myself thinking what a good thing it was that Kincaid wasn't a physician. His bedside manner sucked rocks.

"So Hal and I are just hanging out there to dry?"

"Pretty much. The best we can do is a drive-by a few times a night."

Defeated, I hung up. Drive-bys weren't going to do us any good.

I had to admit that I was as scared as I'd ever been in my life, for Hal as well as myself. It took my mind completely off my fear of being accused of murdering Sally Shore. *Shit, maybe I'd actually be safer in jail.*

How the hell did Robbie get into my office? Nobody had seen or heard him. Nobody had let him in. Nobody had taken the flowers and put them in there for him. The outside door to my office was always locked if I wasn't in it. The door from the lab was usually unlocked, but the outside door to the lab was also locked if nobody was there. So, how did he get in? He had to have a key, but where would he have gotten it?

Maybe he'd borrowed the one Dr. Shore used to get into my office.

What a horrible thought. Robbie and Sally Shore in cahoots. Yeah, yeah, I knew she was dead, but if Robbie could melt through walls, he could sure as hell commune with the dead.

Maybe she was a zombie and he was a vampire. He could put those buck teeth to good use. Just file 'em to points, and he'd be good to go.

Chapter 24

God bless the King, I mean the faith's defender!
God bless ... no harm in blessing ... the Pretender!
But who pretender is, or who is King,
God bless us all! That's quite another thing.

—John Byrom

Right in the middle of my surgicals, I received a call from the chief of neurosurgery at Massachusetts General Hospital.

He sounded elderly and benevolent. "Dr. Day? What can I do for you, my dear?"

I explained my problem, and what he told me almost—but not quite—took my mind off getting killed and/or widowed by Robbie and his rifle.

"Sally Shore was the best fellow we've had in this department since I've been here, and I've been here nearly thirty-five years," he said firmly. "Her death was a tragic loss—to Mass General and to neurosurgery."

"Her death?" I echoed. "Who told you about her death?"

"My dear, I was there," he explained, his voice shaking

slightly. "I operated on her. I did everything I could. But it was no use."

"Wait a minute," I begged. "Obviously we're not talking about the same person. The Sally Shore I'm talking about died here just a couple of weeks ago. She applied to our staff. I have her file right here. It says she did a fellowship in neurosurgery at Mass General from 1994 to 1997."

"That's right," he said. "She died just after she completed her fellowship. A ruptured berry aneurysm of the circle of Willis. So tragic. She did a great deal of research on that particular problem. She managed to save every patient she operated on. It was so ironic that she should die of the very same thing, and that I, her teacher, was unable to save her."

"Oh, dear," I said inadequately. "I … er … don't suppose there were *two* Sally Shores at Mass General during that time?"

"Not in neurosurgery."

"Were there any other female residents or fellows?"

"No, my dear. Not too many females choose neurosurgery, you know, even now. She was the first, and we did not have another for several years."

I was grasping at straws now, unable to reconcile what I was hearing with what I knew. "Did your Sally Shore have a daughter?"

"Not to my knowledge. She was very dedicated. She didn't even have a boyfriend. No time for one." He chuckled. "Too bad. She was a pretty little thing. Blonde, blue eyes …"

That did it. There was no way that our Sally Shore

could ever have been described as a pretty little thing with blonde hair and blue eyes.

I thanked him, apologized for taking up so much of his time and hung up. Then I sat there for a moment trying to make sense out of what I had just heard.

Wow! So, our Dr. Shore was an impostor! No wonder she'd made so many mistakes.

I couldn't wait to tell Pete.

Predictably, he asked me to come to the station, which I did—later in the afternoon when they were finished in the operating room and wouldn't need me any more.

The Commander shook my hand and told me, with a grin, that he'd never felt worse or had less. "Pete says you've got something to tell us."

"I certainly do," I said. "I just found out that the late Dr. Shore was an impostor."

"What?" they both said.

"How did you happen to find that out?" the Commander asked, shifting the toothpick to the other side of his mouth.

I explained about the Credentials Committee. "I just called Mass General to check up on her references and found out that the real Dr. Sally Shore died in 1997."

"What?" they chorused.

"Well, I thought you'd like to know she isn't who we thought she was. Maybe she's not even really a doctor. If we can find out who she really is, it might help us find out who killed her and why." I was so excited, I stumbled over my words.

The Commander hitched his chair closer to the desk and leaned on his arms. He took the toothpick out of his mouth and broke it into tiny pieces. I hadn't seen him do that before. "Well, young lady, that is quite a piece of information. We're gonna have to chew on this awhile. Anything else we can tell you, Doc?"

"Yes. What about the hit-and-run in our parking lot?"

"Pete?"

"No, Bernie's working on that one. I'll get him." Pete got up and left the office. He returned almost immediately with Lt. Kincaid, who said, "What's up, Ray?"

Then he saw me. I could almost see his jaw clench. "Doctor, if you've come to harass us about providing round-the-clock protection, you've made a trip for nothing."

"What the hell are you talking about, Kincaid? Dr. Day wants to ask you about the hit-and-run in the hospital parking lot. How are you coming along on it?" inquired the Commander.

Kincaid looked confusedly from me to the Commander and back again.

"Yeah, Bernie," put in Pete. "Remember, we interviewed Toni about that at the hospital? The time you got sick?" He chuckled, reminiscing, and added for the Commander's benefit, "Toni was working on a gangrenous bowel, and it made Bernie sick."

"No shit," the Commander commented, looking interested.

I smiled. "They don't call it 'gross' pathology for nothing."

The Commander chuckled.

If looks could kill, all three of us would have been dead several times over. Kincaid was obviously embarrassed about the incident.

"She was the one that Dr. Shore fired," I added.

"Now that is interesting," said the Commander, hitching forward in his chair. "Could there be a connection between these two cases?"

"Actually, it was Dr. Cabot who fired her, but he did it because Dr. Shore wanted him to. She claimed Lucille had been rude to her, and she threatened to leave if Dr. Cabot didn't fire her. So he did."

"I don't understand," said Kincaid. "If she'd been fired, what was she doing in the parking lot at that time of night?"

"Oh, she was working. She got her job back. Turned out Dr. Shore's story was a pack of lies."

"When did she come back to work?" asked Pete.

"The day before she was run down."

"Jesus!" exclaimed Pete.

"Pretty inconvenient for you," observed the Commander wryly. "Did you have anybody else to do her job?"

"Yeah. Me."

"So are you still doing it?"

"No, strangely enough, I only had to do it for one day. Someone showed up who was qualified, and we hired her."

"Damned convenient," mused the Commander.

"Isn't it, though?" I said.

"Almost as if it was planned," added Pete.

"But that's not all," I said. "The replacement gave us a false name on her application. Turns out her last name's really Cabot."

"Cabot?" Pete and the Commander looked at each other. "Any relation to the doctor?"

"She says not," I said.

159

Kincaid cleared his throat. "If we could get on with it," he said fretfully, "I could get back to work. I have a million things to do."

"Please proceed, Lieutenant," the Commander said graciously, leaning back in his chair and lacing his hands across his abdomen.

"Up until today, we had no leads. But just this morning," Kincaid paused portentously, "just this morning we pulled a car out of the canyon."

"A white Cadillac convertible with Massachusetts plates?" I inquired innocently.

Kincaid gaped at me as though I had shot him. "How ... how did you know *that*?" he gasped.

"Just a lucky guess."

"Oh, now, you can't get away with that, girl," said the Commander, shaking his head. "You know something. Out with it!"

"I visited Lucille on Saturday," I explained. "She's home now, you know. She told me that she keeps having a dream about a white Cadillac convertible. And Dr. Shore drove a white Cadillac convertible with Massachusetts plates. And it's not in the parking lot any more."

"She told the Boise police she couldn't remember anything."

"She still can't. She just keeps having this dream."

"I see." Kincaid sounded skeptical. "Unfortunately, it's been in the water, so if there was any blood or tissue on it, it's probably been washed away."

"Was there anybody in it?" I asked.

"No. Should there be, Miss Know-It-All?"

"No, not necessarily. But if you find who drove it

into the canyon, you'll probably find your hit and run driver."

"And I suppose now you're going to tell me how to do that?"

I was about to say no, when the Commander interrupted. "What was that comment about round-the-clock protection all about, Kincaid?"

Kincaid's expression was pained. "You'd better ask the doctor about that, sir."

"It's a long story," I began.

"We've got time," the Commander said. "We're not going anywhere. Are we, Kincaid?"

Now Kincaid looked really pained. Maybe "pissed" would be a better word for it. He clamped his jaw shut and shook his head.

So I told them about Robbie.

The Commander's jaw dropped, and his expression was shocked. "Why haven't you told us about this, young lady? This is serious business."

"I did. I told Lieutenant Kincaid."

Kincaid stood up and started pacing. "Commander, I told her we were too short-handed to give her protection around the clock. This guy's threatening her and her husband with a high-powered rifle that can shoot over five hundred yards." He stopped, faced the Commander's desk, and turned his palms up. "I don't *know* what we can do about that. If you do, please tell me."

The Commander sighed. "No, Lieutenant, you were right. There isn't anything we can do. Doctor, is there any connection between this Robbie and Dr. Shore—or whoever she is—that you know of?"

I shook my head.

"Well, we'll keep you posted. And if you think of anything else, please tell us." He stood up and held out his hand. It was a dismissal, and I took the hint. Pete walked me to the door.

"You really stole Bernie's thunder," he said. "You know, Toni, you know entirely too much about this case. It's kind of spooky."

"Sorry," I said.

"Well, you want to be careful who you talk to. If I were you, I'd let the police ask the questions from now on."

"Gladly," I said.

Chapter 25

Teas,
Where small talk dies in agonies.
—Percy Bysshe Shelley

My feet were killing me.

I had been standing on them all day at work, and now, here I was again, standing for hours—this time in high heels—making inane small talk with more people than I could count.

Unobtrusively, I made my way to a secluded corner behind a potted plant and sank with a sigh into a chair. I put my drink on a table, leaned back, and closed my eyes.

It was the annual doctors' and lawyers' St. Patrick's Day bash at the country club. Hal and I had barely had time to change before it was time to go, and I hadn't had time to tell him everything about my day.

Conversations swirled around me. Hal was regaling a group with one of his favorite jokes. Further away, Elliott was telling a couple of other lawyers about a case he'd been involved in recently.

"He doesn't know why he did it. He doesn't play golf,

and neither do any of his friends. They just thought it would be fun to break into the pro shop …"

"…the doctor says, you're in luck, I just got this new machine. You just give me a urine specimen. So he does, and the doctor puts it in the machine and says, you've got tennis elbow. And the guy says, that's ridiculous, I don't even *play* tennis …"

"See, the country club up there in Sun Valley has golf bags for their rental clubs that all look the same. And after a year, they sell them and get new ones and change the bags. Like, last year's bags were blue, and this year's bags are burgundy, and you can tell them a mile off. So this guy and his buddy go in there and rip off about ten of them …"

I gradually became aware that someone on the other side of the potted palm was crying softly and being comforted by another woman. While I dislike eavesdropping on conversations not meant for my ears, and I feel uncomfortable witnessing someone else's emotion, my feet really were killing me, and I didn't want to move again … so I didn't.

"I just don't know what's gotten into him lately," said the tearful voice. "He doesn't talk to me any more. And he seems to spend all his time at the hospital."

"Well, honey, don't they all?"

"… so he goes back to his regular doctor, and the doctor says, you're in luck, I just got this new machine …"

"What the hell is he going to do with the fucking things? He can't sell them. He can't even give them away. So he hides them on the back porch of his condo. But the goddamn road goes right around up the hill in back of the building, and there they sit, right out in front of God and everybody …"

"I always thought you two had the perfect marriage."

"So did I, until the last couple of months." Sobs. "If I didn't know better, I'd think he was having an affair."

Poor thing. The same old story. But I couldn't move, or she'd know I had been listening, and I didn't know which was worse.

"… he says, I can't go right now, I'll bring it in later. Then he goes home and pees in the cup, and he has his wife pee in the cup, he has his daughter pee in the cup, he even gets his dog to pee in the cup, and then he masturbates into the cup, and then …"

"… he didn't get home until four in the morning, and his coat was soaking wet …"

Now that sounded interesting. I pricked up my ears and made an effort to breathe more quietly.

"… this guy says to the landlord, looks like one of your tenants really likes golf, he's got about nine or ten bags out on his porch. Funny thing, though. They all look the same …"

Giggles of anticipation.

"Maybe he couldn't start his car? Or maybe he got stuck in the snow or something and had to walk home?"

"… the doctor comes out after about half an hour and says, okay, your wife's got gonorrhea, your daughter's pregnant, your dog's got worms, and if you don't stop jacking off, you're never going to get rid of your tennis elbow!"

Gusts of laughter.

"But the car was in the garage! And when I asked him about it, he told me to get off his case."

"What I'm saying is, it doesn't take a freakin' Sherlock Holmes to figure that one out. So the judge decided to charge him as a juvenile so it won't go on his record and embarrass his parents, who are filthy stinking rich and can buy and sell Sun Valley ten times over, but it won't do any good. Felony *stupid*, that's what this kid's problem is …"

"Honey, I'm sure there was a perfectly logical explanation …"

"You're probably right, Gloria, and I'm making a big deal out of nothing. I guess I'd better go to the little girls' room and fix my face."

"I'll come with you."

Tyler approached me, smiling for a change.

"Hi, Toni. Nice party, isn't it? Seen my wife?"

I shook my head. He sank into the chair on the other side of the table and put his drink down next to mine. "Toni, did you do an autopsy on Dr. Shore?"

"Nope. Somebody else did."

"How come?"

I wasn't about to tell Tyler it was because they considered me a suspect. "That's the way the police wanted it. They wanted someone with experience in forensic pathology to do it."

"Well, don't you …"

"Well, no, how would I? Our patients don't usually get themselves murdered, now, do they?"

"*Murdered*? What do you mean, *murdered*? What makes you think she was *murdered*?" Tyler was on his feet, standing menacingly over me, fists clenched. Involuntarily, I cringed.

"What's going on here?"

Hal and Elliott suddenly loomed up behind Tyler, and Tyler suddenly looked a lot less menacing. I heaved a sigh of relief and felt silly. Surely Tyler wasn't really going to do me physical harm right here in the country club. I must be overtired or something.

"We were discussing Dr. Shore," I said shakily. "Tyler was just inquiring as to why her autopsy was done in Boise instead of here."

"A lot of other people have been wondering that too," said Elliott.

"Why? What did they find?" Tyler asked.

"Nothing," I said. "Absolutely nothing," I added, firmly, shaking my head at Hal, who looked like he was about to say something. "It's just that they wanted a forensic expert to do the autopsy just in case it was murder, and as it turned out, the expert was having a coronary bypass and the post got done by a locum who probably had no more experience than I do."

Tyler pulled out a handkerchief and mopped his forehead. "Why does it have to be so damn hot in here?" he complained. "I better go find my wife."

"See ya later," said Hal.

Tyler left, and Hal sat in the chair he had vacated. Elliott pulled up another one.

"What was that all about?" Elliott asked.

"He asked me if I did the autopsy on Dr. Shore, and I told him why the police didn't want me to do it, and he got all upset. I suppose you'll say I overreacted, but I really thought he was going to hit me or something."

"No, hon, it looked pretty bad from across the room too," said Hal.

"If anybody overreacted, Tyler did," Elliott observed. "What exactly did you say to him to get him all excited?"

"I said I didn't have experience in forensic pathology because our patients don't usually get themselves murdered, and that's when he jumped up and started yelling at me."

"Murder seems to have been the freakin' operative word," mused Elliott. "I wonder why?"

"Hey, you guys."

I turned to see Stan Snow standing next to the potted palm, smiling broadly.

"Got somebody I want you to meet," he went on, stepping aside to reveal his companion.

Robbie.

Chapter 26

That fellow seems to me to possess but one idea,
and that is a wrong one.

—Samuel Johnson

Oh, no. Not again.
I was very glad I was sitting down, because I felt
as if I might faint. Or throw up.

Stan continued to perform introductions while I
clung to the arms of my chair and took deep breaths.
"And of course you know Toni, and this is her husband,
Hal Shapiro."

"So," Robbie said, shaking hands with Hal and
looking at me, "this is your Jew boy, huh?"

I jumped to my feet, fists clenched. "Robbie!" I
protested, scandalized. "How dare you?"

Hal took my hand and pulled me away from Robbie.
"Easy, hon."

"Well, *that* was pretty freakin' inappropriate," Elliott
said.

Stan's round face was scarlet with embarrassment.
"Rob, what's gotten into you?"

Jodi and Cherie Snow, who had joined us just in time

to hear Robbie's comment, simply looked at each other, speechless.

Hal put his arm around me and steered me toward the door. "Come on, honey, let's get out of here."

Robbie spoke from behind us. His diction was slightly slurred. "Toni, I need to talk to you."

I turned. "I don't want to talk to you, Robbie."

"Come on, Toni. Now that I'm here, you can't seriously tell me you'd take Grizzly Abramowitz over me, can you?"

Grizzly Abramowitz? Flaming asshole.

"Oh, yes, I can. Leave me alone, Robbie."

"Toni, don't do this. I love you."

"I don't love you, Robbie. I don't even like you. Now please leave me alone."

"Toni, darling …"

Hal stepped forward. "You heard her," he said quietly. "Now do what she said. Leave us alone. Or you'll regret it."

Robbie took a step back, but his expression didn't change. That toothy smile was the last thing I saw as the door closed behind us.

"You're shaking," Hal said as we made our way out to the parking lot. "He still upsets you that much after all this time."

All I could do was cling to him. I didn't trust myself to speak.

"Come on, sweetie," Hal continued. "You'll feel better once we get to the car."

I sank gratefully onto the car seat. I felt lightheaded. I think I was hyperventilating. I bent over and put my head between my knees.

"Are you going to be sick?"

I shook my head. "No, I don't think so."

"The infamous Robbie," Hal said, starting the engine and guiding the Cherokee smoothly out of the parking lot. "He really *is* just a little twerp, isn't he?"

I sat up and shook my hair out of my face. "Yes, but he can still shoot a gun."

"Gun? What are you talking about?"

"Oh, my God. I called you this morning. Didn't your secretary tell you?"

"My secretary's out with the flu. Nobody told me you called. What did you call about?"

"I saw Robbie at the hospital today," I said. "He threatened me."

Hal swerved over to the side of the road and stopped the car. "Threatened you? How?" he demanded.

"He said you should stay away from windows."

"What the hell does that mean? Oh, my God, is that what you meant by saying he can shoot a gun?"

"That's what I meant," I said.

"Jesus." Hal rubbed his hands over his face. "Do you think he means it?"

"I don't know. The Robbie I used to know wouldn't have, but now I just don't know. There's something ... *evil* about him now that wasn't there before."

"For God's sake, Toni, he raped you! Don't you think that's evil?"

I had to admit that he had a point.

Hal put the Jeep back in gear and pulled back onto the road. "I need to talk to Elliott. There must be something we can do. He can't go around threatening to shoot people like that. Can't the police do something?"

"Hal, I called the police. Right after I called you. They can't do anything but drive-bys once in a while."

"Oh, that's ridiculous."

"But that's what Bernie Kincaid said when I called."

"Yeah, well, Kincaid's an asshole. I'll call Elliott as soon as we get home."

It was the first thing I saw as we came into the kitchen from the garage.

A bud vase with a single yellow rose, right in the middle of my kitchen table.

Chapter 27

As I was going up the stair,
I met a man who wasn't there;
He wasn't there again today,
I wish, I wish he'd go away.

—Hughes Mearns

Hal called the police. Then he went around checking all the doors and windows. They were all just as we had left them.

He poured each of us a Scotch, neat. He took his in a single swallow, while I sipped mine, wrapped in an afghan on the couch, where I had given way to a terminal case of the shakes.

Robbie had actually been here, in my house. I felt violated, almost as if I'd been raped again. Would I ever feel safe in this house again?

How the hell did he get in?

I had restrained myself, with an effort, from hurling that rose, bud vase and all, into the garbage. It might have fingerprints. The police might want to actually see why they had been called.

After what felt like several centuries—actually about

173

ten minutes—the doorbell rang, and Hal opened the door to admit two uniformed policemen I hadn't met before. The larger of the two reminded me of Merlin Olsen and introduced himself as Darryl Curtis. They interviewed both Hal and me and took the bud vase away with them in a plastic bag.

After they left, I told Hal about my visit to the police station; and that led to the revelation that Dr. Shore wasn't really Dr. Shore.

"Maybe I've been unfair to Kincaid," Hal said. "He was telling the truth."

"So, you don't think he's an asshole any more?"

"Oh, no, he's still an asshole."

Even after all that, Elliott wasn't home yet. Hal called him repeatedly for an hour and then gave up. We went upstairs to bed and stayed away from the windows. But neither of us got much sleep.

The phone rang several times during the night. Each time, Hal got up to answer it. Each time, the person hung up. Finally, at about four, Hal unplugged the phone.

"If anybody from the hospital wants you at this ungodly hour, they can just come right over here and knock on the door," he growled.

In the morning, at the relatively ungodly hour of nine o'clock for a Saturday morning, Hal dragged me next door and roused a snarling, hung-over Elliott out of bed.

Elliott looked awful. He was still in his pajamas, his hair standing on end, with bags the size of Texas under his bloodshot eyes. I hoped he didn't feel as bad as he looked, but he probably did, because he acted as if the canary-yellow caftan Jodi was wearing hurt his eyes.

"What the fuck is this about, Shapiro?"

Hal told him.

"You mean that nerdy friend of Stan's is the freakin' asshole that's been stalking Toni? Shit, I should have figured that out from what he said. I guess I had too much to drink."

Jodi laughed. "What makes you think that, sweetheart? You and Stanley were trying to drink each other under the table. I think you won."

"Bullshit," growled Elliott, holding his head. "Stanley had lots more to drink than I did."

"Hal," I said, tugging at his arm, "maybe we should do this later."

"No, no, I'm all right," Elliott protested, waving a hand in our direction. "Talk."

Hal did.

"I can understand why the cops can't do anything," Elliott said. "Everything Kincaid said is true. But we can get a restraining order. Keep the sonuvabitch from coming anywhere near either of you."

"Restraining order?" scoffed Hal. "I've always heard they're not—"

"Worth the paper they're written on. Yeah, Shapiro, I know. But it's what we have. If he gets caught violating it, he could go to jail and lose his license to practice law. That's quite a deterrent."

But first, he has to get caught, I thought sourly.

How the hell do you catch an invisible man who walks through walls?

Chapter 28

Thou canst not say I did it; never shake
Thy gory locks at me.
—Shakespeare, *Macbeth*

When I got to work Monday, Kincaid was waiting for me.

He told me to come to the station and make a formal statement. As it happened, that was no problem; there were no scheduled frozen sections that morning, which didn't mean there wouldn't be an unscheduled one. I took my cell phone with me, just in case, and made sure it was turned on.

Kincaid ushered me into a conference room. The Commander and Pete sat at the table and rose when I entered. Then we all sat down again. Nobody smiled. I began to feel ill-at-ease.

The Commander said, "Doctor, we're going to be taping this. The law requires that we inform you of that fact."

I nodded, and he reached over and turned the tape recorder on.

I began to relax as the Commander took me over

familiar ground. We reviewed everything we had already discussed in regard to the Shore case and Lucille's accident. Then the questioning took a bizarre turn as Kincaid took over.

"How did you know, Doctor, that the car we pulled out of the canyon was a white Cadillac convertible with Massachusetts plates?"

"I didn't. I guessed."

"And how did you know that Dr. Shore was given a lethal dose of succinylcholine?"

"I didn't. I still don't."

"What do you mean?"

"All I know is that she died of respiratory failure, and that she received an injection that she didn't have a reaction to that her nurse didn't give her, and that Surgery came up short on their inventory two weeks in a row, and that you can't test for it. So I think she could have been, but I don't know she was. Do you know something I don't?"

"I'll ask the questions if you don't mind, Doctor. How did you know that the fatal dose was given to her in her allergy medicine?"

"You know what? I don't think it was."

That brought Kincaid up short. "What do you mean?"

"I think it was given to her straight out of the ampule; because she always had an allergic reaction and got a big welt on her arm after her allergy shot. If the poison was in her allergy medicine, she would still have gotten a welt, and we'd still think she died of natural causes." I paused as another thought occurred to me. "Or maybe not."

Kincaid looked confused. "What are you talking about?"

"If she died before she had time to develop a welt, she wouldn't have had one, so maybe she got the succinylcholine in her allergy shot after all. She couldn't develop a welt postmortem. Anyway, all I know is that the bottle is missing. And I know that, because her nurse told me."

They shifted uncomfortably in their seats, and none of them would meet my eyes, even Pete. Finally the Commander spoke. "You should know, Doctor, that we have received some new evidence. We checked with Roland Perkins to see who paid for Dr. Shore's funeral expenses." He paused. "It was your Dr. Cabot."

I nodded. Somehow, that didn't surprise me.

"We had a nice chat with Dr. Cabot. He apparently thought quite highly of the deceased." Again he paused. I nodded. I knew that. He continued. "He wanted to know if we thought she had been murdered. He said he thought she might have been, and when we asked him if he had any idea who might have done that, he mentioned you."

"Oh, for God's sake," I exclaimed. "The man had no idea she was murdered until he heard it from me at the country club." My outrage increased as I reflected that if I had kept my mouth shut, I wouldn't have to be here now, hearing my own words turned against me. Unless Tyler already knew and was just playing with me. But his reaction seemed way too spontaneous to be faked. "Do you mean to say he came right out and accused me of murder?"

"Not exactly. He just said you were the only one on the medical staff who couldn't seem to get along with her. He couldn't think of anyone else who might have a grudge against her."

"Did you ask him if he knew she wasn't who she said she was?"

Kincaid appeared nonplussed. "No, I didn't. What's that got to do—"

I interrupted him. "Well, maybe you should. Maybe he knows who she really is. And while you were at it, did you happen to ask him if he knew who ran over Lucille in the parking lot? Or are you going to accuse me of that too?"

Kincaid was momentarily at a loss for words; but his face reddened, and an explosion seemed imminent.

At this point, my cell phone rang. I checked the read-out. Surgery. I answered it. A frozen section. What else? "I have to go," I said.

The Commander reached over and snapped off the tape recorder. "I think we're done here, Lieutenant, at least for now," he said. "You can go back to work now, Doc, but stay in touch. We *will* need to talk some more before this is over."

Pete offered me a ride back to the hospital, which I accepted.

As I left, I glanced back. The Commander and Kincaid were arguing, almost nose to nose over the Commander's desk. Kincaid looked up and caught my eye. His expression made my blood run cold.

Pete saw it too. "You'd better be careful, Toni," he said seriously. "Or Kincaid'll be the one coming after you with a rifle, not Robbie."

I stared at him. He didn't seem to be joking.

"I don't know what his problem is, but he's gonna get you behind bars or die trying."

"But he can't do that," I began, but he interrupted me.

"You should get a lawyer, Toni. Just in case. I'd feel a lot better if you did."

He wasn't smiling.

I decided to take his advice.

I called Elliott's office as soon as I got back to work. Right after I finished with the frozen section.

My techs clustered around me when I walked into the lab, clamoring for information; but there was not much I could tell them. I did mention that it might be helpful to know if anyone on duty that night saw Dr. Shore alive after I left, and they promised to start asking around and getting people to talk. "We don't mind doing it, either," Connie said. "After all, if they put you in jail, God only knows what they'll replace you with."

"Right," said Brenda. "Maybe another Dr. Shore."

"Oh, please," said Margo, shuddering. "You can count on us, Dr. Day."

And I knew I could count on every one of them, except for one person who sat silently in the back of the room, her eyes wide, her face white.

Natalie was obviously scared stiff; but of what, I could not imagine. Not of me, surely. After all, she had nothing to do with this.

Or did she?

Chapter 29

Diplomacy is to do and say
The nastiest thing in the nicest way.
—Isaac Goldberg

Elliott ushered Hal and me into two comfortably upholstered chairs in front of his massive desk. I looked around curiously and realized this was the first time I had actually been in Elliott's office.

Hal was not in a good mood. "I don't know why we couldn't have talked about this at home," he complained. "Now we're gonna have to pay you a shitload of money just to talk about the same stuff here. What's the point?"

"The freakin' point, Shapiro, is to keep your wife out of jail. I'm sure Toni told you that Pete Vincent advised her to do this. That was good advice. She's so close to this case that she can't see the big picture. That's what I'm here for."

Hal was not appeased. "I still don't see why we couldn't have done this at home."

"Right," Elliott said. "With Jodi and the kids around, interrupting all the time. It's not that I'm worried about Jodi knowing all this, but the kids don't need to hear it and spread it around at school. Talking about it here keeps it privileged information."

I spoke up before Hal could continue picking a fight with Elliott, which he seemed determined to do. "What 'big picture' am I not seeing, Elliott? It seems pretty clear to me. Somebody killed Dr. Shore, or whoever she is, and put her body in my office, and Tyler is going around saying that I must have done it because nobody else had a problem with her, which is a crock, because lots of people had problems with her, and the police would know that if they bothered to talk to the other doctors, but they won't because Kincaid hates me. What's so complicated about that?"

"Whoever-she-is is just one freakin' reason it's complicated," Elliott said. "My primary purpose here is not to solve the murder but to keep you from being accused of it."

"Good. That's why we're here," I said.

"So let's get on with it," Hal suggested. "All this small talk is costing us money."

"Don't worry about the money yet, Shapiro," Elliott advised him. "It will depend on how much time I have to spend on this case on your behalf. But you're right. We do need to get on with it. Toni, why don't you tell me from the beginning everything you can think of about your relationship with the deceased?"

"From the beginning, like when she first started working there?"

Elliott nodded. I thought for a moment.

"Well, the first thing that happened was that she yelled at my techs when they tried to help her collect specimens correctly. When I tried to talk to her about it, she told me she didn't like my attitude, she didn't know why the other physicians kept me here, and that I'd better slap my techs into line or she would. She said she'd never had to put up with non-physician personnel telling her what to do, and she wasn't about to start now."

Elliott nodded again. "Go on."

"Then Dr. Cabot started bringing me her complaints and telling me about how well-trained she was and how much we needed her and would hate to lose her."

Elliott stopped me. "Dr. Cabot complained to you on her behalf? She didn't complain to you herself?"

"No, she never did. She'd yell at my techs, and she'd complain to Tyler, but never directly to me unless I sought her out. Elliott, you already *know* all this."

"I know, but this is for the record. I need to get everything in some kind of order."

"Okay. Well, then Lucille got fired."

"What was the reason?"

"Dr. Shore accused her of refusing to come in on call and set up a throat culture, and she said Lucille used obscene language. Lucille denied it. I talked to the ward clerk and the charge nurse, and they both confirmed Lucille's story, so she got her job back."

"Was that when Dr. Shore wrote the letter to you and Dr. Cabot?"

"Yes, and I went to Monty's office to talk to him about it, and Tyler and Jack Allen were there, and they told me not to worry about the lab; but then they said Dr. Shore would probably be joining the staff permanently, and I told them they'd have to choose between her and me."

Elliott looked startled at this. "Wow. Just like that, huh?"

"Just like that," I said.

"Did you know about that, Shapiro?"

Hal nodded. "Oh, yes, she told me."

"What was your reaction?"

Hal shrugged. "Well, once I got over the initial shock, I was proud of her for calling their bluff; although I really hoped it wouldn't come to that."

"You do realize," Elliott said, "that this could be construed as a motive? How much of a hardship would that have been?"

"You mean living on my salary? It'd be tough. We'd probably have to move to a smaller house. It costs a fortune to heat that old ark we live in. Not to mention the upkeep and maintenance of century-old plumbing and retrofitted electrical wiring. We'd have to give up a few luxuries. But I really think that if it had come to that, it wouldn't be long before Dr. Shore screwed up to the point where they'd let her go and want Toni back. Either that, or they'd decide they needed Toni more than they needed Dr. Shore. Worse comes to worst, she could get a job someplace else and we'd have to move. It'd be a bitch, but we'd manage somehow."

Elliott was silent for a few moments while he made some notes on his legal pad. Then he looked back to me. "Then what happened?"

"Then Lucille got run over, and Natalie came."

"The very next day, wasn't it?"

My throat began to feel scratchy. I wondered if I was coming down with a cold. "Could I have something to drink?" I asked.

"Sure," Elliott said, pushing aside his legal pad and getting up. "But we don't have any Scotch here, you know." He strode over to the door and stuck his head out. "Betsy, could we have some coffee and ice water in here? Thanks." He came back and sat down again, pulling his legal pad back in front of him. "That must have seemed awfully convenient."

Betsy came in carrying a full tray and placed it on the table between us. Elliott thanked her, and she left.

"Oh, it did. It seemed too good to be true." I poured myself some ice water. Hal helped himself to coffee. "But then she switched two breast cases to make it look like I'd misread a frozen section as cancer when it wasn't and caused a patient to have an unnecessary mastectomy."

"Oh yeah," Elliott said. "I remember you telling us about that. But you got that straightened out, as I recall."

"I did," I said. "But then Tyler called me at home and threatened to call me at home every time a patient's lab work wasn't on the chart, and I went in to the hospital to see what I could do and found Dr. Shore in my office with a cup of coffee."

Hmm, I thought, *that sounds good*, and I poured myself a cup. "She accused me of accusing her of malpractice … I know, that sounds dumb." I shook a packet of sugar into my cup. "But she did, and then she started threatening me with what she was going to do to the lab when she got on the staff." I tore open a creamer container and dumped it into my cup. "So I kicked her out and came home. Then the next morning, I came to work and tripped over her body. Have I left anything out?"

"That seems to sum it up pretty well," Elliott said. "Shapiro? Can you think of anything else?"

Hal shook his head. "Nope. That pretty much covers it."

Elliott shoved his legal pad aside and leaned forward with his elbows on the desk. "Okay. Let me recap and make sure. Dr. Shore—we'll continue to call her that for now—comes to your place of work and starts antagonizing you and your techs. Dr. Cabot sings her praises and defends her and even fires your histotech on her behalf. She complains about you and your lab to anyone who will listen, and she writes a letter complaining about you and the lab, which is probably seen by multiple physicians, in an apparent effort to undermine you and question your competence. Then, after everybody knows about the antipathy between the two of you, somebody kills her and puts the body in your office, hoping that people will think you killed her. Then, just in case that doesn't work, Dr. Cabot tells the police that he thinks you killed her because nobody else has a grudge against her."

"But she's been dead for two weeks," Hal said. "He didn't even *know* she was murdered until he talked to Toni at the country club Friday night."

"I thought he was going to hit me," I said. "But this is ever so much more effective. If he had hit me, I could have had him arrested. But this way, *I* get arrested instead."

"You're not arrested yet," Elliott said.

"It doesn't make sense," Hal said. "The only reason he had for getting rid of you was to get Dr. Shore on the medical staff. Otherwise, like you say, he's had ten years to do it and didn't. But now that she's dead, he no longer has a reason to get rid of you. So why do this?"

"What I want to know is why Kincaid is so anxious to put me in jail," I said. "Are the police going to stop looking just because Tyler accused me? He didn't tell them anything they didn't already know from me. But the minute *he* says anything, they run right out and drag me down to the station. Who the hell is he that they fall all over themselves to cater to him? So he's a doctor. Big deal. So am I."

"That may be," Elliott said. "But his wife is a Baumgartner. That makes a difference. It shouldn't, but it does. This is a small town, and the Baumgartners are very influential. It doesn't do to antagonize them."

"Whereas it's perfectly okay to antagonize the Shapiros," I replied.

"Honey," Hal said, "you're being melodramatic."

"Maybe if we knew who she really was, all this would make more sense," I said.

"Well, then, that's what we need to do," Hal said. "Find out who the hell she was and what her relationship is to that asshole Tyler Cabot; because maybe he killed her and accused Toni just to cover his ass."

"That may be true, but that's not the reason we're here," Elliott interrupted. "What I'm saying is, the purpose of this meeting is to keep Toni out of jail, not solve the mystery of who Dr. Shore really was."

"But if we solve the mystery, we'll find out why she was killed, and that will lead to who killed her," Hal objected.

"And how long will that take? Suppose Toni gets arrested in the meantime?" Elliott countered. "Do you think I'm going to freakin' leave her to rot in jail while we play Sam Spade? No, I think we need to establish her innocence and leave the rest to the police."

"Hmph," I grunted. "I can't say I have a lot of confidence in the *police* at this point."

"Toni, get a grip," Elliott said. "Quit blaming the

police. They aren't all Kincaid. So he doesn't like you. Big freakin' deal. He's only one cop. Ray Harris isn't about to let him run the show. So let's forget about him and work on proving that you couldn't have killed Dr. Shore. Go back to the night before you found her body and tell me exactly what you did."

"You know that as well as I do," I replied. "I was at your house."

"Before that. Go back to kicking her out of your office. Did you physically throw her out or just tell her to get out?"

"I told her to get out of my office and stay out of my lab."

"And did she?"

"Yes, and then I locked up and went home."

"What time was that?"

"Quarter to eight." A sense of familiarity came over me. "You know, Kincaid asked me all this."

"Never mind Kincaid."

I took a swig of my coffee, which was now cold. "Okay. I got home at quarter to eight. Hal left me a note, so I came over to your house. Then we left at about ten and came home together."

"Then what?"

"We went to bed."

Elliott pulled his legal pad back and made a note. "So the only people who can substantiate your whereabouts between quarter to eight and ten are Hal and me and Jodi. After ten, only Hal can. Too bad. That wouldn't do us any good in court."

"Because he's my husband, you mean."

"Right. But surely there are people at the hospital

who saw Dr. Shore after you left. All we have to do is find them. Does the hospital have security cameras?"

"Are you kidding? We barely have security." I told him about the Old Fat Brigade who staunchly guarded the walls of our hospital while sipping from their hip flasks. "You can always ask them what they saw." Or didn't see because they were sleeping on the job, as I suspected happened all too often.

"We will," Elliott assured me. "Was Dr. Shore on duty that night?"

"I don't know," I said. "I don't know her schedule."

"We'll check that out too," Elliott said, making another note on his pad.

"Who's we?" Hal asked.

"We retain a firm of private investigators," Elliott told him. "Obviously I can't run around like freakin' Archie Goodwin and run a law practice at the same time. Anyway, if she was working, there ought to be other hospital personnel who saw her. If she wasn't on duty, where would she be?"

"At home, I should think," I said, realizing that I had no idea where Dr. Shore lived. At a motel? "Monty should know. He probably made the arrangements or knows who did."

Elliott made another note. "What was the time of death supposed to be? Does anyone know?"

I shook my head. "Unfortunately, the autopsy report doesn't say. The body was completely cold when the police arrived, so the time of death could have been any time between when I left and when I found her the next morning."

"Not really," Elliott said. "It had to take some time

for her to get completely cold. You're a pathologist. How long do you think it took?"

Not having been trained in forensic pathology, I was a trifle hazy on details like that, but I made a stab at it. After all, Elliott could always find himself an expert if he really needed to know. "I think the body temperature drops one degree per hour, but it depends on the ambient temperature where the body is. I mean, if they left her outdoors for a while, she'd get cold much faster than if she was someplace warm."

"That can't be right," Hal objected. "For a body to go from 98.6 degrees to, say, seventy degrees would take twenty-eight hours. There couldn't have been more than nine hours between when Toni left the hospital until she found the body the next morning."

"If the core temperature wasn't taken until she got to Boise where the pathologist got hold of her, it could have been longer than that," I said. "Besides which, she had a two-hour ride in a hearse, which couldn't have been very warm."

"The autopsy report doesn't give a core temperature," Elliott said. "It only says that rigor was fully advanced, however long that takes."

"That depends on the ambient temperature too," I said.

Elliott made another note. "So that angle won't do us any good. Too bad about Frank Robertson; he would have checked. This other guy probably didn't have any freakin' forensic experience at all."

I thought about that, and about whether Dr. Nicholas Schroeder's forensic ineptitude would work to my advantage, but for the life of me I couldn't see how.

Chapter 30

My strength is as the strength of ten,
Because my heart is pure.
　　　　　　　　　—Alfred, Lord Tennyson

s I prepared my first frozen section of the day, I was acutely aware of Natalie working silently and efficiently across the room from me.

I glanced at her from time to time, but her glossy black hair hung like a curtain, obscuring her face from my view. I had no idea what was going on in her mind, but I knew that something was bothering her.

What could it be? Was it because I blew her cover?

Well, so what? What did she need cover for in the first place? Surely having the same surname as one of the doctors was just coincidental.

But what if it wasn't? What if she really was related to Tyler?

And again, so what? I knew there were people working in the hospital who were related to other employees and even to some of the doctors—their college kids during the summer and Christmas holidays, for example.

Tyler didn't have kids. At least, he didn't have any

with Desiree. He could have had some before he came here, with a previous wife, perhaps, or a girlfriend.

Or girlfriends. There could be any number of little Cabots running around back in Massachusetts.

Natalie was from Boston. Was that a coincidence?

I was so deep in my thoughts that I jumped when the phone rang. It was Surgery.

"Haven't you got anything for us yet?"

This would not do. This idle speculation was interfering with my work.

I finished the frozen sections and cleaned up my mess. Then I went back to my office and tried to read Paps, but it wasn't easy. I just couldn't concentrate. I went back to speculating.

Dr. Shore was from Boston too. Dr. Shore was divorced and had a daughter who was about to get married.

Natalie was afraid of being found by an abusive ex-boyfriend.

I thought about Dr. Shore's long black hair. I thought about Natalie's long black hair.

Both had incredibly white teeth.

Dr. Shore had brown eyes, but Natalie's were blue. A very intense blue.

Like Tyler's. All of that could be coincidence too, but I didn't really believe it. There were too many coincidences.

What if Natalie was Dr. Shore's daughter? And Tyler's?

It would explain so many things. Like why Dr. Shore had come here instead of Boise or Salt Lake. Like why Natalie had showed up just in time to replace Lucille. Like why Natalie had screwed up that breast cancer case.

Okay, Toni, now you're just being paranoid. I could

hear Hal saying it just as clearly as if he were standing right next to me.

Maybe so, I argued. *But just because you're paranoid doesn't mean someone isn't out to get you.*

If Dr. Shore had been Natalie's mother, Natalie had to be under incredible stress. I tried to imagine myself in her place. Twenty-two years old, in a strange town, at a new job, not knowing anybody except my mother, and nobody was supposed to know. To have my mother die and not be able to grieve openly.

Then another thought wormed its way into my subconscious and caused me to break into a cold sweat.

Assuming that Dr. Shore and Tyler were in cahoots, and knowing that Tyler was going around saying he thought I had killed Dr. Shore, it was likely that he had said it to Natalie as well.

I felt as if I had been poleaxed.

Here was Natalie, secretly grieving for her mother and believing that her boss, with whom she worked side by side every day, *had killed her mother.*

How the hell did she manage to get everything done so efficiently and still act normal?

I was almost twice her age, and I knew perfectly well that I would have been a basket case. The girl must be made of iron.

Should I try to talk to her, I wondered? What would I say? *Sorry for your loss, but I didn't kill her?* And why would I say that when I really didn't know that Dr. Shore was Natalie's mother, that I only suspected it? If I was wrong, then Natalie wasn't grieving, and I didn't need to say anything.

I decided to keep quiet.

I hoped I wouldn't regret that decision.

Things were a little hectic the next morning. We were shorthanded, and I embedded and cut my own surgicals.

Natalie had been admitted to Intensive Care at midnight. She'd taken an overdose of sleeping pills, prescribed for her by Tyler Cabot. Her stomach had been lavaged in the emergency room, but she was still unconscious, and nobody knew if she would live or die.

Dale had found her, and he was with her now. He wouldn't leave, and Margo gave him the day off. She also finished up his night on call for him.

I tormented myself by wondering if I couldn't have prevented this. If only I had talked to Natalie instead of keeping quiet. She might have opened up and told me everything. I might have been able to convince her that I was not the enemy. If Natalie died, I would never forgive myself, and I was sure that Dale wouldn't either. Then he would quit and go elsewhere, and I would be short two techs. And I would have nobody to blame but myself.

"Hogwash!" snorted Hal, when I expressed all this to him at home. "What makes you think you could have changed anything? If Natalie considered you the enemy, she would have refused to talk about it or denied the whole thing. There's no guarantee that you could have changed her mind. Stop torturing yourself."

"But I could have talked to Dale," I argued.

"You don't know that she's told Dale any more than she's told you. Didn't he come to you awhile back wanting to know if *you* knew what was the matter with Natalie?"

I had to admit, he had a point. Maybe Dale didn't

know any more than I did. Less, actually, since he didn't know any of the things I'd discussed with the police. Of course, I didn't really *know* anything myself. To be perfectly honest, nobody really knew for a fact that Dr. Shore didn't die of natural causes in the first place. There was only circumstantial evidence that she didn't.

But people had been hanged for circumstantial evidence before, and it could happen again—to me— unless I could clear myself. If not, losing two techs would become academic. It would no longer be my problem.

I called ICU several times during that day—and night, since I couldn't sleep anyway—to check on Natalie. Finally, at four in the morning, they told me that Natalie had regained consciousness. Exhausted, I fell asleep, but I had to get up again at six-thirty to go to work.

Dale came in while I was embedding. "Natalie should be back tomorrow," he said.

"Oh, good," I said, with relief. "I've been so worried about her."

"Me too," he said.

I went back to my embedding, but Dale didn't leave. He clearly had something on his mind. I put the full mold on the cold block and gave him my full attention. "What is it, Dale?"

"Well," he hesitated, "remember that time I asked you if you knew what was bothering Natalie because she wouldn't tell me?"

"Yes, I do."

"Well, she still hasn't told me what it is, and it's making her sick, Dr. Day. I mean literally. She tries to eat and then throws up. She's lost twenty pounds. She's been taking sleeping pills. I was kinda half-expecting her to do something like this. That's why I went and checked on her while I was on call last night. I really care about Natalie, Dr. Day. I want to marry her, but I can't if she goes on like this. I have to know what I'm getting into."

"Understandable," I said. "But I'm afraid I don't know any more than you do."

His face fell. "But you work together … I thought she would have said something … but I guess not."

"Well, I do have some ideas. Dale, do you suppose she'd talk to me if I went up with you?"

"Do you want me to go up with you?" Dale seemed surprised.

"I think it'd be better. In fact, I think it's essential."

Natalie saw Dale before she saw me, and her eyes lit up. He bent down and kissed her, and she clung to him. I felt a lump in my throat. I moved to the other side of the bed, sat down, and did some rapid blinking and surreptitious flicking of tears from my eyelashes before I looked up.

Dale loosened Natalie's arms from around his neck and straightened up, still holding her hand. "Honey, Dr. Day's here, too," he said.

Natalie turned her head, saw me, closed her eyes and turned her head away.

"Honey, I thought you liked Dr. Day," Dale said. "I thought you'd tell her what's wrong. You won't tell me."

Natalie shook her head stubbornly, her eyes still closed.

"See?" I said to Dale. "She won't tell me either. Natalie, do you know how lucky you are?"

Natalie opened her eyes in amazement. "Lucky?" she asked.

I decided to go for broke. What did I have to lose? "Yes, lucky," I said. "When a girl loses her mother, it really helps to have a strong man who loves her to lean on. And you have one. Don't you think you owe Dale an explanation? After all, he saved your life."

Natalie's eyes filled with tears.

"Dr. Shore was your mother, wasn't she?" I asked gently.

Dale's jaw dropped. Natalie buried her face in the pillow, and her shoulders shook with silent sobs.

"How did you ..." Dale began, but I shushed him.

"Natalie, I didn't kill her," I went on. "I didn't like her, but I didn't kill her."

Dale stroked Natalie's tangled hair until she had cried herself out. Eventually the storm passed, and Natalie sat up, dried her eyes, and blew her nose.

"You can't imagine how awful it's been," she said. "Nobody was supposed to know she was my mother. I couldn't even grieve for her. We couldn't even have a regular funeral, because people would wonder why I was there."

"Who's we?" I asked. "Dr. Cabot?"

"How did you know?"

"I know he paid for the funeral expenses."

"I didn't have enough money," she said and started to cry again. "He was the only friend she had in this place. Nobody liked Mom, Dr. Day. You should have heard the things the other techs said about her, and I couldn't even stick up for her."

"She could be pretty provocative," I said.

"I know," Natalie said. "Mom was really screwed up—mentally, I mean. She always had trouble getting

197

along with people. She couldn't hold on to jobs for very long. When I was a kid, we were always moving. She was always telling me people were against her and that they didn't know a good doctor when they saw one. Whenever we moved, she'd tell people she left the last place because the quality of medical care wasn't good enough and she was afraid she'd get sued for other people's mistakes."

"That sounds familiar," I said.

"Mom thought she'd finally found a place to settle down. She said Dr. Cabot guaranteed her a place on the medical staff."

"Did she say why he would do that?"

"She said he was a very old friend."

"That's all? A friend?"

"That's what she said." Natalie looked puzzled. "Why?"

"Natalie, you have the same last name. Dr. Cabot is your father, isn't he?"

Natalie didn't have a chance to answer. A nurse came in to take her vital signs and shooed us out.

Dale seemed shell-shocked. In the privacy of the elevator, he finally spoke.

"She's got his eyes," he said.

Chapter 31

Our ancestors are very good kind of
folks; but they are the last
people I should choose to have a visiting acquaintance with.
—Richard Brinsley Sheridan

I couldn't believe I had actually been right about Natalie being Dr. Shore's daughter. But Natalie didn't know if Tyler was her father. She'd been told her father was dead.

I was all ready to storm the police station and demand they investigate Dr. Shore's background and find out who she really was. Elliott restrained me with difficulty.

"Toni, stay out of it," he advised. "The one thing you don't want to do right now is set foot inside the police station. They already told you they didn't care who Dr. Shore really was."

"But that was before they decided she'd been murdered!" I protested. "They need to find out who she really was, and what her relationship to Tyler was, and why she came here in the first place, and they need to talk to all the other doctors, because I *wasn't* the only one who didn't get along with her."

Elliott waved his hands in front of his face. "Toni, please, one freakin' thing at a time. For one thing, Mass General won't have employee records going back twenty-two years, not on computer, anyway. And even if they do, there won't be anybody still there who will remember—or care—who Tyler Cabot was dating. As for finding out who Dr. Shore really was …" He threw up his hands. "We don't even have a name."

"Natalie must have known her mother had a different name," Hal said. "In 1997 she was fourteen years old. And what about birth records?"

"Not only that," I said. "She must have known her mother wasn't a doctor. She couldn't have stolen the real Sally Shore's identity until 1997. How did she explain to her child that she was suddenly a doctor without having gone to medical school sometime?"

"Maybe she *was* a doctor," Elliott speculated. "All you know is that she isn't the same Sally Shore who was a neurosurgery fellow at Mass General in 1997. It doesn't necessarily mean she *isn't* a doctor—just not *that* one."

"Maybe what we need to do is trace her work history," I said. "She gave us a curriculum vitae. And if she came from a locum tenens agency, they'll know where she's been. I'll ask Monty. And I'll talk to Natalie too."

"No, you won't," Elliott contradicted me. "I'll ask the questions from now on."

I agreed to let Elliott ask the questions, but I lied.

I got on the Internet and brought up the Idaho State Board of Medicine website to see whether Sally Maria Shore, MD, was licensed in Idaho and found out that she also had active licenses in Oregon, Washington, Wyoming, and Montana, all obtained within the last six months. She had inactive licenses in Illinois and Massachusetts.

That was odd. I could see why her Illinois license was inactive, but Massachusetts? If she had been practicing in a group in Boston before coming to Twin Falls, she would have needed an active license ... unless that was all fiction too. I checked for disciplinary actions on any of those licenses and found that there were none on record.

Tyler was on vacation for a week, which suited me just fine. I had no idea what I would say to him if I ever came face to face with him, and I was glad I wouldn't have to worry about it for a while.

It was eerily quiet in my office. My techs were staying away from me, and so were the doctors. The phone didn't ring all day. Even with all my extracurricular phone calls, I had no trouble getting everything done. Too bad I couldn't enjoy it. I knew I was being avoided because nobody else knew what to say to me, either.

Natalie was back to work and still very quiet, but she seemed less tense than before. I kept my conversation with her strictly work-related, because I was just as uncomfortable as she was. I stayed out of Histology as much as possible and just let her get on with it. This was one area where I was happy to let Elliott ask the questions, although I had to restrain myself from calling him and saying, "Well? Well? What have you found out?" It was far too soon to find out anything. These things took time, and time was what I didn't have.

Monty informed me that Dr. Shore had called inquiring about locum tenens work and had given Tyler as a reference. When the Board saw her curriculum vitae, they had snapped her up. He had never gotten around to checking the references on it. As far as he was concerned, it was a moot point.

I made a copy of her curriculum vitae, all of the reference letters, and anything else that had addresses and phone numbers on it while I still had her file on my desk. Elliott would need all the help he could get if he was going to check all these out, and he would have one hell of a phone bill. She had done locums in *seventeen* different hospitals in the Pacific Northwest in the past six months.

Then I went home exhausted.

Dale called while Hal and I were eating dinner. He sounded unusually agitated. "I didn't want to disturb you at home," he began, "but Natalie had a call from the district attorney this afternoon. He wants to interview her about Dr. Shore. She's scared, Dr. Day. Could we possibly come over and talk to you?"

"Well, sure, I guess so. We're just finishing dinner. We're not going anywhere, are we?" I looked at Hal, who shook his head. "Come on over."

"We'll be there in ten minutes," Dale said, and we hung up.

"They're coming over?" Hal asked. "What for?"

"They want to talk to me," I replied. "The district attorney wants to interview Natalie."

"Are you sure you want to get mixed up in that?" Hal asked. "It might hurt your own case. Why don't I call Elliott?"

"They might not talk freely if he's here," I objected. "I think Natalie might need legal advice, which you and I can't give her," Hal said firmly. "It might not help …"

I sighed. "But it wouldn't hurt," I finished for him. "Okay, go ahead and call him."

Jodi and Elliott arrived as I was loading the dishwasher. Jodi came into the kitchen, and Elliott made a beeline for the couch.

The phone rang.

"This better not be Robbie again," Hal said darkly as he answered it. "Hello?"

But nobody was there, and Hal swore as he hung up.

"That asshole is still calling you guys?" Elliott asked.

"Every night," Hal said. "Right about this time."

"Didn't you get a restraining order against him?" asked Jodi.

"We did. He's not to come within five hundred yards of either Toni or Hal." Elliott said.

"But he can still call them up and harass them?"

"If we knew it was him, we could add that to the restraining order," Elliott said.

"Well, how are you gonna know that if he just hangs up?" demanded Jodi.

"The phone company can trace the calls."

"Yeah, they'll trace them to Stan's house," I objected. "No way to prove who actually called. I tell you what, why don't I answer the next time? Maybe he'll talk to me."

"No way," Hal said.

"All right, what's your solution, Mr. Know-It-All?"

"All right, all right, you two," interjected Elliott. "No need to get violent. I have an idea. You say he always calls right about this time, every night?"

"So far," said Hal.

"So I'll come over about that time and listen in on the extension. How would that be?"

"Fine," I said impatiently. "Can we talk about something else now? Natalie and Dale will be here any minute now."

The doorbell rang before I even finished the sentence. As I went to answer it, I wondered how in hell I was going to be able to concentrate on the matter at hand with Robbie rattling around inside my head.

Dale and Natalie burst through the door as if propelled by the gust of icy wind that came into the room with them, hugging themselves against the cold and blowing on their hands. Dale, unbelievably, wore shorts, and I marveled at the resilience of youth. It made me shiver just to look at him. Natalie wore jeans and a letterman's sweater that was obviously Dale's. She pulled it tightly around her, and I noticed how thin and drawn her face was. She was shivering. I took them both over by the fire. Hal made hot chocolate and brought us each a cup.

I performed the introductions. "I know you wanted to talk to me alone," I apologized to Dale and Natalie. "But I'm under suspicion, and it might not be a good idea for you to talk about this without a lawyer present. Elliott is my lawyer, and he already knows everything I know, and he needs to know everything you know in order to help me."

"That's right," Elliott said. "And if you're going to be talking to the district attorney, you don't want to do that without a lawyer either. Fritz Baumgartner can be a real sonofabitch. You could easily say something you don't mean and get yourself and Toni into more trouble."

"Fritz *Baumgartner*?" I echoed. "Any relation to …"

"I think his old man and Desiree's old man were cousins, isn't that right, Jodi?" Elliott asked.

Jodi nodded.

My heart sank. "That's all I need," I said. "A district attorney who is related to Tyler, who is trying to get me put in jail. How can we fight that?"

"Well, there is such a thing as legal ethics," Elliott said. "Yes, Shapiro," he went on, seeing Hal's skeptical expression, "lawyers do actually have them. If Fritz has a conflict of interest, he'll turn the case over to his deputy."

"And who is that?" Hal asked.

"Bert Kincaid."

"*Kincaid*?" I echoed again. My heart sank even further. "Oh, no."

"What—oh, your pal on the police force. I don't think he's related. There are other Kincaids around here. Didn't you say he was from California? Anyway, I don't think you need to worry about nepotism in the prosecution. But you do need to be careful what you say, Natalie. What we need to do is go over this case and make sure we're all on the same page." He reached into his attaché case and pulled out a yellow legal pad.

"Now, I know that Dr. Shore was your mother and that she was murdered, and the police think so too, thanks to Toni, who convinced them by coming up with a plausible but totally unprovable method, and connected it in their minds to the hit-and-run in the hospital parking lot, thereby getting herself implicated—with help from a certain Dr. Tyler Cabot."

Natalie's eyes were wide and bewildered. "Wait. I

don't understand. What hit-and-run? What does it have to do with me?"

"Lucille," Dale said. "You didn't know her. She used to have your job. Then she got run down in our parking lot. She almost died."

"That's awful," Natalie said. "I've heard the other techs talking about her, but I never knew exactly what it was all about. Is she okay now?"

"She's home and on the mend," I said. "I don't know when she's going to be able to come back to work."

"The only thing that has to do with you," Elliott said, "is that your mother's car is believed to be the car that ran her down. It disappeared from the parking lot after that, and a few days ago the police pulled it out of the canyon."

"My God," Natalie whispered, her hands over her mouth. "I wondered what happened to it, and I asked Dr. Cabot, but he said he didn't know."

"Well, the police have it impounded now. Since it's been in the water, there's no evidence linking it to Lucille. And we'll never know who drove it. But it's probably not in very good shape. You probably better forget about it, as far as using it is concerned. The repairs may cost more than the car is worth. Was there insurance?"

"I don't know."

"Natalie," Elliott went on, "tell me how it was that you happened to come to Twin Falls? Did your mother ask you to come?"

"Yes, she did. She said there was a job opening and that, if I hurried, I might get it before anybody else did. She said she would e-mail me a ticket and that I should come right away."

"What was the rush, did she say? And why did she think you would want to quit your job in Boston and come here?"

Natalie hugged herself and rubbed her arms. "She knew I wanted to leave Boston," she said. "I was engaged to this guy, and we had a fight one day and he hit me. I broke off the engagement, but he wouldn't leave me alone, and then he started threatening me. I jumped at the chance to get away."

"Oh, so that part *was* true," I said with a significant look at Hal, who shrugged.

"You didn't believe me?" Natalie asked me with a hurt expression.

"I'm sorry, Natalie," I said gently. "I was skeptical of everything at that point. You see, Hal and I had talked about how conveniently you showed up to replace Lucille, and I thought you were a Trojan horse."

"A what?"

"It was the day that we had the big mixup on the breast biopsies," I said. "I thought you did that on purpose to get me in trouble. Hal told me I was crazy and that it was just an honest mistake."

"It was Mom's idea," Natalie said. "She told me that she had a good chance to get on the staff, except that there was this pathologist that kept making her look bad. So she said that if I got the job, I had to find a way to discredit you so that the other doctors wouldn't listen to you any more, and maybe you'd even get fired."

The bottom dropped out of my stomach. Despite all the theorizing, deep down, I guess I had never really believed it was anything more than an honest mistake.

"Christ on a crutch," Hal said. "You *were* a Trojan horse."

"It would have worked, too," I said, "if I hadn't found tumor in a lymph node."

"I felt awful about it," Natalie said. "Once I met you, I didn't want to do it, but I had promised Mom. I was glad it didn't work, Dr. Day. And you could have fired me, but you didn't. Mom wanted me to try something else, but I refused. I couldn't do it again."

"Thank God," I said with feeling. "I'm not sure I could have survived a second time."

"We had an awful fight," Natalie said, her voice breaking. "And then she died. And I couldn't tell anybody she was my mother." She sobbed as Dale put his arms around her. "Not even you."

"It's okay," Dale said softly, into her hair, as he rocked her. "Shhh, now. It's okay. I love you. Everything will be okay."

Elliott gave Natalie a moment to collect herself and blow her nose before asking the next question. "Natalie, how much do you know about your mother's medical background?"

"She was in medical school when I was born."

"Where was that?"

"In Chicago. At Loyola."

"Do you remember your father?"

"No. Mom said he died before I was born."

"Who took care of you while she was in school?"

"We had a live-in housekeeper."

Hal and I looked at each other. *We* couldn't afford a live-in housekeeper. How on earth did she, as a medical student? Who had paid for it?

"Was your mother from a wealthy family?" I asked.

"I don't know. I never met any of her family. I didn't know my grandparents, even. But we always seemed to have enough money somehow."

"From your father's family, maybe?"

"Maybe. I don't know. I never met any of them, either."

"Was your father a doctor?"

"Hey!" Elliott interrupted, glaring at me. "Who's asking the freakin' questions, here?"

"Sorry. I got carried away."

"You may as well answer Toni's question, Natalie," Elliott said. "I would have asked it myself, if Toni hadn't taken off with the freakin' interrogation."

I shot him a dirty look and got up to fix myself a Scotch.

"Darling," Jodi drawled. "Could you possibly use another word? *Interrogation* sounds so threatening. One almost expects rubber hoses to materialize."

Elliott ignored her. "Natalie?"

"Mom said he was."

"How did he die?"

"I don't know. Mom wouldn't talk about him. She said it was too painful."

Hal got up and came over to the bar. "Fix me one too while you're at it," he whispered. "I have a feeling we're gonna need it before this is over."

"I don't know," I whispered back. "She seems to be doing okay now."

Elliott continued. "She never said what his name was?"

"She said it was Thomas Cabot. She always called him Tommy."

"Was Sally Shore your mother's real name?"

"No. It was Sally Schott. Sara Lee Schott, but everybody called her Sally." Natalie's voice quavered and her eyes filled with tears. "I'm sorry. It just keeps hitting me that she's really gone."

Dale's arm tightened around her, and he kissed the top of her head. *Thank God she's got him,* I thought. This would be much harder without somebody to lean on.

Like I have Hal. I slipped my arm around his waist and hugged him. He hugged me back and kissed the top of my head. It made me smile right out loud. For a minute.

"Did she use the name Cabot in medical school?" Elliott asked.

"No. She graduated as Sally Schott."

"Then what happened?"

"Then she started her internship at Cook County. Straight surgery. It was really tough. She was hardly ever home."

"Did she finish it?"

"No. She got sick. They called it a nervous breakdown. She was in a mental hospital for a month."

Not nearly long enough, in my opinion.

"At Cook County?"

"No, it was a fancy private one. I don't remember the name of it."

"And how old were you at this point?"

"Five."

Christ on a crutch. How does a five-year-old deal with not having her mom for a month? It must have seemed like an eternity.

"Then what happened?"

"Then we moved to Boston. She started her general surgery residency at Mass General."

"Did she finish that?"

"No. She got sick again."

"Another nervous breakdown?"

"Yes."

"And what year was this?"

"About 1990, I think. I was eight."

"And then what happened?"

Under Elliott's skillful guidance, Natalie spun a depressing tale of job after job working in emergency rooms and moving from place to place, going to a different school every few months, until her mother placed her in a private school at age twelve.

Perhaps that was why Natalie was able to handle the stress at work as well as she did. She'd had so much practice. Poor kid.

"I was homesick at first," Natalie said, "until I realized that the school was more of a home to me than any of the places I had lived with Mom. I made friends for the first time, and they were my friends for the next six years. Some of them are still my friends. Then I got into Boston College, got my degree in medical technology, met my boyfriend, and got my job at Mass General."

"Did you keep in touch with your mother during this time?"

"Oh, yes. I always knew where she was and what she was doing."

"So she knew about your problems with your boyfriend—or should I say ex-boyfriend—when she called you up out of the blue and told you to high-tail it for Idaho?"

"Yes, she did."

"So she knew you would come right away?"

"Yes, she did. But when I got here, it was really weird. She told me she was using the name Sally Shore, not Schott, and that nobody was supposed to know she was my mother, and she wouldn't tell me why. And she told me not to use the name Cabot, either, because there was a doctor named Cabot on the staff. Then she told me I was supposed to sabotage the pathologist."

Jesus, Mary, and Joseph, I thought. *And the camel.*

"Holy shit," Hal said.

"Do you know why she picked the name Sally Shore?" I asked.

"Oh, that was probably my fault," Natalie said. "My coworkers were all sitting around talking one day when it was slow, and one of the techs was telling me that she remembered a resident named Cabot on the house staff, years ago, and then they all started reminiscing about interns and residents they had known, and somebody mentioned a neurosurgery resident who had died, and her name was Sally Shore, and it stuck in my mind because it was so close to Mom's name—and I told her about it."

"When was that?" Elliott asked.

"Oh, last year sometime." Natalie yawned. "Oh, excuse me."

"I think she's about to turn into a pumpkin," Hal observed.

I looked at my watch and saw with a start that it was nearly midnight.

Elliott took pity on us. "I think we can stop here for now," he said. "Natalie, you don't have to talk to the district attorney. In fact, I think it would be best if you didn't. You can say your lawyer advised you not to."

"But I don't have a lawyer," Natalie said.

"You do now," Elliott said.

Chapter 32

Thus grief still treads upon the heels of pleasure;
Married in haste, we may repent at leisure.
—William Congreve

I awoke with a start.

The sun was shining in through the bedroom window, and I heard voices downstairs. It was nearly eight o'clock, and I was late for work. I leaped out of bed, ran into the bathroom, and then realized it was Saturday. *Thank God.* I hastily put on jeans and a sweatshirt and went downstairs to find Elliott and Jodi at the breakfast table, drinking coffee. Hal was frying bacon with Killer lying at his feet. Geraldine was on Jodi's lap. Spook was nowhere in sight.

"Did you guys spend the night here or what?" I demanded.

"And good morning to you, too, darling," drawled Jodi.

I poured myself a cup of coffee and sat down at the table, rubbing my eyes. "I have a feeling of déjà vu," I said. "Did last night really happen?"

"I'm afraid it did," said Hal. "Do you think Natalie was telling the truth?"

Elliott laughed mirthlessly. "I'm sure she was. It's too freakin' bizarre not to be true. Nobody could make all that up."

"Well, it fits with what we already know," I said.

"And the district attorney would never believe it," Elliott said. "He'd try to tear her apart. She's fragile enough that he might be able to get her to say things that would incriminate you further."

"Like what?" I demanded.

Elliott made an impatient gesture. "I don't know like what. Like you making threats against her mother."

"I never made any threats in her presence," I protested, and then I remembered. "Except that I did tell her to stay out of my lab or the hospital wouldn't be big enough for both of us, and I told Monty and Jack and Tyler that they would have to choose between Dr. Shore and me."

Elliott got up and retrieved some papers from his attaché case. "I had one of my associates interview Bruce Montgomery, Charles Nelson, and four of the doctors. They pretty much backed up what you said. But Charlie Nelson did hear you make threats, and he told people about it. I'm afraid your assistant administrator is a bit of a gossip."

I knew that. Our Charlie has a mouth like a sieve. It was stupid of me to say those things to him, of all people. They just came out, and there was no taking them back.

"So, to sum it all up, other members of your medical staff didn't like her, but you were the only one whose job was threatened by her. Nobody else said they couldn't work with her. Nobody else was worried about the lab.

Nobody else threatened her. So your motive still stands out from everybody else's. Fritz will have no reason not to jump on that and use it for all it's worth, circumstantial as it is."

"What about George Marshall?" I asked. "He was the one who mentioned all the malpractice suits we may be getting because of her. Somebody needs to talk to him."

"We can do that, but Bruce Montgomery already addressed it. He told my associate that she would have been let go if she hadn't died—for that very reason."

"I wish I'd known that when I had my confrontation with her." I sighed.

"At that point, nobody knew," Hal said. "There's no point in agonizing over it."

"I'm not," I snapped. "I'm agonizing over going to jail."

"We have a lot to do before that happens," Elliott said. "We need to check out Thomas Cabot, for one thing. Sometime during the eighties, in the Chicago area. Does Tyler have a brother, by any chance?"

"I've never heard him mention one, but that doesn't mean he doesn't have one. And *I'm* not about to ask him."

"He doesn't," Jodi said. "Desiree told me once that they were both only children."

"We don't know what Thomas Cabot's position was at the time, either," Elliott went on. "Natalie said she thought he was a doctor, but he could have been a medical student. He could have been her mother's classmate."

"Or he could have been an intern or resident in whatever hospital she did her clinical rotations in."

"It would help to know what year," Elliott grumbled.

"Nobody's going to want to look through ten years of records."

"She's supposedly my age," I said. "I started medical school in 1987, but I was already a medical technologist. She probably started in 1986. No, that's impossible. If she was in medical school when Natalie was born, and Natalie is twenty-two, that means she had to be in medical school in 1982, and he had to have gotten her pregnant in 1981."

"Then she's got to be older than you," Hal said. "Unless she started medical school at sixteen."

"I'll check 1980 through 1982," Elliott said, making notes.

"You better check hospitals too, in case he was an intern or a resident at the time."

The phone rang. Hal cursed and reached for it, but Elliott detained him. "Wait, let Toni get it," he said.

"What … oh, okay." He handed the receiver to me. With foreboding, I said, "Hello?"

"Finally!" said Robbie. "I was beginning to think you didn't live there any more. Where have you been?"

"Hi, Robbie," I said, frantically gesturing at Elliott, who sprinted upstairs to the extension in the hall. I heard the click as he picked it up. I sincerely hoped Robbie didn't hear it too.

"Where have you been?" he persisted.

"What do you mean, where have I been?" I demanded in return. "What business is it of yours where I've been?"

"Because I've been trying to talk to you for days. That's why I keep calling. To talk to you. To you, not that hirsute, Hebrew-spouting hippie of yours."

I had to smile in spite of my distaste. The idea of Hal spouting Hebrew was ludicrous in the extreme. I wasn't sure he even knew the words to "Hava Nagila." But that was neither here nor there.

"Did it ever occur to you, Robbie, that I might not want to talk to you? I don't, you know."

"You loved me once, Toni. You could love me again, if you tried."

I shuddered. "I can't imagine why I would want to try. I'm a happily married woman."

"Yeah, right. To a Jew. How can you possibly be happy married to a Jew?"

"Unlike you, Robbie, anti-Semitism has never been my problem."

"I can't imagine that your mother was happy about that either."

"She wasn't, but she got over it. *Everybody* got over it. Everybody, apparently, except you. Get over it, Robbie. I will never, ever, in this lifetime or the next, ever love you again. I don't care if you shoot Hal or not, it won't change my feelings. Is there any part of that you don't understand?"

"Toni, my darling love, *you* don't get it. I will never, ever, in this lifetime or the next, stop loving you. I will never, ever, in this lifetime or the next, stop trying to get you back. No matter what it takes. Is there any part of that *you* don't understand?"

"What do you mean, no matter what it takes? Besides shooting my husband, you mean? What are you going to do, shoot my mother too?"

"All I know is that whenever I think about you with that Jewish prick shoved up inside your—"

"Toni. Hang up. Now." Elliott's tone brooked no refusal. I hung up.

Hal put his arms around me, and I buried my face in his shirt front. "You're shaking," he mumbled into my hair.

"I know," I mumbled into his shoulder. "I feel like throwing up."

Jodi went to the liquor cabinet and returned with a snifter of brandy. "Here," she said. "This'll stop the shakes."

I sipped it tentatively, not sure I could keep it down.

"That was pretty gutsy, honey," Hal said. "I can't believe how casually you challenged him about shooting me and your mother."

"It wasn't casual," I mumbled against his shirt front.

Elliott came downstairs after about ten minutes. His face was set. I'd never seen Elliott look so serious before.

"Well?" Hal demanded. "What are you going to do?"

"Add phone calls to the restraining order and go from there," Elliott responded.

"Big deal," scoffed Hal.

"It's only a starting point. If he gets caught violating it, he could go to jail, and if he goes to jail, he could lose his license to practice law."

"Hmph." Hal was still skeptical.

"He seems to think that if you were out of the picture, he could get Toni back."

"Which is nonsense," Jodi said.

"Of course it is. It's the classic 'if I can't have her, nobody else can' scenario. So I made a few threats of my

219

own. He's not stupid. I don't think you'll be hearing from him again."

He sounded confident, but I had my doubts. Robbie seemed to be impervious to threats. I had a feeling that he'd manage to find a way around anything Elliott could do. I hoped I was wrong.

After Elliott and Jodi left, Hal got the paper and settled himself in his recliner, while I cleaned up the breakfast dishes. When I was finished, I poured myself another cup of coffee, curled up on the couch, and tried to read; but after several minutes of staring at the same page without remembering a word I'd read, I put the book down. "Hal," I began.

Hal sighed and put the paper down. "Toni, I don't want to talk about it."

"We have to talk about it," I persisted.

"No, we don't," he said. "I've had enough of that jerk. Let Elliott handle it."

"Hal, he threatened you. Doesn't that bother you?"

"Of course, it bothers me! Why wouldn't it? But there's nothing I can do about it. And he didn't just threaten me, either, he also threatened you."

"Me? How?"

"Elliott said it was the classic 'if I can't have you, no one else can' scenario. So let's suppose that he succeeds in getting me out of the way. Now the coast is clear. He goes after you. You reject him. Who do you think his next target's gonna be?"

"Hal," I said in a small voice. "I'm scared."

Hal threw the sports section on the floor. "Come here," he said. I climbed onto his lap and he held me tight and rocked me like a small child. "I'm scared too," he admitted. "All we can do is watch our backs and leave the rest to Elliott. Okay?"

"Okay."

After a while, I climbed off Hal's lap, picked up his paper and gave it back to him, and returned to the couch—where I again tried to read, and again found myself staring at the same page without remembering a word I'd read.

"Hal," I began again.

With a sigh, Hal put down the paper. "What, Toni?"

"What do you think are the chances that Thomas Cabot killed Dr. Shore?"

"Why would Thomas Cabot kill his ex-wife? Especially now, after twenty-two years?"

"Maybe he's married and doesn't want his wife to find out? Or maybe he's been paying alimony all this time and doesn't want to any more? Or maybe she was blackmailing him. Maybe his wife doesn't know he has a daughter."

"For God's sake, Toni, it's 2005. Lots of men have children by previous marriages."

"Maybe they weren't married," I speculated. "Maybe it was just a one-night stand. Getting pregnant out of wedlock is a big deal if you're Catholic. You can't take birth-control pills, and you can't get an abortion. Grandma Day used to threaten me about that all the time," I continued, "You had no choice but to have the baby, even if you were raped. If Dr. Shore was at Loyola, she was probably Catholic. And she could have been kicked out of school too."

"Well, we know she didn't get kicked out of school, because she graduated."

"Maybe she forced him to marry her so the baby would have a name and her honor would remain intact. Then she wouldn't have gotten kicked out of school."

"Well, that would explain why Natalie's name isn't Schott."

"But," I argued, "we also know that she wasn't married when she came here. She told everybody she was divorced. Catholics aren't supposed to get divorced, but a lot of them do nowadays. Or maybe Thomas Cabot wanted to get married to somebody else, and she wouldn't give him a divorce, so he killed her."

"Right," Hal snorted. "He comes to Twin Falls in the dead of night, creeps into the hospital, goes right to the emergency room, finds her and kills her? No, even better, he creeps up to Surgery, never having been inside the place before, mind you, finds the succinylcholine, goes down to the ER, finds her allergy stuff, puts the succinylcholine in it, and gives her a shot? And she just sits there? Her ex-husband shows up out of the blue after twenty-two years with a fucking needle in his hand and she just sits there and lets him stick her, for God's sake?"

"Hmm, yeah, I guess that doesn't make a whole lot of sense. Too bad it wasn't Tyler she was married to instead of Thomas. She'd *have* to have been divorced from Tyler, though, because he's married to Desiree now and has been for fifteen years or so."

"He's also married to the Baumgartner fortune," Hal pointed out. "If Dr. Shore was married to Tyler, and they aren't divorced, his marriage to Desiree wouldn't be legal."

"And he wouldn't be entitled to any of that lovely money," I mused.

"A dandy motive for murder, don't you think?"

"No shit, Sherlock," I said.

Chapter 33

Virtuous and vicious every man must be,
Few in the extreme, but all in the degree.
—Samuel Pope

Saturday afternoon was uneventful. Hal and I spent it upstairs in the office, me paying bills, Hal grading papers.

The doorbell rang as we were getting dinner ready. I had just gotten a package of frozen lasagna out of the freezer and stuck it in the oven. Hal answered the door.

"Oh, for chrissake," I heard him say.

"Who is it?" I called out from the kitchen, where I was cutting up vegetables for a salad.

"Nobody," he said. "There's nobody there. And the porch light's out, besides."

He got another bulb from the hall closet, collected a flashlight and a stepladder, and went back outside to change it. I had my head in the refrigerator looking for the crumbled blue cheese when I heard a loud cry and a crash.

"Hal? Are you okay?" I called. There was no answer. "Hal? Honey?"

Silence.

Oh, no. You don't suppose ... My heart jumped up into my throat.

I ran out onto the front porch to find Hal sprawled prone and the stepladder overturned.

I knew it! I knew it! Robbie shot him. Oh, God, oh, God ...

"Oh, my God," I cried as I ran to him, shards of glass from the broken lightbulb crunching under my feet. He was unconscious, and when I touched his head, I felt something warm and sticky. I picked up the flashlight lying next to him, but of course it didn't work, and I couldn't see much in the light from the streetlight. I knelt next to him, hoping I wasn't kneeling on broken glass, and tried to roll him over on his back, without much success. At least he was breathing. I was about to go back into the house and call an ambulance when he stirred, groaned, and tried to sit up.

"Shit, my head hurts," he complained, and then, "I'm bleeding. What the hell happened?"

"I don't know," I replied, my voice shaky from relief that he was still alive. "I just heard a crash. Don't you remember anything?"

"Something hit me. I came out here and set the stepladder up, and I was trying to figure out how I was gonna hold the flashlight and change the bulb at the same time, and something hit me on the head. That's all I remember."

"Something? Or someone?" Someone like Robbie, for example. I needed to get Hal into the house fast, just in case Robbie was still hanging around with his high-powered rifle waiting for a clear shot.

He shook his head irritably and then clutched it, groaning again. "Shit, that hurt. I don't know. Something, someone, I don't know. God, I feel sick."

For the moment, Hal was shielded by the porch railing; there was no way he could get up and walk into the house in his present condition.

"Lie down," I told him, getting to my feet. "I'll get you a blanket."

I retrieved a comforter from the upstairs linen closet, covered him up, and then called for an ambulance, which seemed to take several years to arrive. I knelt beside him in the shadow of the porch railing, anxiously scanning the darkness for signs of Robbie. I felt silly calling for an ambulance when we lived less than a block from the hospital, but there was no way Hal could even walk to the car, let alone to the hospital, especially with a rifle-toting madman hanging about. It was a relief to turn him over to people who handled this sort of thing all the time.

At the hospital, they took Hal away to x-ray his head, and a young nurse whom I had never met before asked me questions, which I answered in a daze.

When Hal returned from X-ray, Dave Martin came in to stitch up the laceration on the top of his head. "What did you do, Toni, throw a brick at him?" he asked jokingly as he started to clean the wound.

"What are you talking about?"

Dave held up something in forceps. "There's pieces of brick here. Do you have a brick porch or what?"

"No. Let me see that!"

It was definitely a fragment of red brick, and as I looked over Dave's shoulder, I could see several more like it in the wound, which looked to me like the Grand Canyon. I stared at Dave, my eyes wide.

He stared back. "Toni? What is it?"

"You need to call the police. This wasn't an accident."

"Are you serious?" Dave asked. "Are you telling me that Hal was attacked? Right there on your front porch?"

He looked at me for several long seconds, decided I was serious, and directed a nurse to make a phone call. In due course, Pete arrived.

"Toni. I don't believe it. What's happened now?" He sounded stressed. I didn't blame him. I was feeling a tad stressed myself.

"Come on in," Dave said. "I'm just sewing up a laceration here."

"Somebody hit Hal with a brick," I said. "On our porch. He was trying to change a lightbulb."

"Did you see anybody?"

"No, I just heard the crash when he fell."

"So how do you know he was attacked? Couldn't he have just lost his balance or something?"

"I didn't lose my balance, God damn it!" Hal objected from underneath the sterile drape. "Somebody hit me and knocked me out."

Dave Martin concurred. "He wouldn't have this type of injury from a fall. And besides, I've been picking pieces of brick out of this wound. They're in that dish over there."

"There are no bricks on our porch," I added.

"Okay, okay, I get it," said Pete. "Hal, did you see anybody or hear anything unusual before you were attacked? Was somebody lying in wait for you?"

"No," Hal said indistinctly from under the drape. "I don't know. It was dark. The porch light was out. That's why I was out there in the first place, to change the fucking lightbulb."

"Toni?"

"I'm no help," I said. "All I heard was the crash."

Dave whipped the drape off. "All done," he announced.

After Dave had checked on Hal's skull series and CT scan and given the all-clear, Pete took us home in the police car. No need to thank him, he said, since he had to check out the scene of the crime anyway.

Hal went straight to bed, and I ended up holding a flashlight for Pete while he searched for incriminating evidence, which consisted of innumerable glass fragments and the brick. He hefted it in his hand, and said, "Too bad we can't get fingerprints off this. Maybe we'll have better luck with the light fixture."

"The light fixture?" I asked.

"Yes, the light fixture," Pete said. "When was the last time you changed that bulb?"

"Just before Halloween," I said.

"Why would it be burned out so soon?"

Suddenly, I got it. "Oh, my God. You think maybe somebody unscrewed it so the porch would be dark."

"Now you're catching on," Pete said. "Let me get the evidence kit out of the car and check it out. You get inside and stay there."

I stood in the shadow of the doorway and watched, while Pete got up on the stepladder to inspect the light fixture with a flashlight.

"I was right, Toni. The old bulb is still here and it's

loose. That must have been the new bulb that broke. You wanna hold the flashlight for me while I dust this?"

Ten minutes later, Pete had dusted the light fixture, photographed the fingerprints, swept up the shards of the new bulb, removed the old bulb, and had everything "bagged and tagged," as he put it.

"I'm gonna go home now," he said. "Soon as I drop this stuff off. No offense, Toni, but I don't especially want to see you again tonight."

I laughed. "No offense, Pete, but I'm getting kind of sick of you too."

Chapter 34

God's in his heaven
All's right with the world.
　　　　　　　　　—Robert Browning

On Monday Hal insisted on driving me to work, which I thought was silly, since it's only a block. But Hal was adamant.

"It's still dark outside," he pointed out. "Anybody could sneak up on you out here." He drove me right up to the emergency entrance and did not leave until he had seen me safe inside.

I wondered who was going to be watching Hal's back while he walked from the faculty parking lot to his office. To take my mind off it, I called the medical staff secretary and requested Dr. Cabot's credential file. She brought it up almost immediately. As I thought, he had attended Harvard Medical School from 1982 to 1987 and done his entire postgraduate training at Massachusetts General Hospital between 1987 and 1991, after which he had come to Twin Falls. He had never attended Loyola or trained at Cook County. At least, if he had, there was no record of it. I also noted his birth date, August 31, 1960, and that he had also gone to college at Harvard, from 1977 to 1981.

The more I thought about it, the more it seemed that something was wrong with Tyler's file. I kept turning pages until it finally hit me. If Tyler had graduated from college in 1981 and started medical school in 1982, there was a year unaccounted for. Then I noticed something else. If Tyler had started medical school in 1982 and graduated in 1987, that meant he took five years to complete medical school.

I took the file to the nearest copier and made a copy of Tyler's curriculum vitae for Elliott. Maybe the missing years were significant, and maybe they weren't, but it was another Interesting Thing; and I felt—since my continued freedom was at stake—that all Interesting Things needed to be investigated.

I turned from the copier and ran right smack into Tyler, who had been standing behind me, causing me to drop his file. He picked it up and waved it in my face. "What are you doing with *this*?" he demanded, holding it just out of my reach.

I felt my face get hot, and I broke out in a sweat. The copies I had made were still on the floor, and I took the opportunity to regain my equanimity while I picked them up. "I'm Credentials chairman, remember? It's time to renew your privileges, remember? I have to review your file and sign your renewal application so you can practice here another year. Want to give it back now?"

He continued to hold it away from me. "What were you copying out of it?" he asked.

"This is something else," I lied, hoping I looked convincing, since Hal and my mother could always see right through me. "Something entirely unrelated that's none of your business. Want to give that back now, please, unless you don't care to have your privileges renewed this year?"

He shoved the file into my hands without a word and strode away. My knees shook, and I fought hard not to collapse on the spot. I headed for the nearest bathroom, where I composed myself. *I really have to become a better liar or I won't even survive to be put in jail*, I thought as I blotted my face and my pits with toilet paper.

Tyler got back at me, though. He sent me a patient for a bone marrow.

Terence Ross had presented himself to Tyler for a routine physical and turned out to have pancytopenia; that is to say, he was severely anemic with a low white count and a low platelet count.

I like to talk to the physician and review the patient's medical history before doing bone marrows. I like to see a current blood count and see for myself just how high or low everything is. On rare occasions, I can convince the physician that a bone marrow isn't necessary, that it's possible to diagnose certain things with blood tests and not put a patient through a scary and potentially painful procedure. Tyler's patient Emma Grainger, the lady with colon cancer, had been a perfect example of that situation.

Terence Ross, on the other hand, really did require a bone marrow, and I like to know enough about a patient's history to be able to explain to him why he has to have one. Clinicians, in my experience, rarely tell the patient anything, and so the explanations fall to me, the pathologist. I recalled too many times when the news of the patient's cancer diagnosis had come from me instead of from the physician actually caring for the patient.

Terence Ross's chart was relatively thin for an eighty-four-year-old. He seemed to be in excellent health up until he developed pancytopenia. I went back through his lab work to see how long ago and how rapidly his counts had dropped. He hadn't had much lab work. The only CBC within the past year had been done on February 28, the day that Dr. Shore died, a month ago. Everything was relatively normal at that time except his white count, which was elevated.

Curious, I leafed through the chart to see what the occasion had been and found an emergency room visit. Terence Ross had developed pneumonia as a result of the flu and had been put on antibiotics and sent home; but after taking his first dose of the antibiotic, he had developed hives. He had returned to the emergency room, where he was given corticosteroids, Benadryl, and a different antibiotic and sent home again.

Both visits had been dictated and signed by Sally M. Shore, MD, and the patient had been discharged home from his second visit at 12:45 a.m. on March 1.

Ordinarily a story like this would earn a big "So what." Lots of elderly patients who got the flu developed bacterial pneumonia. Lots of people developed allergies to antibiotics too.

What was so special about this particular case was that I had been the last person to see Dr. Shore alive on the evening of February 28. And I had discovered her dead body—on the morning of March 1.

What the hell had Pete and Kincaid been doing that they hadn't questioned anyone who worked in the emergency room on the night Dr. Shore died? It seemed a simple matter to find out who worked that shift on that night and question them. They could find out what patients Dr. Shore had seen that night, and question them. They could subpoena charts and make copies of the pertinent records.

After I finished with the surgicals and Paps and got that bone marrow out of the way, I vowed, I was going to march myself right down to the station and have a word or two with those lazy bums.

No, on second thought … why wait?

I called Pete at the station.

"Did either you or Kincaid interview anyone who worked the swing and graveyard shifts in the emergency room on February 28 and March 1?"

"I didn't," he said. "I think Bernie did. Just a minute, let me see if there's a report in here." I heard him typing rapidly on a keyboard. "Here's a report from just before he went on vacation. Let me see…yeah, he's interviewed quite a few of the emergency room personnel from the swing shift, and none of them saw Dr. Shore."

"How about the graveyard shift?"

"I guess he hasn't gotten to them yet. Damn. He didn't say anything to me, so I didn't follow up. I'm really sorry, Toni, I'll get right on that."

Damn Kincaid anyway. I drew a deep breath and tried to remain calm as I told him what I had discovered. "So, can you come and check this out for yourself?" I asked him. "And interview the Rosses?"

He promised to do it no later than that afternoon. I thanked him politely and concentrated on not slamming the phone down. Then I called Elliott, and asked him the same thing. He said that either he or Stan would contact the Rosses at the earliest opportunity.

Satisfied, I got back to the business of doing a bone marrow.

Terence Ross had acute myeloblastic leukemia. It was in the aleukemic stage, which meant that there were no leukemic cells in the blood yet, but there would be soon. The bone marrow was virtually replaced by myeloblasts, the earliest precursor of the white blood cell.

I called Tyler and gave him the bad news. He asked me to package up the slides for the patient to pick up that afternoon, as he planned to send him to Boise that very day.

I wondered why. At eighty-four, Terence Ross was a very poor candidate for chemotherapy. Elderly patients don't tolerate it well. And he was much too old to be considered for a bone marrow transplant. His prognosis was grim, and I was glad I wouldn't have to be the one to break the news to him and his wife. That would be Tyler's job, and Tyler would do it very well. He was very good at that sort of thing.

"*The guilty fleeth where no man pursueth*," quoted Hal when I told him about Tyler as we were getting ready for bed.

"He wasn't exactly fleeing," I pointed out. "He was attacking."

"Want another one? *The best defense is a good offense.*"

"I thought that all along," I said. "Why else would he

act like he did at the country club that night? Why else would he be trying to implicate me?"

"Why didn't you come right out and ask him what he was doing in 1981 and why it took him five years to finish medical school? Those are perfectly reasonable questions. It's not like you to let him intimidate you like that."

Hal was right. But this was different. "Intimidated, my ass," I said. "He scared the shit out of me."

Chapter 35

And much of Madness, and more of Sin,
And Horror the soul of the plot.
— Edgar Allan Poe

The phone rang as I was dictating the surgicals the next morning.

"Hi there, young lady," said a deep voice, which I recognized as that of Roland Perkins. I wondered why he would be calling me and then remembered with a sinking feeling that he was county coroner.

"Hi, Rollie. What's up?" I inquired without much enthusiasm.

"I've got a couple of folks here that I'm going to need autopsies on," he said. "Your friend Pete Vincent found them dead in their home yesterday."

"Who are they?"

His reply hit me with the force of a sledgehammer in the stomach.

They were Terence and Kathleen Ross.

They were my alibi.

Black spots swam before my eyes. Rollie's voice sounded far away and faint. "Toni? Are you there?"

I pulled myself together. "I'm here. I need to call you back, Rollie. I need to talk to Pete."

"He's right here," Rollie said. "I'll put him on."

Pete sounded apologetic. "I got to them as soon as I could, but it was pretty late," he explained. "Nobody answered the door, so I went to the neighbors on either side and asked if they knew anything, and they didn't. But one of them had a phone number for their son, who lives in Ketchum, so I called him. He came down and opened up the house, and we found them dead in bed, side by side, like they died in their sleep. When are you gonna do the autopsies, do you know? I want to be here when you do them."

I did both autopsies that day at the mortuary with both Rollie and Pete assisting me. It was kind of like old times when Pete was a student at Canyon Community College. These autopsies were different, though, because we had to handle them as potential homicides. I took blood and urine samples for drugs and did a rape kit on both bodies. From time to time during the autopsies, Pete would strip his gloves off and take photographs.

I found nothing to explain either death. For their ages, Terence and Kathleen Ross had amazingly little pathology. Terence Ross had mild arteriosclerosis without coronary occlusion, diverticulosis of the sigmoid colon, an enlarged prostate, and an enlarged liver and spleen caused by his acute leukemia. Kathleen Ross's heart showed some evidence of hypertension. Both had had their gallbladders and appendixes removed, and Kathleen Ross had had a hysterectomy. Neither had evidence of any of the usual causes of sudden death, such as pulmonary embolus, acute myocardial infarction, or cerebral hemorrhage. However, both had a puncture mark on the left upper arm.

I pointed them out to Pete, and there was no need for explanation. "Where have I seen this before," he commented as he documented them with his trusty camera. I then excised them and put them in with the other tissue samples.

I took the tissue samples back to the hospital and put them into formalin. They would have to fix for several days before I could prepare sections. The brains would have to fix for two weeks. Pete took the blood and urine samples and the rape kits back to the station with him.

I filled out the provisional report form. Under "Manner of Death" I wrote "Homicide."

I called Elliott as soon as I got back to my office. He was in court, and had been all day. I didn't get to talk to him until after supper, when he and Jodi came over at our invitation. He was understandably upset.

"I was in court all day, and I didn't get a chance to talk to the Rosses, and neither did Stan," he said defensively. "I did get a thirty-minute recess this afternoon and gave them a call, but they had a doctor's appointment and couldn't do it. I wonder what doctor they were going to. Maybe I could interview him."

"Tyler," I said.

"Oh, shit. That guy is everywhere," Elliott said.

"Terence Ross had acute leukemia," I said. "I imagine Tyler was going to tell him so. I called him as soon as I saw the smears, and he said he was going to have them go straight to Boise."

"Could he have died of it?" Jodi asked.

"He would have eventually, but not so soon," I said. "Without treatment, he could have lasted a couple of months, maybe. No, Pete and I both think it was homicide. They both had injection sites on their arms, just like Dr. Shore."

"If they had a doctor's appointment, couldn't they have had shots?" asked Elliott.

"Terence might have, but not Kathleen. She didn't have an appointment. At least I don't think she did. I need to see their charts. Do you have them, Elliott?"

"I haven't subpoenaed them yet. I need to do that," Elliott said, making notes on a paper towel.

"You haven't done that yet?" I asked, my voice rising in apprehension.

"Well, no, not yet. What are you getting so freakin' uptight about?"

"For God's sake, Elliott! These people were my alibi. And he was real chatty. He talked about everything and anything. That's how we got on the subject of Dr. Shore in the first place. She saw him twice in the emergency room on February 28. Don't you think he told Tyler all about it? Don't you think Tyler'll make sure that chart never gets found?"

"Toni, you're overreacting," Hal said.

"I don't think so," I said. "Tyler is trying to get me put in jail for this murder. Don't you think when Mr. Ross told him all about this emergency room visit, he might have mentioned how interested that nice lady doctor who did the bone marrow was and how many questions she asked? Don't you think Tyler might realize that Mr. Ross could give me an alibi? And perhaps do something about it?"

"Toni, you've outdone yourself," Hal said. "You've reached a new level of paranoia. You're suggesting that Tyler killed two patients because one of them could give you an alibi. Are you serious?"

"If he killed Dr. Shore, it's not inconceivable that he would kill again to cover his tracks," I said.

"Calm down, Toni," said Hal. "Wasn't there a tech with you when you did the bone marrow?"

"Oh, yes, yes, thank God," I said. "She heard everything." Suddenly I was panicked again. "Elliott. You've got to talk to her *now*."

"Why can't it wait till tomorrow?"

"If all this is true and Tyler really is the murderer, she'll be in absolutely horrible danger. He could kill her next!" My voice shook with the effort not to burst into tears.

Elliott sighed. "Shapiro, does she get like this often?"

Hal smiled. "Only every other day."

"Damn you, Hal. That's not fair," I said and, to my horror, exploded into loud sobs. Jodi put her arms around me.

"Mr. Sensitivity you're not, darling," she remarked. "What did you have to say that for?"

Hal was genuinely bewildered. "What did I do?"

"How would you like it if it was *you* who might be arrested any minute?" demanded Jodi indignantly. "And *you*, you chauvinistic jerk, you're supposed to be her *lawyer* and what do you do? Make fun of her. It wouldn't kill you to go talk to Toni's tech. I don't think she's overreacting at all. Here she finds somebody who can give her an alibi, they go see Tyler, and the next day they're dead. That might not be just a coincidence, you know!"

Elliott held up his hands and made a time-out sign. "Okay, okay! Take it easy! It's two against one here. I'll get hold of her right now. Do you know her address and phone number and her last name?"

I told him. "And you don't need her address, she's working tonight."

"Are you suggesting I just walk into the lab and …"

I disengaged myself from Jodi, wiped my eyes on the backs of my hands, and blew my nose on the Kleenex Hal handed me. "I'll go with you."

"Toni, slow down!" Elliott panted behind me as I sprinted across the parking lot to the emergency entrance.

"Walk faster," I called over my shoulder, and then turned back to see Robbie coming out the emergency entrance. *Shit. Of all the people I don't want to see right now …* I slowed to a stop and waited for Elliott, hoping that Robbie hadn't seen me or that he wouldn't recognize me behind my dark glasses—but no such luck.

"Toni! Hi! What are you doing here so late at night?" Then he noticed Elliott. "And what are you doing here?" he inquired in a much less friendly tone.

"I could ask you the same freakin' thing," Elliott returned. "You're not supposed to come within five hundred yards of Toni, her home, or her work."

Robbie smirked. "Well, for your information, Clarence Darrow, nobody has served me with that restraining order yet. So don't tell me where I can and cannot be. Besides, this is a hospital. If I need medical care, where am I supposed to go?"

"What medical care?" Elliott demanded. "You don't look sick to me."

"It just so happens that I stepped on a tack in my bare feet, and had to get a tetanus shot. Want to see?"

"Elliott," I interrupted, too panicked over the possible danger to Brenda to obsess over why that restraining order hadn't been served. "Let's go. We haven't got time for this."

"Okay," he said. "Stay away from her. I'm warning you," he said to Robbie, then followed me into the hospital.

"She's upstairs drawing Millie McIver," the night phlebotomist said, staring curiously at my dark glasses. "She's got the worst veins in the country. Dr. Cabot ordered all this blood work, and I stuck her twice and couldn't get anything, so she—"

"Dr. Cabot is here too?" I asked a little too sharply.

"Well, yes, he's on call tonight," she said. "Are you okay, Doctor?"

"Now what?" Elliott asked.

"Come with me," I replied and headed for the stairs.

"Where are we going?"

"Upstairs. There's no time to lose!"

Millicent McIver was in room 204, a private room. She was a long-time patient who had to have blood work on a regular basis, and everyone in the lab loved her and hated her at the same time. She was a sweet lady who brought us homemade fudge and cookies on every conceivable occasion, and she did indeed have the worst veins in the country. She endured multiple stickings every time she came in. And, of course, she was Tyler's patient.

Brenda was nowhere to be seen. Millie hadn't seen her. The charge nurse hadn't seen her, but she asked around. One of the other nurses volunteered the information that she had seen her going into the doctors' dictation room with Dr. Cabot, which had struck her as odd. It struck me as odd too, and my heart leaped up into my throat. Were we too late?

"Hurry," I begged Elliott, and we ran down the hall to the doctors' dictation room. It was locked.

"Stay here," I ordered. "I'll get the key."

I sprinted back to the nurses' station and asked the charge nurse for the key. It took her about a year and a half to find it, or so it seemed. I tapped my toes and drummed my fingers impatiently on the counter and paced in tiny circles while I waited for her to ask every other person on duty if they knew where it was. Nobody did. I was getting more panicky by the second, knowing with absolute certainty that Brenda was in there on the floor, slowly suffocating from the effects of the succinylcholine injection that Tyler had just given her, still conscious but unable to move or cry out for help. I hoped desperately that Tyler didn't have the key. Doctors were supposed to have their own keys—except for the radiologist and me, because we had our own Dictaphones and never used the dictation room.

Finally, several geological ages later, she found it, pretty much in the same place where she'd started looking for it, and handed it to me. I snatched it from her with barely a nod and raced back down the hall. Wouldn't you know, it stuck in the lock, and I was unable to turn the knob. In my frustration, I almost started crying again. Luckily, Elliott was better at keys than I; he managed to get the door open. There was nobody on the floor. I nearly fainted from relief and then felt exceedingly stupid … until Elliott, with consummate diplomacy for him, said, "Maybe she's in one of the other rooms. Let's keep looking."

Perhaps Jodi's scolding had had some effect on him.

Nonetheless, we didn't find Brenda.

My sense of dread intensified.

Chapter 36

Some circumstantial evidence is very strong,
such as when you find a trout in the milk.
—Henry David Thoreau

Frustrated, we went back downstairs to the lab. Brenda was there. I had to restrain myself from throwing my arms around her and making an absolute fool of myself with relief.

She had drawn Millie's blood while we were trying to get into the dictation room, and she was putting blood tubes into the centrifuge when we got back to the lab. "What can I do for you, Doctor?"

I introduced Elliott. "You can tell him all about what Mr. and Mrs. Ross were telling us about their emergency room visit on the night Dr. Shore died," I said.

"Well, sure, but why not just ask them?" she wanted to know.

"Because they're dead," I said. "I did autopsies on them today."

"Oh, my God! You're kidding!"

I nodded silently and Elliott added, "She's not kidding."

"Okay, then," Brenda said. "Anything I can do to help."

While Elliott questioned her, I wandered back to my office. Might as well do a little paperwork while waiting, I figured. But as soon as I entered the room, I felt that something was wrong. The hairs prickled on the back of my neck. Of course, the thought that somebody might be hiding in there waiting to ambush me was ludicrous in the extreme. A mouse would have a hard time hiding in my office. There wasn't a space big enough anywhere in that room that wasn't filled. But the feeling persisted.

Had Robbie been in here? Had he planted a bomb or a trap of some sort?

I turned on the light. The feeling didn't go away. I couldn't understand it. I hadn't felt it yesterday. I continued to stand in the doorway, looking around. I noticed, with annoyance, how dusty my bookcases were. Housekeeping vacuums the floor and not much else. They didn't seem to want to touch my bookshelves, even though I had asked them multiple times to dust them. There was no good reason for them not to; I didn't keep specimens in glass jars on them, or anything else disgusting. I had a silk flower arrangement on one low bookcase and a framed portrait of Hal and me, taken on our tenth anniversary, on another. The flower arrangement was crooked, I noticed.

I straightened it, and noticed smudges in the dust. The bookcase seemed to be out from the wall a little further than the others. Why would that be, I wondered. Did Housekeeping pull them out to vacuum behind them? I tried to peer down into the space between the bookcase and the wall, and saw the usual collection of dust kitties. No, I decided, Housekeeping hadn't done it. I shrugged and started to push it back into place, but it didn't slide very well on the carpet, and I decided to get Elliott to help me when he was done with Brenda. I busied myself initialing laboratory quality control and proficiency testing reports until Elliott came in.

"You needn't have worried, Toni," he said, sitting in my visitor's chair. "She did go into the dictation room with Tyler, but only because she didn't have orders on the patient she was supposed to draw, and Tyler had the patient's chart in there. She hasn't mentioned to anyone that she assisted with that bone marrow, and hasn't told anybody about the conversation you had with the patient. And she won't now. She's not in any danger as long as she keeps her mouth shut. Looks like you've got your alibi; and don't forget, there's still the chart with the ER note."

I heaved a sigh of relief. "I feel a lot better now," I said. "I guess we can go. Can you help me shove that bookcase back against the wall before we go?"

He agreed, but it didn't slide for him either. "It seems to be hanging up on that corner," he said. "It won't go in straight. Maybe if we pull it out all the way and straighten it, it might go in easier."

We did so, and I decided to clean out the dust behind it before pushing it back. I fetched a surgical towel from Histology and was in the process of dusting the baseboard when a gleam caught my eye. I scooped up a handful of dust kitties in the towel, and nestled in the midst of them was a glass ampule. The top had been broken off.

"What's that?" Elliott asked.

"It seems to be an ampule," I said. "What in the world is it doing there?" I recalled that I used to keep ampules of epinephrine in my desk drawer when I was taking allergy shots, but that had been a long time ago, and I had never used one. I thought I had thrown them all away. I turned the ampule sideways, still holding it in the towel, and attempted to read the name on the side. My heart stopped.

Anectine
(succinylcholine)
20 mg/ml.

Wordlessly, I showed it to Elliott, who began to pick it out of the dust with his fingers. "Don't touch it!" I said sharply. "Just look at it."

He looked. Our eyes met. No words were needed.

Not Robbie, I thought.

Elliott turned away, grabbed the phone, and dialed a number.

"Ray, this is Elliott," he said when the other party answered. "I think you need to get over here to Dr. Day's office. Right now. No, not on the phone. Just get over here. I'll tell you when you get here." He hung up.

"Toni," he said soberly. "I'll never doubt you again."

Within an hour my office was crawling with police detectives. By that I mean Pete and the Commander, but considering the size of my office, that *was* crawling with cops. They dusted the bookcases for fingerprints. They took all the books out of my bookcases. They pulled the bookcases out from the wall. They crawled under my desk. They went through my desk drawers and my file cabinet. They unscrewed the light fixture in the ceiling. They removed the air-conditioning vent and looked around in the duct. There was not an inch of space left undisturbed. There were footprints on my desk. The air was thick with dust, and I was in the throes of a major allergy attack.

The Commander stood in the middle of the room, hands on his hips, toothpick in mouth, and watched Pete as he finished reinstalling the light fixture. To their credit, they did put everything back. Technically. Meaning that to the casual observer, my office looked okay, but on Monday morning when I came to work and tried to function, I would not know where anything was. My heart failed me at the thought of trying to rearrange everything now.

Then they fingerprinted Elliott and me for exclusion purposes.

The phone rang. It was Hal. "Is everything okay?"

I looked at my watch and saw with a start that it was nearly ten o'clock. I gave Hal the *Reader's Digest* condensed version of what was going on.

He was silent for a long second and then said softly, "Holy shit." Then he said, "Stay there. I'm coming over."

"Bring me an allergy pill," I said.

"Was that Hal?" asked Pete.

"Yeah. He's coming over."

"Well," said the Commander, shifting his toothpick to the other side of his mouth, "I guess we've done all the damage we can do here." They had found nothing more.

"Toni, do you have any idea when this ampule was put behind your bookcase?" asked Pete, pulling out his notebook. The ampule, now safe in a plastic evidence bag, rested on my desk.

"I have no idea. It wasn't here when you guys searched

my office before?" I really didn't need to ask. I knew the ampule hadn't been there before. I hadn't had that creepy feeling until tonight.

"I could have sworn we looked behind all the bookcases before," Pete said. "We didn't see it. We certainly wouldn't have left it there if we had."

"Well, I didn't notice the bookcase was pulled out until tonight, but that doesn't mean it wasn't before. Sometimes I just don't notice things."

"That's for sure," said Hal, looming up in the doorway to my office. "Jesus Christ, Toni, your eyes are nearly swollen shut. Here. Go take your pill."

I took it and headed for the nearest drinking fountain. When I returned to my office, I found a conference going on. I sat in one of the chairs out in the hallway/waiting room and waited for my pill to take effect. Just being out of the dust in my office was a big help. The things that were being said in there, however, were not.

"There's nothing to rule out the possibility that she put it there herself."

"We just found it," Elliott protested. "We were trying to straighten the bookcase, and we just found it."

"She could have staged the whole thing."

"Do you guys *hear* yourselves? Think about it. Toni kills Dr. Shore and then takes the empty ampule of succinylcholine and puts it behind her bookcase to hide it. She does this even though it would be just as easy to take it out in the parking lot and stomp on it. Or just throw it in the dumpster. Or in the freakin' trash can. Why the fuck would she keep it and hide it in her own office? Do you think she's that freakin' stupid?" Elliott had clearly had enough of this conversation.

"Well, no, but …"

"What I'm saying is, no matter who did it, there is only one reason to put that ampule there, and that is to frame Toni Day. She is the one person who has no reason to put that ampule there. You arrest her and she'll sue you for false arrest, and the papers are going to have a field day. Is that what you want, to be the laughingstock of the Magic Valley?"

"Now wait a minute, Counselor. There's no need to get belligerent with us. You know Pete and I don't want to arrest Dr. Day, but Kincaid's got a burr up his ass on this case. For some reason, he's convinced the doc is guilty. However, if he tries to get a warrant, I can go to the judge and tell him that the rest of us don't feel that way, and that will probably end it right there. Of course, Kincaid'll have to know I did that, and he'll be even more of a pain in the ass than he usually is, but …"

"It's worse than that," Pete added. "Until now, we had no proof that a murder was actually committed. Now, we not only have the proof, but we have confirmation of exactly how it was done, now that we have that ampule, and it was just as Toni said."

"Wait a minute, son," cautioned the Commander. "Don't get carried away. All we have is an ampule that once contained … whaddyacallit, succinylcholine, behind a bookcase in Dr. Day's office. We have nothing linking it to any crime until we find fingerprints on it and find the drug in the deceased's body, and since there's no way to test for it, that's not gonna happen."

"Exactamundo," said Elliott. "It's all freakin' circumstantial. There's never going to be any absolute proof. If any arrest is made, a jury is going to have to decide based on circumstantial evidence if a crime was actually committed, and if so, whether the suspect is guilty or innocent."

"That's gonna take a grand jury," the Commander said.

"Grand jury?" Hal asked. "How is that different from a regular jury?"

Elliott fielded that one. "A grand jury isn't used at a regular trial. A grand jury goes over all the evidence and takes testimony. They can have the district attorney ask questions or ask questions themselves and then decide if a crime was committed—and if there is reasonable justification for bringing someone to trial for that crime. The only problem with that is there's no defense attorney present."

"So, why arrest Toni? I thought she had an alibi. Isn't that why you're here?"

Thank you, Hal. My hero.

"You're right," Elliot said. "In all the excitement, I'd forgotten that. But she'll be a key witness. Our friend Tyler will be a witness too. There'll be a lot of witnesses." He paused. "Maybe that's not such a bad idea. Maybe we ought to just go ahead and call a grand jury. Maybe we can finally get to the bottom of this case. I'll talk to Fritz tomorrow."

"What's this about an alibi?" asked the Commander. Elliott told him.

"Why the hell didn't you say that before!" the Commander growled and dispatched Pete to interview Brenda, who was just finishing up and about to go home.

"Between you and me and the bedpost," the

Commander confided to Hal and me, "we don't have a snowball's chance in hell of solving this case. It's like trying to grab a handful of fog. The only thing that would help us break it is if the killer kills again."

"At least Toni's off the hook now. Right?"

"Right. Unless he goes after her next."

Chapter 37

It was déjà vu all over again.

—Yogi Berra

The next morning, I called Medical Records and asked for Terence and Kathleen Ross's charts. Dr. Shore didn't dictate her ER notes, so the paper chart was the only record.

Terence Ross's chart was checked out to Dr. Cabot, they told me. Would I like them to go get it from him? Yes, I would, very much. I dreaded the thought of asking for it myself. I didn't want to be anywhere near Tyler if I could help it.

I prayed that Terence and Kathleen had not mentioned anything to Tyler about Dr. Shore. Maybe they had done all their chatting with his nurse. She would have no reason to pass it on to Tyler. Would she?

In due course, the charts arrived. I opened Terence's to the front section where emergency room visits were documented. There it was: February 28. Patient checked in at 2015. Checked out at 2155. Checked in again at 2345, checked out at 0015 on March 1. A note written and signed by S. M. Shore, MD, timed 0045. There was my alibi, in black and white.

I called Elliott. He was in court all day again. Could he call me back? No, never mind. If he was in court all day, I might as well wait and talk to him tonight. I felt like I was sitting on a keg of dynamite. I desperately wanted that chart out of my hands and into Elliott's. If Tyler or anyone else called Medical Records and asked for that chart, I would have to have a plausible reason for not letting them have it. Of course, since the patient was dead, who else besides Tyler would want it?

I dared not leave my office with that chart in it. I knew it would disappear and never be found once Tyler found out how important it was. It might as well have "Toni's alibi" written on it in neon letters a foot high. I had to get it into safe hands. I called Pete. Luckily, he was in.

"Hi, Toni," he greeted me. "Are you as pooped as I am?"

I wasted no time on amenities. "Can you come over here? I have a piece of evidence I think you should see."

"Can it wait until this afternoon?" he wanted to know.

I felt myself getting panicky again. "No, I don't think so. Are you going to be there for a while? I'll bring it to you. Can you meet me at the door? In fifteen minutes? Please?"

I was taking a terrible chance, taking a patient record out of the hospital. I could lose my privileges if I got caught.

I could lose my privileges if I got put in jail for murder, too.

Pete must have felt my urgency, for he met me at

the door. "So, what's this new piece of evidence that's so important?" he asked teasingly. I handed him the chart. "What's this?" he asked, and then he saw the name on it. *Ross, Terence.*

He got serious. "Let's go into Ray's office," he suggested.

The Commander stood up to shake my hand. "Never felt worse or had less," he replied to my routine inquiry. "And how are you feeling today, after what we put you through? And how's Hal?"

"We're both fine," I said, relieved to have the chart out of my hands. "I brought you some new evidence that clears me. This is the chart of a patient that Dr. Shore saw in the emergency room the night she died, at 12:45 a.m. The ER note is in there with her signature."

"Is this the couple who Pete found dead the other day?"

"Yes," Pete said. "Toni did autopsies on them yesterday. They both had needle marks on them just like the one Dr. Shore had. We're ruling them homicides."

"Could you please make a copy of that note for your file?" I begged. "Elliott hasn't gotten around to subpoenaing this chart yet, and he's in court all day. I'm afraid to let it out of my sight until you do."

Pete volunteered to do so, and he vanished, only to be replaced by Lieutenant Kincaid, who glanced coldly at me and said to the Commander, "What's *she* doing here?"

"Bringing us evidence," the Commander replied. "And what's got *your* undies in a bundle? You just came back from a vacation. You should be all bright-eyed and bushy-tailed."

Kincaid did not reply but turned and left the room as

Pete came back in. He handed the chart back to me and the copy to the Commander and sat down.

"Bernie's getting a divorce," he informed me. "His wife's in California. He had to go down there because his wife took him to court. I guess it was nasty. We're all kind of staying out of his way."

"I see," I said. "And now I really have to go. I've got to get that chart back before anybody knows it's gone."

When I got back, I went through both charts, extracting pertinent medical history for the autopsy reports. There was nothing in Kathleen's chart that had any bearing on my alibi, I reflected, just Terence's. And now the police had that evidence.

Nobody asked for either chart. When I went home that night, I left Kathleen's chart on my desk but took Terence's home with me, intending to give it to Elliott. As I turned to start up the walk to the house, I thought I saw a shadow move behind one of the maples. I stopped and waited, but saw nothing more. I shrugged it off as a figment of my overactive imagination or possibly a squirrel, and then the thought occurred to me that I may as well take the chart right to Elliott's house and leave it. As I made this decision, something hit me very hard on the back of the head. Pain exploded behind my eyes, and everything went snowy and gray, like an old black and white television with bad reception, and then black.

I awoke to a painfully bright light shining in my face and gradually became aware that someone was groaning loudly. I wished whoever it was would shut up. As my vision gradually cleared, I saw Hal leaning over me with concern. Then I realized the person doing the groaning was me and that I had a terrible headache. I tried to speak, but all that came out was disjointed garbled sounds. It hurt to move my tongue. I tasted blood.

Hal disappeared. In his place was Dave Martin. "Toni? Are you awake?"

"I think so," I tried to say. It sounded like I was talking through a mouthful of cotton. I reached up to touch my head and became aware that I had an intravenous line in my arm. There was a clock on the wall. It said 11:45. *That can't be right*, I thought and said, "Is it really quarter of twelve?" But of course nobody could understand that either.

"Don't try to talk yet, Toni," Dave said. "You've had a blow to the head that knocked you out. You've been unconscious for six hours. You've got a laceration on the back of your head, which has been sutured, and you've had an X-ray of your neck and CT of your head. Nothing is broken, but you've got a hell of a concussion, and you've bitten your tongue. That's why it's swollen. The police have been here and made a report. They'll be back tomorrow to talk to you."

"Where's Hal?" I tried to say and raised my head to look for him. Wrong thing to do. A giant wave, a veritable tsunami of nausea swept over me, and I vomited. Dave, in a fluid motion that suggested that this was something he'd done many times, shoved an emesis basin under my chin just in time. I resolved to never move my head again as long as I lived.

I spent the night in the hospital. It was the longest night of my life. Nurses came in every fifteen minutes to wake me up and shine a light in my eyes. My head hurt abominably, and I vomited several more times, which made it hurt even more. I wished they would just give me a pain pill and let me sleep, but I knew they couldn't. I had monitored many a concussed patient in my medical school days, and I knew exactly what to expect.

I was also really bummed that I hadn't gotten off as easily as Hal had. He'd been able to go home and get a full night's sleep, and he hadn't puked up once.

Several eons later, morning came, and with it, discharge. Hal came to take me home. I spent the day in bed, but at least it was my bed. I was vaguely aware of people coming and going downstairs but couldn't seem to stay awake long enough to care who they were or what they wanted. Hal came in from time to time and woke me up, as directed by the concussion care instructions the hospital had given him, but otherwise he left me alone. I hoped he was getting some sleep, too, somewhere else.

From time to time, I became aware of animals on the bed with me. They too kept coming and going, barking and racing down the stairs every time anybody came to the house. By evening, I roused myself enough to eat a little chicken soup and kept it down. Hooray.

Hal sat on the bed, stroking my hair, which was still encrusted with blood. "Want to hear what's been going on around here today?" he inquired. "Are you up to it?"

"I think so," I replied, and it came out relatively clearly. My tongue wasn't so swollen anymore, but it sure did hurt. I decided to let Hal do all the talking for now. I could ask questions later—like next month, maybe.

"Well, for starters, today is Tuesday. I cancelled my classes so I could stay home with you. When I got home last night I found you lying on the grass under the maple out front in a pool of blood. I thought you'd been hit by a car. I thought you were dead. Scared the shit out of me.

I had no idea head wounds could bleed so much." Hal's voice shook slightly, and he cleared his throat. "Did *I* bleed that much?"

I shook my head no and wished I hadn't.

"Anyway, I couldn't wake you up, but at least you were breathing, so I picked you up and carried you into the house and called the hospital. They called an ambulance."

Seems silly to call an ambulance when we live less than a block away, I thought for the second time, but I guess they couldn't just wheel a gurney over here and back. Actually, Hal had taken an awful chance moving me in the first place. Suppose I'd had a spinal injury? But I said nothing, and Hal continued.

"It caused quite a stir in the neighborhood, the ambulance pulling up and guys carrying you out on a stretcher. Everybody was out on their porches, watching. Elliott came home about that time, and he came with me to the emergency room. He was the one who called the police. He said you'd left him an urgent message." He paused expectantly, but I had no idea what he was talking about. I couldn't remember yesterday at all. "Anyway, they checked you over, and found that your only injury was the hit on the head, and they wanted to know who had attacked you. They wanted to call the police, but Elliott said he'd already done it. Pete showed up about then and filled out some papers, and then I guess he was going to interview the neighbors. Toni, honey, do you have any idea who's doing this?"

I shook my head again and winced. The nausea came back, faintly, briefly. I knew he was wondering if the same person who'd attacked him had attacked me, but speculation was too much work and made my head hurt.

"Whoever it was didn't take your purse," Hal went on. "So it wasn't your routine mugging. Whoever it was did it for some other reason. Did you have anything else with you when you came home?"

"I don't know," I said. I couldn't remember.

Downstairs, the screen door squeaked, and someone came into the house. Killer and Geraldine leapt off the bed, jarring me, and ran down the stairs, barking. A shout combined with a musical "yoo-hoo" announced the presence of Elliott and Jodi. "We're up here," Hal shouted back, and they came up the stairs accompanied by the dogs. "Is she decent?" Elliott inquired.

"Come on in," Hal said.

"I thought, if you were up to it, I could help you shower and wash your hair," Jodi offered.

I slowly sat up in bed and swung my legs over the side. The dizziness returned but not the nausea. I allowed as how, if I didn't make any sudden moves, I could manage it. She helped me into the bathroom.

Downstairs, the doorbell rang, and the dogs took off down the stairs again. *How the hell did I manage to sleep through that racket,* I wondered. Hal grumbled, "What is this, Grand Central Station?" And he and Elliott went downstairs.

With Jodi's help, I managed to wash the blood out of my hair, shower, and even shave my pits. Once I was clean, I felt much better. Wrapping myself in a thick, terrycloth robe with the hood pulled up over my wet hair, I went downstairs, Jodi holding onto my arm in case I felt faint and stumbled on the stairs. I made it down without incident and found Hal and Elliott in conference with Pete Vincent.

"How are you doing, Toni?" Pete greeted me. "You look a hell of a lot better than you did last night at this time."

"Do you have any idea who did this to you?" Elliott asked.

"She doesn't know," Hal said, saving me the trouble of shaking my head no.

Elliott continued. "Do you remember what you called me about yesterday?"

"I don't remember anything about yesterday," I said. "The last thing I remember is *Hal* getting hit on the head."

"That's called *retrograde amnesia*," Hal said confidently as if he'd been using medical terms all his life. "Not uncommon with head injuries."

Pete handed me a crumpled slip of pink paper. "We found this under the bushes out front," he said. "Recognize it?"

I recognized it as a lab report from the hospital and saw the name on it. *Ross, Terence.* Suddenly, the lights came on in my head. "His chart," I said, excitedly. "I remember. I brought his chart home. I was going to give it to you, Elliott. My alibi is in it. Where is it?"

"We didn't find a chart," Pete said. "This looks like it fell out or blew out and got blown under your bushes. If there was a chart, it's gone."

"Somebody attacked her for a *chart*?" Hal said with disbelief. "Who the hell would do that?"

"Whoever's trying to frame her for the murder," Elliott

said. "Probably the same person who put the ampule of succinylcholine in her office."

"This makes no sense," I objected. "If I got attacked for a chart, what did Hal get attacked for?"

"Toni, please. One freakin' catastrophe at a time."

"Anyway," Pete went on. "I interviewed your neighbors. Would you believe that with all those elderly people that live in your neighborhood who were all out on their porches when the ambulance came, nobody saw who attacked either one of you? I also went back to the hospital and asked your tech on call if anyone had come looking for you after you left. She said the only person was Dr. Cabot. She heard something in your office and went to investigate, and he was looking through your desk drawers. She asked him if she could help him, and he said he was looking for a chart. She pointed out the one on the desk, but he said that wasn't the chart he was looking for. He said he needed the chart because he was seeing the patient in a few minutes. What's the matter, Toni? You look like you've seen a ghost."

Tyler. The blood drained from my face, and I felt faint. I clutched Geraldine, who had somehow gotten into my lap without my noticing, and she yelped. It brought me to my senses.

"He must have attacked me for that chart, because it had my alibi in it, and now it's gone. My alibi is gone. He succeeded. Now I'm right back to square one."

"No, you're not, Toni," Pete said. "Don't you remember? No, I guess you don't. You brought that chart to me at the police station, and I made a copy of that emergency room record. Your alibi is safe. Not only that, but I interviewed the tech that helped you with the bone marrow."

"So did I," Elliott said. "It's all on record."

"So that asshole Kincaid is not going to be able to accuse her of faking her own head injury to avoid suspicion?" Hal inquired sarcastically.

"Jesus Christ, Shapiro, you're as bad as your wife," Elliott said disgustedly.

"She's taught me well. Not to change the subject or anything," Hal put in, "but what are you guys going to do about this? Toni's life is in danger here. Can't you protect her?"

"I wish we could," replied Pete. "But we don't have the manpower to assign an officer to her. All we can do is make periodic checks, and that wouldn't stop anybody if they were really determined."

"Hold it, you guys," I said. "My life's not in danger. If Tyler wants me to go to jail for killing Dr. Shore, he's not going to kill me. I'm no good to him dead. It's my *alibi* he wants, not my life."

"You can't be sure of that," Hal argued. "He could have killed you with that blow to the head. If you didn't have such a hard one …"

"If he'd wanted to kill me, he would have," I argued back. "In the time it took for him to hit me over the head, he could have just as easily shot me full of succinylcholine. He could have done the same thing to you too. But he didn't."

"It makes no freakin' sense for Tyler to attack Hal," Elliott said. "What would that accomplish, other than to upset Toni? How would Tyler benefit by getting rid of Hal?"

"Who knows what Tyler thinks? Maybe that's just

another way to get back at me for giving Dr. Shore such a hard time."

"What I'm saying is, who else do we know who would like to get Hal out of the picture?"

"Nobody I can think of," I said, and as I did I had just a fleeting thought that Hal's life was in danger too … but from whom? I simply couldn't remember.

"Well," Hal replied, "you will when the amnesia wears off. We've been all through this. It's Robbie, of course. So much for restraining orders."

"God damn it, Shapiro, I hate it when you're right."

"Looks to me like you'd better be trying to protect Hal, not me," I remarked.

"So, Pete, whose fingerprints did you find on the porch light?" Hal inquired.

Pete had been so quiet that I had forgotten he was still there. "No fingerprints," he replied. "Just smudges."

"So he wore gloves," I said. "It's still pretty cold at night."

"So what we have here," Hal said, "is somebody trying to kill both of us, and we're speculating that Robbie's trying to kill me and Tyler's trying to kill Toni. At least I can't imagine that Tyler'd want to kill me or that Robbie'd want to kill Toni."

"I don't think Tyler wanted to kill me," I objected. "He just wanted that chart."

"You know, as much as I hate to admit it," Elliott said, "I think she's got a point. He's got the chart now, at least I think he does, and as far as he knows right now, Toni has no alibi. I don't think he's going to do anything to her as long as he thinks she doesn't have an alibi."

"So all we have to do," I said, "is keep him thinking

that I'm going to be convicted of murdering Dr. Shore, and he'll leave me alone."

"The only problem with that," Elliott said, "is that *everybody's* going to have to think that. And the only way to do that is to have you taken into protective custody."

Horrified, I said, "You mean I have to go to jail?"

"No, no, you won't have to do that," Pete reassured me. "We can work something else out. I'll talk to Ray tomorrow."

"Well, you're not going to work tomorrow, I know that much," Hal said firmly.

"Actually, I think it would be a good idea for you to take a leave of absence from work," Elliott said. "That'll give us time and keep you out of sight for a while."

I tried to argue but to no avail. In the end, tired and with my head pounding mercilessly, I agreed to the course of action Elliott recommended.

Not five minutes after Jodi and Elliott left, the phone rang. Hal answered it. Nobody was there.

Chapter 38

A secret's safe
'Twixt you, me, and the gatepost!
—Robert Browning

onday morning, I called Monty and told him I was being indicted for murder and would need to take an indefinite leave of absence during the proceedings.

There was a long silence, and then Monty spoke. "My God, Doctor, are you serious?"

I assured him that I was.

"Well, then, what are we going to do about your practice? Send everything to Boise? That's gonna really slow things down. The docs are gonna hate it."

"Why don't you call one of those locum agencies?" I suggested. "That way, it'll be just like having me there, and it'll be cheaper in the long run than sending everything to Boise."

Dubiously, he agreed, and I hung up the phone with relief. That was the easy part.

The rest would not be.

It was too soon for anything to be in the paper, but I looked anyway. Hal had gone off to work, and I was alone in the house with the animals. I was at loose ends and bored out of my skull already at eight o'clock. I had never, unless I was deathly ill and in bed, been home alone in this house on a weekday. I had worked every day of my life, and now, suddenly, I was a lady of leisure.

My head didn't hurt nearly as much today as it had last night, and I was wide awake and full of energy. Napping was not an option. Neither were soap operas and game shows. I guessed I could get dressed and maybe have another cup of coffee and finish watching the *Today Show*. That would take me until when? Nine o'clock? Then what? What the hell was I going to do with myself today? And tomorrow? And the next day? Time stretched ahead of me, an endless vista of emptiness.

And what about Hal? Robbie might try again, and this time he'd use something a little more efficient than a brick. If he decided to shoot Hal in the faculty parking lot, there'd be nothing anybody could do to prevent it.

I was just sinking into a nice little morass of self-pity when the doorbell rang. I answered it in my bathrobe, Killer and Geraldine at my heels, and with a jolt saw the police car parked in the driveway. Pete and the Commander stood there on the porch.

"Well, young lady," the Commander said, smiling, "are you going to keep us standing out here all morning?"

"We brought doughnuts," Pete added.

Embarrassed, I invited them in and poured them coffee, then excused myself to go upstairs and get dressed. I was much more comfortable in sweats.

"What's going on?" I said, joining them at the table

and helping myself to a doughnut. Geraldine jumped into my lap, and Spook materialized under my chair, weaving around my ankles, meowing. I scratched his back, and he purred.

"You guys didn't just come over for coffee and doughnuts," I said. "To what do I owe the honor of your company?"

"Plotting," said Pete.

"Pete told me about the little plan you all hatched here last night," the Commander added. "I think it might be worth a try, but we need to figure out the details."

"You know, I've been thinking," I said. "Maybe we've got our priorities wrong. Shouldn't you be trying to find out who really killed Dr. Shore, instead of protecting me?"

"We haven't stopped working on that, if that's what you're thinking," replied the Commander, fishing a toothpick out of his shirt pocket. "We haven't stopped working on who killed the Rosses, either. And then there's the little matter of who attacked *you*, don't forget."

"I'm not likely to," I said with feeling.

"See, this is what we're thinking," the Commander went on, hitching forward in his chair and leaning on the table. "Your Dr. Cabot is probably guilty as sin, but we can't prove it. We can't even show probable cause. He's been slicker'n snot. But he's got to slip up sometime. We'd just as soon he didn't do that by killing anybody else. As long as he thinks you're gonna fry for what he did, he can relax. And then he might get careless. He might brag to somebody, or something. He's an arrogant bastard, your Dr. Cabot is."

"He's not *my* Dr. Cabot, damn it," I said.

"Sorry. Figure of speech. Do you see what I'm getting at?"

"Yes, I see. I've already arranged to take a leave of absence from work, and I told Monty that I was being indicted. Now what?"

"We've already let that slip to the *Clarion*," Pete said. "It'll be in tomorrow's paper. We didn't get it in soon enough for today."

"Yeah, I know. I looked."

"Now," the Commander continued, "the next thing that happens when someone gets indicted for murder is that they go to jail."

With alarm, I said, "But Pete said I wouldn't have to go to jail!"

The Commander raised his hands in a calming motion. "You don't. But it has to *look* like you did. The paperwork has to look authentic. You have to be arrested and booked. And there has to be an arraignment, that's when you get indicted, and then you have to be bound over for trial, and then there has to be a trial. There won't be one, of course, but we have to go through the motions as if there will."

A thought struck me, and I said, "Why can't I be out on bail?"

"There's no bail for murder," Pete said.

"Shit. So what do I do?"

"You come with us now, and we'll get the ball rolling."

Suddenly, I was scared. "How do I know I won't end up in jail anyway? What if something goes wrong? What about Lt. Kincaid?"

"Don't worry," the Commander said. "I took care of *him*."

"What about Elliott? I want him to be there."

"He'll be there," Pete said. "I already called him."

I cooperated magnificently. It was quite a show. They took me out to their car in handcuffs, Pete holding me by one arm and the Commander by the other, while I struggled and wailed and sobbed and cursed. They practically had to drag me. The commotion brought the neighbors out to their porches. Mrs. Merriweather across the street hollered, "Want me to call Mr. Maynard for you, Toni?" And the Commander snapped, "She can call him from the station, like everybody else." And Pete added, "Please go back inside. This is not your concern." Then they opened the back door of the police car and unceremoniously shoved me inside.

Lt. Kincaid was nowhere in sight when we got to the station. Clad in an orange jumpsuit, I was taken downstairs to the jail and put into a cell—at gunpoint and in cuffs and leg irons. I continued to struggle and yell and cry, and the reporter from KMVT Channel 11 diligently recorded the whole performance. I was almost enjoying it, but that changed abruptly when they actually put me in the cell and locked me in.

The jail cells were in the basement of the Twin Falls police station, which had been built somewhere around the turn of the century. The walls were bare stone, cold and damp. There was a single tiny window, high up, covered by bars, through which I could see a fragment of newspaper plastered against the bars by snow. Each cell contained two sets of bunk beds made of iron pipe, each with a paper-thin mattress, a rock-hard pillow, and a threadbare filthy blanket. In the corner was a stainless steel toilet, apparently the only thing that had been changed since the place was built in 1898. The stink of urine and vomit was almost palpable. There were only four cells, all in a row along one side of a narrow hallway. They were all empty but one, in which I could hear someone snoring.

Pete and the Commander were nowhere in sight, and neither was Elliott. A policewoman removed the cuffs and leg irons, while a guard held a gun on me. As they locked the door, I said, "Hey, I'm not supposed to be in here," and the guard said, "That's what they all say," and the policewoman giggled. Then they were gone.

That's when the performance began in earnest. Panicked, I pounded on the bars and screamed, "Let me out! Hey! Goddammit! Where the fuck's my lawyer? Let me out, you sons of bitches!" and any other expletives I could think of. After a while, exhausted, I sank to the floor, sobbing.

"Oh, cut it out," growled the man in the next cell, who was now awake. "I'm not gonna spend all day listening to you whine."

"Leave me alone," I mumbled.

"I mean it. Shut the fuck up, or else."

I felt ashamed, the same way I had as a child when my mother chided me for whining; and then I realized how ludicrous that was. I was being chewed out by a felon in a cage, for God's sake, and I realized what every actor knows: the show must go on.

"Get off my case, asshole," I snapped in the huskiest whisky voice I could manage, which wasn't difficult since I had been crying and my nose was all stuffed up.

"I told you to shut up, bitch."

"Oh yeah? Who died and made you king, dickhead?"

"I don't have to listen to you whining all day, cunt."

"Yes you do, fuckhead. You're in a cage just like me."

"So, what're you in for? Stealing lingerie from Macy's?" he sneered.

"Don't you wish, big boy."

"You better shut up, bitch. I'm not gonna tell you again."

"Good," I said. "I was getting tired of it."

"You better not get smart with me, bitch. I can tear you into little pieces. You'll wish you'd never been born. I'll beat your pretty face to a pulp. I'll carve it up with a hunting knife. No man will ever look at you again."

My blood ran cold, and I shivered. Thank God this animal was in a cage.

"Is that what you're in for?" I asked.

"I beat up my girlfriend. She was steppin' out on me. Nobody does that to the Bruiser and gets away with it," he bragged.

"I hear you," I said, suddenly inspired. "My boyfriend did the same thing to me. But he'll never do it again."

"Yeah?" he said, interested in spite of himself. "What'cha do to him?"

"I strangled him with a pair of her panties and carved my initials on his scrotum."

I heard what I thought might be a little gasp.

"With a razor blade."

"Jesus Christ," he muttered under his breath.

"Nobody does that to Stella and lives to tell about it," I added, just for good measure.

He was silent. I guessed he'd leave me alone now. My wild imagination had stood me in good stead. Hal would be proud.

I attempted to kill some time by trying to read the fragment of newspaper that was stuck in the window. The date on it was last December's, and the article was about a female lawyer in Boise who had killed two children while driving under the influence. I remembered Hal telling me about the case, since I never bother to read the papers, and I remembered Elliott talking about it too. There was apparently some doubt about the validity of the blood alcohol level, or something, I forget what.

But remembering that case reminded me that I could hardly hope to get out of this without the whole town knowing about it. Like that lady lawyer, I was a professional, and I was supposed to have killed not two children but another doctor, and not under the influence, but in cold blood. I would undoubtedly make the *Boise* papers. The thought did not cheer me.

I paced my cell, getting angrier and more upset by the minute, convinced that Pete and the Commander had forgotten all about me. I hadn't gotten my phone call, and I hadn't asked for one, since Pete said he'd already called Elliott. But Elliott hadn't been there, and still wasn't there. It slowly dawned on me that the police had tricked me. This arrest was not a ruse to prevent Tyler from attacking me; it was for real. In which case, the arraignment would also be for real, and so would the trial. And until the trial could be scheduled, I would languish indefinitely in a jail cell with only the Bruiser for company. And he wasn't much company now that he was ignoring me; not that he'd been all that great before. I wondered about starting another scintillating conversation and was trying to think of something to say, when Elliott showed up accompanied by the policewoman.

"Well, it's about damn time," I began, when the policewoman snapped the cuffs back on me. "Hey, what are you doing?"

"Don't start with me, lady," she snapped. "Unless you'd like the leg irons too?"

Elliott, who had been uncharacteristically silent during all this, said curtly, "Behave yourself, Toni."

Startled, I began to object, and as his eyes met mine, he slashed the edge of his hand across his throat, out of sight of the policewoman. I got the message with relief. We were still acting.

"Hey, I thought your name was Stella," bellowed the Bruiser.

"It was," I said flippantly. "I changed it."

"Stella?" muttered Elliott, under his breath.

"Later," I muttered back.

"Smartass bitch," growled the Bruiser.

"Shut up, Bruiser," said the policewoman.

Pete was waiting at the top of the stairs. "I'll take it from here, Shelley," he said.

"Now what?" I asked as Elliott and Pete accompanied me out the door and into a waiting police car.

"We're off to your arraignment," Elliott said.

"What took you so long?" I demanded, once the car doors were closed. "I was worried sick."

"I'm sorry, Toni," Elliott said contritely. "All these freakin' arrangements took more time than I thought they would."

"Can I get these damn cuffs off now?"

Pete, who was driving, turned his head and said, "You'll have to keep them on a while longer, till we get inside the courthouse. The newspapers and the TV station will be waiting for us. You gotta look authentic."

"And no matter what they ask you, you say 'No comment,'" Elliott added.

I sighed.

"So who's Stella?" asked Elliott.

"My alter ego," I said and told him what happened. Pete laughed so hard I thought he was going to drive us into a lamppost. "I thought ol' Bruiser was awful quiet," he said when he caught his breath.

Once we got to the courthouse, Pete escorted me up the steps, holding one of my arms firmly, Elliott holding the other. Suddenly a reporter with a notepad, a photographer with a camera, a skinny black-haired girl with a microphone and Kabuki-white makeup, and a pimply young man with a video camera converged in front of me, all talking at once.

"Doctor! Look over here!" Flashbulbs flashed, and I flinched and turned away.

The microphone was shoved in my face, and the black-haired witch shouted, "Doctor, did you kill Dr. Sally Shore?"

"Get that thing out of my face," I snapped.

"No comment!" yelled Elliott. "No freakin' comment, goddammit!"

Heads down, we plowed our way through them and entered the courthouse.

The Twin Falls County courthouse was built in 1913, and its age was showing. The walls were dingy yellowish-brown and mottled with stains from decades of sweaty bodies sitting on the benches. There were water stains on the ceilings. Portions of the baseboards were missing. The linoleum floors were scuffed, and the black-and-white diamond pattern was all but obscured. Electricity and running water had been retrofitted, and conduits and pipes ran up and down the walls and traversed the ceilings in a disorganized maze. I pitied any electrician or plumber who had to work on them. The building's best feature was the wide polished mahogany banisters that flanked the stairs. Every time I had come here in the past to renew a driver's license or a car registration, I had admired those gleaming banisters and wished I had the nerve to slide down them. But their beauty was lost on me today as we ascended to the fourth floor in a creaky elevator.

The district attorney was waiting for us at the door of one of the several courtrooms on that floor. Inside, the room was empty. No spectators. No jury. No judge.

And best of all, no reporters; just Pete, Elliott, me, and the infamous Fritz Baumgartner. Elliott introduced us.

The district attorney had none of the beauty and glamour of his cousin Desiree. He was short, squat, and glaring. Bullet-shaped bald head. Rolls of fat on the back of his neck. Wire-rimmed glasses. A lipless slash of a mouth. He looked like a caricature of a German SS officer; hardly the type to inspire confidence in me, Toni Shapiro, whose husband was a Jew.

But when he smiled, his face came alive and his eyes twinkled. He shook my hand. He said he was glad to meet me at last, he'd heard so much about me from Desiree's husband.

"I can just imagine," I said.

"No, no," he assured me. "It was all good. He said you were an excellent pathologist and pretty besides."

Pretty? Me? Tyler said that? But I decided not to argue the point. I merely smiled and inquired, "What happens now?"

"Heh-heh," chuckled the district attorney. "What happens now is that Elliott smuggles you out of here by the side door and takes you home."

I looked at Elliott. "And that's it?"

"Not quite," said Elliott. "Once you get home, you have to stay out of sight. The papers and the TV stations will say you've been arrested and indicted and that you are being held in jail pending trial. So, until something breaks and we can arrest Dr. Cabot, everybody has to *think* you're in jail."

I stared at him, aghast. "But Elliott," I finally said, "that could take weeks! Months!"

"More like days," Fritz Baumgartner said.

"Days?"

"Elliott can tell you all about it. Now you better get out of here before the fourth estate finds out where we are."

We went back down by the freight elevator, and Elliott brought his car around to the loading dock to pick me up. I wore a long black trench coat, borrowed from Elliott, over my orange jumpsuit. Nobody saw us. He drove me down the alley in back of the house, and Hal let me in by the gate. Tall elms, now fully leafed out, shielded us from the prying eyes of our neighbors. Killer and Geraldine weren't much help, though, barking and whining and racing around, calling attention to themselves.

Once inside the house, I tore off the trench coat and

raced upstairs to get the loathsome orange jumpsuit off me as quickly as possible. Clad in my comfortable black sweats, I came back down to find Elliott and Pete sitting at the table while Hal made sandwiches. I realized with a start that it was only one o'clock in the afternoon. It seemed as if I'd been gone for days. I grabbed a turkey-and-Swiss and a handful of chips, and joined the group.

"You did great, Toni," Pete said. "Ray said he hopes we never have to arrest you for real."

"He's not the only one," I said. "So what was Fritz talking about, Elliott?"

"We have a plan," Elliott said. "There has been nothing in the paper about the Rosses' deaths being ruled homicides. The police don't usually release anything to the paper until the autopsy report is received. You haven't completed your report yet, have you?"

"How? I haven't been there since Monday. And now I'm on an indefinite leave of absence."

"So now what?" Pete asked. "How are we going to get a completed autopsy report if you can't complete it?"

"There's supposed to be a locum tenens. You could call and ask. He can call me if he has questions."

"No, he can't," Elliott said. "You're supposed to be in jail, remember?"

"Shit." This pretending-to-be-in-jail stuff was shaping up to be a real pain in the ass, I reflected. "I guess he's on his own, then."

Over sandwiches and chips, Elliott outlined the plan. I listened with some degree of skepticism. The investigation wasn't complete, so something might turn up. That seemed awfully chancy to me. How did he know that what might turn up would clear me? But when I voiced my objections,

Elliott merely said, "Just leave it to Fritz," and wouldn't tell me any more.

Hal went back to the college after lunch.

The rest of the day passed like cold molasses in January. Hal had gone to the library and checked out an armload of mysteries for me to read; then he got in a supply of potato chips for me to snack on. I spent the rest of Thursday flaked out on the couch, munching and reading, and realized that this could not become a daily routine or I would soon outweigh Hal. So I planned to start jogging during the night when nobody would see me. At least, that was my plan.

As with so many plans, life interfered.

Chapter 39

The game is afoot.
—Sir Arthur Conan Doyle

*H*al didn't come home.

He was supposed to be off at four thirty, but by six he still wasn't home. I called his extension and got an answering machine saying that Dr. Shapiro was available between the hours of 9:00 a.m. and 4:30 p.m.

When he still wasn't home by eight, I called the extension for campus security and talked to whoever was on duty, which was an exercise in futility. The rent-a-cop I talked to said he'd check around the campus, but he didn't sound the least bit enthusiastic about it, and it was a big campus. I had no idea what "check around" entailed, but I was willing to bet it wasn't a very thorough check. I asked him to call me if he found out anything. In my naiveté, I actually thought someone would go right over to Hal's office and look around.

When I had heard nothing by ten, I called the police. There was nobody on duty that I knew. The person who answered the phone informed me that missing persons have to be missing for at least twenty-four hours before they can do anything.

Shit. How the hell was I going to get through the night? I wouldn't sleep a wink. Where could he be? Why wasn't he home where he belonged?

Frustrated and becoming more frantic by the minute, I called Elliott. He told me sternly to stay put, and he would see what he could do. *Stay put, my ass.* Near tears, I promised I would, but as soon as it was late enough that I could be relatively sure there'd be no college students having romantic interludes in the bushes, I planned to go over to the college and check around for myself. If I took Killer with me, I should be safe enough, and all the buildings would be closed and dark and nobody would see me. Unfortunately, I hadn't taken into account the fact that we only had the one car and that Hal had driven it to the college, which was at least two miles away. But when I jogged, I jogged at least that far every day.

So, at midnight, I put a flashlight in my jacket pocket and Killer on his leash and jogged the two miles to the college. As I rounded the loop, I saw a car turn into the entrance and hid Killer and myself behind a bush until it had passed, which took for-friggin'-ever at the campus speed limit of fifteen miles per hour, at which point the soles of my running shoes were clogged with mud. Nobody would have any trouble following my footprints.

Keeping Killer on a very short leash, I crept through the underbrush and between shrubs until I reached Hansen Hall, where Hal's office was located on the second floor. Of course, the building was dark and locked, and I went around it trying all the doors and windows on the first floor, to no avail.

Just then the car came back. I ducked behind a bush, pulling Killer after me. The car pulled over to the side and stopped, and someone got out. Killer immediately began to whine and wiggle, and as soon as the person started walking I recognized Elliott. He was following my footprints. When he heard Killer, he stopped and listened for a moment and then called out my name in a stage whisper.

"Toni? Where are you?"

"Here I am," I whispered back as Killer and I came out from behind the bush. Killer jumped up on Elliott, soaking his windbreaker with muddy paw prints. Elliott gently pushed him away.

"What the hell are you doing? I told you to freakin' stay put!"

"I could ask you the same question!"

Killer growled.

"Freeze, you two," came a voice out of the darkness. "Don't you move a goddamned inch, you hear me?"

Killer started barking and straining at his leash. I fought to hold him back; he weighed nearly as much as I did. "Down!" I told him.

A flashlight beam blinded me.

"All right, frisk 'em!"

Elliott and I were pushed against the building, searched, and handcuffed. When we were finally allowed to turn around, we saw that we had been apprehended by Earl and Howie's evil twins, two big-bellied campus security guards with heavy flashlights and service revolvers on their belts.

Killer had stopped barking, but continued to growl.

One of the evil twins now held his leash, and he didn't like it.

"All right, you two, we're just gonna take a little stroll over to the security office and you're gonna tell us what the hell you're doing sneaking around at this time of night."

"First, you're going to tell us why we're being treated like common criminals," Elliott retorted. "Is this what you do when you catch students in the bushes?"

"We've had a missing persons report," said the other guard. "A faculty member has gone missing. So when we saw this one"—he shook me—"trying to break into Hansen Hall ..."

"Yeah," said the other, "and we were just on our way to search his office when we found you two. So what are you doing here?"

"We're looking for him too," Elliott said.

"And you are?"

Elliott identified himself, showing his driver's license. "I'm his attorney. His wife called me."

"And you, ma'am?"

"She's my wife," Elliott said before I had a chance to open my mouth.

After approximately two more eons of interrogation and a phone conversation with the city police, the campus police decided to let us go, Elliott drove me and Killer home with a strict injunction to stay out of sight. Did I realize that I had nearly blown my cover tonight?

Maybe that was what someone wanted me to do.

Friday morning, there was no new information about Hal's whereabouts and nobody left to call, so I called my mother and told her Hal was missing, and could she please come?

"Of course, I can come, dear, but what do you mean, Hal is *missing*? Has he left you? Or is he having an *affair*? You *surely* don't mean he's been kidnapped or murdered or tossed into the canyon or anything like that? Could he have had a heart attack in his office and just be *lying* there…?"

Jesus. My mother could think of even worse case scenarios than I could.

"Mum, I don't know. Nobody knows. He just went to work yesterday and never came home, and nobody's seen him since."

"Kitten, have you called the police?"

"Yes, I have. Mum, I'll tell you everything when you get here, okay?"

Half an hour later, she called me back to say she would be here on the five o'clock flight and asked if I'd called Hal's parents.

I arranged to have Jodi pick her up, since I was supposed to still be in jail. I was counting on Elliott to help me tell her what was going on.

I dreaded calling Hal's parents, since I knew Ida Shapiro wouldn't allow me to just give her the bare bones like I had my own mother. I would have to tell her every little detail, and then they would also insist on coming up here, and I would have to go through it all again. Furthermore, I didn't have a kosher kitchen, and I would have to hear about that all over again, after which they would decide to go to a hotel and make me feel guilty because I couldn't accommodate my own husband's parents at such a stressful time, and what kind of a daughter-in-law was I.

Hal's mother usually called on Saturday night, and I hoped that somehow Hal would be back by then, and I wouldn't have to call them. But what if he wasn't back, and they called and found out he'd been missing for what, three days, and I hadn't thought to call and tell them?

So I called them.

Talk about guilt. Ida Shapiro was the West Coast distributor of it.

She wore me out. Since I could think of nothing else to do, I gave myself up to a major crying jag, which wore me out some more, so I took a nap.

The phone woke me at five. Hoping it would be Hal or at least news of Hal, I catapulted myself off the couch, but it was Robbie.

"Are you lonesome tonight," he sang, hideously off-key. "Where's your Jew-boy tonight? Do you wish I was with you instead?"

"What have you done with him, you son-of-a-bitch?" I screamed. "Where is he?"

But there was no answer. In a rage, I slammed the phone down, but it rang again almost at once. I was all ready to scream at Robbie some more, but it was Elliott, who told me that the police had found no sign of violence in Hal's office or elsewhere in or around Hansen Hall—or any other evidence except for our footprints from the night before. They had been interviewing Hal's students, and so far nobody recalled anything unusual. The Cherokee had been parked in the faculty parking lot since Thursday morning, and he asked if I wanted him to bring it home.

After that, I alternated between rage and tears and entertained myself by picturing various artistic things I could do involving an autopsy knife and Robbie's genitalia, during which he would be fully conscious to enjoy them with me—after which I would dismember him, starting with his fingers and toes, and put him down the garbage disposal a piece at a time. I found that, for the most part, rage felt better than tears.

Jodi picked up my mother from the airport at six and got some fried chicken on the way back. While she carried in my mother's suitcase, my mother stood in the doorway in full view of the entire neighborhood and held out her arms.

"Antoinette, darling, *why* are you hiding way over there, and why on *earth* is it so dark in here?" she began, while I stood well away from the front door and beckoned to her. "Mum, please," I pleaded in a stage whisper, "please get in here and close the door."

"Upstairs in the guest room?" Jodi wanted to know, and I said "Yes, please," as I walked into my mother's arms.

Before I could say anything, however, Elliott drove the Cherokee into the driveway and into the garage. I heard the garage door close behind it as Elliott tapped at the connecting door into the kitchen and then came in.

"Oh, hi, Fiona," he said, seeing my mother. "How was your flight?"

"Would *someone*," my mother said, her curly red hair quivering with outrage, "tell me exactly what is going on here? My daughter sends someone to pick me up when there appears to be no reason for it, and then she hides behind the door so the neighbors can't see her. One would think she's afraid to be seen. I *fail* to see what that has to do with Hal being missing. And by the way, dear, *have* you called the Shapiros yet?"

Oh, she knew me so well.

"I did," I assured her. "They're coming in on the next flight."

My mother nodded. "Very well."

I knew she was pleased that I had called Hal's parents, but she really didn't much care for them. She didn't much care for Jews in general but was too polite to show it. "And will they be staying here, too?"

"I doubt it. I don't have a kosher kitchen, and that's a problem. They always start out talking like they'll stay here, but then they change their minds and decide to go to a hotel at the last minute. So I already made a reservation for them at the Blue Lakes Inn."

I knew the Blue Lakes Inn had kosher meals, and the Shapiros always stayed there when they came to visit.

"Right, then," said my mother, taking off her coat and hanging it on the coat tree. Sitting primly on the couch next to me, she looked from Elliott to me and back to Elliott and said, "Now, kindly *explain* yourselves."

Elliott obliged, and Mum listened without interrupting, a major feat for her. When he had finished, she was silent for a long minute, at the end of which she breathed a reverent, "My stars and garters."

Jodi, who had been bustling about the kitchen, putting out the fried chicken and all the side dishes and setting the table, called us to dinner. We opened a bottle of wine and talked until it was time for Elliott to go back to the airport.

When he got back with the Shapiros, sure enough, Ida

insisted on going to a hotel where they could get kosher meals. I was exhausted, even though I had taken a nap earlier, so Mum and I went to bed at ten. But I couldn't sleep. Whatever was being done to find Hal, it wasn't being done fast enough.

At midnight, I dragged myself out of bed to go jogging, like the night before, taking care not to wake Mum. My route took me through Tyler's neighborhood. I could have jogged somewhere else if I'd wanted to, and I knew I shouldn't be there, but I was curious.

One could not fail to know which house was Tyler's. It was the most ostentatious one on a street full of multimillion-dollar homes. It looked like the Parthenon, with fancy columns and manicured landscaping full of topiary, sitting on a lot at least twice the size of any of the other lots near it. A circular driveway lined with lights curved right up to the entrance. The portico was like a fairyland with nets of tiny white lights.

I would have known it was Tyler's house, even if the driveway and the street were not filled with cars and every window filled with light. The front door was open, and Desiree stood there saying good-bye to people as they left. A young man ran back and forth, fetching cars and driving them up to the door. I stood watching in wonder. Valet parking, I ask you. Everyone was dressed up, men in tuxedos and women in long dresses and high heels, showing off their best jewelry.

I stood in the shadows, watching. Hal and I never got invited to parties like this. These were the cream of society, the ultra-rich. I didn't recognize anybody, so I figured that the guests were from Sun Valley and that Killer wouldn't call attention to me by recognizing someone and barking.

So I nearly shot my heart right out of my mouth when he suddenly growled and someone laid a hand on my shoulder. I jumped and whirled round to see Fritz behind me, holding a finger in front of his lips. I took the hint and didn't utter a sound, which was more than I could say for Killer, who whined softly and wagged his tail. Fritz beckoned, and I followed him into the shadows around the back of the house.

"What the hell are you doing here?" he demanded, sotto voce, when we were out of earshot of the departing guests. "Are you trying to blow your cover after all the trouble we've gone to?"

I shook my head, then realized Fritz probably couldn't see me and said, "No, I was just out jogging. Hal's still missing, and I couldn't sleep."

Fritz put an arm around my shoulders. "I know, Elliott told me. You must be worried sick."

"I am, believe me. So why aren't you inside with everybody else?"

"I wasn't invited. I just showed up. Since Desiree's my cousin, I figured she wouldn't just kick me out. I needed to be inside the house to let Pete and Bernie in. They're searching the upstairs rooms. They'll do the downstairs after all the guests have left."

As he spoke, a dim form slid noiselessly out the sliding glass door at the rear of the house that led out onto the deck. When it materialized behind Fritz, I recognized Pete. Killer, who had settled down, started whining again, and I shushed him.

"We got something," Pete whispered, brandishing something that looked like … could it be? … a hospital chart.

"Is that Terence Ross's chart?" I whispered.

"It sure is," Pete said. "Found it upstairs in Dr. Cabot's study."

"Well, it's a start," Fritz said. "I was really hoping you'd find a syringe or an ampule of succinylcholine or …"

"Or the missing bottle of Dr. Shore's allergy medicine?" I suggested.

"We're still looking," Pete said. "If all else fails, at least we've got circumstantial evidence that Dr. Cabot assaulted you, and we can arrest him for assault and battery."

"Good," Fritz said. "I'll hang onto this. You keep looking."

Pete disappeared.

"Now what?" I asked Fritz.

"Now you and your dog just turn around and go home," Fritz said. "There's no need for you to be here."

"Not on your life," I argued. "I want to see this." Anything to take my mind off Hal.

Fritz shrugged. "Suit yourself. Just don't get in the way."

I considered the wisdom of taking Fritz's advice and just going home, but I discarded it as I envisioned the logistics of taking Killer home and leaving him there and then getting the Cherokee out of the garage to drive it back to Tyler's house. The ruckus that would ensue would surely wake my mother and possibly the neighbors as well. So I sat on the back doorstep and snuggled Killer close to me for warmth. The sweat I had worked up jogging was now cold and clammy on my skin.

Suddenly I heard the sounds of a scuffle inside the house. I jumped to my feet. Fritz was at my side in nanoseconds, stealthily opening the slider wide enough to let us inside the house.

The sounds were coming from the entry hall. Fritz, with hand gestures, indicated that I was to keep myself and Killer out of sight, and then strolled casually through the kitchen and dining room right into the middle of the melee.

"Fritz, where have you been?" demanded a distraught Desiree. "Make them stop!"

"What the hell is this all about?" demanded Tyler. "Get your hands off me!"

"Now, now," interjected Fritz, "what's all this about, officers?"

"We've got enough to take him in," Pete said. He sounded slightly out of breath.

"What the fuck are you talking about?" Tyler snarled. "Take me in for what? I haven't done anything!"

"Well, then, Dr. Cabot, suppose you explain what this was doing in your medicine cabinet?" Kincaid inquired, waving a small glass object in Tyler's face.

"Who's that?" Desiree suddenly demanded.

Killer and I had been stealthily moving nearer and nearer to the fray, and despite our efforts to stay out of sight, Desiree had spotted us.

Fritz turned around and, seeing me, beckoned. "You may as well come out," he said.

I did so, keeping Killer on a very short leash—and a good thing too, because once Killer got within sniffing distance of Tyler, he started growling.

Desiree jumped back, her beautiful face twisted with distaste. "Get that dog out of my house!" she demanded. "I don't allow animals in my house."

"Toni, you stay right where you are," Fritz told me. "Show her what you found, Detective Lieutenant."

At the mention of my name, Tyler, now handcuffed, shot me a look so vitriolic that I involuntarily took a step back. "Why aren't you in jail where you belong?" he snarled.

"To make room for you," I replied sweetly, moving closer to Fritz—just in case.

Pete handed me a small bottle that I immediately recognized as one containing the stuff allergy shots are made of. A somewhat smudged prescription label bore Dr. Shore's name, the names of the allergists that had prescribed it (nobody local) and the dilution.

Fritz, still carrying Terence Ross's chart, spoke behind me. "I'd advise both of you to keep your mouths shut," he said. "Desiree, go call your lawyer. Tyler, go with these men. Desiree and I will take care of everything—right after I drive Toni and her dog home. Come on, you two."

Obediently, Killer and I followed Fritz out to his car, which was parked quite a distance from the house. Obviously Fritz had not availed himself of valet parking.

Killer and I could have jogged home, but I was in no mood to spend any more time outdoors, plus I felt glad of the company. It wasn't every day that I actually witnessed an arrest, and I was feeling the reaction set in. I found myself trembling, and my legs felt like jelly. I was also freezing. Lycra spandex doesn't insulate real well.

Shivering in the passenger seat, I felt my euphoria draining away like the heat from my body. My fears about Hal made me shiver even more.

"Fritz," I said, "what else did Elliott tell you? What are

the police doing to find Hal? Have they arrested Robbie yet?"

I saw Fritz wrinkle his brow in the light from the streetlights. "Robbie? Who's Robbie?"

Crap. Elliott didn't tell him about Robbie. And I sure didn't feel like going into all the gory details. "An old boyfriend," I told him. "He's been threatening Hal. And he's here. He's staying with Stan Snow."

Fritz glanced at me. "And you think this Robbie kidnapped Hal?"

"I'm almost sure of it," I said. "He's been threatening to shoot Hal through a window with a high-powered rifle. What's a little kidnapping compared to that?"

Fritz pulled up in my driveway and stopped. "If you're right," he said, "then Hal may be in more danger than we thought."

Well, that was comforting.

As I let myself into the house with my key, I invited Fritz in for coffee. Geraldine, decidedly put out by not having been included in the evening's festivities, started barking at us.

"Now what happens?" I asked, pouring two cups of cold coffee from what was left over from this morning, or, I realized, that would be yesterday morning. I put them both in the microwave, and sat at the kitchen table to wait. Fritz joined me.

"Well, now we have to go through the formality of dropping charges and releasing you."

"What does that mean? Do I have to go back to jail to be released?" I asked.

"No, no," he assured me. "It's just a matter of paperwork. I'll take care of it when I get back to the station and let the paper know about it too." The microwave beeped, and I retrieved the cups of coffee and put them on the kitchen table.

"Kitten? Is that Hal I hear?" Mum, awakened by Geraldine's barking, came down the stairs in a fluffy green bathrobe that set off her red hair. "Oh, no, I guess it isn't," she observed. "Who *is* this gentleman, darling?"

I introduced them. Mum sat down, shook Fritz's hand and then said, "Antoinette, really, *must* you entertain men at this time of night?"

Fritz laughed. "It's not that, Mrs. Day. Toni was out jogging and accidentally got involved in our police operation."

"My goodness," exclaimed Mum. "And did you catch the *perp*, or whatever it is you call them these days?"

"We did," I said. "Tomorrow I get 'released from jail,' and I won't have to hide anymore."

"Thank heavens for that," said my mother. "Now, what are you going to do about my daughter's husband, Mr. Baumgartner?"

Fritz took a healthy swig of coffee and winced. "Jesus, that's hot. I was telling Toni about that while we were on our way here," he said, "but I didn't have a chance to finish. Elliott tells me that all of Hal's students have been interviewed, all the faculty that use that building, the campus cops, his teaching assistant … nobody saw anything out of the ordinary. His office was searched, and they came up empty there too. But Toni seems to think that somebody named Robbie had something to do with it."

My mother made a face of extreme distaste. "Robbie? He's here? Since when?"

So much had happened lately that I couldn't remember exactly how long Robbie had been here. "A couple of weeks or so," I replied.

"Has he been bothering you?"

I told her about Robbie's appearances at the hospital and the country club, the yellow roses, and the phone calls. As I spoke, her expression of distaste morphed into one of outrage. At the mention of the high-powered rifle, she exploded.

"Why on *earth* haven't the police done something? He should be in jail!"

"They know about it, Mum. There's a restraining order against him. But they can't arrest him because he hasn't done anything yet, and they don't have the manpower to keep him under surveillance or give us personal protection."

My mother scowled. "Well, in that case, I wouldn't be surprised," she said darkly. "He wasn't a very nice boy. He raped her, you know."

Fritz, startled, put down his coffee cup so hard it sloshed, and turned to me. "Raped you? When did this happen? How come I didn't know about this? He should be prosecuted."

He looked so outraged that I actually laughed. "It was a long time ago," I reassured him. "While I was in college."

"So the bloody sod seems to think," Mum put in acidly, "that if he gets rid of Hal, he can get you back?"

"That's what he says," I told her. "He claims he's still in love with me."

"But this is terrible," Fritz said. "It sounds like the old "if I can't have her nobody else can either" scenario.

If that's the case, Hal is in much worse danger than I thought."

"That's exactly what it is," I said.

Fritz stood up. "I've got to get to the police station and figure out what to do with Desiree and Tyler. Thanks for the coffee." And he left.

"Well!" said my mother. "Somebody finally listened to you. It's about bloody time. Now, darling, let's get to bed. You need sleep."

I knew I needed it. I just didn't expect to get it.

But I slept soundly, in spite of myself.

Chapter 40

If once a man indulges himself in murder, very soon
he comes to think little of robbing; and from robbing
he comes next to drinking and Sabbath-breaking,
and from that to incivility and procrastination.
                                    —Thomas De Quincey

The *Clarion*, through a terminal case of failure to communicate, had two articles, both in the "Around the Valley" section, both entitled "Physician Charged with Murder," a situation guaranteed to make even the most astute reader say, "Huh?" The first read:

> TWIN FALLS-Formal charges were filed in District Court against Antoinette Day, MD, in the murder of Sally Maria Shore, MD.
>
> Dr. Shore was found dead in her office at Perrine Memorial Hospital on March 1, 2005. Her death was ruled a homicide after evidence was brought to the attention of the Twin Falls police that implicated Dr. Day. Further evidence against Dr. Day was found in her office last Sunday, and an arrest was made.

Dr. Day is currently being held without bail in the Twin Falls City Jail until a trial date can be set.

The second one read:

TWIN FALLS-Tyler Thomas Cabot, MD, was arrested late last night at his home for the murder of Sally Maria Shore, MD, on March 1, 2005.

Murder charges against Antoinette Day, MD, were subsequently dropped, and she has been released.

Mum and I burst out laughing. Our precious *Clarion* would have everybody totally confused and wondering what came first, the chicken or the egg, so to speak. But I didn't care. My husband was still missing, and that took precedence.

Hal's father, Max, called from the hotel to find out if there was any news of Hal and invited us to breakfast at the Blue Lakes Inn. I accepted on behalf of Mum and myself, even though spending time with the Shapiros was the last thing either of us wanted to do.

Ida Shapiro, a tiny woman wearing a wig in a shade that that did nothing for her olive complexion and dark eyes and no doubt did not exist in nature, buttonholed me the minute I sat down at the table. "So, Toni dear, what are the police doing to find my son?"

I told her everything I had learned from Fritz, and didn't mention Robbie. There was no point in giving Ida Shapiro any more ammunition. "I'm sure they're doing all they can," I assured her—without adding that they didn't have the wherewithal to do what the Long Beach police department could do in similar circumstances.

Max, a burly bear of a man with snow-white hair and contrasting black eyebrows, put an arm around me. "And how are you doing, my girl? Are you okay?"

And that in a nutshell was the difference between Hal's parents. Ida didn't like me and was concerned only for Hal. Max cared about both of us.

Conversation was forced, and Mum wisely kept quiet. Once breakfast was over, we couldn't get away fast enough. I had plans for the day and I wanted to get going.

But Elliott came over right after we got home with the newspaper in his hand. I offered him coffee. He offered me the newspaper.

"I've read it," I said.

"Did you know Dr. Cabot's middle name was Thomas?"

"Of course. It's in his credential file."

"Well, in case you've forgotten, according to Natalie Cabot, my other client, her father's name was Thomas Cabot. Now, you may think that doesn't mean anything— there could be other Thomas Cabots—but I've done some investigating. It so happens that in 1982 in Chicago a certain Tommy Cabot was charged with rape. The victim's name was Sara Lee Schott. Both were students at Loyola-Stritch School of Medicine. It was quite a scandal at the time, especially as the girl became pregnant as a result and Loyola is a Catholic school. Abortion was, and still is, out of the question. However, because of the rape charge, the girl was not expelled, but the boy was. The charges were subsequently dropped—in return for the boy marrying the girl in order to give her baby a name, and the Cabots providing support for the girl to complete her education and raise her child." Elliott sat back in his chair and sipped his coffee, a smug expression on his face.

"That's what Hal said!" I exclaimed. *Damn, I miss him. Where the hell is he? Please God, let him still be alive…*"But if there's no record, how did you find all this out?"

"Connections," Elliott said. "I have a buddy from law school who works in Chicago. One of the senior members of his firm was involved in the case. He remembered it because the girl was a real screwball … definitely not the Cabots' class of people."

"Lucky," I commented. "What are the odds? Were they ever divorced?"

"No record of it," Elliott said.

"So Tyler's marriage to Desiree really *isn't* legal?"

"So it would seem."

"Well, that clinches it," I stated. "There's your motive; all that Baumgartner money, right out the window if Desiree ever finds out."

"Not necessarily," Elliott pointed out. "Don't forget the Cabots are wealthy too."

"Oh, yeah," I said. "That explains why Natalie and her mother had a live-in housekeeper, and why they could afford to put Natalie in a private school. But if she was holding a marriage over his head—a marriage that he'd never been divorced from and didn't want Desiree to know about, there's no end of the things she could demand of him. Like being on the medical staff of Perrine Memorial Hospital and getting her daughter a job."

"And being protected against any possible disciplinary actions by the medical staff," said Elliott. "She probably figured she'd never have to hunt for another job in her entire freakin' life."

I remembered how Tyler had broken into a sweat and refused to look me in the eye when he told me that *I* would have to convince Dr. Shore to let Lucille have her job back. I'd wondered at the time if she had something on Tyler. It looked like I was right about that.

No wonder he wanted to get rid of her. I imagined having to defend someone like her from the ire of every other physician on the staff for years on end until she decided to retire. I felt myself breaking out into a sweat at the very thought of it.

"Too bad he didn't divorce her," I remarked.

"They were Catholic, darling," Mum reminded me.

"I know that, but Catholics get divorced all the time nowadays," I objected. "I know if they do, they can never be remarried in the Catholic church, but apparently some people don't care about that."

"Evidently Tyler did," Elliott said.

"But he married Desiree," I argued. "Divorce may not be allowed in the Catholic church, but at least it's legal. Bigamy isn't. How can he reconcile *that* with his religion?"

"How can he reconcile rape and murder with his freakin' religion?" retorted Elliott.

I gave up. I couldn't imagine it. It made no sense. That plus worrying about Hal was giving me a headache. I massaged my forehead to make it go away, but it didn't work.

"One wonders how he could live with himself," my mother said.

"Well, that's that," Mum said after Elliott had gone.

"Not quite," I told her. "I still have to find Hal."

"Surely, darling, you can leave that to the police? Especially after Fritz told them about Robbie last night?"

"He's been missing since Thursday night," I said angrily. "This is Saturday, and he still isn't here."

"Antoinette, just *what* do you think you're going to do?"

"I don't know, but I can't just sit here. I have to do something."

"Kitten, you *can't*. I refuse to let you put yourself in danger when you know the police are doing all they can."

I got to my feet. I argue better standing up. "Mum, that's just it. They don't have enough cops to devote anyone to finding Hal. They have other cases to work on. Doing 'all they can' may not be enough, and while they're doing it, Hal could be dead or dying somewhere, and they'll be too late." My voice began to break while I said this, and I turned away to hide my tears.

"Antoinette, *really*," my mother began. But I envisioned Hal's bloated corpse being found after someone complained about the smell. Along with the tears came rage.

"I'm going to find him, Mum," I told her. "Are you going to help me or not?"

Chapter 41

The dog, to gain his private ends,
Went mad and bit the man.
The man recovered of the bite,
The dog it was that died.

—Oliver Goldsmith

Mum got to her feet. "Well, then. What are we waiting for?"

Inside, I sat Mum at the kitchen table and grabbed a notepad and a pen off the counter. "We need a plan," I told her. "Let's do what you always do."

Mum grabbed the pen out of my hand and pulled the notepad over in front of her. "Make a list," she said.

Mum was famous for her list-making.

"Number one," she prompted.

"Call the police. To see if they've done anything we haven't heard about."

She wrote it down in her precise handwriting.

"Next, call Stan Snow. That's who Robbie's staying with. Find out if he's still there."

She wrote it down.

"Call Elliott. He should know what we're doing. Also, if I can't get hold of Stan, he might know where he is."

"Good thought," she said, and wrote it down. "So, what now, love?"

I sighed. "I guess now I call the police. We can add more things to the list later." Once Mum got going on making a list, the list tended to assume a life of its own.

Darryl Curtis answered the phone when I called the police station. "Hi, Toni. What can I do for you?"

When I told him, he offered to pull the file for me. "I'm not working that case, but there should be a report or two that might help. What do you want it for? I'm sure Pete's doing all he can to find your husband."

"I know he is," I said. "But what if new information comes in while he's out? What if there's a new lead to follow? Who follows it?"

"Well, today, that would be me," he said. "Why? Do you have something?"

"I have a pretty good idea who's behind it," I told him. "Robert Simpson. He's an old boyfriend who's been stalking me and has threatened to shoot Hal with a high-powered rifle. He's visiting Stan Snow."

"Oh, that guy. The yellow rose in your kitchen, right? Want me to pull that file too?"

"Please. We'll be there in ten minutes."

"We?" Darryl asked, but I hung up on him. I didn't want to spend another nanosecond on chitchat.

"Get your shoes on, Mum," I said, getting up from the table.

I introduced Darryl to my mother, and he invited us to sit. The two files were on the desk in front of him.

"Before I let you see these, I need to know what you plan to do with the information," he said.

I assumed my most innocent demeanor. "We just want to know where the investigation stands," I said.

"Okay," Darryl said. "But I could have told you that on the phone, you know."

"I know. I just want to see if they're anywhere near finding Hal. I can't just sit around and wait all day." As soon as I said it, I knew I'd gone too far.

"Oh, now wait a minute," Darryl said. "The Commander'll have my ass if I let you two go running around getting into trouble and we have to come and bail you out. Why don't you just go home and let us handle it?"

I pretended to give in. "Okay. If you let us see the files, we'll go right home. Promise."

Mum would have seen right through that, and probably did, because as Darryl hesitated she drew herself up to her full height of five-foot-one and turned her British up full blast.

"Young man, my daughter gave you her word. Now hand over those files at once."

Startled, Darryl shoved them across the desk. "You can take those into the conference room," he said. "It's more comfortable in there, and you won't be disturbed. I'll be right out here if you have any questions."

Robbie's file was a waste of time.

Oh, yeah, my complaints to Kincaid were written up in detail. In black and white, they seemed ludicrous. Kincaid's skepticism fairly leapt off the page at me, although the words themselves couldn't have been more correct and totally appropriate for a routine police report of a citizen complaint.

Pete's report of the break-in of our house and the yellow rose on the kitchen table was not much help. No signs of a break-in were found on any of our doors and windows, there were no fingerprints on the bud vase, only smudges; and no fingerprints anywhere else either. Obviously Robbie had worn gloves. How he'd gotten in remained a mystery. Perhaps he had somehow obtained a key. But how?

Pete's report of the attack on Hal likewise yielded no clues. The brick was useless. There were no useful fingerprints on the lightbulb or the light fixture and only partials of Hal's fingerprints on the shards of the broken bulb.

Casts made of footprints around the house failed to match any of Robbie's shoes. *But surely they match somebody*, I thought. *Tyler, perhaps? Or maybe Robbie borrowed a pair of Stan's shoes.* I made a mental note to ask about that when all this was over.

Robbie himself, when interviewed by Kincaid, denied everything. Stan Snow told Kincaid he was pretty sure Robbie had been present at his house at the time of both incidents, but couldn't swear to it. But he did give permission for the police to search his house and office, saving them the trouble of getting a warrant.

No high-powered rifle was found in Robbie's possession. Stan had a couple of shotguns for duck hunting, but that was all.

Kincaid had been thorough. He'd found nothing incriminating at Stan's house or his office.

Pete had gone over to the college to check out Hal's

office. At first glance nothing was amiss. He saw no signs of struggle. Aside from a pile of exams to grade and the usual pencil holder, stapler, coffee cup, etc., his desk was clean. He had dusted the desk and everything on it for fingerprints, and found only Hal's. The coffee cup was empty and had been rinsed and dried. There were no extraneous bits of paper hidden among the student exams. He had even vacuumed the carpet, and found nothing but dust and a few hairs. They were blond-gray and probably Hal's. He had also interviewed most of the students in Hal's classes. Everyone expressed surprise and shock that Dr. Shapiro was missing. Unless they were very good liars, the students knew nothing.

But one detail made my blood run cold. On Hal's desk he had found a bud vase containing a single yellow rose.

Chapter 42

O dark, dark, dark, amid the blaze of noon.
Irrecoverably dark, total eclipse
Without all hope of day!
—John Milton

When we got home, I realized that I had forgotten to get Stan Snow's home phone number. So I called the police station, but instead of Darryl's voice I got the bored voice of the dispatcher, who informed me while audibly chewing gum that Officer Curtis was out on a call. I asked her to give him a message to call me, but she didn't fill me with any confidence that she would actually pass the message on.

My next call was to Elliott, but there was no answer. Now I could only hope that Stan was in the phone book and not unlisted like most professional people, myself included. There were several Snows listed, but no Stanley. Only the office number was listed.

Shit. I was batting zero here. "Damn it," I said to Mum. "I'm not waiting until tomorrow to get hold of all these people. By tomorrow Hal may be dead." My voice broke as I said that. I hoped that it wasn't already too late. *Oh, God, please …*

The officious bitch at Information refused to give an unlisted number unless it was an emergency. It didn't help that I didn't know Stanley's address either. Was I now going to have to break into Elliott's office to find them?

Mum firmly vetoed that idea. "But my dear, you *can't!*" she protested. "It's in a bank building downtown and will no doubt have an alarm going *straight* into the police station. You will surely get arrested. I won't have it."

There was no use arguing with Mum; I knew that from many years of experience. It was easiest to pretend to give in to her and change the subject. In any case, she had given me an idea.

I called the police again. Darryl answered. I told him I needed to talk to Stan Snow on a private matter and asked for his phone number and address. He gave me the phone number but balked at giving me the address. "Why do you need that if you're just going to talk to him?" he asked. I couldn't think of a decent answer to that question without actually telling him the truth, which was that we were going to break into Stan's house looking for Hal. I felt pretty sure that Darryl wouldn't be too happy about that.

I called Elliott again. This time he answered.

"They've gone to Las Vegas for a few days," he told me. "A second honeymoon, or some such freakin' nonsense. They should be back on Monday."

I asked for Stan's address. Elliott refused to give it to me. "What do you need that for, Toni? Are you planning to go over there and break in looking for Hal? No freakin' way."

Well, shit.

I called Stan Snow's number. A recorded message informed me that nobody could come to the phone and that I should leave my message at the tone. I hung up. Then I called Information back and asked for the address that went with that phone number, and miracle of miracles, the officious bitch gave it to me.

"We're in!" I exulted, and Mum gave me a suspicious look.

"Antoinette," she began in her severest tone. "You had better not be planning to break in anywhere else."

"I have to," I protested. "Robbie is staying at Stan's house. He could be holding Hal hostage there. I have to know!"

My mother was adamant. "You're not going *anywhere*, young lady, unless you call that nice young policeman and tell him where you're going."

I sighed. I guessed that made sense. I just didn't like the idea of letting Darryl in on it until I knew for sure that Hal was there. I mean, why bother the police if he wasn't even there?

But what if Robbie was there? Just because the Snows were gone didn't mean he had gone with them, and he probably hadn't if it was a second honeymoon, and if he was there alone, there was no reason for him to answer their phone. The unwelcome thought came to mind that he hadn't answered the phone because he was busy torturing or killing Hal, but I refused to dwell on that for fear I would panic and have a major meltdown, rendering me worthless for search-and-rescue purposes.

So I gave in and called Darryl, and again I got the nasal gum-smacking voice of the dispatcher. I told her to tell Officer Curtis that I would be at Stan Snow's house trying to rescue my husband. She promised, in the same bored tone, to pass the message on when Officer Curtis came back. She was obviously and totally unimpressed, and I would have to take my chances that she wouldn't decide it was a crank call and just ignore it.

"Okay, Mum?" I asked. "Satisfied? You know you don't have to come with me if you don't want to, but I'm going whether you do or not. Got it?"

My mother got up from her chair and came over to the couch and sat next to me, putting her arms around me. "Antoinette, my darling child," she said. "Forty-one years ago, I would have gladly thrown myself in front of that car to save your father. Losing him was the worst thing that ever happened to me, and now it's happening to you. Of course I'm going with you, you silly goose. How could you *possibly* think otherwise?"

Well, that just blew my stoicism *right* out the window. I broke down and sobbed on her shoulder like a small child, while she rocked me in her arms. It was she who finally let go of me and said in her most British tone, "Now then. Shall we?"

I drove the Cherokee slowly down Stan's street, checking addresses on one side of the street while Mum checked them on the other side. She spotted it first. I drove on down the street and parked around the corner so the Cherokee could not be seen from Stan's house. Mum and I strolled casually up the street, trying to act natural. I'm not sure we succeeded, but we didn't see anybody around, so it probably didn't matter. Stan's house, a large

313

split-level house with a three-car garage set back from the street, had overgrown shrubs all around the front obscuring the ground floor windows. There were no cars in the driveway.

Mum and I crawled through the bushes checking out doors and windows. I saw no windows at ground level, which told me that there was no basement; however, there could have been a crawl space. What luck! A bathroom window on the first floor was open about six inches. It was a casement window, which meant that it opened with a crank from the inside, and there was a screen on the inside. Even if I could manage to get the screen off and crank the sucker open all the way, there was no way Mum could squeeze in through that space, and it was going to be a pretty tight squeeze for me as well. Not to mention that it was about five feet off the ground; being only five-three myself, this was a real issue for both me and Mum.

I reached up and managed to pry the screen loose at the bottom. They were the same kind as the ones on my house. As it slipped to the ground, I thought I heard a sound from within. I stopped and listened, not sure it wasn't a figment of my fevered imagination.

There! There it was again! It sounded like a groan.

Either that or there was some kind of motor with a belt that was slipping. The fan on the furnace, perhaps? A malfunctioning heat pump? Somebody running the garbage disposal?

I looked around the yard for something to stand on. Aha! There it was. A wheelbarrow leaning up against the fence near a woodpile. It had a flat tire, but it would still do for Mum or me to stand on to reach the window crank. I rolled it underneath the window, and Mum held it steady while I climbed into it and stood up. The added height was enough to allow me to crank the window wide open but not enough to climb in. Maybe if I filled it with firewood and climbed up onto that, I could do it. Mum and I fetched logs until we had created a pile that overtopped the wheelbarrow by at least two feet. Mum was panting by the time we finished. "My stars and garters," she exclaimed, pushing damp hair out of her eyes. "I'm not sure I'm up to all of this cloak and dagger business."

"You're doing fine," I told her. "I'm going to start calling you Mrs. Peel."

Mum was a great admirer of Diana Rigg. She accepted the compliment with a regal little nod.

I hoped we had stacked the logs securely enough so they wouldn't roll when I climbed up on them. I was just hoisting myself up when I heard the sound again. This time I was sure it wasn't machinery; it was a groan.

Mum thought so too.

I scrambled to the top of the log pile and pulled my top half through the opening. My shoulders barely made it, and I had serious doubts that my hips would get through without help. "Mum, give me a push," I said. She put her hand on my butt and shoved, but no dice. I pushed myself backward until my feet touched the log pile. Once safely back on the ground I sat down on the edge of the wheelbarrow and started taking off my shoes.

"Antoinette, what are you doing?" asked my mother.

"You'll see," I replied. "Here, hold these." I shoved my pants into Mum's hands.

This time I managed to get my hips through the

opening and tumbled headfirst onto the bathroom floor. "Kitten?" Mum called anxiously. "Are you all right?"

I scrambled to my feet and stuck my head out the window. "I'm fine. Give me my pants and shoes, and I'll let you in the back door."

Once Mum was inside and I had put my jeans and sneakers back on, we stealthily checked all three levels and saw no sign that anyone was in the house. A closet next to the stairs between the first and second level contained a water heater and a water softener. The groaning sound seemed especially loud there and seemed to come from right under my feet. I dropped to all fours and felt around on the floor. I felt an edge, but I couldn't see anything. Damn. Why hadn't we thought to bring a flashlight? "Mum, see if you can find a flashlight, please?"

Mum disappeared and I heard her opening and closing drawers. After a decade or two (actually about five minutes), I heard her say "Aha!" and she came back with a flashlight. "We're in luck," she told me. "It actually works."

When I played the light around on the floor of the closet, I spotted something shiny. I reached for it, and found a ring set into the floor. It was attached to a trapdoor, but in order to get any purchase on it, I was obliged to stand in an awkward bent-over position because it was under the stairs. What possessed those idiots to put it in such an inconvenient place? Were they expecting the house to be inhabited by midgets? Did they expect people to send their *children* down into the crawl space if anything needed to be done down there? *Assholes.* I had enough trouble fitting in here; there was no way a full-grown man could do it. I grabbed the ring and yanked on it repeatedly. It didn't budge.

Just as I was cursing the idiots who built things to be so fucking difficult, and Mum was saying, "Kitten, what on earth are you doing in there?," the trapdoor finally came open. My head hit the underside of the stairs with a clunk, but not to the point where I saw stars. The next groan confirmed my suspicion that it was indeed coming from under the floor where I stood.

"Mum, he's in here!" I called excitedly.

"In where, dear?" she called back.

"In the crawl space! Hal! Hal, is that you?" I shouted. I was rewarded with another groan, or perhaps it was a snarl. The trapdoor was actually a section of the floor that could be pulled completely out. With some difficulty, I managed to do so and set it against the wall behind the water heater.

"Is there anything I can do to help?" Mum asked. In the light of the flashlight, I could see the dirt floor of the crawl space, but no stairs or ladder to climb down to it. It appeared to be about five feet down. I figured I could just jump down. Getting back out would be another thing.

"Mum, I'm going in," I said to her, and she responded, "Be careful!" I sat on the floor, dangling my legs into the space. Gingerly I eased my butt over the edge and let myself down the rest of the way. I shone the flashlight all around and saw only dirt. I called to Hal again and earned another groan. This time it came from the south. I turned the flashlight in that direction and saw a furnace. "Hal!" I called again and saw something move—a foot. I heard another groan. This time it almost sounded like words, and I was almost positive one of them was the

F-word. I went back to the opening in the floor and found Mum sitting on her heels right by the edge. "Call the police and get an ambulance," I told her, breathless. "He's down here."

"All right, dear," she said, scrambling to her feet. I heard her footsteps on the floor overhead as I moved toward the furnace where I had seen the foot. The dirt was much closer to the floor here, and I was obliged to crawl on my hands and knees the last few feet, where I gasped in horror at what I saw.

Hal was there all right. I recognized the shoes and the clothes. His hands and feet were bound with duct tape. There was a plastic bag where his head should have been, secured around his neck with duct tape. It was a miracle that he was still alive. Besides the plastic bag over his head, he must have been freezing. It was damp and cold beneath the house.

I tried to loosen the duct tape with my hands, but my fingers were so cold and numb I could barely make them work. Hal rolled over on his side and mumbled something that I couldn't understand, but he also moved his head in such a way that I could see that there was a hole in the plastic bag. *That* was why he'd survived! The bag must have ripped when they'd moved him, or maybe it was already torn and they hadn't noticed it. I assumed "they," because Robbie couldn't possibly have moved Hal without help. I put my fingers in the hole and tore the bag wide open.

Hal had been blindfolded and then gagged with a rag stuffed into his mouth and held in place with more duct tape going all the way around his head. The blindfold was easy, but the gag was another story. Try as I might,

I couldn't loosen it. *Shit!* I felt totally helpless. Had our situations been reversed, Hal could have cut me loose with his pocketknife; but I didn't carry one. But wait a minute! Maybe Hal's was still in his pocket, unless that asshole Robbie had taken it ... No, it was still there. I pulled it out of his pocket and managed to cut off the gag without cutting off Hal's head in the process. Actually I didn't leave a scratch on him. Instead, I ripped the duct tape off and yanked the rag out of his mouth all in one fluid motion, causing him to yelp with pain. "Shit, that hurts!" he exclaimed. He worked his tongue around his mouth and tried to lick his lips. "You didn't happen to bring water, did you?" he inquired in a rusty voice, slurring his words slightly.

I burst into tears and hugged his head to my breast, until Hal said with asperity, "You know, sweetie, we could do this much better if you untied my hands and feet." *Well, of course we could.* But as soon as I cut his bonds and removed the plastic bag from around his neck, I heard angry voices and sounds of scuffling overhead. Perhaps the Snows had come back early and were not too pleased to find Mum in their house, or maybe ...

Oh, no. What if Robbie...? Just then I heard something that sounded like a slap, then something heavy hitting the floor, and a cry, almost a scream.

"Mum!" I cried, and Hal shushed me.

"Quiet," he hissed. "He doesn't know you're here. Let's keep it that way."

"He knows Mum," I argued back. "Why would she be here without me?"

"Get behind the furnace and turn that flashlight off," he commanded. "I'll take care of him."

"Are you sure you're strong enough?" I whispered, but Hal drew his hand across his throat in an unmistakable signal to shut up, so I got behind the furnace and kept quiet.

Next thing I heard was Robbie's voice. "Toni? Are you down there?" I didn't answer. "Toni, answer me!" I remained quiet. "You can't get away, you know. If you're down here, I'll find you." *Just try it, you son-of-a-bitch*, I thought and contemplated bashing him on the head with the flashlight. But then he laughed contemptuously. "Why should I bother? You can both just rot down there." And with that, the trapdoor fell back into place, cutting off what little light we had.

"Now what do we do?" I hissed as Hal crawled back behind the furnace with me and put his arms around me. "We'll think better if we stay warm," he said in a normal tone of voice. "He's probably got your mother tied up too." At his words, memory kicked in. "Mum called the police. At least I hope she did. She was going to call for an ambulance too. All we have to do is wait until they show up."

"Good," said Hal. "Unless that asshole Robbie manages to convince them that nothing is wrong and that it must have been a crank call."

"Surely Mum will make enough noise to prevent that," I said.

"That depends on where he put her," Hal replied. "I'm surprised he didn't throw her down here with us … Hey! Hear that? Sirens!"

I heard it. Sirens, coming closer and closer and stopping. Car doors slamming, heavy footsteps outside, and someone pounding on the door. Robbie's footsteps, the door opening, muffled voices. Hal and I crawled over to the trapdoor and tried to push it upward, but it didn't budge. So we started yelling, while I pounded on the trapdoor with the flashlight.

It worked. The footsteps and the voices got closer. There were some scuffling sounds, and then the trapdoor lifted to reveal Darryl Curtis, Bernie Kincaid, and two paramedics looking down at us.

Darryl shook his head. "Toni, I thought I told you to stay put."

"You didn't really expect her to, did you?" asked Kincaid.

"Then it's a good thing she didn't do what you told her," Hal countered.

"Where's my mother?" I asked.

"Right here, dear," said Mum's voice as Darryl and the paramedics pulled me and then Hal out of the crawlspace. Mum was sitting on the floor, calmly pulling the remnants of the duct tape off her wrists.

"I never liked that boy, as you know, Antoinette, but this is really too much! He's become an absolute *thug*. Do you know that he actually struck me and knocked me down? I do hope, young man, that he receives an *appropriate* punishment." This last remark was directed at Darryl, who merely replied, "Yes, ma'am."

"So it *was* Robbie," I said with satisfaction. I looked around and didn't see him. "Where is he?"

"Handcuffed and sitting out in the patrol car," Kincaid answered. "He won't be bothering you anymore, Toni."

"I don't really need an ambulance," Hal objected to the paramedics, who were trying to get him to lie down on the gurney. But they were adamant, and in due time off they went to the emergency room, Mum and me following in the Cherokee.

With the police presence, Hal was accorded immediate attention. As soon as he was whisked into a room, Pete and Darryl took Mum and me out into the hall while Kincaid stayed with Hal. "We need to talk to you," Pete said. "Is there somewhere else we can go?"

"Sure. How about my office? It's right around the corner."

I put Mum in the visitor's chair, and went down to the break room for coffee. Once we were all situated, Pete said, "We'll need to talk to Hal too, but obviously we can't right now, so we'll start with you."

Under their questioning, I told them about what had transpired inside Stan Snow's house. As I described the method we used to climb in through the bathroom window, Pete put a hand over his face. "Do you realize that if anyone saw you and reported it, you could have been arrested?" he asked me. "Are the both of you plumb crazy?"

But he changed his tune in a hurry when I described the plastic bag over Hal's head. "That's attempted murder," he stated. "Robbie could have killed both of you, too."

"He wasn't there," I said. "He came in later and tied Mum up, and then you guys came."

"That's because I called them," Mum said. "And I called the ambulance, too."

Darryl shook his head in amazement. "You were both lucky," he told us. "What if Robbie had had an accomplice?"

"He wasn't there," I said. "I didn't see anybody else. Maybe Mum did."

"Fiona?" Pete said.

"No, Pete, dear, nobody else was there except that awful Robbie. And to think Antoinette almost *married* him. Ugh!" Mum shuddered delicately.

"Mum," I reminded her, "that was twenty years ago."

"Yes, dear, and he also beat and raped you twenty years ago," she pointed out.

Pete cleared his throat. "Did Robbie know anyone in town besides you and the Snows?"

"I don't know," I said. "I suppose it's possible that the Snows introduced him around. We did see him with them at the country club not too long ago."

Pete made a note in his notebook. "Well, I guess we're going to have to wait until the Snows get back. Do you know where they went?"

"Las Vegas," I said. "Elliott says they should be home Monday."

When we got back to the emergency room, Dave Martin told us that aside from being slightly hypothermic, Hal seemed to be just fine, and perfectly able to answer a few questions. To my disgust, Kincaid wouldn't allow Mum and me to be present. I intended to find out from Hal what they had asked and what he had told them, but when we were finally allowed to take him home, he was so exhausted that he went straight to bed.

He slept for twelve hours.

Chapter 43

And almost everyone when age,
Disease, or sorrows strike him,
Inclines to think there is a God,
Or something very like him.

—Arthur Hugh Clough

When I woke up Sunday morning at 5:00 a.m., it was raining.

I decided to skip jogging and went back to sleep. I got up at eight and built a fire in the fireplace. My plan was to curl up on the couch with a cup of coffee and a book and let Hal and Mum sleep for awhile.

I picked up the *Clarion*, and what I saw on the front page nearly made me choke on my coffee.

Apparently Tyler *couldn't* live with himself. He'd committed suicide in his jail cell.

Usually they take everything away from prisoners that they could possibly use to harm themselves: penknives, nail files, shoelaces, pills, you name it. But Tyler, with incredible strength and purpose, had torn his orange jumpsuit into strips, tied them together, and hung himself. He was naked when they found him.

I felt sick. How on earth was Desiree handling this? I tried to imagine myself in her place and failed. It was beyond unimaginable. I felt like crying.

Even after Tyler had given me hell for ten years, even after he had tried to pin Dr. Shore's murder on me, even after he'd attacked me and given me a concussion, he had still been one of my colleagues in the fraternity of medicine; he had been a part of my life. His patients would miss him too.

So would my other colleagues, who were now going to have to absorb his patients into their already full practices. Recruiting a new internist would take at least a year.

I also felt guilty, as if I had somehow caused this, which was ridiculous.

Geraldine climbed into my lap and licked my face. Killer sat on the floor next to me and leaned up against me. Somehow dogs always seem to know when their people are feeling bad. I hugged them and felt marginally better.

"Well," Mum said, later when I showed it to her, "suicide is usually an admission of guilt."

"He must have been really desperate," I said.

"Maybe he just couldn't stand the humiliation," said Mum.

"I wonder how things are going to be at the hospital," I remarked. "I'd love to be a mouse in the wall and hear what everybody is saying."

"Well, you realize, kitten, that there's no reason why you can't go back to work now," my mother pointed out.

"That's true," I said with some regret. It seemed too soon. "I'll call Monty tomorrow."

My coffee cup was still half full when Hal came downstairs, ravenous. I poured him a cup of coffee and a glass of orange juice and toasted him an English muffin, while he filled me in on what had happened to him.

When he'd left his office Thursday, a student had approached him with a message. It was purported to be from his teaching assistant, who wanted Hal to meet him in the basement of the administration building on an urgent matter. Hal was curious, so he went.

"It's like an ant farm under there," he told me. "Hallways going off in all directions with all those storage rooms, all numbered, but no indication of what's supposed to be in them. The message didn't say where to meet, so I wandered around for a while, calling out his name, before someone hollered at me."

"Do you still have the note?" I interrupted.

He gave me an exasperated look. "I don't know. I don't remember."

I persisted. "Did you recognize the student who gave you the note?"

"No, Toni, I didn't. Now, can I get on with it?"

His voice had risen, and I took the hint and shut up.

He took another bite of English muffin and washed it down with more orange juice. "So you went in," I prompted. "Then what?"

"The room was full of all these shelves piled with files and boxes. I still couldn't see anybody, so I went down an aisle between two shelves, and a box full of books fell on me and knocked me down. Then, when I tried to get up, somebody grabbed me from behind, tied me up, gagged me, blindfolded me, and then put a plastic bag over my head."

"Did you know who it was?" I asked.

He coughed. "I know it was at least two people. I put up quite a fight, but I couldn't shake them off, and I never saw their faces. Then they put the fucking bag over my head, and I knew I'd be running out of air soon, so I stopped fighting." His voice sounded slightly hoarse.

He took another bite, and I said, "Were you scared?"

"Of course I was scared! Wouldn't you be? I thought I was going to die a horrible death, suffocating in a plastic bag. You know, you see those labels all the time, and you never think it could happen to you ... so then they started trying to carry me out of there and dragged me into the elevator, huffing and puffing ... I mean, how stupid can you get? They could have left my feet untied and made me walk out, but no, the assholes had to try and carry me ... and then they dumped me in the back of a van, and the bag caught on something and the seam split. They didn't notice, and I wasn't about to tell them."

"That was lucky," I said. "For both of us."

"No fuckin' shit," Hal agreed with feeling, and coughed again. He sounded congested. "So I just kept still and pretended to be unconscious, and they drove away. After a while, the van stopped, and they hauled me out of the back, and carried me into a house, and then dropped me down a hole into a really cold damp place, and then dragged me in the mud until they got me to where you found me."

I shivered. "So you had been lying there since Thursday night, until we found you Saturday afternoon. It's a wonder you didn't freeze to death."

"I thought I was going to," he said. "When I heard

327

your voices, I thought I was delirious. What took you so long?"

"Well, for one thing, the police refused to do anything until you'd been missing for twenty-four hours."

"Oh, for chrissake."

"So I called campus security, and they said they'd check around and let me know, but they didn't, so I called Elliott, and he said he'd see what he could do and that I should stay put."

"Oh, now let me guess. You didn't."

I got up and refilled both our coffee cups. "Of course, I didn't. I went over to the college to see for myself, and Elliott was there, and the campus cops arrested us."

"Fucking assholes," Hal growled.

"But Elliott talked them out of it," I continued. "And then on Friday night, Tyler was arrested, so now I'm officially out of jail."

Hal swallowed coffee and winced. "Jesus, that's hot. So we don't have to hide you any more."

"Right. So then, yesterday, Tyler committed suicide in his jail cell."

Hal put his coffee cup down so hard it sloshed onto the table. "He did *what?*" This outburst precipitated a fit of coughing.

I grabbed a paper napkin and wiped it up. "Committed suicide. It's in today's paper. Honey, are you okay? You sound like you're coming down with a cold."

"Maybe. I don't know. Is there more?"

"Elliott told me that he's the same Tommy Cabot who raped a fellow student named Sara Lee Schott in 1982 and got her pregnant and had to marry her and got kicked out of Loyola for it."

Hal put both hands over his face. "Toni, stop. I can't process all this."

"Elliott said he talked to an old law school classmate who's in the same law firm as the lawyer who handled the case."

"How long has Fiona been here?"

"I called her the day after you disappeared. Your parents are here too. They're at the Blue Lakes Inn."

Hal put a hand over his eyes. "*Oy vey.*"

"We had breakfast with them yesterday before we rescued you."

Hal stood up and swayed, putting a hand on the back of his chair to steady himself. "Jesus. I have to talk to them. Did you tell them I was home?"

Oh, the guilt. I hadn't even thought of it, and neither had Mum. "No, I didn't. I just didn't think of it. I got you to bed, and Mum and I just crashed. We were exhausted. I'm so sorry, sweetie. Your mother's going to hate me more than ever."

He patted the top of my head. "Don't worry. I'll tell them what happened. It'll be okay." He walked unsteadily over to the phone.

"Hal? Are you okay?"

"I'm fine," he assured me and had another coughing spell. It sounded worse than the last one. He dialed, and I heard him tell his mother that he was home, that Mum and I had found him, that the kidnaper had been arrested, and that he'd tell her all about it when he felt better. He was still coughing when he got off the phone.

He ate the last of the English muffin and drained the orange juice. "I think I'm going to go back to bed," he said. "I'm feeling kind of woozy."

After he went back upstairs, Mum came downstairs and fixed herself a cup of tea. "Good morning, kitten," she said. "Do you feel as stiff as I do?"

I had to admit that I did feel pretty stiff. Every muscle ached. I could only imagine how Hal must feel. "Hal came down and had some breakfast," I told her. "But then he went back to bed."

"I don't blame him," she said. "I may do the same."

After she had consumed an English muffin and her tea, she stretched out in the recliner and was soon fast asleep. I put my afghan over her, and she didn't even move.

I had intended to call Monty Monday morning, but the more I thought about it, the more I realized that what I really wanted was a nice, juicy gossip-fest with Charlie.

Hal had definitely come down with a cold, which had gone to his chest; so he decided to stay in bed. I heartily concurred. The extra sleep would do him good.

So, when the fire died down and I felt I'd had enough coffee, I got dressed in jeans and turtleneck, put on a waterproof anorak with a hood, and walked over to the hospital in the rain, hoping Charlie would be in his office. He was, and he greeted me with a smile.

"Well, Doc, are you ever a sight for sore eyes! What brings you out on a day like this?"

"I just wanted to talk," I said. I didn't feel like discussing Hal's kidnapping just yet. It would show up in the *Clarion* soon enough. "I know about Tyler, and they dropped the charges against me, and I could come back to work now, but I don't know if I want to."

"Let's get out of here," he said. "We can talk over lunch."

We walked downtown to Dougal's, a small, dark, cozy bar a block from the police station, where the booths were private, and we could have beer and sandwiches—just the place for a rainy day. Charlie shrugged off his raincoat and hung it on the wall next to the booth. I pulled off my anorak, and he hung it up for me.

"I needed this," he sighed as he sank into the booth opposite me. "The hospital's a nightmare today."

"I can imagine."

"No, you can't. Dr. Cabot had seven patients in the hospital, and the other docs are bitching and moaning about having to assume responsibility for them. The front desk is inundated with calls from patients wanting to know what they're going to do now that Dr. Cabot is dead. The clerks are trying to reschedule them with other docs, and the docs are having a fit about accepting them, especially if they're Medicare, and most of them are. We have to let people off for the funeral tomorrow, so we're going to be short-handed. The newspaper and the TV station keep calling and sending reporters around, and we're trying to do damage control. It's not doing us any good to have one of our physicians turn out to be a murderer. Once the shock wears off, the public is going to start wondering about the other docs. What are we supposed to say?"

"You're kidding."

"I wish I were. At my last hospital, one of the physicians turned out to be a pedophile, and you wouldn't believe what people said. For a while, every doctor on staff was suspect. There wasn't anything we could say. As far as we knew, the other docs were okay, but up until somebody complained, we thought *that* doctor was okay too."

"Is anybody saying anything about me?"

"A couple of the docs said they didn't much care for your locum, and they wished you were there. Your techs miss you. Other than that, no. Why?"

"Well, I was arrested and charged with murder too. What's being said about that?"

"Jesus, Doc, I'm sorry. I was so wrapped up in our problems, I forgot all about that. What was it like in jail? Did they treat you okay?"

"About how you'd expect. The fact that I'm a doctor didn't cut much ice." I decided not to tell the Bruiser story just yet. I was supposed to have been in jail all last week, and I was afraid I'd let something slip if I said too much, so I merely added, "It was beyond awful. I couldn't sleep, and the food was terrible."

"You've lost a lot of weight," Charlie commented. "You look almost gaunt."

Our sandwiches arrived. Charlie's was a meatball sub, and mine was turkey and Swiss on a kaiser roll with guacamole. "I won't stay gaunt long if I keep eating like this," I said and took a huge bite.

At that point, the door opened, and Pete and the Commander walked in. I waved at them, and they came over.

"Hey, you old bastard," the Commander greeted Charlie.

"Hi, Toni," said Pete. "Hi, Charlie."

"You can't have her," Charlie said.

My mouth was full, so I slid over on the seat and gestured at it. Pete sat down next to me. "How's Hal doing?"

he asked, and I said, "Fine" and shook my head minutely at him when he tried to continue that conversation. The Commander slid in next to Charlie, fished a toothpick out of his pocket, and stuck it in his mouth.

"Well, young lady, it looks like you survived your stay in our facility," he said. "Hell of a thing about your Dr. Cabot. That was the last thing we expected."

"I'll bet," I said.

"Rollie decided he didn't need a post," Pete added.

"Thank God," I said with a shudder. "That would have been a hard one to do."

"You wouldn't have to do it," Charlie said. "Your locum could have done it, if it needed to be done."

"So, I guess there's no doubt that Dr. Cabot killed Dr. Shore?" Charlie inquired.

"Not any more," the Commander replied. "We found enough evidence to arrest him for that, and also for assaulting this young lady."

"You mean that night you spent in the hospital with a concussion? You think *Dr. Cabot* did that?" Charlie asked.

"He did it, all right," Pete said grimly. "We found the chart in his desk at home. We've got it at the station now."

"Poor Desiree," I said. "How is she taking all this?"

"She's under sedation at home," Charlie said. "Dr. Allen has been taking care of her. Her cousin's wife is staying with her. I understand she's been beating reporters off with a stick. Her cousin's wife is, I mean, not Desiree."

"Jesus," I muttered.

The Commander said, "There's no doubt that Dr. Cabot killed Terence and Kathleen Ross, either. We found definitive evidence; a syringe with Dr. Cabot's fingerprints on it, under the bed."

Pete shook his head. "I can't believe he didn't wear gloves. He's a doctor, for God's sake."

Then the talk shifted to basketball, which was still going on, even though the college's season had ended in March. I didn't contribute much, since I rarely watched sports on television. I began to feel uneasy, but I couldn't figure out why. I was pretty sure it had nothing to do with basketball, however.

After lunch, Charlie and I walked back to the hospital and went into his office. I sat in his visitor's chair as I had that fateful night back in January. "About coming back to work," I began.

"There's no rush," Charlie said. "Your locum has a contract through April 15. We have to pay him whether he stays or not, so you might as well have a vacation. I should think you'd be happy," he added, looking closely at my face. "You don't look happy."

"Oh, I'm happy," I protested. "I just have a funny feeling, and I don't know why."

At that moment, a tall, thin, white-haired man appeared in the doorway and said, "Do you have a minute—oh, I'm sorry, I didn't know you had company."

Charlie laughed. "She's not company. She's Dr. Day, our regular pathologist. Doc, this is your locum, Dr. Nicholas Schroeder."

I rose from my chair and held out my hand. "I'm happy to meet you."

He towered over me. He had a long pale face, a hatchet nose, thin lips, and pale-gray, almost-colorless eyes. He gave me a long assessing look and unsmilingly shook my hand. "Likewise," he said coldly. He turned to Charlie. "We do have a contract, you know."

"Not to worry, not to worry," Charlie said. "She's not coming back until your contract is up."

"Very well then. I'll come back later. There are a number of things that we must discuss." Dr. Schroeder nodded curtly at me and then left.

I stared at his retreating back view and then at Charlie. "What a cold fish," I said. "No wonder the techs miss me. Is he a good pathologist?"

"I guess so," Charlie said. "It's not his expertise the docs are complaining about. It's his personality. They can't just drop in and talk to him like they could with you."

"Well," I said, gathering up my purse and anorak, "I guess I'll go, so you two can have your little heart-to-heart."

Charlie grimaced. "I can't wait."

I walked home, enjoying the brisk air and dampness. The rain had stopped. Everything looked clean and washed. The clouds were beginning to break up. We would have a nice sunset.

So that's my locum, I thought—a human icicle. They really will be glad to see me back, I told myself with an inward grin. Dr. Nicholas Schroeder. Where had I heard that name before?

Hal was still in bed when I got back.

"I didn't try to wake him," Mum told me. "I thought he needed the sleep."

He probably did; but I went upstairs anyway to check on him. He was breathing heavily, more so than usual, and he looked flushed. I sat down on the side of the bed and put my hand on his forehead. He was burning up.

He awoke at my touch, tried to speak, and began to cough uncontrollably. I fetched a thermometer from the bathroom and took his temperature: 104.

Oh, my God, I thought and took his pulse. His heart was racing, and his respirations were rapid and shallow. I hunted out my stethoscope from medical school days and listened to his lungs. I heard rales on both sides.

Hal had pneumonia. Double pneumonia, unless I missed my guess.

"Sweetie?" he whispered between coughs. "I feel like crap."

I called for an ambulance.

Mum, who had her nose deep in a book, looked up when she heard the siren.

"Goodness gracious!" she exclaimed. "That sounds like it's right outside the house!"

"It is," I told her as I peered out the front windows. "I called the ambulance. They sure didn't waste any time, did they?"

Mum brought the recliner upright. "Kitten, did I hear you say that you called for that ambulance?"

I opened the front door to admit the paramedics with a gurney. "I did. Hal's really sick. I think he has pneumonia. Right up the stairs and the bedroom on the left," I told the paramedics.

Mum was on her feet. "Kitten, I'm so sorry! But I can't say I'm surprised after he spent all that time in a cold, wet crawlspace. Darling, is there anything I can do to help?"

At this point, the paramedics descended the stairs

with Hal on their gurney. I noticed with foreboding that he was not objecting to going with them. In fact, as they went by me, I saw that he was unconscious, and his lips were blue. "We didn't get to him any too soon," one of them said.

I closed the door after them and burst into tears. Mum put her arms around me. "Kitten, what happened? He seemed fine yesterday."

"He seemed fine this morning," I sobbed. "I thought he just had a cold. But when I went up to check on him just now, he had a fever of 104 and his lungs sounded awful! And now he's comatose and cyanotic. Oh, God, Mum! We went through all that Saturday to rescue him, and now he might die anyway!"

Mum held me tight and smoothed my hair. "Kitten, kitten, get hold of yourself. He's not going to die, you know. They'll give him oxygen and antibiotics, and he'll be fine." She held me by the shoulders and looked into my face. "Dry your eyes, now, love, and let's go to hospital. The doctors will need to talk to you."

By the time we got there, Hal was in Intensive Care, intubated and on a respirator, with an IV and an arterial line. I tried to tell myself that he didn't look quite so blue, but that could have been a trick of the light. Jack Allen materialized on the other side of the bed. "Toni, good, I need to talk to you," he said. "How long has this been going on?"

His brusque manner got my back up. "Just today, what do you think? He's spent two days tied up in a cold, wet, muddy crawlspace. We just got him out Saturday."

Jack shook his head. "Toni, what are you talking

about? What was he doing tied up in a crawlspace for two days?"

Mum drew herself up and drilled Jack with a green glare. "He was *kidnapped* Thursday night, Doctor, and not found until Saturday."

Her imperious manner and British accent penetrated even Jack Allen's pomposity. Anyone else would have gotten a sarcastic "Oh, really? You don't say," but he actually seemed sympathetic when he said, "My God, Toni. You must have gone through hell. Who did it? Did they catch whoever it was?"

"Only one of them," I said, and Mum shot me a startled glance. "Hal told me yesterday that at least two people were involved."

"Goodness gracious," said my mother.

"So are we going to have to have a police guard, do you think?" Jack wanted to know.

"Wouldn't be a bad idea," said a new voice as Pete and Darryl came around the curtain and stopped at the foot of the bed.

An alarm started beeping. A nurse hurried to the bedside, disconnected the hose, and began suctioning the endotracheal tube. An obscene amount of evil-looking, yellowish-green mucoid material came out. Pete and Darryl immediately turned away, hands over mouths. Mum merely murmured, "Oh, dear."

The nurse sealed some of the disgusting stuff into a sterile container for cultures. "We'll need fungus and TB as well as the routine stuff," Jack told her.

"Fungus and TB?" inquired Mum. "Why on earth?"

"It's routine," I told her. "And he was down in a damp

crawlspace, and God only knows what he could have gotten into down there. They can't afford to miss anything."

"I'm getting some blood serologies, too," Jack told us. "For viruses. This isn't just an ordinary pneumonia. His chest X-ray shows almost a complete white-out in both lungs. We've got him on 100 percent oxygen, but he's still cyanotic. We may have to use PEEP."

PEEP … positive end-expiratory pressure … used to force oxygen into the lungs when they couldn't absorb enough on their own. The fact that they might need to use it on Hal was not a good sign.

"We've got him on broad spectrum antibiotics," Jack continued, "but until the cultures grow we won't know which antibiotics are the best choice."

"What if it's viral?"

"Christ, I hope it's not," Jack said. "Then we just support him and hope for the best."

I knew that, but I had hoped Jack knew of something new and revolutionary to use. I also knew that whatever was causing the pneumonia could also irreparably damage Hal's lungs, and that eventually the 100 percent oxygen could too. Not to mention the brain damage from chronic hypoxia.

All the time we had been there I was aware of all the patients in the other beds, many of them also on ventilators, and I knew from my medical school and internship experience that most of them wouldn't make it, or if they did, they'd be vegetables.

I suddenly couldn't get out of there fast enough.

Pete had stationed himself in a chair just outside Hal's cubicle and was still there when we left. "I'll be here until midnight," he assured us. "Then Darryl will relieve me."

It was nice to know that Pete was protecting Hal from Robbie's accomplice, or accomplices.

Too bad Pete couldn't also protect him from whatever was ravaging his lungs.

Chapter 44

No one is such a liar as the indignant man.
— Friedrich Wilhelm Nietzsche

Darryl Curtis had replaced Pete by the time we arrived the next morning.

Hal's condition was unchanged. He was still unconscious and unresponsive, but not quite so blue. "He's on 100 percent oxygen with five centimeters of PEEP," the nurse told us. I stood looking down at him, and my eyes filled with tears. After all we'd been through, I might still lose him. A sob escaped me, and Mum put her arm around me. I struggled to control myself as Jack came up beside us.

"No improvement, I'm afraid, Toni," he said. "In fact, he's a little worse. We've got him on antibiotics and corticosteroids, but his chest X-ray shows a total white-out now. So we've got him on PEEP, but we can't get his PO2 over 85 without putting him into respiratory alkalosis." Meaning that, even with these extreme measures, Hal was still not getting enough oxygen; his lungs were pretty much non-functional.

"ARDS?" I asked. Adult respiratory distress syndrome

was the adult equivalent of hyaline membrane disease of newborns, and it could occur with any number of bacterial or viral respiratory infections, as well as serious infections of other types. The picture Jack was painting for me sounded typical. Unfortunately, most people didn't survive it—at least not without cardio-pulmonary bypass, and that wasn't available in our little community hospital.

Jack nodded somberly. "Probably. At least his temperature's down—101 at last check. Things could turn around. It's early yet, and he's in good shape for a man his age."

I knew Jack was trying to make me feel better, but I had never forgotten the first autopsy I did after my arrival in Twin Falls; a twenty-five year-old single mom who had died of ARDS.

Mum and I went home shortly after that. She made tea, and we sat sipping it at the kitchen table.

"Kitten, I wish there was something I could do to make this easier for you," she said.

I couldn't imagine anything that would make losing my husband easier. "Just being here is enough," I told her. "Although killing Robbie might help."

"Antoinette, really," she began, but I cut her off. A white-hot rage began to replace my feelings of loss.

"This is his doing, you know," I told her. "Hal wouldn't be sick if it wasn't for Robbie. I wish he could be charged with murder if Hal dies. I wish he could get the death penalty." My voice rose. "I swear to God, he's gonna pay for this if I have to kill him myself."

My mother covered my hand with hers. "Antoinette, darling, please don't talk like that. At least, not outside this house. Someone may take you seriously." She squeezed my hand. "Rather like they did when your Dr. Shore died, don't you know."

I grunted. She was absolutely right, of course.

She changed the subject. "Did you talk to your administrator yesterday?"

"No, but I had lunch with Charlie, the assistant administrator," I said. "I also met my locum, Dr. Nicholas Schroeder. I didn't like him. Charlie says the other docs don't much like him either. Oh, and by the way, Pete and the Commander had lunch with us too. They said there was no doubt that Tyler had killed the Rosses, because they found a syringe under their bed with his fingerprints on it."

"I don't understand, kitten," said Mum. "Why did they need to stage all that jiggery-pokery and put you through that ordeal at the jail if they had such an incriminating piece of evidence?"

"Maybe they found it after that," I said.

"Well, then, that *really* doesn't make sense," Mum persisted. "How could they miss something so obvious the first time they looked?"

She had put her finger right on what had been bothering me. I picked up the phone and called Pete. "When was that syringe found in the Rosses' house?" I asked him.

"Their son brought it to us. He'd found it under the bed."

"So that was after you had released the crime scene?"

"Yes, that's right."

"How come you guys missed it when you searched the house?"

Pete sighed. "I don't know. We searched under both beds. There was an awful lot of crap under there, but no syringe, I swear."

"Could someone have planted it to incriminate Tyler?"

"It's possible."

"Well, like you said, he's a doctor. Surely he would have worn gloves. There shouldn't be any of his fingerprints on it at all."

"Holy shit. You know what that means?"

"Maybe the real murderer is still out there."

"Not just that," said Pete. "I mean, if we arrested the wrong person, and then he committed suicide in jail, do you realize what that would do to our reputation? As a police department, I mean? Besides making us look really bad, the family could sue us for false arrest and wrongful death. Especially since the Cabots are related to the District Attorney. It's gonna raise a *huge* stink around here."

"I'm sure," I agreed. "And maybe the real murderer is still out there too."

Pete sighed. "So now we have to figure out who else could have murdered Dr. Shore and the Rosses? Who would have a reason to do that besides Dr. Cabot?"

"Maybe they're totally unrelated crimes."

"Christ. That would mean we'd have to start all over," Pete said.

"Isn't it possible that the son killed his parents for some reason totally unrelated to Dr. Shore?"

"Then why would he try to incriminate Dr. Cabot? He doesn't even know him," Pete argued.

"Maybe he does," I suggested. "You don't know

344

anything about him. The son could be the key to this whole case, for all we know."

"He certainly deserves a closer look," Pete agreed.

I hung up the phone. Mum looked at me quizzically. "Whatever made you think of the son, love?"

I threw up my hands in frustration. "Only that he's also been in that house. It makes as much sense as anything else we've thought of. Only how the hell did he manage to get his hands on a syringe that had Tyler's prints on it?"

Oh, how I wished I could discuss all this with Hal. But his condition was still unchanged when Mum and I dropped by later in the afternoon.

Jodi and Elliott came by after work, and Elliott informed us that Robbie had been arraigned that morning on a charge of kidnapping, and that the preliminary hearing would be scheduled in two weeks. Apparently, in Idaho, cases required a preliminary hearing within fourteen days of arraignment to determine if it would be tried in magistrate court at local level or district court at state level.

I sounded him out on the possibility of charging Robbie with murder and giving him the death penalty if Hal died, but unfortunately, according to Elliott, it would be considered second-degree murder at most, and those cases didn't generally end up on Death Row. Then the discussion turned to Tyler's possible innocence.

"Have you been putting LSD on your potato chips or smoking hash?" inquired Elliott. "Because you're obviously hallucinating, is what I'm saying."

"I agree it doesn't make any sense," I argued. "That's the problem."

"Isn't it possible," Elliott mused, "that there's someone else who *is* involved in both cases and could have planted that syringe?"

"For instance?"

"Oh," Elliott waved his arms expansively, "just for the hell of it, let's say, his wife, his daughter, his office nurse ..."

I stared at him uncomprehendingly. "You're suggesting that Desiree or Natalie or Donna could have done this?"

"Why not?"

"For one thing, Donna's the only one who could possibly know where to find succinylcholine, and that's only because she used to work in Surgery. Natalie wouldn't know anything about that, and neither would Desiree. And I can't believe that Donna would be so attached to Tyler that she would murder for him and then try to incriminate him. Unless he's been having an affair with her."

"That's a good point," Elliott said. "You realize that if he could have an affair with Donna, he could have had affairs with other nurses or any other female employees, including surgical nurses. And isn't there a surgical secretary? And housekeeping personnel who work in Surgery?"

I clutched my head. "Stop! You're giving me a headache. This is all so confusing!"

"'Hell hath no fury like that of a woman scorned,'" quoted Elliott.

"I just can't believe that any of those women would commit murder."

Elliott chuckled. "How about all those freakin' murder mysteries you read? Isn't poisoning supposed to be a woman's crime?"

"Some of the most famous poisoners have been physicians," Mum reminded us. "All *men*, don't you know."

"But Elliott," interjected Jodi, "if Tyler is innocent, *how* did his fingerprints get on the syringe?"

"Good thought," I said. "That would pretty much eliminate anyone who didn't work with Tyler. In fact, that would implicate Donna Foster, because she would be the one who would draw up shots and dispose of the syringes after he used them."

"Then why wouldn't her fingerprints be on the syringe too?" Jodi asked.

"If she was trying to implicate Tyler, she'd wear gloves," I said.

"I think I know her," Jodi said. "Is she about fifty, short, plump, gray-haired, and wears glasses?"

"That's her," I said. "Not exactly the type one would suspect Tyler of having an affair with, I wouldn't think."

"Nobody is above suspicion in the eyes of the law," Elliott said pompously. "Sometimes it's the *last* freakin' person you'd suspect."

"Like the son?" I suggested.

"What son?" Elliott snapped.

"The Rosses' son," I said. "He's the one who found the syringe. Yes, yes, I know," I said as Elliott started to object. "There's no obvious connection between the son and Tyler, but children have been known to murder their parents, and we don't know anything about him. He may have a connection to Tyler that we don't know about. Pete's going to check him out."

Elliott shrugged. "You got me. That really *is* the last freakin' person I'd suspect."

Chapter 45

I do not love thee, Doctor Fell,
The reason why I cannot tell;
But this alone I know full well,
I do not love thee, Doctor Fell.

—Tom Brown

Tyler's funeral was huge.

St. Barnabas Catholic Church was packed, and people crowded the courtyard. A public address system had been set up so that they could hear the service. I sat with Elliott and Jodi about halfway back, leaving the front pews for family and friends. Desiree—tall, tragic, and beautiful in a long black veil—sat in the front pew, flanked by Fritz and Amy Baumgartner. I looked for Natalie but didn't see her. No doubt she had to work.

The service brought back warm memories of my childhood. I hadn't attended church since high school. Although my father had been Catholic, my mother was Church of England, and she'd had me baptized and confirmed in the Episcopal church at the earliest opportunity, against the wishes of my paternal grandparents. I recalled with a smile how Grandma

Day had taught me the "Hail Mary" and the rosary whenever she babysat, and how to say grace properly, and that the Lord's Prayer ended with "deliver us from evil"—all without Mum's knowledge. I will never forget the first time I said Grandma's grace at Thanksgiving dinner instead of my mother's. I was four years old at the time. Mum didn't say anything, but if looks could kill, Grandma and I would have died on the spot.

Over the years, Mum and Grandma ironed out their differences, but there were some mighty interesting discussions about religion during my early years, especially since Grandpa's brother, Uncle Frank, was a Catholic priest and frequently came to dinner, usually on Fridays, probably checking to make sure we weren't eating meat. Grandma and Grandpa were gone now, having died while I was in high school, but I had warm memories of them. They had been very good to Mum and me, even though they weren't financially much better off than Mum and I were, and they did have a house with plenty of room for us.

I could only imagine what Grandma would have had to say about my marrying a Jew. Mum had been bad enough. "But, my dear, you *can't*!" Mum would say. "What about the children? What will people think?" She was also not too enchanted with the fact that Hal was ten years older than I, divorced, and my teacher.

Hal's parents weren't much help. They were aghast that their youngest son was marrying one of his students, and a *shiksa* besides. "But there are so many nice Jewish girls!" they moaned. "Why can't you marry one of them? What about the children?" To which Hal would respond, "I married a nice Jewish girl. It didn't work."

So we were married by a justice of the peace, and once the dastardly deed was done, the parents shut up and accepted it.

I wondered, for the umpteenth time, why, if religion was supposed to be a good thing, it usually ended up causing so much unhappiness. These reflections took me right through the service, and before I knew it, the service was over, and people were beginning to file out of the pews. I spotted Donna Foster in the crowd ahead of me and began to make my way toward her. I wanted to see what her reaction was to Tyler's death. I caught up with her outside and put an arm around her plump shoulders.

"I'm so sorry," I began. "Are you okay?"

"Oh, I think so," she said matter-of-factly. "His patients will miss him terribly, of course, but I've only worked for him for the last three years, you know, and between you and me, dear, he wasn't the easiest person in the world to work for. I'm going to be working for Dr. Martin now. His nurse is getting married and moving to Boise."

"Have you ever been to his house?"

She laughed shortly. "Oh, dear me, no. I don't exactly move in his social circle."

"Do you and he wear gloves when you give injections?"

Donna frowned. "Dr. Day, why are you asking me all these questions? Am I supposed to have done something wrong?"

"No, no, nothing like that." I laughed lightly, as if it were the silliest thing in the world. "It's just something the Infection and Safety Committee is working on." The lie slipped easily off my tongue.

"Oh," she said, mollified. "I always do. He does too sometimes, but not always. Is that all you wanted to know?"

"Who worked for you while you were off?"

"Maria Ramirez."

"Didn't she used to work in Surgery?"

"Yes, but she couldn't get along with Roger. She requested a transfer."

Now there's a surprise, I thought cynically, but what I said was, "Really. So where's she working now?"

"She's a float. She fills in for whoever's on vacation. This week she's working in the ER."

I was going to have to talk to that nurse, I realized, to find out if anything unusual had happened while she was working for Tyler. So instead of going straight home, I made a visit to the emergency room, where I found Maria in the break room enjoying a cup of coffee. She was only too willing to talk about her experiences, both with Roger in Surgery, and following that, Dr. Cabot.

After I had found out everything she knew, I visited Hal.

Still no change.

At least he's no worse, I thought and supposed I ought to feel thankful, but I didn't.

"So how was the funeral, dear?" Mum asked me when I got home.

"Oh, fine, I guess. I didn't pay much attention," I said. "I went to see Hal. He's no better."

"I'm sorry, kitten," she said. "I'm praying for him, you know."

I knew. I'd been praying too.

To get my mind off it, I told her about my conversations with Donna Foster and Maria Ramirez.

Mum was silent while she thought about it. "Let me get this straight," she said finally. "According to this Maria, Tyler and Desiree had a big fight in his office two weeks before he got arrested. And Surgery had succinylcholine missing twice? The week before that, and again back in March?"

"That's about the size of it. I wonder if there's a connection."

"I suppose one could assume that Tyler stole the succinylcholine, and maybe Desiree found out about it and was giving him what-for."

"From what the nurse said, it sounded like he was giving *her* what-for."

"Well, then, it certainly couldn't have anything to do with the missing succinylcholine, then, could it?"

I had to admit that she had a point. And unfortunately for me, I didn't question it.

Tuesday, I decided to pay my locum a visit.

I had butterflies in my stomach as I crossed Montana Street and entered the hospital through the emergency room entrance. So much had happened since I'd last worked that I felt like I was starting a new job. However, once I was inside the door, there was an endless succession of people greeting me, wanting to know how I was, wanting to know when I was coming back, wanting to tell me what they thought of my locum. It took me fifteen minutes to actually get to my office.

My heart was in my throat as I knocked on my closed office door. My last encounter with Dr. Nicholas Schroeder had not been pleasant, and I was dreading confronting him now; but I felt that it was necessary to find out about any pending cases or any problems that might be waiting for me, instead of coming in cold on Tuesday.

Nobody answered my knock, so I went into the lab instead. Margo was in Hematology on her hands and knees with her head under the sink ... again.

"Haven't they fixed that yet?" I inquired.

She jumped and bumped her head. "Damn!" she said, sitting back on her heels and rubbing it. "You scared me to death! How are you doing? Are you back?"

"Not yet," I replied. "Where's Dr. Schroeder?"

"He went to talk to Monty. He's been complaining to everybody about the workload. He says there's no way one pathologist can handle it all. Everybody he tells that to says you had no problem handling it and he should shut up and just do it, but he's been nagging Monty to get another locum in here. And in answer to your question, yes, they fixed it, but now it's leaking again. I think it needs to be replaced."

"I'm sure *that's* going to happen," I said sarcastically. "Maybe I better go see what's going on in Monty's office."

What I found out in Monty's office drove everything else clear out of my mind.

As a result of my locum's complaints about the workload, Perrine Memorial Hospital was going to start recruiting a second pathologist.

I wished I could tell Hal.

I wished I could feel happy about it. But there were still two pesky unanswered questions.

Who was Robbie's accomplice?

And if Tyler didn't kill Dr. Shore and the Rosses, who did?

Until those questions were answered, Hal and I were still in danger. Assuming Hal survived, that is.

Chapter 46

Heaven has no rage like love to hatred turned,
Nor hell a fury like a woman scorned.

—William Congreve

Friday night, Jodi and Elliott had a party.

Hal's condition was still unchanged. Going to a party was the last thing I wanted to be doing while Hal's life hung in the balance, but there wasn't anything else I could be doing that would benefit him. Perhaps the party would benefit me by taking my mind off it for a while. Mum begged off because she had come down with a cold and thought she might have a fever.

I sincerely hoped that was all it was and not the same thing Hal had.

Elliott had strung tiny white lights in his quakies and lined his driveway with luminaria. In the backyard, there were blazing tiki torches. Although it was the middle of May, it was still quite cold at night. The back patio was heated by two kerosene stoves, one on each side, and the sliding door into the family room was open so that guests could come and go.

Most of the guests were lawyers or judges, and the

Baumgartners were there. Elliott and Fritz were over in a corner, deep in conversation. After offering my services in the kitchen and getting turned down, I got myself a Scotch on the rocks at the bar (manned by Kevin Maynard), grabbed a handful of green olives, sat down a comfortable distance from the nearest stove, and just watched.

Stan Snow came out the back door with a drink in his hand, and went over to talk to Fritz and Elliott. Casually I got up and wandered over to them. Fritz saw me first and greeted me.

"Hi there, Toni, how are you? How's your husband?"

"About the same," I told him. "Hanging in there. No better, no worse."

He shook his head. "I'm really sorry. Is there anything we can do for you?"

Like what, I wondered, *a miracle?* "No, not really."

Fritz turned to Stan. "I'll bet you're gonna be more careful about who to have as a houseguest from now on. That last one turned out to be a real pip."

"If Shapiro dies, he'll be a freakin' murderer," said Elliott.

Stan drained his drink. "This has been the worst week of my life," he said. "Cherie is beside herself. And Jason is acting even weirder than usual. Shit, all we wanted was a little romantic getaway, and see what we got for it."

"Who's Jason?" I asked.

"My son," Stan said. "He's always been a problem. He's one of these Goths, you know, all in black, with the tattoos and piercings, and long stringy hair, and the black stuff around the eyes..."

"And how old is he now?" Fritz wanted to know.

"Nineteen. He's going to the college, or at least he's supposed to be. God only knows what he's really doing. He never seems to have any friends, at least none that we ever see."

"Where was he while you were in Las Vegas?" I asked.

"He stayed at home," Stan said. "He and Rob really seemed to hit it off. Heck, we were congratulating ourselves on having Rob there to keep him out of trouble. Little did we know."

There was a murmuring of general commiseration from Elliott and Fritz, during which I discreetly withdrew and slipped into the house. I found a seat in a secluded corner of the living room, pulled out my cell phone, and called the police station. After a scintillating chat with the gum-smacking dispatcher, I was put through to Darryl Curtis.

"I know who Robbie's accomplice is," I told him.

Having done my civic duty for the night, I casually strolled back out through the kitchen door to the bar that had been set up on the patio, where I got myself a Scotch on the rocks and sat down in an unoccupied chaise lounge to sip it and congratulate myself on a fine bit of detective work. *Just wait till I tell Mum*, I thought.

Mrs. Baumgartner detached herself from her husband's side and sat down next to me. She was a plump, pleasant, white-haired lady in, I guessed, her fifties. Her face didn't look as old as her hair did.

"Fritz keeps saying he's going to introduce me to you, but I got tired of waiting. You're Toni Day, aren't you?"

"Yes, I am. And you're Mrs. Baumgartner."

"Amy, please. Fritz has talked about you so much, I really was quite jealous. I just had to meet you, so here I am."

I really didn't know quite how to respond to this but was saved the trouble of answering when Jodi burst out the door with a large tray of hot appetizers with bubbling cheese on top. She put them down on the long table running along the back of the house, pulled up a chair next to Amy, and sat down with a gusty sigh. She wore a purple and mustard yellow caftan with matching purple pendant and earrings, apparently sliced from geodes. They looked like they weighed a ton apiece. Her face was as red as her hair, which appeared to have been styled in Early Eggbeater Punk.

"Whew!" she exclaimed, fanning herself. "It's hot in there. I see you two have met. Isn't Desiree coming, Amy?"

"No. I asked her, but she says she's just not up to it yet. She worries me, Jodi. She won't eat, and she sleeps all day and stays up all night looking at old photograph albums and crying. She's drinking too. I try to spend as much time with her as I can, but she doesn't seem to want to talk; she just wants to sleep. I fix meals for her, and she just picks at them. I don't know what else I can do."

"Me either," said Jodi. "Maybe she just has to deal with her grief in her own way. Maybe she just needs time."

"Well, that's easy for you to say," retorted Amy, testily. "But the problem is, she's not eating, and she's drinking. She's losing weight. She's going to make herself sick."

At this point, I decided to stay out of the conversation. But Jodi seemed unfazed. "We went through the same thing a few years ago when Elliott's father died. His mother just withdrew. Wouldn't eat, couldn't sleep, and wouldn't see anybody. She got addicted to sleeping pills. She was like that for four months."

"Four months! I can't—"

Jodi held up a hand. "After the first month, we stopped going over there. I mean, after all, we have lives too. And eventually she started eating again, started going out and playing bridge again, and kicked the sleeping pills, all by herself. Don't worry about Desiree, Amy. She'll be okay after a while."

"Well, maybe," Amy said doubtfully. "But there's something else, Jodi. I can't quite put my finger on it, but it isn't just grief. It's almost … well, almost like anger. Or bitterness, I don't know. All I know is that it gives me a really bad feeling."

"Like what?"

"Oh, I don't know … like she's planning something. I'm afraid she might do something foolish, something that might hurt her … or hurt somebody else."

"You mean … like suicide?"

Amy gasped. "No! Oh, no! That never occurred to me! Oh, Jodi, do you really think … oh, dear, oh, dear, and this is the first night I've left her alone …"

She was really upset, wringing her hands and nearly in tears. "I've got to go make sure she's all right. Jodi, can you … oh, no, I don't suppose you can, since you're the hostess, can you?"

"Well, no, but Toni can. Who knows, you might *need* a doctor."

Oh, crap.

I spoke for the first time. "I'm not exactly the kind

of doctor you want, you know. And you can call an ambulance as well as I can." I was not too pleased with Jodi volunteering me for Desiree detail. I hardly knew the woman, and our last meeting hadn't exactly been all sweetness and light.

But Amy turned to me beseechingly. "Oh, please, Toni. Please. I'm so scared. I can't do this alone."

"What about Fritz?"

"Oh, Fritz is no good," said Amy disgustedly. "He's absolutely worthless at times like this. He won't go to funerals, he hates being around people who've lost a loved one. He hasn't been to see Desiree since the day of the funeral."

I sighed. "Okay. Let's go."

For someone in a hurry, Amy drove excruciatingly slowly. Just under the speed limit at all times. I was having a real approach-avoidance conflict. I didn't want to be there, but I was developing a definite feeling that the sooner we got there, the better. I began to picture finding Desiree hanging from a rafter in the garage, or in the kitchen with her head in the oven, or in the bathtub with the back of her head blown all over the wall from a shotgun, or …

At that point, we drew up in front of the Cabots' house. It was ominously dark. No light showed anywhere. I heard Amy catch her breath. "Uh-oh," she murmured.

"This is not good, is it?" I ventured.

"No, it isn't. Oh, Toni, I'm so scared."

"Well," I said, practically, "let's go see what's what."

We got out of the car and went up to the front door. It was locked, naturally. Amy was searching through her purse and getting more agitated by the minute.

"I've got a key here someplace," she muttered. "Now where can that have got to? It was right here … oh, for goodness sake," and she proceeded to dump out her purse right there on the Cabots' front steps.

Sheesh, I thought. *What next?*

I sat down and helped her go through the contents of her purse. There was no key other than Amy's house key and car keys.

"Come on," I urged, as she returned everything to her purse. "Let's go around the back. Maybe there's something open there."

But the back door was locked too.

"Now what?" asked Amy fearfully.

"Aren't there any other doors?" I asked. "This is an awfully big house to just have two doors."

"There's a sliding glass door over here, near the hot tub."

No dice. It was locked too.

Then I spotted a balcony on the second floor. And if my eyes didn't deceive me, there was a sliding glass door up there, too. And it was open. And, even better, there was a large tree right there, with a branch sticking out right over it. It actually shaded the balcony. Why, a person could just climb right up that tree and …

Don't be silly, Toni. You haven't climbed a tree in thirty years. And you're not exactly dressed for it.

But at least I was wearing pants and flat shoes. Amy was wearing a long skirt and high heels.

I should have listened to myself, but my curiosity was getting the better of me. Experimentally, I grabbed the lowest branch and swung myself up.

Just like riding a bicycle. Some things you never forget.

Standing on the limb, I noticed another branch within reach. I climbed up on it.

"What are you doing, Toni?" Amy called out.

"Just seeing if I can reach that balcony," I called back.

"Well, don't fall!"

Well, duh.

Only two more branches and I would be on a level with the balcony. It was just a step over from there to the branch that hung out over the balcony. Carefully, I worked my way over to it, and tested my weight on it.

It swayed ominously, and I realized that it might be too fragile to bear my weight. But I had come this far, and I was unwilling to give up now. So I stretched myself out full length on the branch and inched my way toward the balcony. I had just reached a point where I was directly over the balcony, when the branch suddenly broke and decanted me onto the balcony, head first, with a resounding crash. Amy screamed. *Oh, shit,* I thought, *this is going to really, really hurt any minute now.* I lay there, head spinning, and one by one, various body parts began to really hurt. *Really* hurt. *Really* bad. I tried moving various extremities, and after a minute or two, I was pretty sure I hadn't broken anything. My knit tunic top, however, would never be the same again, and I wasn't sure my head would either.

"Toni?" shouted Amy. "Are you okay?"

I assured her that I was and pulled myself to my feet with a heartfelt groan. Slowly, I made my way through the open slider, located a light switch, and found myself in the most luxurious master bedroom I had ever seen.

I stopped and looked around the bedroom in awe,

especially at the round, king-sized bed covered in red satin and the matching red satin canopy with gold tassels. *Where the hell do they find sheets for that thing*, I wondered. A huge, red, sunken, Jacuzzi bathtub occupied one corner and a gold-and-red, velvet chaise lounge the opposite corner. The ornate, gold-trimmed, antique-white bureau and highboy sat on thick, white, plush carpet. Carved, gold molding surrounded the vaulted ceiling. I could see a red pedestal sink with gold fixtures through the open bathroom door, and a gilt-framed, oval mirror hanging on the wall over it.

My reverie was broken by Amy, who was calling, "Toni? Toni! What's going on up there?"

I went back out to the balcony. "Sorry," I called down to her. "I'll go down and let you in the back door."

As quickly as I could, I limped through the bedroom, out into the hall, and down the stairs, turning on lights as I went. I sincerely hoped that Desiree would not come home and find me in her house before I had a chance to let Amy in. Or worse, that she was actually still in the house, brooding in the dark somewhere.

But my luck held, and I let Amy in without incident. Together, we searched the house, including closets and the garage. There was no doubt that Desiree was not here. Her car was gone. Tyler's silver-blue Porsche was still there.

"Well, I guess that's that," Amy said with a sigh of relief. "Toni, what are you doing?"

A horrible thought had occurred to me. I was crossing the garage to look in Tyler's car and make sure Desiree was not in it, her lifeless body dramatically draped across the backseat, when I heard sirens. The next thing I knew, someone was banging on the front door. Amy ran to answer it.

"Oh, Mrs. Baumgartner, it's you," said a familiar voice. "We got a call from one of the neighbors. She said every light in the house was burning, and she knew Mrs. Cabot wasn't here." I recognized Darryl Curtis. "Is everything all right?" he went on, and Amy assured him that it was. "Okay if I look around anyway?" he asked, and Amy just nodded.

At this point, I heard the garage door open and a car drive in. A few moments later, Desiree Cabot came in through the connecting door that we had left open. The place was turning into Grand Central Station.

Desiree wore snug jeans and an ancient black U of I sweatshirt. With it she wore, incongruously, a gold choker chain with a single diamond and diamond studs in her pierced ears. Her golden hair was matted and greasy-looking. She was so thin as to be almost skeletal, and her face was gaunt. Her blue eyes were rimmed with red. She wore no make-up and still looked dramatically beautiful.

"Amy, what the hell is going on here?" she demanded. Then she saw me. "And what is *she* doing here?"

She stepped toward me, and the expression on her face was so hostile that I instinctively stepped back. Even so, I caught a strong whiff of alcohol. Amy didn't seem to notice.

"This is Dr. Toni Day," she said. "Don't you two know each other?"

"I know who she is," Desiree retorted angrily. "What's she *doing* here?"

"I asked her to come," Amy said patiently. "I was

worried about you, and I asked her to come with me. Where have you been?"

"Never mind," Desiree replied. "I can go wherever I please. I don't have to answer to you. And get her out of here!"

"Mrs. Cabot—"

Darryl had been so quiet that I had forgotten he was still there. Desiree didn't give him a chance to say any more.

"I don't need the police. I really don't. Everything is quite all right."

"Well, if you say so," said Darryl. "Good night, Mrs. Baumgartner. Good night, Doctor." And he left.

"Desiree, what's gotten into you? There's no need to be rude," Amy said.

"Will you just get off my case and leave me alone? I'm fine; I don't need you hanging around all the time. So will you please get out of here? And take her with you!"

"How can you talk to me like that, after all I've done for you?" Amy sounded almost in tears.

Desiree threw up her hands. "Okay, okay, I'm sorry! But would you please go now? I want to go to bed."

Amy hugged her briefly, and then turned away. "Come on, Toni, let's go."

"Yes, go," Desiree mimicked. "And don't bring *her* with you next time. She's not welcome in this house."

Amy did burst into tears once we were back in the car. "I'm so sorry, Toni," she sobbed. "She had no right to be so nasty to you. I wouldn't have asked you to go with me if I'd known she'd do that."

I put an arm around her heaving shoulders. "It's okay. Really. It isn't your fault. She was drunk, wasn't she?"

"I'm afraid so. She shouldn't have been driving. But I wasn't going to say anything in front of that policeman."

I withdrew my arm. "You should have," I told her. "She's a danger to herself and others, driving drunk. If you're so worried about her doing something foolish, well, she's doing that every time she gets in that car. You should take her keys away from her, or have Fritz do it."

Amy fished in her purse for a Kleenex. "I suppose so," she mumbled. "Oh, dear," and the tears flowed again.

"Do you want me to drive?" I offered. "You're too upset."

"I can't go back to the party like this!"

"You have to," I pointed out. "How's Fritz going to get home if you don't?"

In the end, I drove us back to the party, but first I took Amy to my house to compose herself and fix her face. I needed to change my own clothes anyway, since my tunic and pants were ripped and soiled beyond repair. By the time we got back to the party, nearly everyone had left. Those who were still there were in the process of leaving. Amy and I went into the kitchen to wait until everyone had gone. I started rinsing dishes and loading the dishwasher.

Jodi came into the kitchen and leaned against the counter. "Finally!" she exclaimed. "I don't know why we do this; it's such an ordeal. Don't bother with that, Toni; I'll do it in the morning."

I continued to rinse plates. "Just a few more and you'll have a full load. Then you can run it tonight and put this stuff away in the morning."

"It already *is* freakin' morning," said Elliott, pulling out a chair and sitting down. Fritz joined him. They had a bottle of Scotch with them, as well as the ice bucket and six glasses. "How about a hair of the dog?"

I looked at my watch and saw that it was after midnight. No wonder I felt so tired. It was crazy, but a drink sounded good. I accepted a Scotch on the rocks and sat down next to Elliott. Jodi had one too. Amy declined and poured herself a cup of coffee.

"So. What have you girls been up to?" inquired Fritz. "Was Desiree all right?"

"No, she wasn't," said Amy. "She was gone when we got there, and while we were there she came back, and she was drunk. She wouldn't tell us where she'd been. And she was just awful to Toni. She said she wasn't welcome in her house. Why would she say such an awful thing?"

"That's easy," said Elliott. "She probably associates Toni with everything bad that has happened to Tyler. This whole freakin' investigation has involved Tyler trying to get Toni blamed for Dr. Shore's murder and Toni turning the blame back on him and getting him put in jail. She probably even blames Toni for his suicide."

"Oh, for God's sake," I objected. "I can't be held responsible for that!"

"She's obviously not herself," Jodi said. "Ordinarily, she's really nice."

"Well, she's only human," Fritz said, "and as if things weren't bad enough, the company's been having problems. We've both had to spend a lot of time in board meetings trying to deal with them. It seems that somebody has been embezzling funds for years, and it's just now become obvious. We have no clue where the money has gone or who's responsible. And she's had to deal with Tyler's problems on top of that. Maybe that's the reason she's been so testy lately."

"You didn't tell me that, Fritz," Amy said. "No wonder she went out and tied one on."

"It didn't do her much good," I observed. "She was still pretty testy when she got home. Of course, coming home to find her house broken into didn't help."

"Why'd you have to break in? You have a key, don't you?"

"Yes, Fritz, I do have a key," Amy said with exasperation. "But I couldn't find it. So Toni climbed a tree and got onto the balcony outside their bedroom door."

"Fell onto the balcony is more like it," I added. "Right on my head."

"You did what?" Elliott said, suddenly at attention. "*You* broke into their house?"

"Well, not exactly. The sliding door was open."

"So you climbed a tree and ..."

"There's a tree right outside the master bedroom window and a branch that hangs right over the balcony, and I climbed it and the branch broke and ..."

"You fell on your head," Elliott finished.

"On the balcony," I added. "But I'm okay."

"That's not the point," he argued. "You committed a crime. Breaking and entering."

"I didn't break in," I repeated.

"Under the circumstances," put in Fritz, "I don't plan to press charges."

"Desiree might," I reflected.

"She won't," Amy said firmly. "For all she knows, I had my key and let us in."

"Come on, Amy," Elliott said. "You think she's not

gonna notice a giant freakin' broken tree limb on her balcony?"

"Maybe she'll think the wind did it," Amy said meekly.

She got no argument on that one. Here in southern Idaho, one thing we always have is wind. Most of the time, we hardly notice it.

I clutched my head with both hands. "God, what a night." I sighed. "All I need now is for Robbie to show up."

"He won't," Fritz said. "He's in jail, remember?"

"Yeah, but his sidekick isn't."

"Tell me more about this embezzlement," suggested Elliott. "How long has it been going on? And how did they find out about it?"

Fritz sighed. "The CFO found some things that didn't add up and ordered an audit. That's how they found out about it. The auditors went back twenty years. They started finding evidence of it in 1991."

"That's fourteen years. Who's worked for them that long?"

"Lots of people. Mostly factory workers who have no access to the finances. There's only one person who did, a bookkeeper, and she was on extended medical leave for a year in 2001. But the embezzlements went on during that year anyway. So it probably wasn't her."

"How was it done?" pursued Elliott.

"Simple. It was stolen from the employee pension fund."

"Do the employees know about it?"

"They do now. They're threatening to strike unless

they get their money back. And there's no money to give them. That's the problem."

"And Desiree knew nothing about it until now?"

"Not until about a month ago. That's when the audit was completed."

"Hmm."

"Elliott, what are you getting at?" I inquired. "Do you think it has anything to do with Tyler?"

"It could. He was being blackmailed by Dr. Shore all those years. Where did he get the money?"

"I thought his family was wealthy."

Elliott shrugged. "Not if they cut him off. They could have. He wasn't exactly their white-haired boy anymore, you know."

Chapter 47

He flung himself from the room, flung himself upon
his horse and rode madly off in all directions.
—Stephen Butler Leacock

Saturday it rained all day. It was windy and cold. Mum and I slept late and spent the rest of the morning on the couch in the living room in front of the fire. It sure felt good. Overnight, I had developed multiple bruises, and I ached all over, especially my neck. I plugged in my heating pad and kept moving it around on all my sore places.

Mum's good night's sleep had done her good. She sounded like a foghorn but assured me that she felt much better, and that the fever was gone. Her reaction to my news about Robbie's accomplice was all that I could have hoped for.

"What an *unsavory* sort of person," she commented. "One feels sorry for his parents. It must be a right bugger, having a child like that."

I tried to lose myself in a trashy novel, but I couldn't stop thinking about Desiree. Questions swirled round in my head. Who was the embezzler? Did it have anything to do with Tyler? What was bothering Desiree to the extent that she was turning into an alcoholic? Was it just Tyler's suicide and the problems at Baumgartner Boots? Or was there something else? What were she and Tyler fighting about that day at the hospital?

Did Desiree know about Dr. Shore? Did she know that Tyler had never divorced Dr. Shore and that her own marriage wasn't legal? That alone would make *me* a bit testy, I reflected. Something that Hal and I might conceivably fight about. Except that I had seen *his* divorce papers.

And where did the Rosses' son fit into all this, if at all?

I couldn't seem to arrange my thoughts in any kind of order. If I could just take one question and answer it, I thought, the answers to the other questions would fall into place. Or would they? Maybe I should do like Kinsey Millhone and write things on index cards and pin them to the wall.

I decided to try. Dislodging Geraldine again, I dragged my aching body upstairs to the study, found a pen and a legal pad, and took it back downstairs to the couch.

Mum looked up from the newspaper. "What are you doing?"

I pulled the afghan over my knees and balanced the legal pad on them. "I thought if I wrote down everything we know, it might help make sense of it. Want to help?"

Mum put down the paper. "Let's go sit at the table where we can write more easily," she suggested.

I groaned. I was loath to leave my cozy couch and afghan and heating pad, but I supposed she was right. She was obviously just dying to make a list.

Once we were seated at the table, Mum with her legal pad and pen and me with my laptop, I suggested that we each write down the facts we knew and then compare them. Mum thought that was a good idea, and we both started writing, or in my case typing, furiously. At the end of about fifteen minutes or so, we compared our results. Rearranging everything into more-or-less chronological order on my laptop, we had the following facts:

1. Tyler and Sally Schott were first-year medical students together at Loyola.
2. Tyler raped Sally Schott during her first year of medical school (probably 1981) and got her pregnant.
3. Sally Schott and Tyler were married in 1981 and never divorced.
4. Natalie was born in 1982.
5. Natalie said that her father's family supported them while her mother finished medical school and training. (How about after that?)
6. Sally Schott never finished a training program due to nervous breakdowns.
7. Natalie said her mother had her second nervous breakdown in 1990 while in the first year of her surgery residency at Mass General.
8. Tyler came to Twin Falls in 1990.
9. Sally Schott started working in emergency rooms in 1990 or 1991.
10. Tyler and Desiree were married in 1991.
11. Somebody has been embezzling money from Baumgartner Boots since 1991.

12. Sally Schott stole the identity of a deceased neurosurgeon in 1997 and became Sally Shore.

13. Tyler had a motive to murder Dr. Shore because she was blackmailing him, and he didn't want Desiree to find out about her.

14. Succinylcholine was found to be missing from Surgery on the occasions of Dr. Shore's death and the Rosses' deaths, according to Dixie Duncan.

15. Dr. Shore wanted Lucille fired and got Tyler to do it.

16. Someone used Dr. Shore's car to run Lucille down in the hospital parking lot and then dumped it in the canyon.

17. Dr. Shore brought Natalie here to fill Lucille's job.

18. Natalie tried to sabotage me because Dr. Shore told her to.

19. Tyler attacked me to get Terence Ross's chart. We know that because Pete and Bernie found it in his study.

20. Tyler had a motive to murder Terence and Kathleen Ross, because they could give me an alibi.

21. Someone put an empty succinylcholine ampule behind the bookcase in my office.

22. Tyler and Desiree had a fight in his office two weeks before he died—overheard by Maria Ramirez—in which Tyler was chewing out Desiree, not the other way around.

23. Tyler was arrested after Terence Ross's chart and Dr. Shore's bottle of allergy medicine were found in his house.

24. Ross's son found a syringe with Tyler's fingerprints on it under a bed after the police had searched the house and released the crime scene.

25. Tyler committed suicide in jail.

26. Desiree is drinking heavily and antagonistic to me.

I pointed to items 9, 10, and 11. "Do you see what I see?"

"Hmm. If the Cabots stopped supporting her in 1991, and she was having trouble holding a job, perhaps that's when she started blackmailing Tyler. And that's the same year the embezzlements started. But what's the connection?"

"I don't know," I said. "But there's got to be one, otherwise it's a hell of a coincidence. And if there is one, then Tyler would have to be the embezzler. But how? He doesn't work at Baumgartner Boots. Desiree would have to do it. But then she'd have to know why. And she couldn't have known, because that was the whole point of the blackmail."

"Unless Tyler somehow managed to bribe an employee," Mum suggested. "Or blackmail one."

"Okay," I said. "Let's review. Tyler comes to Twin Falls, develops a successful practice. He marries an heiress. Meanwhile, Sally Schott, having been forced to discontinue her training due to nervous breakdowns, is forced to become an itinerant emergency room physician.

Since she didn't complete a residency, she couldn't become board certified, but she could lie about it and she was probably gone by the time anybody found out. So, Tyler's doing well, making lots of money, and she's not."

"But how would she know that?" Mum asked.

"Perhaps the Cabots told her. Perhaps when they explained to her that since they had put the both of them through school, they considered their obligation to be at an end. Perhaps they told her about Tyler's new wealthy wife. What a surprise. Especially since he had never bothered to divorce her. Well, well. What a handy little tool for blackmail. I can just see her, leaning back in her chair, lacing her fingers behind her head, smiling that lipstick-stained smile."

My mother got into the spirit of things. "So then she contacts Tyler and informs him that if he doesn't send her a certain amount of money every month, she will tell his new wife that her husband is a bigamist. Tyler can't come up with that much money every month without Desiree suspecting something. Where can he get it without anybody knowing? Of course! Embezzle it from Baumgartner Boots & Bindings, his wife's company! There's a certain poetic justice in that, don't you think?"

"Sure, if you can explain how Tyler could embezzle from a company for which he did not work."

Mum was undaunted. "So let's just assume that he did and figure out how later. Go on."

"Okay. So, for the next fourteen years, this situation continues, and nobody ever finds out. Then, in 2004, the hospital gets an application from a female neurosurgeon with impeccable credentials who's been working at one of the most prestigious medical centers in the country, and who now wants to work at our little hospital as a general surgeon and cover our emergency room besides. What an absolute gift! What hospital board in its right mind could turn down an offer like that? So Tyler, who is now on the board, blissfully unaware of the bomb that's about to be dropped on him, concurs with the rest of the board that such an exemplary physician should be snapped up without delay. Imagine his astonishment and dismay when he meets her for the first time and realizes who she is."

My mother shivered. "Really, it defies description."

"So," I continued, "Tyler now finds himself in an untenable situation. With Sally right here in Twin Falls, the danger that Desiree will find out about her becomes acute; and now his daughter Natalie—whom he's never met, mind you—is grown up and needs a job. Not just any job, but a job at *this hospital*. Furthermore, his first wife turns out to be a terrible doctor who is pissing off patients, employees, and other physicians at an alarming rate; and she expects him to defend her and keep her from losing her job for as long as she wants to work there."

"It's a life sentence," Mum said.

"Right. Tyler's desperate to put an end to this situation. So he gets some succinylcholine from Surgery and—late at night on February 28, or maybe early on March 1—he comes to the emergency room, and during a quiet period when there are no patients, he offers to give her an allergy shot. She accepts, he gives her succinylcholine instead, and she dies. Now what's he going to do with the body? Inspiration strikes. He can dump it in my office. Perfect! Everybody knows how I feel about her and will blame me for her murder. If she's found in my office, it's a lot more suspicious than if she was in her own."

"Making you the last to see her alive and the one to find the body. How convenient," my mother commented.

"Except that I produce an alibi. Terence Ross."

"So Tyler goes back to Surgery and gets some more succinylcholine and kills him and his wife."

"That would account for the two times that Surgery came up short in its inventory. And luckily for me," I said, "the ER visit is documented in Terence Ross's chart; and because I did the autopsies, I had the charts. So Tyler had to get Terence Ross's chart away from me and destroy that evidence; not knowing that the police already had a copy of it."

"So, now the police are relatively certain that Tyler is guilty, but they have no proof. So they set a trap, and Tyler falls into it and goes to jail, where he commits suicide, unable to face the humiliation."

"So now Desiree hates me," I finished. "Plus, someone has embezzled from the Baumgartner Boots pension fund, and the employees are threatening to strike unless they get their money, and suddenly Baumgartner Boots is in deep financial trouble."

"But does she know that Tyler was never divorced and that her marriage wasn't legal?" my mother mused. "And does she know that her husband stole money from her family's company and sent it into financial ruin to pay blackmail to this other woman? If so, how did she find out? Who told her?"

That was the Final Jeopardy question.

Chapter 48

Every murderer is probably somebody's old friend.
                                        —Agatha Christie

Hal woke up on Monday, my first day back at work.

Mum and I were there to see him open his eyes and look at us. After that, he tried to reach for my hand, but his hands were restrained. So I took his hand and squeezed it. He squeezed back. Tears blurred my eyes and ran down my cheeks. I swiped at my face with the back of the hand not holding Hal's, and Mum handed me a tissue. Jack showed up while I was mopping my face.

"He's a lot better," he told us. "We can actually see clear spots on his chest X-ray. He's maintaining a normal pO2 on 50 percent oxygen without PEEP. If this keeps up, we'll be able to take him off the vent in a couple of days."

"Oh, thank God," I said, and to my horror burst into uncontrollable sobs. Mum put her arms around me and held me close, while Jack looked exceedingly uncomfortable, as if he would rather be anywhere but here. For him, managing a comatose patient was a piece of cake, but dealing with an overly emotional female colleague was definitely not his forte.

Mum patted me on the back. "Isn't that *splendid*, kitten," she murmured.

Feeling like an idiot and a prime example of why women shouldn't try to be doctors, I dried my eyes and blew my nose, and attempted to control myself.

Our five minutes was up, and Jack had moved on to another patient, so we went back downstairs. Mum went home and I stopped in the ladies room to repair my face before showing myself in the lab.

Histology was a mess.

Construction work had already started for remodeling and adding space to the pathology department to accommodate a second pathologist, as well as a second histotech. The plan was for us to acquire the space formerly occupied by Medical Records, and Medical Records had been moved to the basement. Lucille was back to work, sharing our original space with Natalie. Workspace was uncomfortably cramped.

Now, the wall between Histology and Medical Records was gone, and so were all the shelves on which charts had been stored. The carpet had been taken out. There were fragments of wood and plaster all over the floor and on the countertops, and the dust was unbelievable. I sincerely hoped it wasn't asbestos dust. Natalie and Lucille, wearing masks at my insistence, spent most of the morning cleaning up so that I could at least do a frozen section if needed, and of course, one was needed.

It was a skin cancer, a basal cell carcinoma, and a margin was involved, meaning that some of the cancer was still in the patient, and that the surgeon would have to remove more skin. For some unknown reason, the line was busy when I tried to call Surgery, and it stayed busy for the next five minutes. So I drew a picture of the specimen and its marking sutures, colored the involved margin in red, and ran up the stairs to Surgery, intending to hand the picture to the circulating nurse so she could show it to the surgeon.

To my surprise, the circulating nurse turned out to be Dixie Duncan. She took the drawing, carried it into the operating room, brought it back out, and handed it to me. "He'll send another specimen in a minute," she said with a sigh.

"Are you having a bad day?" I asked sympathetically.

"Yes, I am, and that's throwing roses at it," she stated firmly. "I thought that when I retired, I wouldn't have to work anymore, and it seems that I'm working just as much as I was before. I've been here ever since Maria left. They can't seem to find anybody else."

"Can't they borrow somebody off the floor? That's what they usually do."

"Yes, I know, but guess what. Nobody wants to work back here with Roger. *Big* surprise. Now he's chewing *me* out for coming up short on succinylcholine. Hey, all I do is count it. It's not *my* fault if there's one missing."

That got my attention. "There's another one missing?"

"Yeah, last week. Let me tell you something. If that fat blowhard doesn't get off my case, I'll steal some more and give him a shot of it myself!"

While I was busy signing out Friday's surgicals, Pete called. "Hey, I've been checking out Kevin Ross, and you'll never guess what I found out."

I was momentarily stumped. "Kevin Ross?"

"Kevin Ross, son of Terence and Kathleen, remember?"

"Oh, right. So are you going to tell me he worked for Baumgartner Boots & Bindings?"

Pete sounded deflated. "Jesus, Toni, I hate it when you do that. How'd you know?"

"I didn't. It was a wild-ass guess. You mean he *did* work for them?"

"Yes, he did. Now, can you guess what else I found out?"

"He's got huge gambling debts and—wait, you mean you found out he's the embezzler?"

"No, jeez, take it easy, Toni. Don't go off all half-cocked on me! I talked to the personnel department there and found out that he's got a retarded son who's been institutionalized since 1989. Plus his wife was diagnosed with breast cancer last year and has had chemo and radiation. But he's worked there since 1975 and his record is squeaky clean. He doesn't have a gambling problem. Hell, he's never even been late to work."

Okay, so maybe he isn't the embezzler, I thought, *but he's certainly a viable candidate.*

Later that evening while watching the news on TV, Mum and I found out just how viable a candidate he was.

"A long-time employee at Baumgartner Boots & Bindings of Ketchum has committed suicide after having been implicated in an embezzling scheme. Kevin Ross, age 60, was found dead in his home yesterday of a self-inflicted gunshot wound to the head.

"Ross had been a bookkeeper for BB&B since 1975. A recent investigation into the missing pension plan funds found evidence that Ross had been diverting funds since 1991, with the result that the employees' pension plan fund is all but gone.

"Employees, on strike since mid-May, are threatening legal action if their pensions are not restored. A spokesman for the company indicated that such action would lead to bankruptcy. Desiree Baumgartner Cabot, CEO, was unavailable for comment."

The commentary was accompanied by a picture of Kevin Ross, and I could see that there was a family resemblance.

"Well, there's your connection, kitten," my mother said.

"It still doesn't explain where Tyler got the money to pay blackmail to Sally Shore," I objected. "Not unless Tyler somehow got Kevin Ross to embezzle the money for him. How would he do that?"

"Maybe Tyler knew that Kevin Ross had money problems," Mum suggested. "Maybe Desiree mentioned the retarded son. Maybe Tyler thought he could get Kevin Ross to embezzle money for him by arranging to help Ross with his own money problems."

"You mean like Kevin Ross could embezzle a certain amount, and then they'd split it?"

"Something like that, perhaps."

"That opens all sorts of cans of worms," I argued. "If they were both in on such a scheme, then Tyler could blackmail Kevin Ross too."

"But don't forget, Kevin Ross could also blackmail Tyler."

"That would be a good reason for Tyler to kill Kevin Ross," I pointed out. "But not Kevin's parents."

"No, he did that to get rid of your alibi, dear."

"What if Kevin Ross killed his parents to get their money?"

"Oh, you mean if Tyler *didn't* kill them? Where would Kevin Ross get succinylcholine?"

"Maybe they weren't killed with succinylcholine. All we know is that they both had injection sites on their arms. You can't test for succinylcholine. He could have injected something else, like insulin, that wouldn't be detected either."

"But why would he have insulin?" Mum asked. "Was he a diabetic?"

"He could have been. Lots of people are. Or he could have stolen some from somebody else who was diabetic, or faked a prescription and gotten it from the local drugstore."

"But kitten, if Tyler didn't kill them for your alibi, why would he need to hit you over the head to get the chart?"

"Well, we certainly can't blame Kevin Ross's death on Tyler, now, can we?"

"No, but we could blame it on Desiree."

"How?" I countered. "He wasn't murdered; he committed suicide!"

"Isn't it possible to murder someone and make it look like suicide?"

"Maybe so, but why would Desiree kill him? If he's dead, he can't tell anybody what he did with the money.

Maybe there would have been a chance of getting some of it back."

Mum shook her head. "Not if he gave it to Tyler and Tyler gave it to Sally Shore. Heaven only knows where it is now."

I shrugged. "It's pointless to speculate. Everybody's dead but Desiree. Unless she spills it, we'll never know."

Chapter 49

The Moving Finger writes, and having writ,
Moves on: nor all your Piety nor Wit
Shall lure it back to cancel half a Line,
Nor all your tears wash out a word of it.
—Edward FitzGerald

Robbie's preliminary hearing, which had been postponed because of Hal's illness, was scheduled for the following Monday morning at 10:30. Jason Snow's preliminary hearing was to follow.

Jason was, indeed, Robbie's accomplice in Hal's kidnapping. Darryl, upon receiving my phone call, had called Pete and the two of them had gone to Stan's house while Stan and Cherie were still at the party and arrested him. At first he denied everything, but after a night in a jail cell and about an hour of intensive questioning by Kincaid, he caved. His attorney, Elliott's other partner Russell Stevenson, cautioned him not to talk, but Jason couldn't wait to get it all off his chest.

Hal, who had been off the vent for two days and whose condition was rapidly improving—so much so that he'd been transferred out of Intensive Care to a private room—insisted that he would attend those hearings if he had to drag his fucking IV pole along with him. So he'd been given a pass from the hospital but would have to go back when the hearing was over, as he was still not completely out of the woods.

I smiled inwardly as I recalled the animated discussion between Hal and Elliott about what Hal should wear: pajamas and bathrobe, to emphasize his illness, or regular clothes to maintain his dignity. Hal had decided to wear regular clothes and was dressed in slacks, sport jacket, shirt and tie. However, he had lost weight in the hospital, and his clothes were noticeably large on him, besides which he was seated in a wheelchair with the fucking IV pole and the oxygen tank attached, thereby projecting himself as both dignified and ill.

From my vantage point in the front row between Hal and Mum, I got the back view of three men: Fritz Baumgartner in his tailored gray suit with rolls of neck fat wedged between his collar and his shiny bald head; a tall, thin, dark-haired lawyer whom I did not recognize, also in a gray suit; and between them, Robbie, his crew cut freshly trimmed and his slight figure dapper in his navy-blue blazer and gray trousers, dwarfed by the size of his two companions. All three sat at a table right in front of the bench.

Over on the left side of the courtroom on a long bench flanking the judge's stand sat Jason, in an orange jumpsuit and handcuffs, his wrists chained to the railing. Jason had languished in a jail cell for the last week because Stan, royally pissed, had declined to bail him out.

Elliott, Stan, and Russ sat behind us. Elliott had told us earlier that Stan could not actually serve as Robbie's defense lawyer since his house had been used in the crime, and Stan would probably be called upon to testify at some point; it would be considered a conflict of interest. I saw Bernie Kincaid and Darryl Curtis, both in uniform, on the other side of the room.

The judge, whom I also did not recognize, entered the room through a door to the right of the bench. "All rise!" called the bailiff, an unkempt-looking man whose sagging belly protruded from under his poorly fitting uniform jacket. Handcuffs hung from the back of his belt. I wondered if he was in any kind of physical shape to overpower a defendant who put up any kind of significant resistance, even one as insignificant-looking as Robbie. In fact, I wondered if he was any relation to Howie or Earl.

We all rose and then sat back down when the bailiff told us to. The judge conferred briefly with the two lawyers. They spoke in low voices, and I couldn't make out what they said; however, the court reporter seemed to have no trouble hearing them and typed away blithely. I imagined she'd heard it all before.

The judge raised his head. "In the case of Idaho versus Simpson, Mr. Baumgartner, you may call your first witness."

Fritz called Hal to the stand. The bailiff wheeled him up to the bench, from where he slowly got up and ascended to the witness stand, taking care not to get tangled in the IV tubing or the oxygen tube leading to his nasal cannula. He took the usual oath and sat down. Fritz continued to stand behind the table as he addressed him.

"Please state your full name and spell your last name."

Hal did so, in a soft husky voice.

"State your address."

"205 Montana Street, Twin Falls."

"Please state your occupation."

"I teach chemistry at Canyon Community College."

"Please tell the court what happened to you on the afternoon of Thursday, April 7."

"Well," Hal began, "when I was leaving work, a student came up to me and handed me a note."

"Did you know for a fact that the person who gave you the note was a student? Did you recognize the person?"

"No. I assumed he was a student. He looked about the right age."

"Do you see that person in the courtroom?" Fritz continued.

Hal looked around. "No, I can't say I do." Jason, seated practically behind him, was out of his field of vision.

Fritz continued his questioning. "Dr. Shapiro, did you keep the note that the student handed you?"

"Yes," Hal said.

"Is this the note?" Fritz asked, holding a piece of paper in front of Hal's face.

"That's it," Hal said.

Fritz turned to the judge. "Request to put this into evidence, Your Honor?"

"Granted," the judge replied. "Let the record show that the note given to Dr. Shapiro on April 7, 2005, is Exhibit One."

The bailiff placed the note in a folder.

"Dr. Shapiro," Fritz continued. "Can you tell the court what the note said?"

"Yes," Hal replied. "It said, 'Meet me Admin basement. Urgent. Something you need to see' and was signed by my teaching assistant. At least I thought it was at the time."

"Your teaching assistant's name is Todd Grant?"

"Yes."

"And the note was signed 'Todd Grant'?"

"It was signed 'TG.'"

"No more questions for this witness, Your Honor," Fritz told the judge. "But I will need to recall him later on."

The judge dismissed Hal, and Fritz called Todd Grant to the stand. A tall, good-looking, blond young man, Hal's teaching assistant could have been a younger version of Hal. On the stand, he was shown the note and denied having written it.

He then called Stan Snow, who testified that the defendant had been a guest in his home for the past two weeks and had remained in his home with his son Jason, while he and his wife had spent a few days in Las Vegas. He then called me.

After the preliminaries, he took me through the events of Saturday, April 9—right up to finding Hal in the crawlspace of Stan Snow's house. At that point, the other attorney took over for cross-examination, and I tensed. What if he asked me about my relationship to Robbie? But he didn't.

"Dr. Day, I'm Daniel McCreary, counsel for the defense. I'd just like to ask one question, if I may?"

I nodded.

"Did you, at any time while you were in the Snows' home, actually *see* the defendant?"

"No."

"No more questions, Your Honor."

The judge dismissed me, and Fritz called my mother to the stand. Mum looked demure in her green tweed suit and pearls, but the look she gave Robbie as she took her seat could have curdled milk.

Mum's testimony was a good deal more damaging to the defendant than Hal's or mine had been, because she had actually seen Robbie. Although she could not confirm Robbie's guilt in the kidnapping charge, at the very least she could get him charged with assault and battery.

The counsel for the defense had no questions.

The judge remanded the case to Fifth District Court, banged his gavel, and the hearing was over.

The next hearing followed almost immediately, after everyone was allowed to take a five-minute bathroom break.

As Jason Snow clanked his way to the table, Russ Stevenson rose and went to join him. Fritz was already there. The other lawyer was gone.

Hal was called back to the stand, and his progress from the wheelchair to the witness stand was noticeably slower and more difficult than before. Fritz rose and walked over to the stand, and reminded Hal that he was still under oath. Hal nodded.

"Dr. Shapiro, do you see the individual who gave you the note purported to be from Todd Grant anywhere in this courtroom?"

"Yes," Hal replied, "it's the defendant."

"No more questions, Your Honor."

Fritz went back to the table and sat down.

"Your witness, Mr. Stevenson," said the judge, and Russ rose and went over to the witness stand.

"Dr. Shapiro, did you at any time during your kidnapping on April 7 or during the subsequent time in the Snows' crawlspace actually *see* the defendant?"

"No," said Hal wearily, "but I heard him."

"Really, Dr. Shapiro," said Russ patronizingly, "how could you know whose voice you were hearing with your head inside a plastic bag?"

Several people in the courtroom gasped audibly.

"He spoke to me when he gave me the note," Hal said, "and there was a hole in the bag. I could hear him just fine." His voice had dropped to a whisper, and he seemed to sag in the chair. The judge noticed.

"If there are no more questions," he said, "I think it's time to get Dr. Shapiro back to the hospital."

Russ nodded. "No more questions, Your Honor," he said, and he and Elliott helped Hal back into his wheelchair. They wheeled him up the aisle to the door, where Mum and I waited. "I'll take it from here," I told them.

The ambulance waited outside the courthouse, and as I wheeled Hal out to it, the same newspeople that had been present at the time of my fake arraignment converged upon us.

"Dr. Shapiro, do you know why were you kidnapped? Did you know the kidnappers?"

"Dr. Day, did your husband's kidnapping have anything to do with Dr. Shore's murder?"

"Dr. Shapiro, what did they want? Was there ransom involved?"

"Dr. Day, was the defendant really an old boyfriend of yours?"

"Get out of our way," the paramedic said. "Can't you see this man's ill?"

"No comment," said Hal, who was safely inside the ambulance by this time.

"No comment," I echoed.

"Sod off," said my mother.

With that, we climbed hastily into the ambulance, which sped off to the hospital.

"Mum, *really*," I murmured to her, "your *language*!"

Mum and I had lunch in the hospital cafeteria before I returned to work and she walked home. I had to cram an entire day's work into an afternoon, and it was five o'clock before I knew it.

I called Elliott as soon as I got home, and he and Jodi came over after they had finished dinner.

"I'll bet you're glad that's over," Jodi said to me.

I nodded, but before I could speak, Elliott said, "Of course, you know it isn't really over; this was just the preliminary hearing. During the trial they'll be asking you all about your relationship with Robbie, trying to damage your credibility. They'll try to make it look like ... oh, I don't know, a freakin' quest for vengeance after a love affair gone wrong."

I shuddered. "Maybe, but they won't be able to discredit Hal. Or Mum."

"Perhaps not, but they'll be seen as sympathetic to your cause."

"Just a minute," Mum said. "Are you trying to tell us that Robbie might get away with this, just because he used to be Toni's fiancé?"

"Oh, no, I don't think so," Elliott said, "but they can make Toni look bad. They'll try to bring the rape into the record, and make her look like a tramp."

"That's not a crime," I scoffed, endeavoring to appear unconcerned, although I shuddered inwardly at the very thought. "Last time they tried to make me look like a murderer."

Chapter 50

I fled, and cry'd out, DEATH!
Hell trembled at the hideous name, and sigh'd
From all her caves, and back resounded, DEATH!
—John Milton, *Paradise Lost*

*J*odi and Elliott invited Fritz and Amy to dinner Friday night, and then invited Mum and me to join them.

The Baumgartners were late. By the time they arrived, we were on our second drinks. And they brought Desiree with them.

My heart sank. I wondered if I could make it to the bathroom before she saw me and perhaps climb out through the window and go home, but it was too late. She had seen me. She was not smiling, but her expression was not as hostile as it had been the last time I saw her, and while Amy was making her apologies, Desiree walked over and sat in a chair right next to me.

I stared at her apprehensively. I couldn't imagine she had anything to say that I wanted to hear. But I was wrong.

"Toni, I'm so glad you're here," she began. "I can't

begin to apologize for the way I acted the other night, but I'd like to try."

"You don't have to do that," I said uncomfortably.

"I know there's no excuse for being so rude to you," she continued, "but I was under a lot of stress, and I'd had a few drinks, and I wasn't myself. I think, in a way, I was holding you responsible for Tyler's death, but that was wrong. I'd like to try and make it up to you in some way. Let me take you out to lunch. Tomorrow? Please? Just us girls?"

I shrugged. "Okay, sure, if you really want to."

"I really want to. Come to my house about noon, okay? You *do* know where I live, of course?" She said this with a grin that dispelled any doubts I might have had about her sincerity.

I grinned too. "Yeah, I think so."

Jodi brought out a tray of hot cheese canapés and passed them around. As Elliot helped himself, he said, "So, Baumgartner, what's so freakin' important at the office that you had to be late for dinner?"

Fritz chuckled. "Nothing that would interest *you*, Maynard. I just got a call from the District Attorney up in Sun Valley about that guy who committed suicide the other day."

Amy broke in. "Honey," she said anxiously, "do you think it's nice to discuss that in front of Desiree?"

"I don't mind," Desiree said. "I already know about Kevin. I also know what's been in the papers, and it's not true."

"What's not true?" I asked.

"We're not going bankrupt," Desiree said. "The employees will be getting their pensions. It's true that there isn't enough money to pay their pensions if they all retired at once, but there *is* enough to take care of those who are retiring now. By the time the others are ready, there will be enough money to take care of them too. The strike is over, and they're all back to work now."

"So how come you didn't tell the papers that?" asked Elliott.

"I didn't know it at the time. We just found out about Kevin last week, and I had meetings with the accountants all week, and they showed me how it was going to work. So we were able to reassure the employees, and they all went back to work today, but I wasn't about to try and explain all that to the papers. They'd just twist it around to sound like we were doing something illegal, and we're not."

"But, Desiree, honey," Jodi said, perplexed, "if everybody thinks Baumgartner Boots is going bankrupt, won't it hurt your sales?"

Desiree laughed. "Not hardly. We're going to have a big sale, and everybody will think it's a going out of business sale, even though it's not. And then the papers will tell everybody that the strike is over, all the employees are back to work, and it's business as usual."

"Desiree seemed practically her old self tonight," Jodi said after the Baumgartners had left. "Do you suppose it was the booze talking the other night?"

"Some people do get mean when they drink," I agreed.

"The thing is," Jodi said. "I've been at parties with Desiree before, and I've never seen her get mean before. I wonder what got into her this time."

"When people are drunk," my mother began, "aren't they more likely to say what they mean, and not the other way round?"

"In my experience as an attorney with the odd divorce case," Elliott put in, "when people get mad, they're more likely to say what they mean. They don't need to drink."

"So are you guys trying to tell me something?" I asked, looking from one to the other. "Are you trying to tell me that Desiree really does hate me after all? Because she invited me to lunch tomorrow, you know."

Jodi laughed. "Just make sure she doesn't slip a cockroach into your salad."

"You could pretend to get the stomach flu," Elliott said. "There's always some freakin' virus going around."

"You're kidding, right?" I said.

"Maybe not," Elliott said. "At least she can't shoot you full of whatchamacallit, the stuff that killed Dr. Shore."

"Succinylcholine," I said. "And that reminds me. I was up in Surgery today, and Dixie Duncan told me that they had some succinylcholine missing last week. Who's stealing it now? It can't be Tyler. Tyler's dead."

I took Mum home and went to visit Hal. When I arrived at the hospital, I found his room darkened and Hal sound asleep. I stood in the doorway, debating whether to wake him up or just go home, and decided that he needed the sleep more than I needed to wake him up, and went home.

"Don't you think that was a rather disquieting little conversation about Desiree, dear?" said Mum as we settled into bed. "I can't help wondering if she has an ulterior motive. And then there's the matter of the missing succinylcholine. I don't really know what one has to do with the other, kitten, but I'd feel a lot better if you didn't go to lunch with her tomorrow."

Chapter 51

Like one that on a lonesome road
Doth walk in fear and dread,
And having once turned round walks on,
And turns no more his head;
Because he knows a frightful fiend
Doth close behind him tread.
                              —Samuel Taylor Coleridge

I didn't listen. I went to lunch with Desiree.

As I drove to her house, I must admit I had a misgiving or two. *They're full of shit*, I told myself sternly. *They're pulling your chain. Get over it!*

So I parked the Cherokee in the circular driveway in front of her palatial mansion, which looked a lot friendlier in the sunshine, and resolutely walked up to the front door and rang the bell.

After what seemed like an eternity, Desiree opened the door, smiling, and invited me in. She was dressed in jeans and a black tank top. She wore diamond studs in her ears and the same diamond choker she'd worn the night Amy and I broke into her house.

"I hope you don't mind, Toni, but I thought we'd have

lunch right here instead of going out. I have this recipe for Chinese chicken salad that I'm dying to try on somebody, and you're going to be my guinea pig!"

It was meant as a joke, I knew, but the bottom dropped out of my stomach. I tried to smile, but it probably looked more like a grimace.

"I can't wait to taste it," I said politely.

"I've got everything set up out here in the sun room," she went on, leading the way. The room she led me into was on the back of the house; it was all glass, even the roof. I hadn't noticed it the night I'd been there.

She seemed to read my mind, because she then said, "I bet you didn't know this was here, did you?"

I shook my head. The bottom dropped out of my stomach again. I was beginning to feel queasy, and I hadn't even eaten anything yet. I hoped I would be able to eat something, just to be polite.

Desiree had lunch set up on a glass-topped, round table surrounded by four padded chairs with a bright, blue-and-green floral pattern. An ice bucket stood on the table with a bottle of wine in it.

"Jodi told me you like Johannisberg Riesling," she went on. "Shall I pour you some?"

The bottle was already open, I noticed. She noticed me noticing and said reassuringly, "I've already had some. It's very good. Late harvest, 2004, see?"

"I'm sure it's very good," I said. "But I don't drink alcohol in the daytime, and besides, I'm driving. I'd just as soon have a Coke, if you've got one." Which was a big fat lie, but I wasn't about to drink anything out of that bottle.

Desiree hesitated momentarily. I seized the

opportunity. "Or I could just come with you and see what you do have," I suggested.

Desiree shrugged. "Okay, come on," she said, but she didn't sound as if she meant it.

I didn't care. Between what Hal and Elliott and Jodi had said and the connection between Baumgartner Boots and the Rosses, I didn't trust Desiree any further than I could throw her, but I was hoping that in the course of conversation she would let something slip about who really killed Dr. Shore and the Rosses.

Desiree's kitchen was every woman's dream come true. It was all done in pastels, and I couldn't help thinking of Tyler and his matching shirts and sneakers. With a picture window, white marble countertops, oak-paneled appliances, and tile floor, it appeared to have come straight out of *Architectural Digest*. A lime-green salad bowl and two smaller matching bowls sat on a butcher block in the middle of the kitchen. I peeked into the salad bowl and saw that the salad was already mixed. Delicious-looking chunks of white meat, mandarin oranges, and slivered almonds were visible between leaves of red-leaf lettuce. It was really a shame that I wasn't going to be able to eat any of it.

"We've got Diet Coke, Dr. Pepper, and iced tea," Desiree announced, peering at me over the refrigerator door. I walked around it and looked in. The iced tea was in a pitcher with lemon slices floating in it. Dr. Pepper and Diet Coke were in cans. "Diet Coke, please," I said, and she handed me one. "Want a glass?"

"No, thanks, I like it right out of the can," I told her. Another big fat lie. I hate drinking out of cans; I just thought it would be healthier for me to do so here today.

She took a cruet of dressing out of the refrigerator, shook it up, poured it on the salad, and tossed it while I watched. God, it looked good.

"Are those almonds?" I asked as she was tossing.

"Yes," she said. "Why?"

"I'm allergic to almonds. Sorry, I should have mentioned it before." Big fat lie number three.

"Oh, no, I'm the one who should be apologizing. I didn't ask you."

"I didn't mention it, because I thought we were going out to lunch, otherwise I would have told you," I assured her.

"I could fix you some salad without almonds," she said. "There's some more chicken and lettuce and mandarin oranges and plenty of dressing …"

"Just show me where everything is, and I'll do it myself," I suggested. "You've done enough work."

She shrugged and pulled a Tupperware container and a bag of lettuce out of the refrigerator, handed them to me, and retrieved a small can of mandarin orange slices out of a cupboard. Picking up the salad bowl, she said, "I'll just take this out to the sunroom while you're doing that," she said. "Shall I take your Coke for you?"

I refused politely and quickly mixed myself a bowlful of chicken, orange slices, and lettuce. I dumped some Wishbone Italian on it from a bottle I found in the door of the refrigerator and some Parmesan cheese I found next to the stove. Grabbing my as-yet-unopened can of Diet Coke, I followed Desiree to the sunroom.

"Why don't you sit there," she said, indicating a seat on the far side of the glass table closest to the glass wall.

I shook my head. "I have claustrophobia," I explained. Big fat lie number four. If Desiree succeeded in killing me today, I was no doubt headed straight for hell. "If it's okay with you, I'd just as soon sit over here." I pulled out a chair on the opposite side of the table, with my back to the rest of the room.

I didn't dare look at her face. If she had been planning to poison me, she must be terminally frustrated by now.

I sat down, popped my can of Diet Coke, took a healthy swig, and burped. That's why I hate drinking out of cans. "Sorry," I said, still not looking at her face. With a fork, I attacked my salad, which was surprisingly good, considering its impromptu origin.

"I'm glad you're enjoying that," Desiree said. "I'm just so sorry about the almonds."

"Don't give it a second thought," I mumbled through a mouthful of chicken, waving my fork in the air.

She put her fork down. "I don't know why I waited until now to invite you over. Tyler and I socialized with all the other doctors and their wives, but somehow we never thought to include you and Hal, and I want to apologize."

Bullshit, I thought. I knew perfectly well why. Tyler didn't like me, that's why.

I swallowed my mouthful, and laid my fork down too. "And I want to tell you how sorry I am for your loss. All of this has to have been horrible for you."

She pushed her salad away and reached for the wine bottle. After refilling her glass, she took a gulp and set it down a little too hard. Some wine sloshed onto the table. "You have no idea," she told me.

"How did you two first meet?" I asked and took another bite of chicken.

"At the hospital," she told me. "I was just out of nursing school and doing my clinical rotations when he came here." She sighed. "It was love at first sight for both of us."

I had forgotten that Desiree had been a nurse. "Did you keep working after you were married?"

"For a while. Until Tyler started making enough money for me to quit. But it didn't last long, because my grandfather died, and I had to take over running the company."

Baumgartner Boots and Bindings, she meant, the family company of which she was currently CEO.

"Did you ever work in Surgery?" I asked.

She finished her wine and poured another glass. "I worked everywhere. Surgery, ICU, CCU, the medical floor, and the clinic. I was even Tyler's office nurse for a while." She laughed shortly. "That didn't work out at all." She took another swig. "I loved my husband, but he was an absolute prick to work for." She was beginning to slur her words.

"You said you had to keep working until Tyler started making enough money for you to quit," I prodded her. "I thought he came from a wealthy family. Was I wrong?"

"Oh, they were wealthy, all right, but they didn't give any of it to Tyler. They cut him off at the pockets." She started to laugh. "He said his dad told him he had to stand up and be a *man*, an' make it on his own before he'd be getting any." She giggled. "An' he's still not gettin' any. Get it? Not gettin' any …" She started to cry.

I reached over and patted her hand. "I'm so sorry, Desiree. You must miss him terribly."

"Miss him, my ass! I don't miss his ass." Desiree was now well and truly sloshed.

"That asshole was hardly ever home. One night he didn't come home at all. So I started calling the hospital to check on him. If he was there, I hung up. Then I went there and spied on him. Ha, ha! And one night it paid off. I heard him talking to a woman in his office. I listened. She was talking about their daughter. Tyler had a daughter! I heard her talk about how she had never bothered to divorce him and that his marriage to me was illegal, and how would he like it if she paid his wife a visit one day and told her all about it! I was devastated! He said, 'What do you want from me? I already pay you five thousand dollars a month! I damn near killed a lab employee so that our daughter could have her job. What else can you possibly want of me? What will it take to get you out of my life?' She just laughed. She said he would never get rid of her, and he would have to do whatever she wanted or she would tell me everything. "

Desiree paused to pour herself another glass of wine. Her hands were unsteady, and she slopped a little onto the table. She ignored it and continued ranting.

"How do you like that?" she demanded. "He was married all the time! And he had a child by her! I wanted children, but he told me he didn't want them. He told me he'd had a vasectomy." She broke down and sobbed. "My husband was a bigamist! He was the only man I've ever loved! How could he?"

"Well, he certainly didn't love *her* any more," I said comfortingly.

Desiree looked up at me. Her gaze was unfocused. "He sure as hell doesn't! He's dead. She's dead. Boy, I sure took care of them, didn't I?"

Surely I hadn't just heard what I thought I'd heard.

Suddenly I couldn't wait to get out of that house. I put my napkin down and slid my chair back. "I think I'd better go," I began and got to my feet.

"Oh, no, you don't!" she hissed. She reached across the table and grabbed for my arm. I jerked away and she missed.

"Desiree, what are you trying to do?" I said. "Don't you think you should go lie down and sleep that off? Do you want me to call Amy?" I kept moving toward the door as I spoke.

But Desiree had other ideas. Moving faster than I would have expected of someone in her condition, she shot out from behind the table, grabbed me, twisted my arm up behind my back and forced me to my knees. I yelled in pain. "What the hell do you think you're doing?" I screamed at her. "Let go of me!"

But her grip only tightened. "I'm gonna take care of you too, you busybody bitch. Why couldn't you mind your own business?" She started to cry again. "Why couldn't you just eat your salad and drink your wine like a good little girl, and then I wouldn't have to do this?" she sobbed. "Why do you have to make everything so difficult?"

I was right! She was planning to poison me!

I went limp. She loosened her grip. I rolled toward

her and managed to extricate my arm. Then I kicked her in the stomach.

I heard the wind rush out of her lungs as she crumpled to the floor and then threw up.

Okay, I'm out of here now …

I struggled to my feet and ran out of the room and through the house to the front door. It was locked. I twisted the thing in the middle of the doorknob, but no dice. I turned the deadbolt. The door opened, but the guard chain was on, and it only opened about six inches. As I closed it and took the chain off, I heard Desiree come up behind me. I backed into her as I swung the front door open and knocked her off balance. As I did so, I felt a sting in the back of my arm.

Not stopping to check it out, I ran for the Cherokee and locked myself inside. My arm burned as I turned the key in the ignition and pulled away from the curb.

Now what? Should I go home, or should I go straight to the police station? Or should I just call the police? What to do, what to do … I couldn't seem to think. The car was getting kind of hard to steer too …

Then I saw Desiree's garage door go up and the silver-blue Porsche drive out. *No time for thinking! I had to move! I couldn't let her catch me. God only knew what she'd do to me if she did …* Before I had even completed the thought, I was speeding through Desiree's upscale residential neighborhood and right out onto busy Blue Lakes Boulevard, heading straight for the police station.

I never got there.

Chapter 52

Out of the jaws of death.
—Shakespeare, *Twelfth Night*

I opened my eyes, but the light was so bright it hurt, and I closed them again. I became aware that I couldn't close my mouth and that I was extremely thirsty. I tried to lick my lips, but there was something in the way. Oh, yeah. I was intubated. Then something pushed air into my lungs. Intubated and on the vent. I must be in ICU. Fine. I was so tired. I decided to sleep some more.

The second time I awoke, it was dark. I was still intubated. I couldn't raise my hand. Either hand. I took a breath. I heard a machine click on. I exhaled. The machine clicked off. The machine clicked on again and pushed air into my lungs. Someone came into the room. A light went on. I closed my eyes against it. A voice said, "Doctor? Dr. Day? Toni? Can you hear me?"

I squinted against the light. A face swam into view. It was a nurse, and I knew I knew her, but I couldn't think of her name. She fiddled with some bags that were hanging from an IV pole and then smeared something on my lips. It felt good. I went back to sleep.

When I awoke the next time, it was daylight. I became aware that my back was killing me, and I tried to roll over. Nothing doing. The fucking endotracheal tube wouldn't let me, and my hands were tied down. I pulled against the restraints, and a nurse came hurrying over. She pushed me back flat on my back and did something to the back of my hand that stung. My back was still killing me. I drew my knees up. That helped. The nurse pushed them down. I glared at her. Dammit, my back hurt, and she wasn't helping.

The nurse glanced at me, and her eyes met mine. She gasped. She ran out of the room. I heard her shouting in the hall, "She's awake! She's awake!"

Hal came into the room next, followed by my mother. They both bent over me, stroking my face and my hair. They both had tears in their eyes. "Oh kitten, we were so afraid you weren't going to ever wake up," Mum said. Hal kissed me on the forehead. "Welcome back, honey," he whispered. "I missed you."

Jack Allen came in. "So, you finally decided to join us, huh? Toni, look at me," he commanded and shined a penlight in my eyes. He listened to my chest. Then he said, "I'm going to turn off the vent and see if she can breathe on her own. The sooner we get that tube out, the better." He fiddled with something behind the bed, and the clicking stopped. "Toni, can you take a breath for me?"

I did so. My chest hurt. Then I took another. Everybody smiled. Jack said, "Right you are, then … out it comes," and he ripped tape off my cheek and pulled the tube up out of my throat, and I gagged and retched. Only mucus came up. The nurse was holding a basin under my chin. I began to cough. Shit, that *really* hurt. More mucus came up. I spit it out. It had some blood in it. The nurse wiped my mouth. Hal and Mum were hugging each other. I continued to breathe and wondered why the hell my chest was so sore.

Suddenly, I was really exhausted. I fell asleep again.

When I woke up the next time, I felt a lot better. My back didn't hurt so much, and my chest didn't either. I tried to sit up. It hurt, but I succeeded. I looked down at myself. My hands were still in restraints. There was an intravenous line in the back of my right hand. That must be what stung. Another nurse came in. "Oh, you're up!" she exclaimed. "Your husband and mother are waiting. I'll get them." She disappeared.

Hal came in first. "Morning, hon," he greeted me. He was dressed in regular clothes, not in a hospital gown, as I expected. There was a bandage on the back of his hand where his IV had been.

"Hi, sweetie," I said, hoarsely. "Why are you dressed like that?"

"Jack discharged me day before yesterday," he told me, enveloping me in a bear hug. Mum came in just in time to hear me tell him that if he could get the fucking restraints off my hands I could hug him back.

"Antoinette, really, such language!" my mother exclaimed, scandalized. Then she recovered herself and hugged me too, tears running down her cheeks.

The nurse bustled back in, took one look, said, "Well, we certainly don't need these any more," and quickly removed my restraints. "Now then," she said, hands on her hips, "are we hungry yet?"

I suddenly realized I was starving. "Yes, we are," I replied demurely.

The nurse left, and Pete materialized in the doorway. "Is she up?"

"Come on in," Hal said.

Pete looked at me, assessing. "Toni? How do you feel?"

I shrugged. "Okay, I guess. I'm still here, anyway."

"Do you remember anything about what happened?"

"I remember being at Desiree's," I said. "And I remember her chasing me through the house and out the front door. And that she was drunk. I made it to my car and drove away before she could catch me. And then … I'm not sure."

"You don't remember me chasing you down Blue Lakes at ninety miles per hour with my lights and siren going?"

I gaped at him.

"And how about crashing your car into a tree in City Park?"

I looked at Hal. "I crashed the Cherokee?"

Hal patted my hand, the one without the IV. "Don't worry about it, sweetie. Cars can be replaced."

I shook my head. "Why don't you tell me what happened? I don't seem to be doing so good in that department."

Pete rubbed a hand over his face. "Jesus. I don't know how you managed not to hit anyone else. Do you remember where you were trying to go?"

"To the police station." Of that I was sure. Small details were beginning to appear in my subconscious; not so clearly that I could put them in words, but they were giving me some rather uncomfortable feelings.

"Desiree was chasing me in her car," I added. "Or rather, Tyler's car, the Porsche. Did you see her?"

"Not until City Park," Pete said. "I've never seen anything like it. Except on Keystone Kops. I stopped about twenty yards behind you and behind another tree in case your car exploded, and Desiree's car crashed right into the back of my car and then exploded. I ran like hell and didn't even get singed, but, Christ, it was scary."

My supper arrived: a heaping plate of macaroni and cheese, a dish of overcooked broccoli, and raspberry Jello.

"Go ahead and eat that while it's hot," Pete urged. "Want me to leave?"

I shook my head. "No, no, I want to hear what happened. What about Desiree?"

"She's dead," Pete said. "She never had a chance. But I thought you were dead too. I got you out of the Cherokee, and you didn't move. You weren't breathing, and you were cyanotic, but you had a pulse, so I started mouth-to-mouth, and then Darryl arrived, and he called for the ambulance."

While he was talking, I practically inhaled the macaroni and cheese. I don't think anything had ever tasted so good. I had just started on the Jello when Jack Allen came in.

"Wow," he observed. "If you can keep that down, I think we can take that IV out tomorrow. What a change from yesterday. We'll have you back to work before you know it."

"Work?"

Jack looked quizzical. "Yes, work. Remember work?" He peered closely at me. "Well, maybe it's a little soon. But I don't see why you can't recover at home just as easily as you can here. Tomorrow, we'll take the IV out and have you walk in the hall a bit, and if all goes well, you can go home Sunday. How does that sound?"

"Um," I said, a little embarrassed. "I have to pee."

"No, you don't," Hal said. "You've got a Foley." A urinary catheter.

"We'll take that out tomorrow too," Jack said and left.

I wiped my mouth and drank some water. "Is that all? The ambulance came and took me away and here I am?"

Pete looked uncomfortable. "Not exactly. I gave you mouth-to-mouth, and after a while I stopped to see if you were breathing on your own, and you weren't, but your pulse was going strong, and then I happened to look at your eyes."

"My eyes?"

"They were wide open, and they seemed to be looking right at me." He shivered. "Spookiest thing I ever saw. It was as if you were trapped inside a shell so you couldn't move or breathe, but you were still alive."

Suddenly all those indefinable, uncomfortable feelings coalesced into rational thought. It all made sense now.

"Succinylcholine," I said.

"Desiree gave you succinylcholine?" asked Hal. "I thought you got away from her."

"She'd locked the front door. While I was struggling with it, she stuck me in the arm with something."

Pete and Hal exchanged glances. "You mean that all the while I was chasing you down Blue Lakes you were paralyzed?" Pete demanded.

My memory was coming back. I remembered how I had strained for air, my lungs burning. I knew my diaphragm was almost paralyzed, and that soon I would not be able to breathe at all. My arms felt like lead. By the time I had turned from Blue Lakes onto Shoshone, everything had begun turning gray around the edges. Then everything went black. I did not remember the crash.

But I did remember regaining consciousness when Pete started giving me mouth-to-mouth. The only problem was that I couldn't breathe on my own, move, or speak. I remembered the arrival of the ambulance, being intubated and bagged by the paramedic, the wild ride to the hospital, the sting of the IV being started in the back of my right hand, and being hooked up to the respirator. I remembered people talking around me, but not what they said. Evidently I had been sedated.

When I eventually woke up, I was able to move. Whatever Desiree had given me had worn off by then.

Had I been driving paralyzed? "Pretty much," I said in answer to Pete's question.

"All I can say is, you're damn lucky to be alive."

Mum's voice startled all of us. She'd been so quiet, we'd forgotten she was there. "And all I can say is that it's a good job that Desiree person is dead, or I'd kill her myself."

I had to laugh. Mum looked so fierce. She turned her green glare on me.

"What are you laughing at, young lady?"

Mama bears have nothing on my Mum when it comes to protecting their cubs.

Chapter 53

When you have eliminated the impossible, whatever remains, however improbable, must be the truth.
—Sir Arthur Conan Doyle

So *that* was what had happened to the last missing ampule of succinylcholine.

Pete found it in Desiree's house, along with a half-full syringe on the carpet just inside the front door. Her intentions were all too clear.

Because I had gone to lunch with Desiree against all advice, we now knew that Desiree had killed Dr. Shore, and we knew that Tyler had run Lucille down in the parking lot with Dr. Shore's white Cadillac convertible. But because all those involved had died, we would never know for sure whether it was Tyler or Desiree who had killed Terence and Kathleen Ross. We would never know if Tyler and Kevin Ross had been in cahoots in embezzling from Baumgartner Boots and Bindings. We could only speculate.

Let the dead bury the dead.

So, two weeks later, I went back to work. My locum,

Dr. Schroeder, had returned to fill in until then. The remodeling was nearly completed.

My new partner was due to start work July first. His name was Michael Leonard, and he was coming to us right out of residency, just as I had. He was also Dr. Schroeder's son-in-law.

Natalie and Dale were engaged. The wedding was set for September, and Natalie had asked me to give her away. It sounded strange to me at first, but after all that had happened, there really *wasn't* anybody else that seemed appropriate.

Bernie Kincaid actually apologized for his hostility to me during this whole thing. Apparently, I'm the spitting image of his wife, from whom he was recently and acrimoniously divorced.

Elliott, in his investigation of Tyler Cabot, had found the answer to a question that had bugged me for the past ten years: *why me?* Why had Tyler been so hostile to me all that time? Why had he disliked me so much that he would try to get me arrested for a murder that either he or Desiree had committed?

The answer was very simple, and I should have thought of it myself. Tyler was forced to repeat his second year in medical school because of his grades.

He had flunked pathology.

The End

About the Author

Jane Bennett Munro, MD, is a hospital-based pathologist with a great love for mystery novels, and she has always wanted to write them. In the rural setting in which she has worked for thirty-four years, she has been involved in a number of forensic cases. She lives in Twin Falls, Idaho, and enjoys music, gardening, scuba diving, and skiing. This is her first novel.

Edwards Brothers Malloy
Ann Arbor MI. USA
August 3, 2017